S. FAXON

The Animal Court

NBBP

Third edition

ISBN: 978-1-7357261-0-6

Editing by Lisa Wolff
Cover art by S. Faxon Productions
Proofreading by Theresa Halvorsen

This book was professionally typeset on Reedsy.
Find out more at reedsy.com

For my grandma Faxon and my Salvatore.
Thank you for believing in me.

Contents

Acknowledgement

This book took twelve years to reach this point. I started writing it in high school, received a series of bad advice, then published it originally in my early twenties. The book underwent the changing of the publishing guard during my mid-twenties when I almost lost hope on it, *but*, thanks to the incredible community that now surrounds me, *The Animal Court* is finally at the stage where it was always meant to be.

The drive behind the reboot of this book and ultimately my writing career came when a dear friend of mine asked me on the 3rd of July if she could download *The Animal Court* to her tablet to read on the fourth. In that moment, it dawned on me that no, she couldn't because it wasn't done. And it wasn't done because I'm an indie author and if I don't do it, it'll never get done. Since that day, I have been on a writing marathon.

The evolution in my writing and marketing capabilities that I have undergone in the year that followed has been astronomical. I popped that ebook up, published the sequel, *Foreign & Domestic Affairs*, wrote the draft of my next fantasy novel, *The Blue Dragon Society*, wrote a half dozen short stories and had many of those published, started writing a paranormal thriller, and, best of all, have met *so* many incredible authors and creatives along the way.

This book would not have been possible without the community that surrounds me. My incredible editor, Lisa Wolff, was able to run through this project and leave wonderful editorial comments.

But, without the comments from my dear friend and fellow author, Theresa Halvorsen, and the comments from my best friend Victoria, the book you are about to read would not be a shadow of what it has become.

I'd like to thank my best friend Victoria for sticking with me through the ups and downs, the numerous cups of tea, and the countless hours of Golden Girls marathons. Thank you for being my friend.

To my incredible partner, Salvatore, I owe the world to you. You keep pushing me, motivating me, and loving me through it all.

No matter how difficult it became, I never gave up on this story, and I am so grateful to the community that never gave up on me.

1

A Good Day

shes and embers rained from the sky.

The once-proud manor of a noble family had been raided and razed to dust overnight.

With a scarf wrapped over his face, one of the arsonists walked over smoldering ruins in his newfound pair of boots. They fit snugly, but they were the trophy he'd claimed from the feet of a fool who chose not to join their side. He kicked a small stack of timber that crackled and clacked.

A small flash of fire expelled itself from the pile he kicked and faded as quickly as it ignited.

The sudden burst startled the rebel, and yet he moved on with a shrug. Today had been a good day. Their leader would be proud of the efforts he and his men made.

"Oy," one of his lads called over to him from around a corner of a stone wall that refused to fall.

Looking back at the mess they had created, the rebel continued forward, stomping dramatically through, enjoying every crunch and crackle. With every step, he thought of their cause, of his starving family, of the watery beers that would be raised in their honor for what they had done.

Stepping out from the thick of the rubble and to the field was a pleasant relief from the heat. The bright summer's morning was warm enough without the intensity of the smoke and ash-laden mess behind him.

He approached his group of eleven men, all smeared with soot and looking ragged from their night's toil. The tall grass he walked through hissed in the wind, which played in their favor, pushing the smoke away from their meeting place.

"What should we do with them?" One of the men motioned to the gate of the manor, where five pieces of their hard work remained. He knew this was necessary, but he did not want to continue looking at what they had done.

Pulling down his scarf, the leader stared hard at the five bodies he had helped to hang. "Leave 'em," he answered, spitting in their direction. "Dead nobles are worth a hell of a lot more to us as a warning to others than they are rotting in the ground. Let's go." He began to walk away quickly. He shouted back to his men over his shoulder, "Maybe dead nobles will finally catch the king's attention!"

2

The Prince

I t had been years since Breyton last walked the steps of his family's home. The time away had changed him and the ancient walls of Maltoro Manor. His youngest brother, the king, had finally realized his dream of revitalizing the old halls of the royal castle by the sea. In Breyton's absence, the castle had become a palace beyond imagining.

Breyton's childhood memories of this place were still as bright and alive as they were four decades ago. He remembered how badly he had wanted to be king then. As the eldest, it was his birthright, something he warned his brothers of repeatedly, for one day, he would have power over everything.

What fools we were, Breyton thought with a smile, remembering those days while walking the castle's wide halls. Until his seventeenth year, Breyton entertained every intention of assuming the throne, but maturity that spanned beyond his years changed his mind. He told his father and stepmother, the king and queen, how he wished to pursue a grander leg of education before taking the crown. However reluctantly, his father allowed him the three-year education he desired from the Northern University in the not-so-near neighboring country

Viramont. There he learned much of life, a new language—the common tongue spoken widely throughout the world—and gained a great perspective of international relations. After completing his education, Breyton found himself on the long ship ride back to his motherland. When the then twenty-year-old returned, he immediately requested to join the military to learn strategy for times of engagement. After emerging from eight active and structuring years of service, Breyton's father told him that soon he would be king. However, much to the disgust and displeasure of his father, Breyton, with a spry smile and a firm look in his eyes, said, "No, thank you."

Today, walking down a hall, Breyton laughed as he recalled how furious his father was when he renounced his title as heir to the throne. Many layers of dust sat atop that memory now. But after all the time and all that had come to pass for him and his country, so many things had changed.

"I don't believe my eyes," a voice called to Breyton as he walked through the corridor. "I heard rumors about the three brothers coming together, but I never actually guessed I'd see you again, Lord Breyton Malle-e-us, not here at least." A tall man with a retreating hairline and a somewhat large nose emerged from the around the bend of the hall ahead.

"Oh, I'll be damned." Breyton put his hand to his head and advanced to meet the other man in the center of the walkway. "Is that you, Yuri?"

"At your service, sir." Lord Yuri Philemon bowed dramatically to his long-lost compatriot.

"I wasn't sure," Breyton admitted after a quick embrace. "You're getting so ugly in your elder years."

Yuri laughed and nodded. "The years haven't skipped you either, Breyton. You know, you really shouldn't let crows walk all over your face—they leave prints everywhere."

Neither man looked aged. Both were only in their early forties, and, aside from Breyton's days in an inactive army, neither had ever worked a day of hard labor.

"God, Breyton, it's been years!" Yuri exclaimed, rubbing his brow. "I haven't seen you since…well, since…"

"Since the funeral, yes." Breyton's hope for congeniality slipped as he remembered the last time he was in Maltoro for his wife's funeral. He quickly changed the subject. "So, how goes local politics? Are things as bad as they're saying? How's that king of ours? Has my little brother found his footing in ruling yet?"

Lord Philemon shrugged his broad shoulders and answered, "Your guess is as good as mine. I'm not likely to receive an interview with the king any time soon. You haven't spoken to your brother yet?"

Breyton shook his head. "I've only been here half an hour. Hasn't Herod just returned from some trip?"

Yuri bit his thin lower lip and sighed. "Yes, yes, he has."

"What's happening?" Breyton inquired.

With a heavy sigh, Yuri answered, "Things aren't exactly great here, Breyton. I'm sure you've heard that people throughout the country are beginning to get a bit, I don't know, *restless*. The king and a few of his staff traveled to Doran, Makovsa, Teybrow, and everywhere in between to try and smooth over relations, but I have no idea what their little diplomatic mission really did. Word has it that your brother mostly went from high-born house to high-born house, eating and drinking with the best of them. That he didn't spend any time at all with the actual people."

Shaking his head, Breyton said, "That doesn't surprise me. You know…" Breyton rubbed his thinly bearded chin, thinking on how to phrase the troubles on his mind. "On my way here from the east, I heard several concerning matters."

Something else concerning came trotting around the corner of the hall, running toward Breyton and Yuri.

"That woman is mad! She's mad, mad, *mad!*" a bulbous man with a frightened look in his eyes declared as he passed the two men.

Not a moment later, an extraordinarily lovely young lady came darting around the same corner, hollering, "Come back here! I'm not through with you!" She passed the gentlemen with a quick nod of her head to acknowledge their lordships.

The bulbous man dove into a room off the hall, slamming the door behind him. Everyone remaining in the passageway heard the tremendous thud of the lock on the door, yet still, the lady grasped the knob and rattled it angrily.

"Oh! You blighter!" She yelled through the closed aperture. "Listening is not painful, you know, and perhaps if a few more of you men realized this, you wouldn't be getting yourselves into these messes!"

The scene that passed continued to play for some time, with the lady continuing to shout her ire and jiggle the doorknob. Breyton watched her. He was sure he knew her, but her exact identity was tough to pinpoint. All he could study from the angle he held was that she had light brown hair pulled in a neat braided bun and a well-shaped figure.

"Who is she?" Breyton quietly asked Yuri.

Lord Philemon rolled his eyes and dismissively said, "That girl? You know her, Breyton—that's Gertrude Kemenova, the prime minister's daughter."

"*That's* Absalom Kemen's daughter?" he asked incredulously. After analyzing her for another couple of moments, Breyton added, "She looks nothing like him, which is a bit of a gift. I suppose I wouldn't have recognized her unless I saw her eyes. They're certainly a pair you never forget."

Lord Philemon nodded his head to agree. Gertrude's eyes were unique. Her right was brown and ordinary, but her left made countless passersby crank their heads to have a second look. The young lady's left optic was a deep cobalt blue, much like a wolf's could be.

"What do you suppose she's up to?" Breyton asked. "Seems like she's fairly involved in what's happening around here."

Yuri closed his eyes. "A little *too* involved. She's actually made her way from being a representative of the 'working class,' as she calls it, of the central valley to being at the king's side half the time, advising him on who knows what. She's got some sort of plan she's been going on about for a little over a year now. She thinks her schemes will help stimulate the economy and calm the people a bit. To put them back to work." Yuri sighed. "I can't say I disagree with her plans, but can you believe it? A *woman* in the king's court."

Breyton chuckled. "Sounds like you're jealous that she has the king's ear."

"She has *something* of the king's," Yuri mumbled.

The woman they spoke of bashed the sides of her fists against the door. Then she turned and slid her back down the wall. She melted to the floor as if chains were pulling her down.

"I think advice is needed," Breyton observed.

"Huh, good luck," Yuri scoffed, patting his friend on the shoulder. "That's the most stubborn ass you'll ever tackle."

Breyton laughed and said, "It'll be just like talking to myself then, hmm?"

3

Gertrude and the King

ertrude looked up to the approaching gentleman. He looked familiar to her, but she bit her lip to restrain herself from saying anything. It was not in their culture's custom for the woman to ask a question before the man initiated the conversation with a cordial hello. She did not care for the tradition. It detracted so much time from what could otherwise be a quick dialogue.

However, her spirit lightened as Breyton said, "You know, civility is the grease that keeps this world flowing."

Gertrude laughed, happy to learn that he must not have cared for the custom either. She was glad to retort, "Yes, sir, but it is male arrogance that gets it stuck in ruts."

Breyton shook his head and smiled to show his appreciation for her banter. His straight teeth shined charmingly at Gertrude. It was his warm smile linking those long smooth cheeks that helped her recall who he was. "I remember you. You're the eldest of the Malleus brothers, aren't you?" she asked. "Prince Breyton?"

Breyton nodded, relieved not to be addressed as the brother-who-cowered-from-the-throne as on so many occasions before.

Gertrude sat straighter, cleared her throat, and apologized for having failed to bow when she streaked by him earlier.

He laughed. "I assure you that I do not care for the ridiculous courtly manners. Besides, you were in pursuit," he excused for her. "What was that all about anyway, if you don't mind me asking?"

She shrugged as the former heir kneeled in front of her to be at her eye level. "It's complicated," she answered. "But, um, the short version of it is, over the last few months, while the king and I were on a tour of the country, King Herod left the man I was chasing in charge of distributing certain orders and necessary, oh, what should I call them? Chores, in his absence? But that jackass in there," Gertrude pointed a thumb over her shoulder toward the door, "failed to obey his king. I started to tell him how he could correct his idiotic behavior prior to the Gathering on Wednesday, and he refused to hear a word of it."

Breyton shrugged. "But why help him if he's just some blithering idiot? Why not just tell him to take a long walk up a wall of ice?"

Burying her throbbing head in her hands, Gertrude chuckled. "Because, as wretched as this is, *that* man is one of the only two intelligent men of the Gatherers. Not including the king, of course." She quickly added the last bit to ensure that she would not offend the brother of said king. "He at least realizes that if we don't do something soon, we may start to see the people take more and more desperate actions."

With her hands still covering her face, a shining ring caught Breyton's eye. Gertrude wore a university ring with a large glittering sapphire for its face. "Which university did you attend?" he asked, finding the jewelry to be a way to continue the conversation.

Lowering her hands, Gertrude looked at her ring. "The Northern," she said, sitting up a little straighter. "When I was a child, I read about people in lands beyond our own, of marvelous creatures our country lacks—dragons, fairies, and the like. I realized that because our country was so dull, I'd do everything I could to get an education elsewhere to find life myself, to learn about the world. I made it to the Northern in Viramont. I was the first female student on campus, and it was incredibly scary and empowering at the same time." She beamed a beautiful smile at him. "Those were wonderful, challenging years. I'm so grateful I took the opportunity."

"You know, I attended the Northern myself." He turned his hand to show her his golden university ring. "I recall how dominantly the masculine sort reigned on that ancient castle's grounds. How long were you a student there?"

"The standard three years for a degree in politics and negotiation," she replied. "Though, the asses here seem to be deaf to my negotiation tactics."

What a daring lady, Breyton thought. "How on earth did you convince your father to let you go?" The prime minister was known for his horrible treatment of women.

Laughing, Gertrude could not help rolling her eyes. It was not a straightforward tale to tell. However, before she could answer, someone standing at the farthest end of the hall caught her gaze.

The man she saw strolling down the far end of the corridor stood with his hands tucked into his dark gray coat's pockets. His warm eyes locked on the lady. His calm confidence was revitalizing to Gertrude after so long a time away. Gertrude turned her gaze quickly back to Breyton, fearing to seem rude. "Forgive me for hesitating, but that's a long story, and I'm afraid that I have another place to be right now." Gertrude started to stand clumsily, burdened by the weight of her dress.

Being a gentleman, Breyton offered his hand to help the lady from the floor. As she stood, unnoticed by Breyton, she gave a subtle nod to the black-haired man at the end of the hall.

He nodded and left the passageway.

"Well, Miss Kemenova, it was delightful talking to you, and I would certainly like to hear the story sometime." Breyton wanted to talk to her again about anything as soon as possible.

Busy with the task of straightening out her long and heavy skirt, Gertrude did not pick up on his flirtatious tone, and yet she did not bypass his statement altogether. "Oh, of course, but for future reference, Your Highness, if you wouldn't mind, could you please refrain from addressing me as Kemenova? I try very hard to separate myself from the prime minister's name." It was proper to address unmarried women by their father's surname with the addition of *ova*, meaning "daughter of." Daughters held the honor of "ova" until they were married and assumed the names of their husbands. For Gertrude, keeping her father's name legacy was anything but an honor.

"That's understandable," Breyton acknowledged. "Oh, and to you, too, Gertrude, please don't call me 'highness.' I abandoned that course eons ago."

Gertrude nodded. She thought, *He is so different from his brothers, who flaunt their royalty without hesitation or shame.* For a moment, Gertrude considered commenting on this, but she did have somewhere to be.

Breyton was sorry to see her leave but was determined to be in her company again.

Gertrude rushed off down the hall in the opposite direction of the mystery man. She had a meeting to spy on for the king.

~*~*~

As a child, Gertrude had spent as much time in Maltoro as she did at home. The prime minister's children were not allowed to play outdoors while at Maltoro, so with the company of her two brothers, Gertrude had explored the halls, towers, and stairwells of the castle. In her childhood wanderings, she found every nook and secret passageway Maltoro possessed. As an adult, she utilized the passages in the walls to save time in travel. Through a door behind an artisan tapestry, Gertrude snuck into a stairwell, which led straight to her intended destination: the king's study.

Down the dark, musty stairs, Gertrude went until finally, the path leveled to a short, dead-end hall. A two-way mirror allowed her to see what was happening in the room without its occupants seeing her. Inside, she saw the king with one man as his company.

Seeing the king's guest made her skin crawl. *How is that dirty brute Igor Mislov still in charge of your King's Guard?*

She decided to focus on Herod to push away her discomfort with the other man. The king in his mid-thirties was one for catching the eyes and attention of every soul around him. His bright blue eyes, much like Breyton's, his crown of golden hair with dark brown roots, his small, pointy goatee, and his tight-fitting robes of lilac made him a fashionable king. Though looked down upon by his male comrades, the power of his crown brought them, along with the ladies, running to his side.

Gertrude was not impressed by Herod's clothes, gold, or crown. So what if he had a charming smile and presided over the country? There was an arrogant air about him. Gertrude did not like the way he strutted around like a peacock in front of others. However, there was another side of Herod that Gertrude admired. He treated her differently from the others. While he addressed the multitude with a high-strung, snobbish contempt, Herod spoke to Gertrude as though she were equal to his self-proclaimed godlike qualities, better even.

Herod adored her. He was impressed by her intelligence and drawn to her ability to shrug off any advance he made to woo her. Peacock that he was, his brilliant colors could not impress her. The last few months for her had been a challenge traveling with a man who admired her, but, at the same time, did not respect her enough to act upon her advice.

"We're seeing far more cases of theft in the city," Igor said. He tilted his head up as he spoke so not to drool on himself through the scarred-over tear in his lower lip. "Bakeries mostly, but also breweries and a few attempts on banks as well."

As she listened, Gertrude shook her head. *I can't remember how many times we heard this on our tour of the country,* she mournfully reflected. *The people are starving, and they're getting desperate.*

"We're making examples of the thieves throughout the city," Igor continued. He shook his head. "Though, I don't think that displaying them in shackles in the squares is enough anymore, Your Majesty. We must take a stronger stance to deter any more malicious activity. How would you like us to proceed, Sire?" The bear of a man wiped the drool that ran from his deformed lower lip. Though he thought nothing of it, Gertrude could do nothing but stare at the scar she'd left on his lip whenever he was around.

The king sank slowly into a chair behind his desk. After a moment, he said, "Well, there's certainly enough rope and swords in the world to teach the peasants a lesson or two."

Igor nodded, thrilled to know that the king approved of his methodology.

The meeting adjourned, but Gertrude remained in the cleavage of the wall for several minutes, hoping to calm her building temper with deep breaths.

Eventually, she pulled on a horn protruding from the wall, producing a loud click. The secret door into the king's room creaked open, and she squeezed through. The king was mildly startled by her unexpected entrance from behind his very own life-sized and heavily framed portrait. He rolled his eyes and grabbed his heart. "Good lord, Gertrude! Why can't you use a door like the rest of society?"

She shut her eyes and kept herself from saying *Because you asked me to spy on the meeting.* Instead, she focused on closing the portrait door. She stared at it for a second, wondering how the starving people in the city would react to the king's painting with King Herod himself depicted as holding a bejeweled sword and his shoulders draped in a gold-stitched and fur-lined cape.

"Oh, Your Majesty, you know me," she eventually said as she sat in one of the chairs facing the desk where Herod stood. "I like to do things differently."

With a cock of his head, the king said calmly, "I see you've changed your outfit since we arrived."

Inhaling deeply, Gertrude ignored his comment and changed the subject. "You know, Your Majesty, that route, so to speak, toward violence needn't be administered on so broad a scale as Lord Mislov suggests."

The king rolled his eyes and sat in the chair behind his desk. "Do you ever think of anything other than politics, Gertrude? Are you even capable of doing such?" The king had hoped to have a sliver of what he deemed a normal conversation with her before their scheduled meeting.

Though the king meant well, Gertrude could not help but feel small. As sad as it was, politics were her life. She'd never learned how to perform normal lady things. She could, undoubtedly, run a manor as was expected of a lady, for governing a house was much like governing a country or Council, the only difference being that there was less land to fret over. Revolutions were just as much a threat to a lady of the house as they were for a king.

Finding no need to respond to the question, Gertrude looked around the room, puzzled to find that the king's loyal bodyguard was missing. "Where's Aleksie?" she asked.

Herod dismissed the topic. "That's of no matter. While you have my time, I suggest we use it wisely. Gertrude, you, hmm, I trust you've already spoken to Lord Gibbet about the Council Gathering?"

Displeased that the king remembered to inquire about that subject,

Gertrude had a momentary flashback of her chasing the man down the hall. "Umm...well..." Gertrude's tone told the king all he needed to know.

Herod sighed and exhaustedly uttered, "How in God's name am I supposed to be king if those who are most loyal to me can't even do the simple things I ask of them?"

Gertrude leaned forward in her chair and sternly said, "Your Majesty, the next few months will be the determining chapters of your crown. To deal with the rumored rebellions brewing amongst the people, you must first take control of the upper classes. Even the noblest of nobles around here could gain from a lesson of respect from you." The last few months had proven to her that the king wanted nothing to do with the lower classes. The plan she had been working on for months to modernize their nation and give hope to the underclasses, had been relatively ignored by Herod.

Maybe appealing to his vanity and about a class that he understands will be the way to make him listen, she theorized.

The king mulled over what Gertrude suggested only to realize that he required more clarity. "How do you mean?"

I'll take this. This feels like progress, she thought.

Gertrude answered, "Your Majesty, if you show your court that you will not tolerate error from them, then word of your strength will trickle down through the pyramid. Eventually, even the lowliest of your people will know of how strong you are and that you are not dependent on the outdated counsel from the damn Gatherers...if you'll forgive my tongue, Your Majesty."

He glared straight into her mismatched eyes. "Gertrude, I have to ask you something. Are your curses against the Gatherings targeted at what you consider to be their bad taste in politics or simply your, hmm, how should I say it, *domestic* reasons?"

Gertrude crossed her arms and pursed her lips. She knew exactly what he was implying. "Sire, the situation with my father being prime minister has nothing to do with my direct ambition of convincing you to disband the Gatherers. Rich men decades past their prime living in castles leagues away from the territories they are supposed to represent are the voices of their people? It makes no sense!" Gertrude took a deep breath to deter her passion from too strongly influencing her words. "The people are distressed because their voices in court are not being heard, and they are starving. There's no work. The projects in my plan outline how we can put the people back to work, but until we begin to move forward with these initiatives, they may continue to steal in an attempt to survive. They're rising up because they are trying to get *your* attention."

The king laughed. "They're not children who need their hands held, Gertrude." The laughter abruptly stopped. The king scoffed, disgusted by the thought. "They're only proving what savages they are."

"Those 'savages' are your people! You cannot condemn a herd of sheep for being led to a slaughterhouse! They, like many others, learn from example. *Who*, your majesty, can you possibly imagine are their most prominent influences? It goes back to the Council, who are either not communicating to you or they are blaming you for their failures. Use your power and deter the nobles from tainting your name! You must show your people that you are not a pushover like your father! *Prove* that you will not be dominated by the prime minister, the nobles, or that bloody Council by striking the lords into action. There's no work; there's no food. Convince the lords that they must take steps to generate work, or they can start expecting much worse things than eggs being pelted at them. Please, Your Majesty, prove that you are a better man than your father."

"Or Donovan," the king muttered. It was not the fear of becoming his father, daunting as it was, that rattled his bones. It was the fear of becoming like his older brother Donovan that kept Herod from sleeping.

Herod walked away from Gertrude to the large bay window in his study. He wondered if he had done the right thing in inviting his brothers to the Council. Breyton was not a threat. No, the danger came from Donovan, to whom the crown would fall were any tragedy to befall Herod. The king shuddered at the thought of losing the crown. It was his. It belonged to him, and no one could remove it from his brow. He needed to produce a legitimate heir to secure his line's seat of immortality on the throne. His thoughts returned to Gertrude.

"Your Majesty," she said, trying to pull him back to attention.

Herod turned around quickly to face her. "Gertrude, I'm sorry, but I'm fatigued, and I would like a bit of rest before dinner. However—" He had hoped to ask her for something most dear to his heart at this meeting, but just as he opened his mouth Aleksie came through the door.

"Your Majesty, both of your brothers have arrived!" Aleksie shouted as he entered.

"Both?" Gertrude asked the king, who looked as though he was about to throttle Aleksie. "You didn't invite Donovan, did you?"

The pleading disposition in Gertrude's voice weighed heavily on Herod's heart. He knew when Gertrude stared critically at him that his decision to invite Donovan was ill-played. "He has been invited, yes," the king reluctantly answered. He gave Gertrude a light smile. "Donovan's lands have been the quietest and the most productive of all over the last several years. I'd like his insight in these times. Now," the king donned an energetic air as various men wishing an audience with him began to enter the room. Ignoring the crowd, Herod turned to Gertrude and said, "I think it best that you go take rest, as I certainly won't be getting any."

17

Squeezing past the men who wanted nothing to do with her, Gertrude muttered under her breath as she made it into the hall, "Take care, Sire. There are far too many predators here who see you as easy prey."

4

The Animal Court

D inner in the king's hall was an event to be seen. Like well-dressed animals, the high-borns gossiped and imbibed all that was around them. Though noble men and women, all manner of animals dined in Maltoro's great hall. The large-busted ostriches with their long, fair necks adorned with the finest of glimmering necklaces did not bury their heads in the sand. These ladies held their heads high, and they proudly cocked their breasts.

The hyenas draped in marvelous velvet robes, and elegant jewels took note of the ostriches with keen interest. They laughed gaily to every advance from those well-wined birds.

The boars were not present tonight, for the Gatherers did not meet for a few days, so why show before then? Even the swine who Gertrude had chased down the hall earlier in the day refrained from being present at dinner, finding a sweet bird instead with whom to occupy the time as he pleased.

The monkeys of the court did well in their attempts to climb the social ladders, but their failures were the most entertaining. The other animals would abuse them thoroughly with pecks, kicks, and claws if any of them came too close. The monkeys dared not touch the cheetahs, for a tug on one of their tails could prove to be a fatal final act.

The ever-alert cheetahs had enough experience to properly pick their intended, full-pocketed prey. Tonight, they had their keen eyes set on the currently empty chairs at the front of the hall, the best seats in the house. Never before had the prospect of prey been so numerous before.

The animals in the circus dined and drank heavily. This was their nightly routine. This was the feast of the animal court.

~*~*~

Not far from the dining hall, King Herod stood with Aleksie. The king rubbed his hand over the scar covered by pastel-blue sleeves with white trim. Herod recalled the last time he saw his brother Donovan. His arm with the scar from the duke's dagger still ached from time to time. He wondered if Breyton's hearing ever recovered in his right ear. In that encounter, had Donovan's fist landed any differently, it might have killed Breyton. Instead, the prince suffered significant hearing loss in one ear. It was a worthy price compared to what could have been.

Herod cringed to think of this ever-approaching encounter between Breyton and Donovan. The king was beginning to doubt his prime minister's advice that bringing his brothers together was the best thing to do.

However, Breyton dreaded little.

The prince, for the first time in several years, spotted his brother, standing in the light from nearby torches. Rolling his eyes and smiling, Breyton was not surprised to see his youngest brother dressing as he always had before.

"You never change, do you, you great pansy," Breyton jokingly said to Herod while still a distance away.

The sudden and unexpected echoing of Breyton's voice startled

Aleksie and Herod. Herod clutched his heart to keep it from abandoning his chest as he sharply turned to see the radiant face of his eldest brother.

"The long-lost prince does still exist!" Herod laughed as his brother pulled him into a tight embrace. "It's been too long, my brother," Herod whispered, but only after ensuring he was on the side on which Breyton could fully hear.

"I agree, but in all reality, our lives have been so busy that we hardly notice each other's absence," Breyton spoke the truth, and it cut Herod to the core.

In their youth, they had been the closest of the legitimate Malleus children. Breyton and Herod enjoyed the most time together, even with their age difference, while Donovan kept to himself and his falcons.

"I'm so glad you came," Herod said. "How are you, Breyton, honestly?" he inquired, seeing the wear of the years gone by in Breyton's eyes.

Sighing, the prince answered, "The past few years have been difficult without Inya, and I'll not pretend otherwise. It's been lonely. I was lost for a long time without her. In my wanderings throughout the lands to fill the time, I saw a lot and learned much more than some men find in a lifetime."

Aleksie asked, "And find yourself, did you?"

Scoffing at Aleksie, who never changed, Breyton answered, "Parts, yes—particularly new pains in my knees. On a much more serious note, Herod, on my journey here, I've heard a series of disturbing matters I must discuss with you in private."

Then, like a ghost emerging from the shadows, Donovan appeared.

Aleksie jumped and reached for his sword, fearing that a faceless foe had come for the king.

A quickly placed hand of Herod's fell upon Aleksie's shoulder.

"Be still," Herod told Aleksie, with a tinge of regret and disdain heavy on his breath. "It's just Donovan."

Donovan did not bother to hide his sneer. He did not look at Herod when he said, "*Just* Donovan. I'm surprised to hear so light a greeting after our last meeting."

Breyton felt the urge to throw a fist into Donovan's nose, which he had already broken years ago.

There were no two related entities in the world that possessed greater contradictions than Donovan and Breyton. Though their physical builds were similar in height and shape, those traits were all that claimed them as kin.

"Good evening, Donovan," the king greeted his brother with no enthusiasm. "I trust you are well?"

Donovan shot a look to the crown on Herod's brow and then to his eyes. "Do you mean have I recovered from being passed over for the crown, or have I finally accepted being a duke?"

"Come off it," Breyton tried to reason. "We are brothers first and foremost. Not enemies."

Donovan approached Breyton and looked his elder brother straight in the eye. With no effort to hide his hatred, Donovan growled, "It is because we are brothers that we are enemies."

Aleksie feared for his king. The malice present was thick enough to be sliced. Here in this hall, the peacock drew the shortest stick of the ability to defend himself. "Your Majesty, Your Highnesses," Aleksie interrupted, hoping to dilute the waters. "Your presence is highly anticipated in the dining hall. Shall we relieve the people of their waiting?"

Hoping to help Aleksie protect his king, Breyton nodded and said, "Come. We have guests waiting. I suspect we'll be the most colorful creatures under the tent."

The three brothers marched into the great dining hall.

All noises ceased upon their entry. The laughter and shrieking of the hyenas, the elephants, and the monkeys were all silenced.

Proudly the peacock walked, oblivious to the dangers all around him.

Reluctantly the bear stalked, disgusted by the lowly curs that called themselves nobility.

Observant, the lion prowled, sensing the dark and self-serving intentions of the court.

The brothers of blood settled in their seats overlooking the circus. As their feasts were served, the gluttony of the circus resumed. Every animal was present, except, Breyton noticed, one. Though her absence was of little meaning on the surface, Breyton stopped to ponder, *Where's Gertrude?*

5

Against the Grain

Tenderly the man pressed his body into hers.

Gertrude watched the passion in her lover's eyes as he sought nothing else but to be with her.

He loved her. Everything he did was for her. And she belonged to him, even though he could never belong to her.

Their love was a curse and a blessing, as love often is. It is a paradox that only those who have loved a forbidden one may fully understand with a mournful, blissful reverence.

Tucked in the safety of Gertrude's room, in their secrecy, they possessed more personal intimacy than most ever could. Their two months apart had been the longest they'd gone in some time without seeing one another. When they met this evening, they barely uttered a full sentence before falling lost to their passions.

However, while her body responded to his touches, her mind wandered.

Why are we doing this now? I have so many things I should be doing instead!

As his hand lovingly took hers, she thought, *Stay in this moment with him, Gertrude. You haven't seen him in two months. What's wrong with you?*

His adoration for her swelled. He was close, and yet her mind was nowhere in this room.

Why am I thinking about anything else? Stay here with him.

She locked her eyes on him as his fingers now played to her pleasure.

The clutch she held on his shoulders grew deeper, her breathing more erratic. Her back arched and a soft noise of fulfillment escaped from her heart.

The gentleman retreated, sighed.

She rested her head on the couch's arm, nestling herself more comfortably on the pillow that supported her. She gazed up to the ceiling doused in shadow.

We've been apart from each other so many times before, why does this reunion feel so different?

Her lover brought his lips to softly kiss her chin. As he continued to make her shudder with his touches, Gertrude pushed the thoughts away and smiled as warmly as summer's first sunrise. "Sam," she whispered through her shortness of breath.

Sam's love-filled eyes traced their way to Gertrude's in an instant. He mirrored her smile. "Gertrude." He pulled her face to a kiss. When their lips parted, he said, "I missed you so much. It kills me that I could not be with you."

Stroking her fingers through his short, thick black hair and occasionally caressing his brow and temples, Gertrude softly said, "You know I had no choice in that matter."

Pausing for a moment to place himself more comfortably, Sam took the moment to decide what he wanted to say. "Gertrude, I've heard some stories about your trip with the king."

Gertrude raised her brows, surprised to hear Sam's direct note on King Herod. It was his normal conduct to avoid the mess of politics. "How much did you hear?"

"That things did not go according to plan. That *you* did all of the footwork while Herod got drunk with the nearby high-borns. The rumors are not reflecting well for Herod."

Gertrude gave a curt nod. "That's essentially the summary of it. I managed to make several changes to that plan I've been working on based on my conversations with the people, which was good, but do you recall that agenda I arranged? With meetings of local representatives from here to the marinas in the far east?" She sat up and began to retie her bodice. She had an important dinner to get to and she could not afford to miss it.

"Of course." Sam also began to make himself presentable again, following her lead. "It took you months, if not half the year, to prepare."

Gertrude exhaled deeply. "He missed all of them."

Sam's jaw dropped.

"*All* of them," she reiterated, shooting her eyes to Sam.

"But...people were expecting him. The ramifications of him missing those meetings are..."

"Unimaginable." Gertrude's stomach clenched as she said it. "Actually, no, they're not unimaginable." She stood and fumbled through the pockets on her belt to find a rolled piece of parchment. "I received this just after my meeting with the king this afternoon, before coming here. Why it couldn't have arrived before..." She handed the letter to Sam. "I knew it wouldn't take long before we saw backlash, but I did not expect this." The quake in her voice was enough of a warning for Sam to prepare himself for heavy news.

As he read the note, his heart began to race. "Gertrude." He looked up to her after finishing it. "Tell me this isn't true?"

"I don't know," she whispered. "I sent a man to confirm it with his own eyes. Rumor will probably have it ringing throughout the halls before he makes it back." He offered the letter back to her and for the briefest of moments, she focused instead on the ring on his left hand. Sighing sharply, she decided that this was not the time for her to lecture him again on why she hated it when he wore it when they made love. She returned the letter to her belt and pressed on. "As of right now, we have to assume that this is true. After the shit our king pulled, I would not be surprised if all of our high-born families have nooses and torches to look forward to."

"Those rebels burned down three manors." Sam stood, enraged. "Murdered all those people, and *this* is your reaction?"

"And what would you have me do, Sam?" Gertrude was hurt to hear this from him. "Talk to the king? I've tried for years. Talk to the Council? They won't even let me into the Gatherings. Our biggest chance to right the wrongs was not only lost, it was also flaunted in the faces of the people who put me here, who *believed* in me, in my ability to have the king's ear, and now, because he chose to not listen to me, people that we know are going to die *horrible* deaths. Because Herod's head is so far up his ass that he is deaf to the screams all around him." Gertrude sighed heavily and began to walk toward the door. "Because *I* was not loud enough…many more will die. This is just the beginning, Sam."

"It's not your fault that he won't listen to you, Gertrude." Sam stood beside her. "The people will remember everything you've done for them."

"Ha." Gertrude squeezed his hand and said, "Memories run short and tempers run high when bellies are empty. I so wish you could have been with me these past few weeks, Sam. It would have made some parts easier to bear."

Sam scoffed. "I wish it too, but the king would not have been comfortable in such confines with me, the brother of a traitor."

Placing her hand on his heart, Gertrude said, "Come now, we have to get to that dinner. This is the first gathering of the brothers in years. What time do you have?"

Pulling out his watch from his pocket, Sam looked at it and said, "Time to go."

"Let me guess, we're late?" Gertrude slowly opened the door, peeking out to ensure that the hall was absent of eyes seeing her and her lover emerge.

"Not yet, but by the time we get there, we will be," Sam answered, following her out the door.

"Well," Gertrude said on the back of a chuckle. "I do like to make an entrance."

~*~*~

She told Sam that she had another meeting with the king after dinner, but there was none. She needed a chance to mull over her thoughts privately. With every step she took toward propriety, she made a stride away from her heart's true desire. She knew that one day she would have no other choice but to part from Sam. Even when that would become reality, though, Gertrude knew that she would always belong to him.

How cruel this is, she thought as she walked alone, *that I will always belong to him, yet he may never belong to me.*

Dinner had been a distracting enough experience to clear her thoughts of her personal affairs for a time. Seeing the three brothers at the head of the hall was witnessing not only a historic gathering but one that had the potential to shift the scale further in the minds of the people against them. Donovan was the brother the people feared. Herod, the one they hated. Breyton, the one they wished were king. She wondered how long it would be before he was added to the list of nobles to string up.

How long do any of us have? How will we ever recover from this?

As she walked, she tried to draft statements, statements she knew the king would never be allowed by the Council to make.

Could I bypass all of that and return to the people, to revisit the route that we made and give those statements on behalf of Herod anyway? The only way that Herod would ever know would be if Absalom found out. Ugh, but how do I go about avoiding that?

A maid that Gertrude knew well crossed the hall before her.

Oh, marvelous! Gertrude thought. *I haven't seen Luda for so long! This will give us a chance to catch up, and maybe I can find out what's really been happening here.* She hastened her step to catch Luda before she slipped away.

"Luda," Gertrude called, ten steps behind the woman of about her age.

The maid turned. The smile that Gertrude expected was absent, replaced with a straight expression.

"My lady." Luda curtsied.

The formality surprised Gertrude. They had known one another for years. Customs between their stations had long been forgotten. "Is everything alright?" Gertrude asked as she closed the distance between them.

Luda fidgeted with her hands. Her eyes darted left and right. She hopped forward and whispered, "They're saying that there's eyes in the castle. People looking to see where loyalties lie."

"Loyalties?" Gertrude asked, then wondered, *What new hell is this?*

Luda nodded and checked the hall again. She leaned closer to quietly say, "Between my class and yours. Is there anything else, my lady?" The second half of her statement, though it felt like a yell to Gertrude, was spoken in a normal tone. Luda leaned in once more and said, "I'm so sorry. I know you're my friend, Gertrude, and the greatest one my people have, but...be careful. Things may start to get really bad really quick."

Gertrude nodded. She more than understood. "You take care too. Let me know if you need anything."

Luda nodded, curtsied, then resumed her path.

Gertrude's stomach felt ill.

If Luda's this nervous, maybe we are too late.

The hall she walked straightened into an elongated and open walkway. The corridors were mostly empty at this time, which made for a perfect atmosphere for her silent reveries. This hall contained Gertrude's favorite thinking place. She needed to sit and think, to try to figure out how to possibly convey the building tensions and fears of the people to the king.

With this castle's occupants being too deeply involved in the hurly-burly of their own affairs, Gertrude was surprised to see Breyton in her spot.

Of course, she thought, her shoulders dropping. *My lifelong friend might as well have just told me that she can't talk to me anymore or either or both of us will be murdered, and now I can't even sit on my favorite bench. I suppose I'll just return to my room.*

Breyton sat with a book in hand by the window. He was so invested in his reading that he missed Gertrude approaching. With great speed and thoroughly focused interest, he continued to scan the pages of the novel in his hand.

As her elegant dress slipped by, the vibrant blue in her skirt caught his peripheral vision. Breyton's eyes popped up to see Gertrude attempting to glide by unnoticed.

"Gertrude." Breyton stood up so quickly that his book went flying from his hand onto the ground. It landed with a loud thud.

His sudden movement made Gertrude jump.

Breyton cursed himself for his not-so-gallant way of catching the lady's attention.

"Gertrude, I'm so sorry—I didn't mean to startle you."

"Breyton, forgive me for not stopping to greet you."

Their apologies ran over each other, making them both smile and their cheeks to further pinken.

As she stooped down to pick up the book that landed at her feet, Gertrude continued, "You seemed so intensely involved with your novel there that I didn't want to disturb you."

Breyton took the book from Gertrude and thanked her.

An odd speechless moment passed between the pair before Gertrude realized the time. "Why are you not breaking bread with your brothers? Isn't this your first communion with them in some time?"

It was true, Breyton did abandon their meeting, but this did not stop him from laughing at the lady's flagrant description. "Because, I'm sorry to say, the bread served at that animal carnival is stale and maggot filled."

Gertrude smiled, "Ah, I take it that your meeting with the king and the duke did not go so smoothly, and I see I'm not the only one who sees the court as an array of animals. Tell me, sir," Gertrude said with a smirk, "what beast are you?"

"Huh, I don't know for myself, but I have an idea for you." The gentleman rubbed his thinly bearded chin in contemplation of how best to tell Gertrude what he saw beneath her flesh. "They say that you're a maverick, a wolf; aggressive and reckless, but I don't see that. I think they've got you all wrong." Breyton waited a moment before saying, "A swan. Yes, a swan. You're protective of your position in the pond and you are willing to defend it from any foe, big or small. But, at the same time, you possess a gentility and a grace that is rarely seen nowadays. Yes, Gertrude, a swan is appropriate for you."

Seeing the roses flaring in Gertrude's cheeks, Breyton decided to take his flattery one step farther. "I suppose the blind fools judge you by your wolf-eye, and it may be for the better that they fear you. This way, I may be able to spend more time with you."

Gertrude gave a warm laugh. "Oh, my, you're quick to flattery, sir. Though, you're much better at giving compliments than your brother."

Breyton was somewhat put off by the notion that his little brother had the first chance and took advantage of it with Gertrude. "Has that brother of mine the idea in his head that he's good enough for an honorable lady like you?"

"Hunh," she scoffed, though more to the notion of being given the title of "honorable" than the larger theme of the sentence. "He is king, sir. He could, if he wished, have any lady he wanted, or any number."

His brows knitted. "I typically turn my ear away when the topics turn to the king, but from the tidbits I have heard, Herod's taken tribute to that hobby...May I ask, do you know if it is true?"

Taking hold of her wrist as brief flashes of the women who she knew the king had bedded came to her eyes, Gertrude smiled nervously and reiterated, "He *is* king."

A rock wedged itself in Breyton's gut. Two worries in his heart formed: the first was waged by memories of his father and Donovan; the other tarnished his hope of extending a hand toward further friendship with this lady, fearing that Herod had already been entertained by her. However, passing a conversation with her over that detail seemed trivial. While licking his lips, Breyton could not help to wonder, "How much like my father has my brother become?"

Gertrude and Breyton delved into the histories of the country's kings, the politics of old, and the daunting failures that could be approaching.

"You know, I've never told a soul about this." Breyton began a mild confession as a pleasant breeze from the window rolled in. "I fear for this country. Our high-born claim to know how to govern people, but you have to have a connection to the human soul and to the common good to claim anything like that. Seeing as how the nobility are animals wearing man's flesh, I just...I just don't know how this is all going to pan out for Herod and his bloody Gatherers."

Gertrude shot a raised brow at Breyton.

"Now don't give me that look," Breyton playfully scolded, his tone of voice becoming slightly effeminate, which was rather endearing to Gertrude. "I…my reason for turning down the crown should probably be known." Breyton repositioned himself closer to Gertrude on the bench. She did not mind the touch of his knee to hers. "From all the lessons I have collected over the years, one theme is continuously rearing its head: one man cannot alone govern a country of this size while controlled by a group of buffoons. Especially not a man who limits his vision to deal with the upper classes and who has hardly ever reached the eastern coast."

"Could you be any more specific?" Gertrude interrupted, smiling as she did.

Breyton looked down. "Mind you, I'm not happy to speak of my brother in this way. I'm afraid that for our country to survive as we know it, tyranny may be the next step—democracy has died."

"The question is, was it ever truly here to begin with?" Gertrude asked quietly, looking up the hall, then down the other side. "The people are afraid. I only just had an encounter with someone who is…maybe *was* a very dear friend of mine and is now so terrified of class division that she's afraid to be seen with me. The desperation that's brewing… given our government's inability to act, I guarantee that it will only get worse." Gertrude sighed and then looked to Breyton. "Do you…" She paused, not sure if she should ask this question. "Do you regret it? Not…you know…"

Breyton considered this question. Throughout most of his life, he had not regretted his decision to turn down the crown. However, he was no fool. Though his country home was tucked away from the building storm, his travels here had begun to open his eyes. "I don't believe in regret. There's no point in worrying about things you've done or decisions that you've made, but…" He looked away.

Bumping him with her elbow, Gertrude tried to lighten the moment.

"If you're afraid I'll run to Herod to tell him you think you should be king, I assure you that he would not be my first stop."

Smiling gaily, Breyton shrugged. "Your second one, then? After visiting a town crier? Gertrude, I assure you that my brother would never take offense from anything that I would say. He owes me the crown."

"I understand that. Honestly, it is not your brother that would concern me; I speak extremely bluntly in front of the king because it keeps him humble...ish. It's really more the prime minister whose shadow would be released from hell's fire should anyone threaten Herod's position."

Breyton knew that Gertrude's father was a brute, but he really could not see how someone as strong as her could be so intimidated by an old hound like him. However, Breyton did not want to turn the evening into something sad, so he found a different chord to strike. "Tell me, do you always speak metaphorically?"

A laugh escaped from Gertrude. "It's funny because Sam is always teasing me about my overly flagrant speech."

"Sam?" Breyton inquired, feeling an immediate and surprising surge of jealousy.

Sam was once Gertrude's number-one topic of discussion. She used to babble endlessly about Sam-this, Sam-that, but she was young then and inexperienced. At eighteen, when first she admitted her love to the gentleman, she was naïve and spilled out Sam's name with every other sentence. With age, experience, and whiplash, she became more sensitive to every time she mentioned her lover's sweet name. "Um, yes—he's my personal guard," Gertrude timidly answered.

"A personal guard?" Breyton inquired. "Have you really such threats?"

Nodding, Gertrude answered, "Oh yes. Do you know Igor Mislov?"

Breyton nodded. "Of course. That old bastard has been a part of the

King's Guard since my father or…or maybe it was Absalom who gave him that station…Anyway, he's been around a *very* long time. Why?"

"Have you ever noticed how he drools? Well, that's because when I was fifteen he tried to rape me and I bit the shit out of his lip to escape. My mother hired Sam immediately following, as she knew that Mislov would likely try again. She wasn't wrong, and he wasn't the only one."

Breyton clenched his fists. The rage that filled him toward Igor and Absalom blocked him from saying anything before his company continued. "Since all of that, Sam Maison has hardly left my side."

The name struck Breyton. "Samuel Maison of Legrette?"

The questioner's accurate knowledge of her lover's home startled Gertrude. "The same," she said with a chuckle of disbelief.

"I don't believe it," Breyton exclaimed, slapping his palm to his forehead. A million memories of his time in the service fluttered in his head. After he abdicated the crown, Breyton reenlisted in the army and found himself moving up in the ranks. When he became a colonel and held charge of his own platoon, several boys passed through his command, but four or five lads elected to stay with him for many years. Samuel Maison was one of these men. Breyton knew him to be deceptively capable of engagement, yet Sam could be the gentlest and most loyal man he had ever been lucky enough to meet. "I knew Sam; we served together in the military. A damn good man. How's he doing?"

"He's fine and doing well for himself. When was the last time you saw him?" It felt so foreign to speak of him; no one in court had ever cared about Sam before.

"Years. Nearly a decade, even. I must have been in my mid-thirties. I left the military shortly after I married…" Breyton ran his fingers pensively through his graying beard as he pondered the correct distance of time. "I'm forty-two now, so that's nearly nine years. Sam was only around twenty-four, maybe twenty-five when I left."

Gertrude's brows lifted. Sam was twenty-six when they met. "That *has* been a long time. A lot has happened since then. He's married and he has a son. He fell into a small bit of fortune, too, shortly after he left the military."

"Really?" Breyton asked. "How so?"

"My mother's employment," she answered with a wink and a smile. "It took him a few years to settle some debts his late father left him and now with the help from my mother's generous checks, the span of his lands has expanded and he has become a successful proprietor."

Returning to the castle, though at first a terrible choice to make, was turning surreptitiously for the better. "Well, I'll be damned," Breyton muttered. "Is he here in Maltoro with you now?"

Nodding, Gertrude confirmed Breyton's inquiry. "I was surprised to see him, actually. He was not able to accompany me on Herod's and my tour around the country, unfortunately. The king has a ludicrous reservation against him, which prohibited Sam from tagging along."

Breyton fought the urge to roll his eyes at what sounded like another one of his brother's terrible choices.

"Do you think I could see Sam?" Breyton shyly asked. "It'd be good to see him again."

"Of course. I wonder, he may still be awake." Gertrude pulled out her silver pocket watch from a small clip on her dress expecting to see the time to be somewhere around eleven. However, much to her horror, it was ten after two. Gertrude popped up from the bench.

"Oh, my goodness!" she started. "Could it really already be after two? I'm sorry to end the evening, but I must retire. I have an extremely busy day tomorrow."

The time had passed so quickly and so smoothly. He was sorry to see it end. "Well, in that case, I had better be getting to bed as well. Though I will admit, I could easily keep talking to you for hours more."

The smile that spread across Breyton's face filled Gertrude with a warm swell and a surge of pink in her cheeks. She bowed her head and gently said, "As could I with you." She swallowed hard, for it was difficult not to keep talking. "Good night, sir," she said succinctly as she bowed. As she began to walk down the hall, Gertrude realized how much she did not want to stop talking to Breyton, and yet, she knew, she had to return to Sam.

"Good night, Gertrude," Breyton called after her; then, more quietly, he whispered, "I wish you the sweetest of dreams. I know that mine will be."

6

Rain

With tender care, Gertrude opened the door. As she had suspected, when she entered her room, she saw that Sam was in bed, sound asleep. A wave of adoring passion swelled in her as she quickly closed the door so that no passerby would spot her inappropriate company.

He did look adorable to her, lying deep within the pillows with an opened and well-read book resting on his chest. And yet, that shadow in her stomach began to stretch and grow.

This used to be so much easier, but now...what's changed?

She carefully removed the book from his sleepy clutch and placed it on the nightstand, lit by three flickering candles. Gertrude gently kissed Sam's forehead. She gave a loving squeeze to his ringless hand to softly alert him to her late presence.

Sam shook his head from his sleep, awakened by the lady's touch. He gave his arms and legs a great stretch. Through an elongated yawn, the good sir declared, "I was worried you'd get back around the time I'd have to leave. I couldn't even begin to imagine what sort of task would keep you so long. Was it something Herod gave you? What time is it, anyway?"

"I, er, I did have so many things to do for Herod. Lots of catching up to be done to clean up after our trip," she quickly lied with a ring of truth. "And it's well after two, love," Gertrude mechanically answered as she circled the foot of the bed to her dresser, untying the bodice of her dress in preparation for bed. "Forgive me, Sam, for not being in earlier. I was caught in a conversation I couldn't call myself to end."

"Really?" Sam drowsily asked while rubbing the bridge of his nose. "With whom?"

She decided not to tell Sam of Luda. She did not want to worry him this late. As she continued to unbutton, unlatch, and unlace her clothing, she answered, "To Breyton Malleus."

"Oh? How is he?" Sam asked, pushing his body into a more erect position beneath the sheets to keep himself from falling asleep mid-conversation.

Shimmying out from her underskirt, Gertrude answered distantly, "Very well. How come you never told me that you served with Breyton?"

The tone of his lady's voice had the slightest hint of berating, but Sam was too tired and too distracted by her undressing to notice. Shrugging, he casually replied, "I didn't think it was that big a deal."

Finished with her undressing, Gertrude slid her freed body into bed. "Several years of your life, darling, isn't that serious?" she asked sarcastically. "So am I just a pin-drop in your thoughts?"

"Heavens, no!" Sam rolled over to capture his girl in his arms. He kissed the fidgeting lady several times, then countered, "You'll forever be in my thoughts." He kissed her slowly, then drew back to say, "And you know, in all truth, I do think about Breyton from time to time. He's a good man—one to admire. When I was a part of his platoon, there were four or five of us who would sit around the fire after our duties to listen to his stories. He always had the best topics and tales to keep us entertained. Of those men in the platoon, including myself, there is not one of us who would not willingly follow him to the end of the world and back again." For a moment, Sam paused to briefly reflect on the incredible intellect and maturity Breyton Malleus possessed compared to his brother, the king. "You know, I truly would have liked to have seen Breyton as king, but..." In silence, Sam finished his point.

Slowly, sensuously running her fingers down his chest, Gertrude airily affirmed, "I think he has certainly made it clear that he repudiates the thought of himself as king, which is ridiculous because he is more than qualified for the part. In my nearly twenty-six years, I have never met a man more appropriate for the post than Breyton."

The pair's thoughts drifted into wondering what position their proud country, Vitenka, would be in if a different Malleus was their king.

After that silent moment's meditation, Gertrude noticed the charming stare Sam locked onto her. It was as if he was filled with a tantalizing secret that made him want to burst at the seams. Gertrude bashfully nestled herself deeper into his embrace and tucked her head beneath his chin.

He rubbed her shoulders. Sighing, Sam whispered, "I missed you so. I know we've been apart longer, but this absence seemed harder than any of the others. I was thinking about that day all those years ago—the eve of your first departure to the Northern University. Do you remember?"

Chuckling, Gertrude rubbed her face against Sam's chest and answered, "I can still feel the rain on my face..."

A cool breeze from the lake crossed over the pair, making Gertrude shiver. The new dress she'd received for her ever-approaching eighteenth birthday was hardly appropriate for damp, windy weather like this, but she did not care. The cold and the rain would not distract her from the task that she was so determined to perform. It had to be done, she knew. She simply could not go another day without telling Sam the truth. She would be gone tomorrow.

The pair strode over the crest of the largest hill on the manor's grounds toward the lake. The waters reflected the face of the troubled, gray sky.

With hands still in his pockets, Sam's steps fell a few behind Gertrude's. The young lady progressed down the hill. Near the belt of the hill, halfway to the strand of black pines towering around the edge of the lake, she turned back toward Sam.

"Are you willing to sit with me for a minute, Sam?" she inquired while holding her hands above her eyes to block the light of the afternoon from her sight. "There's something I'd like to talk to you about."

Sam looked to the lake. A great curtain of rain descending from the heavens was beginning to pound on the once peaceful waters. The rain hummed in the ever-nearing distance.

Finding no spot to be greater than the next, she dropped herself on the grass beneath her feet. She patted the ground beside her as an invitation to Sam to do the same. Gertrude's different-colored eyes stared off into the rainy, blurred horizon. Taking several deep breaths and fiddling with her hands, she swallowed hard. Every word that she had rehearsed on uncountable occasions prior slipped from her mind and disappeared into the darkness.

"Sam," she started, but she did not know where she would end. "You...you know that you are the dearest friend that I've ever had, and you're my most constant companion...I mean, you're paid to be, but you seem to enjoy my oddities genuinely, so, over the years, I've grown to be so comfortable with you..." She paused when a significant drop of rain piddled down her face. "Um, I feel like I can trust you with anything. I mean, you already know most of my secrets, but there's still one that I've withheld from you, and over the next year, I know I won't be able to keep it to myself, so I have to share it with someone. On that note..." Gertrude spun herself onto her knees to face Sam as more and more large drops fell upon the pair. "I'm going to miss you, Sam."

The rain began to come steadily down, but Sam saw that the gathering wetness on Gertrude's face was self-produced. The heart in him ached with the sight of Gertrude's tears, which now disappeared amongst the downpour abusing them. "I'm going to miss you too," he blurted out.

The harsh pounding of the rain muted the strong emotion ringing from Sam's voice, but the longing radiating from his eyes struck her. She was not prepared to see such a sight. The glow from his body language, the pain, and the affection, stung into her soul and ripped out her tongue. The rain soaked through their clothes and chilled their bones. All hope for any further speech evaporated from Gertrude's mind. She stared, lost, at Sam and he back at her. Her body was trembling from the intensity of the moment. Panic soon swelled within her.

A dozen words suddenly stumbled out from her mouth in a hurdle of senseless babble.

The heavy curtain of rain distorted her words, making Sam deaf to what she said.

The gentleman shook his head and hollered, "What?" unaware of the fact that Gertrude had just spilled out her soul to him.

Feeling like a babbling idiot, Gertrude ejected her body from the ground and ran off toward the trees at the bottom of the hill, trying to hide her crying face.

Having no idea what had passed, Sam reared up from the ground and followed her. Gertrude's sodden body made it to the cover of the ancient trees before her protector caught up to her side. Childishly, Gertrude leaned against an obliging tree and crossed her cold, exposed arm s.

Not wanting the girl to advance a step farther, Sam grabbed hold of her shoulders and yelled over the shouts of the storm, "What's wrong?"

Shuddering from the cold and the concern in Sam's eyes, Gertrude found in herself another wave of courage. "I love you," she said.

Unfortunately, Sam hadn't a chance of hearing her correctly, for at that *very moment, the thunder rolled and lightning cracked. "What?" Sam yelled as he leaned as close as he could to Gertrude. He was sure that he must have heard her wrong.*

Gertrude clenched her fists and hollered in Sam's face, "Damn it, Sam! I LOVE YOU!"

Had a horse fallen from the sky, Sam would have been less surprised.

Lost in utter shock, he stared with no visible emotion at her. The grip he held on her shoulders grew a little weaker.

Unnerved by the silence, Gertrude shouted, "You mad-ass, don't just stand there, say something! Anything!"

Sam had nothing to say. He pulled Gertrude against him and drew her into a forceful kiss. He gently pushed her to arms' distance and said, "I love you too, you silly blunt fool."

A loud whistling wind swept through the trees as Sam and Gertrude grasped onto each other in a sweet embrace.

"I don't know what I'll do without you," the young lady sobbed into Sam's chest.

The man pulled her closer to his soaked body. Her wet hair, heavy from the rain, slipped out from its formerly neat bun and clung to her face and neck. He brushed it back from her face and thanked heaven for this opportunity to finally touch her soft cheeks.

Gertrude swallowed hard, then gently pushed him away. "Come to Viramont with me."

The question seemed so simple that the immediate answer from Sam's heart was "yes," but Sam was of reasonable thought, and he knew that though he wanted to, leaving his home, his class, to pursue an affair damaged every ounce of ethical rules he had ever absorbed.

"Gertrude, I-I can't. There are too many twists in our case that would prevent me from going with you to Viramont," Sam said, though every word was like a knife to his heart.

"What? But you are Samuel Maison of Legrette! Decorated, honorable

ex-military! The man who sprung from farmhand to proprietor in less than five years! What do you mean you can't come abroad with me?"

The pouring rain and the whipping wind let off for just a moment for Sam to explain himself. The gentleman ran his hand over his face, clearing his eyes from the rain. "Gertrude, if I were to run away with you, which is exactly what you are suggesting, well, first of all, Viramont would not grant us asylum because you are our prime minister's daughter; they are too smart to involve themselves with such a scandal. Second, I am married. Yes, it was arranged, but I can't leave my wife; the laws of our country will not permit it under the circumstances. As to your class, Gertrude, the distance between us...I'm just a farmer in their eyes. No better than the ground they spit on. I am your servant, your mother's most trusted employee, nothing more. And if I dared to 'kidnap' you, which is how the nobles here would twist our act, I would be removed from all decent society and manners of humanity, never to be seen again."

"They're not going to tar and feather you, Sam!" Gertrude argued, squeezing his hands in a desperate, pleading manner. "I doubt my father would notice my absence. He'd probably love the fact that he wouldn't have to pay to support me anymore! Sam, he doesn't even know I'm leaving tomorrow. What makes you think he'd notice that we'd done a runner?"

Once more, Sam pulled his sobbing, soaking Gertrude into his arms. There would be no changing his mind.

Thunder rolled over the hills toward the trees where the two stood.

She hated to admit it, but she knew that he was right.

"I'll write to you all the time," she mumbled against his heart. "Every day. The papermakers in Viramont will scarce be able to keep up with me."

The gentleman tightened his hold on the young lady. "I'll wait on the porch for your posts every day," Sam confessed. He kissed the top of Gertrude's head. "I love you, Gertrude."

Gertrude kissed Sam's hand, then pulled away. Looking at him straight in the eye, she said, "I know, Sam. I've always known. If I have to, I will wait to love you openly and freely until the day when trumpets sound and the heavens part. Until then, Sam, you will always have my heart. Always."

7

In the Tearoom

Sam awoke before the dawn. He could not be seen with the lady in her room by another soul's eyes. The nights were so short during the summer. It seemed like torture to spend so little intimate time beside the woman he loved. Sam unwound his arms from around his sleeping beauty. He paused before leaving the bed to marvel at how lovely she was and to briefly wonder what life would be like if only the fates were a bit more merciful. Divorce from his wife remained out of the question.

Quietly, Sam buttoned up his breeches. As he straightened his silk cravat, he contemplated waking Gertrude to bid her goodbye or to leave her with a silent kiss. He chose the latter, not wanting to disturb the sleeping lady. The bed sank where he placed his knee to lean down and kiss her.

She stretched and looked up to see the stray lights from the outer world reflecting in Sam's eyes.

"Is it morning already?" Gertrude drowsily asked. She latched her fingers around Sam's wrist to prevent him from leaving.

"It is," he answered with a sense of remorse reverberating through his words.

Gertrude pushed herself up on her elbows and forearms, hoping to have a proper word with Sam. "What is your agenda for the day?"

Sitting on the bedside, Sam answered, "The same as yours, like always."

"I'm not sure that you will be able to follow me for a portion of the day, dearest," Gertrude supposed.

"Will you be with Herod or spying again?" Sam inquired as he rested his hand on the other side of Gertrude's legs.

"A bit of both, really," Gertrude answered, but before she said any more, she fiddled with Sam's silk cravat and straightened his collar. "While I'm doing my duty for the king, Sam, why don't you wait in the nearby hall for me. I feel terrible for making you stand around on top of keeping you up so late waiting for me last night, but you'll join me for breakfast, yes?"

"Of course," Sam answered.

The warmth from the pale morning started to fill the room. Gertrude looked over to the window. "You'd better get going, love. The castle'll start stirring soon." Turning back to him, she fiddled with his collar once more.

Sam leaned forward and kissed Gertrude. "Good night, then," he whispered. "There're still a few hours before you're due for breakfast. Do you need me to fetch Yuri Philemon for your morning meeting?" Sam stood from the bed and looked inquiringly at Gertrude.

The lady pulled her legs up to her chest and thought about this offer for a moment. She knew that there was deep tension between Sam and Yuri from past events, but the fact that Sam offered to collect him made her feel less guilty about accepting his offer. She nodded. "Could you, please?" she sweetly said.

He nodded, then walked to the door. With his hands resting on the handle, Sam turned back to Gertrude and said, "Dream that I am still here beside you. Holding you, caressing you. Try to let that soothe you back to sleep. And right before you slip away, hear me say, 'I love you.'"

Sighing and smiling, temporarily lost in her lover's romantic ways, Gertrude wrapped her arms around her knees. "I love you, too, my dear sweet one. Now get out of here, you soft bastard," she added playfully with a wink.

Sam left, leaving Gertrude behind to struggle with her internal war of guilt and joy for being loved.

~*~*~

For Gertrude, mornings were tough enough, but dealing with a pounding headache while operating on four and a half hours of sleep and recovering from an exhausting journey was an unusually heavy load. She could not wait to get her hands around a strong cup of tea. She felt so silly that morning when she pulled her dress on backward, then put a boot on the wrong foot, and a myriad of other mindless moments. She knew that she could laugh the morning off as soon as she genuinely woke up, but for now, she was cranky and bitter for her drowsiness. She pitied any person who came between her and that first cup of tea. However, when she saw Breyton trooping down a hall not too far from her, her mood changed. She ran after him, throwing the customs of her culture to the wind. "Breyton!" she called halfway down the hall.

Breyton immediately turned on his heels at the sound of Gertrude's voice calling his name. "Good morning," he eagerly said. Feeling like a fool already, Breyton cleared his throat and asked, "Did you sleep well?"

The question felt odd as men did not typically ask her such intimate matters. "I suppose so," she succinctly answered. "Um, did you?" she asked.

"Oh yes," Breyton quickly lied. He had spent the entire night awake, dreaming of her. "What can I do for you, Gertrude?" He deepened his voice and slowed his words in an attempt to make up for his quick answers.

"Breyton, would you like to join Lord Philemon, Mr. Maison, and me for breakfast? It's going to be served in the second landing's tearoom." Gertrude's cheeks flared red.

Why did I ask him that? She wondered. *And why on earth do I feel so nervous right now?*

The lady blurted out her words so quickly that Breyton had to pause to recognize what she asked of him. "Er, yes, I'd be delighted," he answered. "Is there any particular reason Yuri will be joining you?"

While she did not particularly care for Yuri, she needed him as an ally. "Of the lords in court, Lord Philemon has one of the most attuned ears for the people. I think he can be a tremendous help toward fixing the mess that we are currently in." She shrugged and said, "So that's that. Shall we?" She pointed over her shoulder back in the direction from where she came.

Breyton had already eaten, but he agreed anyway and happily accompanied Gertrude for his second breakfast and another chance to be in her company.

Upon entering the room, the comforting scents of tea and freshly baked pastries greeted them. The bright circuitous room with a round table in the middle was where Gertrude held conferences. Due to the sensitive nature of the events she hosted here, food for the meetings was always self-serve. Servants did not need to "accidentally" overhear a bit of political news to spread. Gertrude longed to have a proper private study that she could call her own as her place for meetings and correspondence, but the prime minister forbade it. She'd lost track of the times she'd asked Herod to address this matter, emphasizing each time how ridiculous it was for the king's advisor not to have such a space. Knowing now that Herod's crown did not equal a stable spine in the man, she decided to make the best with what she had.

Smiles ignited on Sam and Breyton's faces at seeing one another after so much time had passed. The pair wrapped their arms around one another.

"It's so good to see you, Sam," Breyton said while slapping his old comrade's shoulder.

"I'm glad to see you," Sam replied. Aside from being thrilled to see his old friend again, a great sense of relief filled him to see the smart Malleus with the king's advisor at last.

The men exchanged promises to take the time to catch up as Gertrude took her seat. Her chair was pulled out for her by Breyton, an act that Sam did not fail to notice, for Breyton beat him to the chase.

A knock came to the door, and the cheerful mood shifted. Sam clenched his muscles and started to repeat to himself not to say anything to the man who was about to enter.

Lord Philemon did not wait for the door to open. The cheerful man that Breyton had long known did not enter. He greeted the prince with a silent bow and then turned to Gertrude. "I was asked to bring you this." He extended a sealed parchment to Gertrude and rounded the table to take his seat. With heavy steps, he passed Sam as if the man were no more than a piece of furniture. The silence between them suited both men just fine.

Breyton found this all wrong but refrained from making any comments.

Gertrude had a sneaking suspicion that this message would confirm the rumor of the attacks on the high-born families. Though it felt like an angry storm was billowing to life in her stomach, she split the envelope's seal.

The men watched her skim the note and saw a gray cloud overtake her.

She sighed heavily and looked out the window behind where Sam stood, her eyes unfocused.

"Gertrude?" Breyton called.

She turned her gaze back to the table. Her stomach felt sick, but she had to share this. "I sent a messenger out yesterday to confirm or dismiss a rumor, and it seems as if it is true." She tapped the letter in her hand up and down upon the table. "Three. Three houses. Three high-born families have been murdered because of our inability at court to"—the words that initially came forward were "do anything," but that did not feel right—"to convince others that our people are desperate. I doubt even this will do much of anything." She tossed the letter to the center of the table.

Sam dropped his gaze. Gertrude's long-held fears were materializing, and there was nothing that he could do to help.

"What names, Gertrude?" Breyton asked. "What families? The entire families?"

She nodded. "As far as the letters say, yes. Children have been hung naked from the gates of their household alongside the bodies of their mother and father." Her voice cracked. She was determined not to cry in front of these men, though if ever there was a moment for becoming emotional, this was it. "They're up in the northeast, these families. The Rybins, the Kazakovs, and the Gagarins. We were—the king's party and I were—scheduled to stay with the Gagarins on our trip, but our king thought the surrounding area too rural." She shut her eyes. She hoped that when she opened them, she would wake from this nightmare. Unfortunately, the concern-laden faces that looked back at her said otherwise.

"What can we do?" Yuri asked, praying that his wife and children would remain sound when he returned to his home. "Is it already too late?"

After taking a deep breath, Gertrude said, "I don't believe that all is lost yet. And, Yuri, there is something that you can do. I have reason to believe that the Council's waters will be expanding and that your lands and your name have come up for consideration." A stunned silence followed the announcement. Anointment into the Council was no small feat. A member of the Gatherers possessed a voice in the political realm that the majority of players in this game lacked. She continued, "With the rebels now rising to violent actions, if your name is up for consideration at Council, it would be paramount for the people—for all the people, noble or not—for you to accept."

Breyton was the first to speak. "But Gertrude, all seats are filled. If Yuri is accepted, it would mean that one other member is being prepared for burial, as death is the only way the Gatherers leave."

Sipping from her second helping of tea, hoping to chase away the vision of the violence that could come, Gertrude nodded. She explained, "While on our venture, we learned that Deo Aspiruth is terminally ill. He will not be present at the Gathering this upcoming week."

"But why me?" Yuri probed. "Of all the lords, why me?"

"I'm surprised you have to ask that," Sam said, from his position leaning against the wall with his arms folded over his chest. A look of extreme disdain was seething from his demeanor. "After all, you are Aspiruth's closest neighbor. The Council believes that your people fear you respectfully, and you're such a loyal subject and all, so why not?"

Gertrude's mouth gaped. She could not believe that Sam would dare to speak to Yuri at this moment.

"When did you become a great political expert, Mr. Maison?" Yuri cruelly asked. "Read up on some of your literature, did you?"

Sam put his hand on the tang of his saber, which Yuri missed, but Gertrude and Breyton caught.

"Enough!" Gertrude demanded. "Let us not bring in past accusations that are irrelevant to our present cause." Gertrude shot a look at

Sam. He looked murderous. This was one of the few times his temper ever flared to such an extent. Seeing her gaze calmed him. His hand slipped off his weapon, and he resumed his stance.

Gertrude's intense eyes shot over to Yuri's. "How dare you?" she scorned. "Don't you ever bring that up in front of me again! Don't make me regret telling you about the Council's decision before it's made. Do you understand?"

Yuri leaned back in his seat and nodded his head.

Seeking to relax the simmering tension in the room, Breyton cleared his throat and said, "You know, Gertrude, Sam, Yuri, not to change the subject, but I've something rather important I ought to tell you. Especially to you, Gertrude." Breyton pointed to the lady across the table. He began his story of the trip from his home in the north to the castle by the sea. "I'm sure you all know of the town of Lubstin—it's just east of you two." Breyton looked at Sam and Yuri, whose homes were less than an hour's ride from each other.

The two nodded.

"I stopped there, at the local inn for the night, under a false name for my safety because of what's been happening lately, and as I was getting ready for bed, I happened to overhear something I'm positive I would have been killed for hearing." Breyton reflectively stroked the sides of his chin as he remembered that evening. "On the other side of the wall to my room, three or four individuals were discussing particular plans. They may have just been talking as people tend to do, but it's still a matter to be taken seriously. There were two leaders, it sounded like, and they seemed to be recruiting new members to join their cause against the high-borns. The leaders did not identify themselves, but they certainly spread no ambiguity in discussing their goals."

This was not a tremendous surprise, but if it was important enough for Breyton to bring up, Gertrude decided to ask questions instead of shutting him down. "Against the high-borns? Like by these means?" She held up the letter. A chill ran down her spine as she envisioned countless other families meeting similar gruesome fates.

Breyton shook his head, frustrated by his handicapped hearing, which did not catch all of the details. "I did not hear the details of their plan, but these people did not sound like a bunch of students blowing off steam; they were describing ways to recruit staff from the castle and the city."

"I spoke to a friend of mine who is a servant here," Gertrude said. "She said that there are spies in the castle. This is a person that I have known for *years,* and she was terrified to so much as being seen with *me,* simply because I am a high-born."

"Have you had the opportunity to tell the king already, Breyton?" Yuri asked a moment before Gertrude could.

Breyton nodded. "Yes, and he'll probably talk to you about it sometime today, Gertrude. You have to convince him to back off on the police action and give the people a chance to be heard properly because that is exactly why they are burning houses and hanging people. Their voices are not being heard in those Gatherings!"

"Don't you think I've tried?" Gertrude snapped. "Herod will not listen to me on that matter. I cannot tell you how many times I've told him exactly that in the past several months! It's that damn Council and people like Igor Mislov that started all of our country's problems. They're just there to take advantage of their posts and pretend that they're doing something when all they're doing is getting away with murder. How many more people will have to die before anyone beyond the four of us realizes this?!" Gertrude bit her tongue from saying that Herod was the Council's marionette and that he was too weak to make his own decisions, something that the prime minister found much pleasure in exploiting. "Breyton, can't you say anything? He is your brother. Surely, he will listen to you. And why didn't you tell me any of this last night?"

The two men not involved in this conversation made eye contact, both curious about that last statement. Of course, Sam knew that Gertrude and Breyton had shared an innocent conversation, but Yuri assumed that she and Breyton had relations more than friendship in the dark of night, which would explain why they came in this morning together.

Breyton rubbed the bridge of his nose and sighed. He could not bring himself to look Gertrude in the eye as he spoke. "I can't. Though he brought me here for Council, I can't tell Herod or give him advice in politics. What credibility could I possibly have after giving up my right for the crown?" That was the one reason why Breyton regretted his choice for giving up his seat for power—that and the lost opportunity of eliminating the Council.

8

Interviews with the King

I n the secret nook next to the king's study, Gertrude listened in
on a meeting between the king and two Council representatives
from the eastern corner of the country. She feverishly recorded
in her leather-bound journal every word spoken between the men
in a language that few in their country knew. The inkwell she had
bound to her wrist like a bracelet, left dots of ink running across her
arm and pages. Her quick scribblings in Heltkor, the dialect of her
mother's homeland, looked like gibberish to most, but it was much
more comfortable and quicker to write than the symbols of her people.
Today was not a day that could afford missed documentation.

"Your Majesty, please," Lord Lelik casually pleaded, "there is no
need to believe that these rumors are correct." Lelik pointed to his
comrade Joseph Skizki and continued, "If anything like that were
happening anywhere near our jurisdictions, we would know. Our
men are everywhere." Lelik put his hands over his heart and shrugged
his shoulders. "I assure you, sire, there is no threat from our people."

Herod tapped his fingers on his knee as he sat behind his desk. The
king narrowed his gaze on the two men before him, men he was
supposed to be able to trust, but now after his conversation with

Gertrude before this meeting, he was no longer as confident in their loyalty. "Lelik, I will not ignore this news. The information I received was credible beyond doubt. High-borns are dying."

Upon hearing this, Gertrude looked up from her writing. Before this meeting, she had brought the letter to Herod. She wanted him to see it with his own eyes before talking to these men whose lands bordered those of the slain. *Hunh, it's sort of nice to hear that you think so highly of my reports. It's a damn shame it took a letter confirming that people are dying for you to start seeing what I've been talking about for ages.*

"Nor should you ignore them, Sire," Lelik continued. He scratched the bottom of his unshaven chin and smiled, much like Gertrude thought a snake would. "Your Majesty, would it put you at ease if Joseph and I sent our men undercover through every one of our towns and taverns until these rumors are confirmed, or anyone connected to these alleged events are caught?"

Gertrude wanted to burst through the silence and slap the king to get him to wake up. *It is ludicrous to think that these men will find those responsible for murdering those families when they're casting doubt upon the reality of their deaths.*

"Please, gentlemen," Herod spoke less confidently than Gertrude or even his bodyguard, tucked silently away behind him, had ever heard before. "I implore you to keep an eye out for any civil unrest. If your people have something to say..." Gertrude's quill stopped and levitated a millimeter above the page. She could not dare to guess what Herod was about to say. With a chest full of air, the peacock replied, "Let them speak."

The woman in the adjoining room wanted to leap for joy, for her words had finally penetrated the king. However, Joseph, who had been extremely quiet throughout the majority of this interview, crushed her moment of victory.

"Your Majesty," Joseph's airy voice started as the heavy man reposi-tioned himself in the seat that was too small for his bulbous hips. "Of course, we will do that. Our only purpose in life is to serve our king, and until our hounds sniff out these criminals, perhaps Your Majesty should, I don't know, do something to rouse the spirits of the people."

The king's fingers stopped tapping. The blue-eyed monarch stared quizzically at the two men and asked, "Like what?"

Immediately Gertrude whispered desperately, "Don't say ball, oh please, don't let them say ball!"

The two men exchanged a look of satisfaction, and then they looked back to the king. Joseph suggested, "Well, you could have a jousting tournament, bear-baiting, or maybe even..."

Oh, don't say it, you low-down piece of sh—

Gertrude's silent curse was interrupted by the king's weakness spilling out of Joseph's mouth. "A ball, sire," he said with a mischievous smile.

She shut her journal and capped the inkwell. She already knew his answer.

But Herod hesitated. "Why, Lelik, Joseph, should I invest in such a gay expense while my people are unhappy?" Herod quickly glanced over at the mirror, then back to the men before him. "Would it not look as though I was celebrating their misery?"

Joseph shook his egg-shaped head and, from his crooked teeth, said, "Oh, no, no, Sire, not at all. It would not be a celebration, but rather, a toast for hope."

Lelik smiled and nodded. "Aye, a toast for hope. The people would see that you are moving in the right direction, Sire, that you are willing to step in a new direction and lend the masses your ear. Be the king you can be."

Gertrude swore she could almost hear carnival music as these shameless men toyed with their well-dressed puppet, making him dance and sing to whatever tune they commanded.

Herod leaned back in his chair and tapped his finger to the dimple in his chin. He looked over his shoulder to Aleksie, whose flat expression did not show his thoughts. Herod did not know what to do. He knew that Gertrude would disapprove, but her father would probably highly recommend a ball; they were always opposites.

Herod perked up and slapped his hands on his desk. "Gentlemen," the king said, disregarding everything Gertrude had ever taught him. "I do believe you have something there that I will consider. Perhaps we will raise our glasses at this ball to honor the families who perished, so their memories will not be lost to the ashes."

Gertrude slowly banged her head against the solid wall away from the mirror, trying to wake herself from this nightmare.

"Now, if you two will excuse yourselves," the king continued, "take the proper time to investigate those murders and report back to me everything you learn."

They bowed deeply to their king, whose support they supped like a fine wine. "Oh of course, Sire," Lelik assured him. "Anything for you, Sire." He and Joseph bowed in unison as they closed the door.

Now came the part that Herod dreaded: the after-interview with the one woman he admired and feared the most. Sighing, he gave his right hand the command. "Aleksie, open the door."

Aleksie crossed the room. He found on the painting's frame the secret lever and pulled. With a click, the portrait opened, and standing on the other side was a sight the king hesitated to see.

Gertrude inhaled deeply, and upon the exhale emerged from her spot in the wall without a word. The temper-controlling exercise she practiced regularly helped today, but she now craved a smoke or a drink to soothe her nerves. The young lady tapped her fingers to her journal and fiddled with her quill. She kept taking in deep and silent breaths, but one direct look at Herod broke her concentration. The king stood and walked over to the aperture. "Ah, Gertrude," Herod started, holding out his arms.

Aleksie snuck away to the far side of the king's desk, seeing her fury. Seeing this as well, the king's arms awkwardly lowered to his sides. "A ball?" she asked shortly. "A 'toast for hope'? Your Majesty." Gertrude was about ready to strike the king blind, but her anger management, slow, deep, steady breaths, and a stern look from Aleksie calmed her. She swallowed hard and looked away. She knew that this ball spelled nothing less than doom for their country, but she had to finally admit to herself that there was nothing more she could do to prevent what would be a tragedy. "Your Majesty, I have but one question: do you honestly believe it possible for a ball to boost *the people's*, not the nobles', perspective of everything happening in the country? The people who cannot afford bread. The people who are *murdering* others in an attempt to make a point that they are starving."

Herod had no idea what to think, but he knew that Gertrude would throttle him if he did not answer, so he did his best to provide one suitable enough for her. "Gertrude, if we high-borns show the people that their violence will not deter us, then yes, I do think that we may get through this stage of the situation with emergence of hope."

Gertrude stared hard at the king and thought, *This makes no sense, but I'm tired of correcting him.*

She had spent every day of the past two and a half years trying to correct him. Clearly, there were too many smudges on the sheet to be ignored or removed without further damage. Again she took a great inhale, then said calmly, "Your Majesty, I, I'm not sure how well you will receive this, but I have to say it: you are still a fairly new king; you've only been wearing the crown, after all, for these past five or six years. You have not yet accumulated enough experience to be the best king that you can be. In this time, like all kings before you, you've had to rely on the opinions of your advisors, Absalom's, Aleksie's, the

Council's, mine, and that's something you must start to wean yourself from now."

"Wh-what are you getting at?" Herod asked.

The toe of Gertrude's boot quietly tapped the tiles beneath her. She sighed and tucked the quill into the journal. "Listen, Your Majesty." She walked up to the king. "You're a good man, Herod, and you are smart. But until you deny the angels and demons who whisper their influence into your ears, and until you can connect the lines from your head and your heart, my advice to you, for the time being, is to deafen your ears to all claimed words of wisdom, even mine. I think that the best way I can help you with that, Sire, is to separate myself from the temptation of talking. I'm going to go home for a little while—two months, I think, just enough time for you to grow used to not having my constant burbling."

From somewhere deep inside the core of the king came the comment, "I don't think I'd ever need a vacation from your voice, Gertrude."

Aleksie and Gertrude were stunned from hearing this, for neither knew of the king's infatuation with her. Aleksie nervously ran his hand through his hair—he was confused and slightly concerned about his king's comment to this woman. Gertrude's different-colored eyes stared blankly at the king. If that statement meant what she thought, then she needed a drink even more.

"When are you leaving?" Aleksie quickly asked, to break the silence and the risk of the king saying something he might later regret.

Gertrude had not yet thought of that, but out from her mouth came the first day and time that came to her mind. "Right after the Council Gathering. I'll stay long enough to learn what passes, but after that, I'm going home."

Herod sighed heavily and put the knuckles of his fists on his hips. "Well, in that case, Gertrude, we're going to have that ball tomorrow night."

"What?" Gertrude and Aleksie asked in unison, for neither could comprehend their king's parties being organized in so short a time.

"Well, yes," the king confirmed, his golden hair regaining a bit of its bounce. "Tomorrow is Tuesday, and if you are truly leaving on Wednesday, then the only time we will have for the ball will be tomorrow night." The king closed the distance between himself and Gertrude. He took her hands and kissed her knuckles, something he'd done only once before, on their first meeting. Gertrude did not know what to think, but she was as dumbstruck as he had been a second before.

The king softly asked, "My lady, will you allow me to be your escort for the dance?"

Gertrude did not want to be queen. She did not want to be regarded as attempting to gain more power by sleeping with the king, which would more than likely be the result of a date with him. On top of all those matters, she feared that this ball would drive the wedge between the classes even farther.

"Sire, please." Exhaustion weighed upon her words. "Is there nothing that I can do to convince you to delay this ball?"

"Gertrude," Herod began. "We cannot let cowards dictate our lives. These men murdered children and unarmed men and women. If we let them deter us from living, are they not winning? Those murderers will be brought to justice, and we will crush their spirits by honoring those who fell to their hands."

Gertrude shut her eyes. Every part of her disagreed, but what more could she say? She nodded.

The king was elated. "And you'll be swiveling into the ballroom on my arm, yes?"

Gertrude nodded again.

Aleksie failed to gather his thoughts enough to formulate an opinion in the time allotted before Gertrude left the office.

As she walked down the halls of the castle by the sea, she felt strange. She was stuck in a cascade of emotions: of guilt for leaving the city for the next few months, of regret for not being able to get through to Herod, of total confusion about the king asking for her to be his partner and the gut-clenching fear of what would happen next as a consequence of this ball.

Herod, you damn fool, she cursed silently. *How will I ever be able to convince the people that you are a good man who could be a good king now? I'll have to use my time away to meet with everyone I can to try to sway them to your side.*

Her feet stopped. The distractions of the morning faded. *This is where we were supposed to meet.* She looked up and down the hall, but she was utterly alone. *Where are you, Sam?*

"Why are you still here?" A harsh voice shattered Gertrude's happiness and dimmed all light from her eyes. Her feet stopped on the spot, frozen from fear. She had no choice but to listen to the man who haunted every turn of her life.

9

The Bloody Prime

Gertrude's heart began to race. She looked this way and that, trying to see where his voice was coming from, but it seemed to be echoing out from the very walls.

"What point are you trying to prove?" the voice continued. "When will you learn to listen to me?!"

Turning sharply, with nothing but disgust burning from her body, Gertrude scoffed and growled, "When will you learn that you have no power over me!"

From the shadow of a passed stairway, a tall figure dressed in red emerged. Absalom Kemen, in the crimson cloak he was unrecognizable without, walked toward her. A wicked smile spread between the unshaved cheeks of a man long ago condemned in Gertrude's heart. Demon features lined his black brows and skeletal face, looking nothing like her own. He hissed, "How long will it take you, Gertrude, to realize that you are the laughingstock of all the lands?"

"Me? Ha. The people are starting to talk, Absalom," she said, standing tall. "They know that their misdirected taxes have sewn the wealth that lines your pockets. Wasn't it just last year when you made that expensive purchase of that skulga, that flying horse from hell?

One can only wonder why you'd need a beast that can lift you away with nothing else on the ground that could catch you." The creature was easily spotted as hardly anything in Vitenka was as fantastical as it. When he rode the beast from his home, the people below ran for cover, fearing that the king of the fallen himself was soaring over their heads.

"You do my name great shame!" Absalom shouted.

"I can't do much more damage than you already have," Gertrude returned. "For God's sake, your nickname is the 'Bloody Prime,' and I doubt the people are referring solely to your coat. I seek to repair and clean up the messes you have made while you seem content to continue your childish displays that may very well tear our country apart!" Though her words were daggers, she wished her Sam were here. Where could he be? *What have you done to him, Absalom?*

Absalom stopped advancing, his cloak surrounding him like a halo of blood. He smirked, then asked, "Enjoyed your little junket, did you? The king certainly has been favoring your company these last few months. Did you finally bend your knees to wrap your hands around his head?"

"Shut up! You'll not get to me!" Gertrude demanded, even though he *was* getting to her. Clenching her fists, she continued, "The day Herod approved your divorce from Mother was the happiest day of my life!"

Absalom locked his hand onto Gertrude's wrist. "You're so much like that mother of yours. Useless, dull. Decades may go by ere you realize your foolishness, and it'll be too late for you to settle any mate, for none will want you to bear his seed!"

Gertrude attempted to struggle out of Absalom's grasp, but after realizing that she could not, she glared at her father and said, "That would be a blessing, for it would guarantee my safety from pigs like you!"

Absalom whipped Gertrude around, shoved her front against the wall, and extended her left arm behind her back.

Gertrude squealed in pain. *Oh! Where is Sam?*

"How old were you when I broke your wrist?" Absalom whispered, his lips touching her ear. "Eleven? What was it you had done then, eh? Oh yes, you kicked me when I struck your brother because he paid me great insult."

"He accidentally knocked over your glass, you bastard," Gertrude muttered against the cold wall. She could feel the blood pounding in her shoulder.

Absalom pulled his daughter's arm up harder. Searing white pain surged through her shoulder.

"You were a mistake, Gertrude. Did you know that? I had my two sons, though now they both have become nearly as much of a disappointment as you —"

"ABSALOM!" a voice roared from down the hall.

Absalom jumped back. Gertrude leaped away from him.

Breyton charged down the hall. Gertrude ran to his side.

"I should hope that you were only helping Gertrude to stretch her arm and that you were not trying to injure her in any way." Breyton held his sword so that a few inches of the blade showed.

The threat from the prince was not one that Absalom could either ignore or challenge physically, but that would not stop him verbally. "You should be grateful, Gertrude, that you have so many men to protect you. I knew of Samuel Maison, that blood traitor peck from the country, but Breyton Malleus is a surprise…"

"Absalom." Breyton, red-faced, stood in front of Gertrude like a lion defending his pride. "Being the prime minister grants you no right to insult a prince. Do not forget your place."

"In that case, forgive me." Absalom bowed. "I would never want to insult the man who *could* have been king."

Breyton popped forward, letting more of his sword free.

But the prime minister swooped out of the hall, disappearing back into the shadows where he belonged.

Trust me, Absalom, Breyton thought, returning his sword to its resting place. *Had I been king, you would have been hanged for treason long ago.*

"That bastard. Are you alright?" Breyton asked Gertrude the moment the prime minister was gone. "Did he hurt you?"

The lady could not help but laugh. "Physically? Not today. Emotionally, though, that's a different tale entirely." Gertrude's wrist and shoulder were throbbing, but it was nothing that Sam could not rub out later that night. Looking down at the emerald folded pattern on her skirt, Gertrude whispered an earnest and humble "thank you" to Breyton.

The gentleman gently took hold of Gertrude's forearm to examine the imprinted finger marks Absalom left behind. "Luckily, I heard you two arguing." Breyton tenderly rubbed the throbbing red marks on Gertrude's wrist. "Who knows what he would have done with another minute."

Gertrude watched Breyton's fingers tend to her arm, an act she neither anticipated nor was prepared to accept. Absently she said, "Absalom is too much of a coward to have killed me himself, so that's at least a mild comfort for the time being."

Breyton sighed, and after a moment, he realized what he was doing. In a flash, he released Gertrude's arm and shoved his hands deep in his pockets. Clearing his throat, he said, "Gertrude, if you don't mind me asking, where is Mr. Maison? Shouldn't he be with you?"

Not at all pleased with the situation, Gertrude assumed the defense and quickly said, "I had a private meeting with the king. Herod is not comfortable with Mr. Maison at the moment and has not been for some time now. The king trusts me, but he doesn't trust my bodyguard.

We were supposed to meet here. I can only imagine Sam was chased off by either Herod's guards or..." She sighed heavily and prayed that her Sam was alright. "Or Absalom's." After her encounter, the latter seemed far more likely.

The eldest Malleus brother shook his head. "Sam served with me for years. I trust my life to him and have on countless occasions. Why is Herod such a damn fool? I'll talk to him about this. In these times, 'sympathizers' of the crown should have as much protection as possible, especially you, Gertrude."

The weight of everything happening began to bear down on Gertrude. She wanted to run from this conversation to search all of Vitenka to ensure the safety of her Sam. There was no telling what might have happened to him if her father was involved. "Breyton, please—it's sweet that you are worried for me, really, but I have my mother, who worries for me plenty, and I think it's high time I go home to her."

"Do you mean you're leaving?" Instantly forgetting his first question, Breyton rapidly released others. "Now? Isn't it fairly dangerous? I know that you're the voice of the people, but aren't you safer here, in the city?"

All she wanted to do was to find a beverage that might help her numb the pains of today. This conversation was not assisting that desire. "There's no need to fear for my safety, Breyton—that's why I have Sam," Gertrude replied. Her arm was throbbing quite seriously now.

"But Sam clearly cannot always be there to protect you!" Breyton returned.

"Do you think I don't know that?" she shouted. Every frustration of the day boiled over onto Breyton. "Do you think that I'm stupid? I am more than aware of the threats against my life. My very own father would prefer to see me dead than alive! The only way I get through the day is with the comfort from Mr. Maison's presence and the hope that if I do die tragically, I may be so lucky as to be remembered as a martyr of the people. I do not *always* need a man by my side to protect me from other men. If it is my time to go..." Gertrude paused. She closed her eyes and said with less conviction, "Then let it be. Good day, Lord Malleus." She turned and continued down the hall, headed toward her multifunctional tearoom-office.

She had notes to translate and a drink to pour.

10

Accidentally Seen

"And what are you doing here?" a guard wearing the crimson shade of Lord Absalom Kemen's men asked Sam as he waited in the hall for Gertrude to emerge.

"Nothing that would concern you," Sam replied. He had been anxious enough waiting for her meeting with Herod to adjourn without one of Absalom's thugs heckling him.

The guard placed his hand on the tang of his sword. Stopping a swing away from Sam, he looked around him, up and down the hall, before saying, "That little tart of yours ain't around. What other reason would you have to be in this hall all by yourself if not waiting for a moment alone with the king?"

Sam tensed. He wanted to throw a fist into this ass's face before he could say another word. "I am waiting for my charge," he answered, trying to remain calm.

"So says you." The guard closed the distance between them. "But I don't see her, so how can I believe you?"

The men stared at one another before the guard continued, "The king's office is right down that hall." He motioned with his brow to the nearby turn. "Who's to say you're not waiting to surprise him to put a knife in his belly?" He leaned forward, daring Sam to make a move. "Like your brother would have done."

Sam's knuckles burned white. Focusing on his clenched fists kept him from murdering this thug with his own sword.

"Nah," the man said with less than a hand's distance between their two noses. "You ain't got the guts, but, orders are orders." The soldier took a step back. "With things gettin' tense and all, I've been asked to clear this hall, which means…" He stuck his finger deeply into Sam's shoulder. Sam took it like a wall. The man's finger hurt from the solid contact, but he did not let it phase him. "You have to go."

Sam shook his head. "Is this on our king's orders or from the Bloody Prime?"

"You watch your mouth." The guard shoved his finger again into Sam's shoulder. "Do what you're told, Maison, or be charged with defiance of an order from the highest member of court." The guard took a step back, returning himself to a distance where he could more effectively reach for his sword. "My feelings won't be hurt either way, and the latter will help you join your brother on the list of traitors against the court."

Every muscle in Sam tensed. He wanted to strike this man down, it would be so easy, but he knew better. Though infuriated, he was determined not to start the war himself. Sam obeyed. He did not like leaving Gertrude exposed, but being arrested or slain would take him from her side entirely.

Sam left the halls and walked to the upper bailey. It was close enough to the king's office without the threat of Absalom's guards having justification for chasing him off.

What a day, Sam thought ruefully.

The current situation aside, that damn guard and Lord Philemon had brought back the worst of his memories. He despised the man for the crimes he'd paid to his kin, but unless Lord Philemon tried to kill Gertrude, there was nothing he could do to avenge his brother.

Pacing the length of the bailey, Sam tried hard not to focus on the past. Enough was happening now. It pained him not to be at Gertrude's side after such a long absence.

Sam strolled out into a beautiful summer day with his hands in his pockets.

In these refined gardens, fenced off from unnecessary foot traffic by waist-high shrubs, walnut trees, and heavy white stone benches dotted the pathways. He strolled through the shaded paths and down into the small dimple of land where a pair of nannies sat. The women were perched on the bench nearest the entrance to ensure that the children they were watching would not "accidentally" slip out of the park without them knowing. A misplaced heir of the high-borns would be a double tragedy—one for the grieving parent, and one for the family of the maid, who surely would hang for her poor care of children that were not her own. A small herd of those children, laughing, chattering, and screaming playfully, ran down Sam as he entered the park. He smiled, not minding at all. He suddenly missed his four-year-old son, Alekzandre, dreadfully even though it had only been a week since he last saw him. Sam cared and tended to his son more than his wife did. When the lad was a baby, Mildred had spent countless hours cooing over him and cuddling him close, but after a while, the allure of the baby boy melted away from the woman who wanted a baby girl more than anything. So it was that Gertrude became the surrogate mother for the boy they called Sawsha, her mother became his grandmother, and Sam became an attentive father. Sam would, on most occasions, bring Sawsha with him while he played bodyguard to Gertrude so that he could be as active in his son's life as possible. It was to his ultimate sadness that he left Sawsha with Mildred this time around so that the mother could, as she put it, "properly instruct the boy in social mannerisms." He guessed that the boy would learn the not-so-noble art of gossip.

Sam walked down the tiny, shiny pebble path through the well-gardened park as sparrows flew about, disturbed by the activities of the children. He found a bench tucked away from the mums and nannies, children, and puppies that were joyfully scattered about. He slowly lowered himself to the wooden bench and stretched his long legs out, settling in to stare at the window he knew belonged to the king's study. The smooth wooden back of the bench was comfortable to this former military man who was happy to rest on anything that was not moist or moldy.

He exhaled heavily. His knee rapidly bounced up and down. It would be impossible for him to find rest while he waited. He exhaled again and looked around him. Something curious caught his eye. On the ground level of the castle, two stories below the king's window, he saw a small number of servants gathering with buckets. He watched them dip their wooden-backed brushes and, with no enthusiasm, begin to scrub what looked to be messages painted onto the stone. Sam squinted, trying to make out what the writing said, but the shadows across the wall and the distance prevented him from reading it.

Probably "Down with the High-borns," he ventured. He'd seen it written on enough walls in the city for that to be an easy guess. It did surprise him, though, to see that here, right below the office of the king.

Sam's stomach clenched. He looked at the high-borns in the park, laughing and smiling, oblivious to the threats surrounding them. Possibly even among them.

Anyone of the servants in this park could have written that. From those attentive nannies to those men making no obvious effort to hide that message, every one of them would presently have a motive to support the rebels. How are all of you so entrapped in your perfect little worlds that you don't see this? That you don't hear their desperation?

73

Sam knew that even in places of great warmth and innocence, poison found ways to seep through. Though focused on the scene before him, a pair of voices, quiet, but unnaturally out of place, drew him from the bench and to the wall of bushes behind him. He knew he heard Absalom's and another man's voice as they passed by. Maintaining an air of false distraction, Sam looked beyond the park, for the two men had already come and gone. Out of the corner of his eye, he found them standing in an alley outside the park, where they wrongly assumed that they were out of sight. Sam attempted to watch without being too obvious.

What on earth could Absalom be conspiring about with Donovan? As far as he had previously been aware, the pair had no social connections. He had never even so much as seen them side by side before.

If he had blinked, he would have missed it.

Donovan placed a small leatherette pouch into Absalom's palm. Sam could not begin to guess what lay in the bag—money, poisons, keys? Regardless of whatever it was, Sam knew this private meeting between two dominant powers in a dark alley to be something that Gertrude ought to know about immediately.

The two men departed from each other's company quickly, disappearing into the streets around them like rats when light came their way.

Sam watched the empty alley for a moment longer, but his view was changed when a little curly-haired blond girl tugged on his sleeve. Sam smiled at the adorable child with a blue ribbon in her hair and a flower in her hand. "Hello, there," he greeted.

The girl held the flower up to Sam and said, "My mum told me to give this to you."

Sam did not think it appropriate for him to accept the budding orange poppy in the girl's hand, as he was balancing marriage and a love affair already. However, to at least appease the child, he took the flower. "Tell your mother, 'Thank you.'"

The child smiled, pleased that she was successful in her mission. She ran straight to the other side of the park, where her gorgeous mother sat staring enchanted at Sam. This woman was one of the cheetahs from Maltoro's court. The girl gave her mother the message, then ran off to play.

He could not believe that a high-born like her would so boldly take an interest in him. This was too much. He stood and began to leave the park, determined to find Gertrude.

However, the high-born woman cut off his exit route.

"Good afternoon," she greeted. Her voice sounded like it was lined with honey.

Sam swallowed hard, then bowed his head and replied, "Afternoon."

The woman, with multiple strands of pearls draped over her breasts, stood close to Sam without shame or reservation. "I'm not usually this bold, sir, but I have seen you around the castle on many occasions prior, and never have I had the nerve enough to ask your name."

"Sam, Sam Maison," he answered. His throat was feeling slightly dry.

"Oh, yes. Is it true that you are Gertrude Kemenova's pet?" the woman responded. "I should hope for your sake that you have not bedded that tramp. I would not want her type to damage that which the rest of us find interest in having."

It was amazing to "Gertrude's pet" that this stunningly beautiful woman with such a sweet smile could be so vulgar and vindictive. "Excuse me, madam, but I am married, and I do not wish to be accidentally seen with a woman who fishes for men."

"Married, are you?" the woman quickly questioned, ignoring his ill comment. "Then why do you not wear your ring? Are you afraid, perhaps, that your lovers will be offended by the very sight of it?"

For a second, Sam wanted to kick himself for forgetting to put the ring back on. It was in his pocket at that very moment, but he recovered. "My wife asked me to get it cleaned when I came to the city along with hers. I'm on my way to pick them up now. Good day, madam." Without another word, Sam left the park, leaving the cheetah in her frustration for losing a tasty-looking prey.

"And what are you doing here?" a guard wearing the crimson shade of Lord Absalom Kemen's men asked Sam as he waited in the hall for Gertrude to emerge.

"Nothing that would concern you," Sam replied. He had been anxious enough waiting for her meeting with Herod to adjourn without one of Absalom's thugs heckling him.

The guard placed his hand on the tang of his sword. Stopping a swing away from Sam, he looked around him, up and down the hall, before saying, "That little tart of yours ain't around. What other reason would you have to be in this hall all by yourself if not waiting for a moment alone with the king?"

Sam tensed. He wanted to throw a fist into this ass's face before he could say another word. "I am waiting for my charge," he answered, trying to remain calm.

"So says you." The guard closed the distance between them. "But I don't see her, so how can I believe you?"

The men stared at one another before the guard continued, "The king's office is right down that hall." He motioned with his brow to the nearby turn. "Who's to say you're not waiting to surprise him to put a knife in his belly?" He leaned forward, daring Sam to make a move. "Like your brother would have done."

Sam's knuckles burned white. Focusing on his clenched fists kept him from murdering this thug with his own sword.

"Nah," the man said with less than a hand's distance between their two noses. "You ain't got the guts, but, orders are orders." The soldier took a step back. "With things gettin' tense and all, I've been asked to clear this hall, which means…" He stuck his finger deeply into Sam's shoulder. Sam took it like a wall. The man's finger hurt from the solid contact, but he did not let it phase him. "You have to go."

Sam shook his head. "Is this on our king's orders or from the Bloody Prime?"

"You watch your mouth." The guard shoved his finger again into Sam's shoulder. "Do what you're told, Maison, or be charged with defiance of an order from the highest member of court." The guard took a step back, returning himself to a distance where he could more effectively reach for his sword. "My feelings won't be hurt either way, and the latter will help you join your brother on the list of traitors against the court."

Every muscle in Sam tensed. He wanted to strike this man down, it would be so easy, but he knew better. Though infuriated, he was determined not to start the war himself. Sam obeyed. He did not like leaving Gertrude exposed, but being arrested or slain would take him from her side entirely.

Sam left the halls and walked to the upper bailey. It was close enough to the king's office without the threat of Absalom's guards having justification for chasing him off.

What a day, Sam thought ruefully.

The current situation aside, that damn guard and Lord Philemon had brought back the worst of his memories. He despised the man for the crimes he'd paid to his kin, but unless Lord Philemon tried to kill Gertrude, there was nothing he could do to avenge his brother.

Pacing the length of the bailey, Sam tried hard not to focus on the past. Enough was happening now. It pained him not to be at Gertrude's side after such a long absence.

Sam strolled out into a beautiful summer day with his hands in his pockets.

In these refined gardens, fenced off from unnecessary foot traffic by waist-high shrubs, walnut trees and heavy white stone benches dotted the pathways. He strolled through the shaded paths and down into the small dimple of land where a pair of nannies sat. The women were perched on the bench nearest the entrance to ensure that the children they were watching would not "accidentally" slip out of the park without them knowing. A misplaced heir of the high-borns would be a double tragedy—one for the grieving parent, and one for the family of the maid, who surely would hang for her poor care of children that were not her own. A small herd of those children, laughing, chattering, and screaming playfully, ran down Sam as he entered the park. He smiled, not minding at all. He suddenly missed his own four-year-old son, Alekzandre, dreadfully even though it had only been a week since he last saw him. Sam cared and tended to his son more than his wife did. When the lad was a baby, Mildred had spent countless hours cooing over him and cuddling him close, but after a while, the allure of the baby boy melted away from the woman who wanted a baby girl more than anything. So it was that Gertrude became the surrogate mother for the boy they called Sawsha, her mother became his grandmother, and Sam became an attentive father. Sam would on most occasions bring Sawsha with him while he played bodyguard to Gertrude, so that he could be as active in his son's life as possible. It was to his ultimate sadness that he left Sawsha with Mildred this time around so that the mother could, as she put it, "properly instruct the boy in social mannerisms." He guessed that the boy would learn the not-so-noble art of gossip.

Sam walked down the tiny, shiny pebble path through the well-gardened park as sparrows flew about, disturbed by the activities of the children. He found a bench tucked away from the mums and nannies, children, and puppies that were joyfully scattered about. He slowly lowered himself to the wooden bench and stretched his long legs out, settling in to stare at the window he knew belonged to the king's study. The smooth wooden back of the bench was comfortable to this former military man who was happy to rest on anything that was not moist or moldy.

He exhaled heavily. His knee rapidly bounced up and down. It would be impossible for him to find rest while he waited. He exhaled again and looked around him. Something curious caught his eye. On the ground level of the castle, two stories below the king's window, he saw a small number of servants gathering with buckets. He watched them dip their wooden-backed brushes and, with no enthusiasm, begin to scrub what looked to be messages painted onto the stone. Sam squinted, trying to make out what the writing said, but the shadows across the wall and the distance prevented him from reading it.

Probably "Down with the High-borns," he ventured. He'd seen it written on enough walls in the city for that to be an easy guess. It did surprise him, though to see that here, right below the office of the king.

Sam's stomach clenched. He looked at the high-borns in the park, laughing and smiling, oblivious to the threats surrounding them. Possibly even among them.

Anyone of the servants in this park could have written that. From those attentive nannies to those men making no obvious effort to hide that message, every one of them would presently have a motive to support the rebels. How are all of you so entrapped in your perfect little worlds that you don't see this? That you don't hear their desperation?

Sam knew that even in places of great warmth and innocence, poison found ways to seep through. Though focused on the scene before him, a pair of voices, quiet, but unnaturally out of place, drew him from the bench and to the wall of bushes behind him. He knew he heard Absalom's and another man's voice as they passed by. Maintaining an air of false distraction, Sam looked beyond the park, for the two men had already come and gone. Out of the corner of his eye, he found them standing in an alley outside the park, where they wrongly assumed that they were out of sight. Sam attempted to watch without being too obvious.

What on earth could Absalom be conspiring about with Donovan? As far as he had previously been aware, the pair had no social connections. He had never even so much as seen them side by side before.

If he had blinked, he would have missed it.

Donovan placed a small leatherette pouch into Absalom's palm. Sam could not begin to guess what lay in the pouch—money, poisons, keys? Regardless of whatever it was, Sam knew this private meeting between two dominant powers in a dark alley to be something that Gertrude ought to know about immediately.

The two men departed from each other's company quickly, disappearing into the streets around them like rats when light came their way.

Sam watched the empty alley for a moment longer, but his view was changed when a little curly-haired blond girl tugged on his sleeve. Sam smiled at the adorable child with a blue ribbon in her hair and a flower in her hand. "Hello, there," he greeted.

The girl held the flower up to Sam and said, "My mum told me to give this to you."

Sam did not think it appropriate for him to accept the budding orange poppy in the girl's hand, as he was balancing marriage and a love affair already. However, to at least appease the child, he took the flower. "Tell your mother, 'Thank you.'"

The child smiled, pleased that she was successful in her mission. She ran straight to the other side of the park, where her gorgeous mother sat staring enchanted at Sam. This woman was one of the cheetahs from Maltoro's court. The girl gave her mother the message, then ran off to play.

He could not believe that a high-born like her would so boldly take an interest in him. This was too much. He stood and began to leave the park, determined to find Gertrude

However, the high-born woman cut off his exit route.

"Good afternoon," she greeted. Her voice sounded like it was lined with honey.

Sam swallowed hard, then bowed his head and replied, "Afternoon."

The woman, with multiple strands of pearls draped over her breasts, stood close to Sam without shame or reservation. "I'm not usually this bold, sir, but I have seen you around the castle on many occasions prior, and never have I had the nerve enough to ask your name."

"Sam, Sam Maison," he answered. His throat was feeling rather dry.

"Oh, yes. Is it true that you are Gertrude Kemenova's pet?" the woman responded. "I should hope for your sake that you have not bedded that tramp. I would not want her type to damage that which the rest of us find interest in having."

It was amazing to "Gertrude's pet" that this absolutely stunningly beautiful woman with such a sweet smile could be so vulgar and vindictive. "Excuse me, madam, but I am married, and I do not wish to be accidentally seen with a woman who fishes for men."

"Married, are you?" the woman quickly questioned, ignoring his ill comment. "Then why do you not wear your ring? Are you afraid, perhaps, that your lovers will be offended by the very sight of it?"

For a second, Sam wanted to kick himself for forgetting to put the ring back on. It was in his pocket at that very moment, but he recovered. "My wife asked me to get it cleaned when I came to the city along with hers. I'm on my way to pick them up now. Good day, madam." Without another word, Sam left the park, leaving the cheetah in her frustration for losing a tasty-looking prey.

~*~*~

Barreling through the castle, Sam hurried to Gertrude's tearoom-office. If the meeting was over, he knew that she would go to this

81

room first if she had not found him waiting for her.

With only two halls separating them, Sam could nearly smell her verbena perfume.

"*There* you are, Sam," Breyton greeted from behind as he came marching down the hall.

"Breyton, what's the matter?" Sam inquired without delay. He could tell by the prince's furrowed brow that something had happened. "Is it Gertrude? Is she alright?"

"Well, she nearly wasn't," Breyton answered sternly, almost as if he were Sam's superior officer again. "Where the hell were you, Sam? She needed you."

Had Breyton simply slapped Sam with no word or greeting, the statement uttered still would have dominated in comparison. "Breyton, for God's sake, what happened?"

Sighing with frustration, Breyton answered, "Gertrude had a bit of a run-in with her father a little earlier. Luckily, I walked in on them just in time to keep him from doing any real damage or harm."

Sam ran his hand down his face. "*That's* why Absalom had one of his fucking men chase me off. What did he do to her? Is she okay? Where is she?"

Breyton held his arms behind his back and reported to Sam, "Let me assure you that she is fine—shaken, but fine. He pinned her against the wall, and it sounded as though he had every intention of breaking her arm. Regardless of his inability to complete his task, it was obvious that Gertrude was deeply disturbed by this encounter."

Sam nearly kicked the ground from his fury toward Absalom and his own absence. He angrily reported, "My God, you know, he did that to her once before—broke her arm, I mean. It was years before I was under her service, but I certainly have heard about it time and time again. It occasionally still bothers her."

The two men stopped talking for a moment and stared intently at each other, both attempting to see what lay beneath the surface of their comrade's eyes. Breyton took a deep breath and tried to distinguish whether Sam was just very enthusiastic about his job or there was something more.

Sam's married, Breyton assured himself. *He's a good man just worried about a fellow good soul.*

Sam stood still. He guessed that after such an encounter, Gertrude was far more likely to react with a snap to whoever might have stepped in to save her, which may have discouraged the kind-souled Breyton a tad.

"Well, Breyton, if you have nothing more to say, I have to return to my post beside Gertrude." Sam began to walk past Breyton, assuming his route once more.

"Just one more thing, Sam," Breyton started bashfully. Sam slowed his pace but did not turn around. "How does one win over Gertrude's graces?" Breyton asked. "How do you satisfy her temper?"

Sam was grateful that his back was facing Breyton so that his former commanding officer would not see the flare of pink erupt upon his cheeks. A few ideas came to mind, but none were appropriate to be shared. Sam slowly turned around and held out his arms defenselessly. "Breyton, I'll tell you when I figure that out myself." He gave Breyton a friendly smile.

Breyton turned down his eyes, wishing that Sam could have been a bit more helpful.

Sam felt no pity. *Why on earth would I want to help you get closer to her?*

However, after advancing down the hall a few more steps, Sam looked down at the hand that normally bore his wedding ring.

I am a married man, Sam reflected. *She deserves a man who isn't, especially one like Breyton.*

"Um, Breyton," Sam called back to the prince, the surge of being humbled evident in his tone.

Breyton stopped and turned around to hear what his old friend had to say.

Samuel swallowed hard. If there was a man aside from him worthy of pursuing Gertrude, it was Breyton. "Though she's fearless, she's really not as tough as she seems. Here, she has to be to put up with all of the shit the politicians throw at her. I've seen her calm crowds of people with nothing more than her smile. She's really quite special, Breyton. Just talk to her as an equal, as she deserves, and she'll come around." He smiled encouragingly to his friend, then turned back toward Gertrude. With a sigh, he thought to himself, *What a day.*

~*~*~

Though Gertrude had a job to do, she could scarcely keep her concentration focused. The notes she took on the meetings lay propped up on the round table where she could easily see them. An open journal and quill were kept right under her resting writing arm, yet her eyes stared off into the great oblivion, aimed at the closed window in her multipurpose room. Despite the fact that it was warm, Gertrude lacked the concentration and drive to open the window to let in the ocean breeze.

With a drink in hand she wondered, *Does Herod have a real fancy for me? How odd a thought. And Breyton, certainly Breyton holds some interest in me based on the way he softly touched my arm.*

A tingle ran across her skin as she recalled the touch. She leaned forward on her desk and began to lightly bite the tip of her thumbnail.

There is an energy there, she recalled. *There is something quite special about Breyton.*

A sharp pain in her shoulder ripped her back to the incident she was trying to forget. She rotated her shoulder and took another big sip of her wine.

He had done it again. She always said that he didn't, but how could he not? Absalom had penetrated her walls and left her feeling like a broken child once more. A tear ran down her face. She snuffled and wiped it away. Leaning back in her chair, Gertrude reached for the brown glass bottle she found best to currently keep within arm's reach. As she poured the red wine into her glass, she thought, *Why am I doing this? I haven't made any difference and people will die before all of this is over.* She put the bottle back on the table. *I will go home to be with my mother and Absalom will win.*

A knock came to Gertrude's breakfast tearoom door, ripping her from her thoughts.

She quickly wiped her face and sat up straight.

The knock was followed promptly by Sam himself. He looked so worried, so apologetic. He closed the door behind him.

She stood and walked to him. For a moment, she hesitated, but it was not long before Sam was holding her.

"I heard what happened," Sam quietly told her. "I ran into Breyton and he told me about Absalom." Sam kissed Gertrude's brow. "I am so sorry I was not there—"

"Oh, Sam, there's no need to apologize," Gertrude said while gently pushing herself away. "I'm the one who should tell Herod to get over it so you may remain by my side. I'd just…I would rather not talk about it anymore. I'm fine, *really*, I'm fine." Gertrude took Sam's hand in hers and kissed his knuckles. She returned to her seat.

Sam was not convinced, but he let it be. Her father, Sam knew, had a way of tearing down all of her walls and confidence. The man could make her life so full of misery in an instant and leave with a smile on his face, but Gertrude would not outwardly show that on the inside she was withering in pain.

Her thoughts were heavy from the occurrences of the day while her body felt light from the wine. She knew that talking to Sam would help to take her mind off everything. "How was your day, Mr. Maison?"

she sweetly asked.

Seated comfortably in his chair, Sam hesitated as he brewed an answer. He did not want her to know about his encounter with Absalom's guard to add to the weight on her shoulders. "It was alright," he succinctly answered, remembering almost immediately the message he had to deliver. "Oh! Gertrude!" he exclaimed, sitting straight up in his chair and knocking his knuckle on the table. "I saw the duke, Donovan Malleus, and Absalom together alone in an alley in the upper bailey. This must have happened right before or right after Absalom and you had your encounter."

"That's odd," Gertrude mumbled, leaning back in her chair as she mulled the possibilities of the meeting's meaning. "What did they do? I mean, were they just talking? How long were they there?"

Sam went on to tell her everything he saw, which was not much, but it was enough to draw suspicion.

After a long silence, Gertrude configured a mild theory. "I know that Donovan and his brothers had a nasty fight last they met, but I have never been aware of any connection between the duke and the prime minister."

"Nor have I," Sam responded. "Which only makes it more interesting, I think."

"I'll give Herod this update," Gertrude said. "Thank you for being such a good spy, Sam." She gave her lover a wink and smiled warmly, something Sam gladly received. Looking out the window, Gertrude rubbed her sore wrist, then said solemnly, "It'll be September next week...does this mean that you will be leaving me soon?"

Sam nodded. "I'm afraid so," he answered glumly, "I'll probably go Saturday or Sunday, depending..."

"It's a good thing, then, that we will both be going home in two days," Gertrude indirectly informed him with a smile.

Sam was shocked to hear this. "Home? You mean, home-home, as in the country?" he asked, spilling out his words. "Why? I mean, you've only just finished traveling, and you're ready to start up again?"

Understanding Sam's confusion, Gertrude nodded and answered without meeting his eyes, "It seems that no matter what I do here, my words will never settle properly in Herod's head. So I've decided to take a two-month vacation effective immediately after the Gathering on Wednesday. I'm tired. I want to go home and see the end of summer in peace." Gertrude swallowed a mouthful of wine. She did not want to tell Sam yet about her intent to use the time away to rebuild bridges in the community.

"As if you'd ever truly take time off," Sam guessed. "Your mother's home, your vacation destination, is a remarkably convenient place to meet with people without Herod or Absalom knowing."

Gertrude raised a brow. "You know me too well."

Sam chuckled and added, "Should I also assume that your travail in the king's office was less than smooth?"

Rolling her eyes and slapping her hands to her forehead, Gertrude grumbled out a loud grunt. "Ugh, Sam. It was a total disaster. You'll never believe what happened."

"That good, eh?" Sam inquired with a smile.

She picked up her glass and said, "I'll put it to you this way: I hope you packed something nice to wear along with your dancing shoes, Sam, because tomorrow night, we'll be going to a ball.

11

The Ball

"How bad is it looking out there?" Pushing out the expanse of breath from her lungs, Gertrude practiced her exercise of trying to focus on something else to stay calm. The heavy gown that she wore on so warm an evening did little to ease her discomfort with tonight's activities.

"If they don't burn down the castle tonight," Sam answered over his shoulder, looking out the window to the city streets just beyond the castle's grounds, "I think we should count it as a victory."

From what Sam could see, the crowd was not chanting or armed with torches. It appeared that the people were standing still, silent. A chill ran down his spine. "Whoever's organizing them," he answered after a while, "knows what they're doing."

There were no mass demonstrations, but the king's guard was concentrated on the entryway where the nobles were arriving for the king's ball.

Gertrude left her post in the hall to join Sam at the window while they waited for Herod to arrive. She took a moment to observe what was happening. In the growing shade of night, the crowd looked like two voids on either side of the pathway.

"It is spookier, isn't it?" she asked. "Just seeing them standing there silently." She leaned her head against the window frame. "Perhaps in their silence, they'll be more powerful. Otherwise, it's peaceful now..." she whispered to Sam in Heltkor. "How long will that last?"

"My lady?" a soft voice startled both Sam and Gertrude.

Heart pounding, Sam quickly ascertained that this delicate-featured maid was not a threat and returned his saber to the sheath that his instinct had begun to draw.

The servant Luda held up her hands to express that she came in peace.

I could have killed her, Sam thought. A second chill ran down his spine.

"Forgive me for startling you." The maid turned down her brow and approached slowly, as was protocol from waitstaff to a highborn.

Gertrude looked over Luda and thought, *I hate that you feel like you have to act this way.* She said, "That's alright. I think we're all a bit jumpy these days." Gertrude gave a weak smile to her old friend, then motioned to her to continue.

"The king is ready for you," Luda said. Looking to Sam, she more timidly said, "He asks that I alone escort you, my lady. I'm sorry, Sam."

They had guessed that this would happen, but a sliver of hope existed in Gertrude that someday the king would begin to truly trust Sam.

"Sorry, Sam," Gertrude apologized. "I'll see you inside?"

While he knew Luda, Sam did not want to leave Gertrude's side. He was about ready to slap some sense into the king to make him see at least an inch of reason. Sam nodded intending to follow them anyway.

The ladies began to walk away from Sam. The king's entourage was much closer than Gertrude had anticipated, coming into view only a minute after they'd left Sam's immediate side. As they approached, the maid looked to her right as if to look out the window. She reached her hand to scratch the bridge of her nose and masking the movement of her lips, she quietly said, "I still believe in you, my lady, but know that there *are* spies in the castle tonight. Please be careful." She returned her hand to her side.

The hustle and bustle and excitement of the entourage ahead of them would have covered up the maid's words, but Gertrude understood her hesitancy to speak openly to her in front of so many nobles. Nobles who would rather step over her if she were lying in the street than outstretch a helping hand.

Turning her head to look behind her, Gertrude was not surprised to see Sam following not so far behind.

Luda whispered, "I still fight for you."

The king's attendants emerged from the crowd and pulled Gertrude into the entourage, leaving the maid behind with Sam only a dozen strides away. It dawned on her that Luda likely came of her own accord. The king would never have sent so humble a servant. This demonstration of Luda's determination to have one moment alone with her warmed Gertrude's heart and steadied her nerves. Yet still, Gertrude thought, *I have to warn Aleksie.*

Before her, a crowd of well-dressed nobles whispered and joked about the scene they'd had to cross to enter the castle tonight.

"And what did they think they'd achieve by staring us down like that?" Gertrude heard one man ask, clearly offended and not intimidated by the threat, the loud billow of his voice carrying out across the crowd.

She wove through the crowd, snaking her way between the arched bells of high-born dresses that made her walk feel like a swim through a churning sea of silks.

"It was rather unnerving," a woman directly beside Gertrude whispered to another. "I didn't like it at all."

This sea of nobles was in Herod's tightest circle of companions.

Those he trusted as friends, but not political allies. This entourage would enter the ballroom behind him in their glimmering attire as the only force that supported him, even if just on the surface, at this time. Gertrude was fairly relieved that only a handful of members of the Council were dispersed in this pool, as she felt as if she might explode if she had to face those animals tonight.

The king's attendants led Gertrude to Herod, who looked stunning. From beside his king, Aleksie glared at Gertrude.

"Ah, Gertrude," he greeted. His cheeks had a touch of red about them from the wine he'd already consumed tonight. He reached out his hand to her and with a wave of his fingers, the group of people that had surrounded him walked away. Without the crowd immediately attached to him, Herod led Gertrude closer to the tall, dark wooden doors that when opened would lead into the ballroom. On the other side of the panels, the clinking sound of the royal crier's staff was beginning to assemble the ballroom's already present attendees to order. The show was about to begin.

"Can you believe all that?" Herod said to Gertrude quietly. With a quick, subtle flick of his brow toward the chattering group behind him, he motioned to what he meant. "They're constantly buzzing around me like flies to shit." Herod smiled and winked at her.

Gertrude chuckled, relieved to be seeing the side of Herod she liked the most before having to stand in front of so many eyes on his arm. "You did do a good job just now asking them to back down; you essentially swatted them off in the same way one would a bug," she complimented, matching his light tone. She hoped that she could ease him into talking about the people's demonstration outside and the warning from Luda.

"You know, I'm not as entirely without power as you may believe," he further joked.

Gertrude opened her mouth to say, "On that note," but the king turned to her first. "That being said, Gertrude, I...I have something to ask you, and I don't want you to think that I'm asking this of you as your king." Swallowing hard, Herod took a gentle hold of her hand. "This isn't exactly how I imagined asking this of you, but I don't know when we'd be granted another intimate opportunity like this."

The urge to start shaking her head popped up, but she denied it. "How intimate is this really?" She asked, looking to the group of at least forty people who were barely ten feet behind them, and Aleksie not even five feet away, all of them watching their engagement.

"Gertrude." He had never said her name so tenderly before. He turned to face the door so that none in the crowd would see what he would have to say. Gertrude wanted to run back to the crowd so that she would not have to hear it.

Quietly, with a little shake to his words, he asked, "Would you do me the honor of marrying me?"

No. No, I would not like to give you that honor, her thoughts decried as her feet felt like they were falling out from beneath her. *Luda may have just risked her life to tell me that she believes in me—would she and the rest of the people if I take your hand? Or...could I have the true power of influence over you as your queen?*

"You don't have to answer tonight," Herod assured her, seeing her hesitation.

On the other side of the door, the crier began to announce the titles of the king, preparing the room for his entrance.

Herod squeezed her hand and said, "Let's just enjoy ourselves as old friends tonight, but do think about it, will you?"

The ballroom doors opened for them so fast after the king's statement that she did not have the opportunity to think.

The moment they entered the room, King Herod was the center-piece of the ball.

Gertrude entered the ballroom with her hand hooked to the arm of the king. She felt so embarrassed as she came onto the dance floor that had never shone as bright, all eyes staring at her and Herod on that incredibly warm Tuesday night. Nearly every person was shocked to see that the king chose the prime minister's daughter as his premiering dance partner. The gossip commenced a beat before the orchestra began.

I was just specifically warned to be careful tonight. I wonder what they'll say when they learn that he's asked me to be their queen, Gertrude thought as they neared the center of the dance floor. *That is, of course, if the people don't burn down the castle before this party is over.*

From the orchestra, a flamboyant waltz started to play for the king and his guest. Her elegant cream-colored and gold-lined dress complimented the king's shimmering peacock-hued suit. Alone on the dance floor, Herod and Gertrude waltzed as the crowd watched, though none more intently than Sam and Breyton, both for the same reason.

Herod was an excellent dancer, so good that his nerves about dancing with Gertrude did not affect his performance. The lady was surprised at how natural Herod was on the floor and how relaxed and at ease she felt dancing with him after how heavy the last few weeks had been.

To the new rhythm of the second song, others joined the dancers, but not Samuel or Breyton. The two stood at opposite sides of the dance floor from the other and intently watched from different angles the swan and the peacock dance together. Another song rolled to an end, but Gertrude kept dancing with Herod beneath the luminous crystal and gold chandeliers. She even laughed to the jests the king whispered in her ear.

Countless drinks were served, carried in on large silver trays by servants dressed to match the napkins of the occasion. Breyton helped himself to a glass of sparkling wine, but he felt little to celebrate. He'd nearly collapsed last night when a messenger came and told him that Herod would be hosting a ball. He laughed at first, thinking that it was a prank message from Yuri, but when he realized otherwise he cursed his brother for his childish stupidity. The people, Breyton knew, would be infuriated when word of this gala spread and spread it would like wildfire across the lands. The people just beyond the gates in their silent demonstrations would ensure that. Breyton took a deep drink from his wine. Watching Herod with Gertrude, he wondered, *How much different would things be if I...*

A young widow, a lady Breyton once knew, tapped him on the shoulder and timidly asked if he would care to dance. Pleased with the interruption of his thoughts, Breyton took her hand and led her to the dance floor.

On the tight ballroom floor, the cliques of the animal court shone brightly. The cheetahs and the elephants stood among their social peers, the jackass landowners with the same, and the awkward bunch, the gaggle of those who the cruel uppermost class called "mixed-bloods," huddled together near the long windows in the back.

It was in this grouping of mixed-bloods where Sam stood. He was relatively by himself, for he, as ever, was doing his job watching Gertrude. He kindly refused the drink he was offered, not from a silver platter, but a sip from a flask an inebriated man waved shamelessly about. Sam was not much of a drinker. Occasionally he would partake of hard liquors to numb his nights with Mildred, but those were so rare lately that he hardly ever possessed need for medication.

Though this ball looked the same as any before, the general feeling was different. From his corner, Sam observed, *It's like they're all pretending that everything is fine. They won't even admit to themselves that they know it is not.*

Sam watched everything in the ballroom as it passed before his eyes. So many faces and hues, but only a handful of targets keeping his explicit attention. Though he knew that Breyton had joined the dance floor with a handsome widow, he watched with pointed concentration how Herod held Gertrude's hand and kept his fingers on her waist as they danced. He watched how Donovan danced with many fine virgins, each with the hope of losing said title that night. Most importantly, Sam watched Absalom, who would not dance, take long drags from a cigar as he stood with Igor Mislov in the corner. Mislov would strike his thumb across his chin to wipe the maverick drips of spit without any recognition of his action. Occasionally, a niece of Sam's, a girl a few years younger than Gertrude, would latch onto his arm and in the gaiety, laughter, music, voices, and clonking of shoes, make earnest attempts to drag her uncle out on the dance floor. Sam would smile and wave his hand, swearing that he would catch the next one. During one such distraction, he took his eye away from Gertrude and she was gone.

Sam immediately perked up his head and scanned the dance floor. She was not with the king. Herod stood on the far side of the floor, taking a breather and chatting in a small group, including Aleksie. Sam moved through the crowd, squeezing between the backs of people, maneuvering around the arches of women's dresses, to no avail.

Sam's heart started to beat rapidly as he began to grow nervous, but a tap on his shoulder and a playful laugh put him at ease.

"Here I am, Sam," Gertrude said with a smile that seemed boundless. She hoped her feigned giddiness would hide the swirling eddy she felt trapped within.

Relieved to know that Gertrude was alright, Sam smiled and paused for a moment to admire how she glowed. She held two glasses of wine.

She held one up to Sam, already knowing that he would deny the offer. He shook his head, but Gertrude insisted. Just loud enough so that Sam could hear, she said, "One glass won't hurt, Sam." She swallowed a sip from her own glass, then added, "This very well may be the last happy occasion this country will see for a *long* time...it will do us both well to enjoy ourselves tonight."

Sam took the glass and raised it for a small toast. "To the best of times."

Their glasses touched. The ring reached the ears of no one other than them and their toast ran down their throats. Sam chuckled and asked, "So, is Herod the idol of the night?"

Chuckling behind her own glass, Gertrude mumbled, "Well, he is a ridiculously good dancer, but what else would you expect? A bachelor king is bound to draw attention. Add Herod's personality and you have a genuine royal spectacle that wants nothing more than to be seen."

Behind his glass, Sam mumbled, "Should I be jealous?"

Gertrude did not answer. Instead, she took a long gulp from her glass. She knew that for her heart, Herod was as much a threat to Sam as a mouse was to a bear, but her stomach clenched. She would have to tell him that Herod asked for her hand but now was not the time. She did not want to be responsible for shattering the soft happiness of the night.

The soft happiness. The idea drew in around her from every angle. She looked around the ballroom. From what she could hear, the conversations about people entering had ebbed. No one was talking about the families who had been lost, the whole alleged reason behind this ball. Be it from the wine or the environment, the high-borns in here were already starting to forget. "It's easy to fall into it, isn't it?" Gertrude said distantly.

Sam leaned closer to her to hear over the music. "Fall into what?" he asked.

She took another long, sweeping look around the spectacle before her. "To fall into the illusion that everything is fine, when in fact," she thought of Luda's fear, of the people outside, of the families who were being murdered for crimes committed by these animals of the court, "everything is not." She watched Herod take the floor with another young lady, leaving Aleksie alone.

"Sam, I'll be right back," Gertrude said so fast that Sam barely heard her. She shoved her mostly emptied wine glass into his hands and scurried off.

Gertrude maneuvered around the bell-shaped ball gowns and scooted between two groups of conversations to reach out and tap Aleksie on the shoulder.

Aleksie turned to her, stone-faced.

Dropping her shoulders, Gertrude leaned closer to him and asked, "Why do you hate me so much when I am doing everything in my power to protect *your* Herod?"

His stone face turned red.

"Look," she started quickly, hoping to spare him any embarrassment. "Something quite awful may be in the works here tonight. Just keep an *extra* close eye on him, will you?"

"You don't have to tell me that," he quipped.

Aleksie began to walk away, but Gertrude sank her fingers into his elbow and turned him back to look at her. She leaned close to him and whispered, "As your *future* queen..." She allowed that to sink in with him a moment, knowing that Herod would have already discussed it with him. "I do." She dramatically let go of his arm and returned to Sam's side without another word.

"That looked like it went well," Sam observed. He raised an eyebrow at Gertrude. "Do I want or need to know?"

Gertrude shook her head and plucked a new wineglass from a passing silver tray. "No. Just, let's keep a sharp eye on everything tonight."

She took a deep sip of wine.

Sam watched her drink and said, "Leave that to me."

On the other side of the hall, after drinking his fill of youthful naïve girls, Donovan crossed the floor with Miss Kemenova as his new target. He arrived at her side long after Sam grew aware of his intent, but Donovan, as cruel as he was to those he despised, could feign even the best of gentlemanly manners. With a smile eerily similar to Breyton's, the middle Malleus brother bowed to Gertrude and said surprisingly kindly, "Forgive me, Miss Kemenova, but I do not believe we have ever formally met."

Staring critically at Donovan, attempting to analyze what he was playing at, Gertrude agreed by nodding her head. "No, sir, I do not believe we have."

The duke held out his hand to her and said, "I am Lord Duke Donovan Malleus, a proud nobleman of the south." However reluctantly, Gertrude placed her hand in his. "Enchanted," Donovan said as if he really were. He kissed her hand.

Sam wanted to kill him already and he gladly would, were the situation to present itself.

"May I have this dance, Lady Kemenova?" Donovan asked Gertrude.

The lady did not want to dance with Donovan. She wanted to stay with Sam, but she knew that maybe if she played her cards well enough, she could figure out the business he'd earlier had with her father. "I would be delighted," she answered, giving her empty glass to Sam. "Go on, Mr. Maison—dance with your niece." She winked.

Swiveling out onto the dance floor with a different Malleus, Gertrude received less attention. The orchestra hummed a mellower waltz for Gertrude, Donovan, and the others who spun on the floor. In his youth, Donovan paid significantly less attention to his dance lessons compared to his equestrian and swordsman schooling. Gertrude did not care. The lady was too busy trying to concoct a topic that would prompt Donovan to speak instead of simply staring at her with a pair of eyes that matched Breyton's exactly. She never knew a pair of siblings to look so much alike, yet to be so different.

Donovan smiled. Gertrude's beauty reached even him, but he was not thrilled by it. He could admire her like a piece of art on the wall, only to walk on unmoved. Regardless, he decided to utilize that particular ability to start the conversation: "You know, for the life of me I cannot imagine how the child of Absalom could be so beautiful. You look nothing like him, thank God."

Chuckling ironically, Gertrude said halfheartedly, "Well, thank you."

The crinkled brow that jumped onto Donovan's expression for a second told Gertrude that he expected a different answer. Donovan shrugged and asked, "Was he really so wicked to you and your family as is rumored?"

Though continuing a conversation about Absalom's mishaps was less than pleasant, she wondered if this would be a way to find out what he and this man had been up to today. She answered with an inquiry: "Tell me, sir, do you know where my brothers are?"

The song ended. The orchestra hung up their instruments for a quick breather.

Donovan stared perplexed at his dance partner for a minute before answering with another shrug.

Seeing this, Gertrude responded, "Neither do I. Nor does my mother or Absalom. They decided to escape him, so they left our country, their homelands, and we have not seen them since. Does that put it in perspective?"

"Forgive me for asking you about such a delicate matter," Donovan hastily said, rushing after the lady, who'd promptly removed herself from the dance floor once the music ended. "I'm only ensuring that you truly have no allegiance to your father," the middle Malleus brother whispered. He took Gertrude's arm within his to have a more private conversation with her beside the ballroom's stairwell.

"And why should that matter to you?" Gertrude asked. Turning to talk to Donovan, she pulled her arm from his grasp. His clutch had pulled on her shoulder that still ached.

"Because I know what it is he is planning to do," Donovan alluded. Gertrude's brow raised and Donovan continued. "Your father, as you know, is a power-hungry man with a remarkable amount of influence in his court of Council members."

"Yes, yes, I know." Gertrude waved off this all too obvious comment. Donovan cleared his throat twice. "Excuse me," he quietly said. "The sea air always infects my lungs. Your father, I think you should know, has every intention to have Council vote out the monarchy from power on the morrow."

"Vote out the monarchy?" Gertrude repeated to validate if what she heard was true. She wondered, *Absalom is a total coward, so how could he come up with something so remarkably stupid? If he makes this suggestion and it fails to pass, Herod will have him executed as a traitor to the crown. If it goes through, Absalom must be aware that Breyton and Donovan would fight for the crown until trumpets sounded to protect their family name. Why would he make such a move?*

"I know what you are thinking, and I thought so myself." Donovan hesitated, making quick glances over both of his shoulders. Leaning closer to Gertrude, he quietly said, "That is, until I arrived this week and overheard exchanges between the Council members and their men. I have since learned that in the past few months, your father has been convincing the Council to come to his side. He will make his move tomorrow, but you must tell no one of this, not even Herod."

Holding up her hands and searching for the meaning behind that reasoning, Gertrude quickly asked, "Why on earth would I withhold from the king that his men are intending to throw a coup against him? And if 'no one must know,' why are you telling me?" She found so many things to be wrong with this story.

"I'm telling you because I know that if he attempts this, the hammer will fall on you because you are such a loyalist." Donovan stepped closer, too close for Gertrude's comfort. "You, too, would be targeted if the king does not go quietly."

"You are still failing to answer, sir, why I should refrain from telling Herod of this claim." Her suspicion of Donovan's treachery grew with every word he spoke. "Is it because you intend to lead the parade against your own brother?"

Donovan inhaled deeply, then said, "Gertrude, I know my brother; he will *not* listen. You *know* this. He trusts Absalom and that Council more than he trusts himself. If you have ever had contact with Herod, you know he will not so much as clear his throat without the approval of the prime minister."

"So, you are telling me to warn me, but you are also telling me to keep my mouth shut to spare me the effort and humiliation of telling this news to the king?" Gertrude asked. Her arms were folded over her chest and her lips were pressed tightly together.

"Yes, if you can believe it."

"I don't," Gertrude replied.

The music in the background chimed up once more.

"Fine then!" Donovan's anger burst, but his level of animosity was muted by a singular chord from the orchestra. "Go on, make a fool of yourself, and tell the king!"

"I will," Gertrude barked. "Good night, Donovan. May the last eve before the revolution against your kin be full of merriment and love," she faux blessed, leaving Donovan's presence at once.

From afar, Sam saw Gertrude walk away from Donovan, excusing herself from the ballroom. He jumped to pursue her, but someone stopped him.

A few strides behind her, Breyton gave a subtle nod to Sam, asking him to stand down on this one.

It felt like a blow to Sam's heart, but Breyton was his prince, so he obeyed.

Obedience did not mean that Sam took this interference lightly. The first tray of drinks that passed him did not get away without him taking a glass.

Before Breyton walked through the large aperture to exit from the dance hall, the prince made eye contact with Donovan. The two men stood stiffly. The elder brother scoffed, disgusted with Donovan for whatever it was he had done to upset Gertrude before he left the bright, glittering ballroom for the darkly lit halls of Maltoro Manor.

12

Balconies

As Breyton traced Gertrude's scentless tracks, he passed several couples who'd escaped the ballroom to further their wine-induced passions with a bit of privacy. The sins of the night were of little care or consequence to Breyton, who only wished to find Gertrude. The eldest Malleus brother was fairly certain that he would not see her engaged in such an intimate predicament, but he was not sure if he would find her at all. Maltoro was a vast labyrinth, with numerous nooks and crannies in which a person could quickly disappear. He would have to be quick and vigilant if there was to be any hope of finding this elusive lady.

Up ahead of Breyton's steps, a brilliant blue hue flowed into the hall from the balcony's open doors. A rich scent of tobacco wafted to the prince's nose as he neared, leading him to deduce that it was probably anyone but Gertrude out there having a mid-evening smoke. At first, the gentleman did not think anything about the smoking person on the balcony. However, the figure of a lady caught the attention of his peripherals and sent him jumping a step back to see who it was out there. "Gertrude?" he softly called.

Gertrude was stricken with panic and dropped something light and wooden to the balcony's cobblestone floor. She choked and coughed out a gray tuft of smoke. "Breyton!" she coughed. "You startled the heart out of me. I thought you were Sam." The lady leaned her backside against the stone rail of the balcony as though to relax, but she was not loose in the least.

Breyton slowly joined her on the balcony. "Are you ashamed for people to know?" he quietly asked. "For people to know that you smoke?" It was the only thing he could figure that would make her jump so.

Gertrude chuckled sarcastically and scoffed. That was a part of the reason she was hiding, though the mountain of issues surrounding her also came to mind. She looked away from Breyton to the castle's wall and confessed, "Only Sam. He knew that I did a few years back. He does not now know that I've started up again...he would kill me if he knew." Her pleading eyes asked Breyton to not mention a word of this to him.

Keeping this a secret from a bodyguard seemed an odd choice, but Breyton agreed with a nod.

The chilled air coming from off the sea was refreshing after dancing in the packed ballroom.

Rubbing his hands together to warm his fingers, Breyton asked, "Can you blame him? It's an awful habit, Gertrude."

Shaking her head, Gertrude leaned down to pick up the pipe she had dropped. "Come now," she lightly argued. "It's only tobacco." She began to reach for the pocket in her boot, where more of her tobacco was stored. With the wine she'd consumed whispering in her ear, she pulled her skirt higher up than necessary, revealing her calf tightly covered in a lace stocking.

Breyton inhaled deeply and tried not to look, though the wine he had enjoyed was screaming the opposite to him.

She removed from the neck of her boot a small leather pouch filled with tobacco and quick lights. As she stood, she stuffed the loose, rich-smelling tobacco leaves into the mouth of the pipe. "If you knew me better or if you could spend a day in my shoes, I think you would understand, but seeing as how my boots would not complement your outfits…" Gertrude put the pipe between her lips and puffed it alive with the help of a struck quick light. In between her little puffs, she added, "For now, I'll ask you to forgive me for my habit, sir."

Breyton reciprocated the weak smile. His mind presently remained caught on her lace stockings.

Looking up to the outer face of the castle, and having Luda's and Donovan's and Herod's words weighing on her, Gertrude released a cloud of smoke. "You know, this balcony—well, this whole adjunct of the castle, was a part of your brother's brilliant additions to this house of kings…" She sighed. "Was he only sixteen when he drew up the plans?"

Removing himself from picturing the rest of her dressings above her knee, Breyton ran his fingers nervously over his goatee. "Mmm, um, yes. He was eighteen when he convinced our father to allow him to go through with the renovations."

"Was he?" Gertrude asked, already knowing that last fact. "His plans were genius, simply brilliant. This castle is an architectural marvel and a visual beauty, thanks to him." Sighing, Gertrude swallowed hard and looked squarely at Breyton. "The only flaw in his designs was that these modifications were paid for with the taxes, the sweat, and quite frankly the blood of our nation's people; it was greenly naïve of Herod to assume that they would not at one point seek to get it all back. Or, of how easy it would be for other high-borns to point the finger at him to blame our king for everyone's' misery." Again Gertrude paused, looking more lost now than ever. "How do you think Herod will be remembered? Ignoring the means to his ends, do you think that a hundred years from now, the people will even recognize the genius of your brother's artful eye?"

At first, Breyton did not know how to answer the lady's inquiry. He stumbled to answer, "I hope that he will be remembered as the monarch who turned a potential catastrophe into the nation's greatest triumph." The former-to-be-king shrugged. "I can only imagine that this following year will determine how Herod is to be remembered, Gertrude."

Taking down one long last duff, Gertrude decided to finish her pipe and dashed it out on top of the balustrade. "Excuse me." Gertrude bent down to return her pipe to its secret hiding place in the leather pouch in the neck of her boot. "The past few weeks—hours have been downright awful." She let out a smoky exhale, then continued, "I suspect something terrible is about to happen—if not tonight, then at the Gathering tomorrow. Something ground-shaking, at that."

"Is that everything that's disturbing you?" Breyton questioned.

Well, that certainly is part of it, Gertrude thought, even though she only initially answered with a simple yes. After a moment, though, her thoughts came together and formulated a complete explanation. "I have reason to believe that one member of the Council will put before the other Gatherers that 'the people' want the king to be voted from power, which according to the laws of our constitution is technically illegal, that is, treason."

"That certainly is something for concern," Breyton said. He began to stroke his chin. This news only added to his distaste for the hybrid government of their country.

"With enough support and with everything else happening, this could be the beginning of a full-scale civil war," Gertrude uttered, with panic and stress dragging every word. "I have to tell the king, whether he listens to me or not...I have to tell him. I cannot have it on my conscience otherwise. I just..." She sighed heavily. "I needed a moment to strategize how to tell Herod." Licking her lips, Gertrude sent her beautiful, pleading eyes straight into Breyton's. "To all others, Breyton, this must stay 'mum,' do you understand?"

"I understand," Breyton confirmed. "What I have more difficulty understanding is why you chose to confide this in me. You barely know me."

With an innocent shrug, Gertrude gave Breyton a sweet smile. "Aside from you being the brother of the king, I told you because I trust you."

The wind changed direction. On the back of a suddenly warm summer breeze, the music from the ballroom floated out to the balcony, calling the pair back for a dance, but Breyton was too shocked to know that he had Gertrude's trust to jump on the call immediately.

Seeing the bafflement in the prince's face, Gertrude explained, "Breyton, I...forgive me for being so snappy toward you the other day. I had, *have* a lot on my mind, and you happened to be nearest to the chopping block at the time. I do believe that you are a charming and honorable man."

"Thank you," he graciously said, but he could not leave it there. Something from the music and warmth of the night influenced him to be bold and to ask the burning question in his mind. "You know, Gertrude, not to change subjects, but you've danced tonight with only two men, both of whom are my brothers, so I can't help but feel jealous and a bit left out. So, too, I bet, does Sam. Do you ever dance with him?"

Oh! What a cruel question! Gertrude thought. She knew that Breyton was asking something that had nothing to do with large social gatherings. She stared at him for a while, though not at all with anger. She usually did not have the patience for such games, and had this not been Breyton she would have screamed something along the lines of *what the hell difference does that make, we have a potential civil war on our hands!* But she did not. Instead, she answered most calmly and with great dignity. "No, I do not. It's not appropriate. I mean, yes, we are good friends, but in the eyes of *this* crowd, he is my servant." Gertrude paused, and then with a smile said, "He's likely losing his mind with worry for me at the moment. We'd best head back inside."

Breyton was not convinced. "Of course. And indeed I am certain that he's worried for you, but he knows you're with me. I signaled him to stand down before I stepped out. Actually," Breyton turned his gaze up to the stars before saying, "I was rather grateful to jump on a chance to be alone with you."

That tingling energy ran across her skin once more. The wine in her blood lowered her ability to properly process the thought before she said, "Do you fancy me?"

"What?!" Breyton exclaimed. He felt his stomach muscles tighten as though he had been bludgeoned. He smiled, ran his hand over his head, scratched his arm, and looked straight at the ground.

Smiling, she playfully said, "You asked your invasive question, now I'll ask mine." She was glad to have caught him so off guard, and yet, she thought, *I will say this of the Malleus men: you certainly would be my pick by far, but I'm not sure I can process all of this right now.*

Breyton laughed. His defenses had also been lowered by the amount he had drunk tonight. "To be perfectly honest, Gertrude, you make me feel like a dewy-eyed youth."

She smiled. Her cheeks flushed. The wine told her that this was possibly their last opportunity to share in this type of moment, so she decided not to let it pass by. Gertrude grabbed hold of Breyton's arm and dragged him toward the dance hall. "Come on, you—if you are green with jealousy toward your brothers' having a dance with me, then we shall remedy that."

~*~*~

From the balcony that overlooked the ballroom, Sam watched his girl dance with his former commander. She was smiling in the way she used to when he and she were in their early days of romance.

Is she falling for him? Sam wondered, a streak of jealousy coursing through him. He turned his head away, shut his eyes. *Too soon,* he assured himself. *They've only just met. He probably just talked her down after being with his horrible brother, that's all.*

Sam sighed and opened his eyes, but what greeted his vision did little to put his soul to rest.

He thought he imagined it, for it could not be true. A servant on the bottom floor carrying a silver tray of glasses slipped something more than wine into one of the cups. Darting his eyes quickly around the rest of the ballroom, Sam tried desperately to see if anything could confirm what he saw. It seemed unimaginable for a servant to tamper with a drink, but Sam witnessed the whole incident, right down to the man slipping something back into his pocket. The servant was heading straight for the king.

13

Meetings in the Night

W ith no time for hesitation or politeness, Sam pushed his way down the stairwell through the crowd. Shoving his way around the long dresses of the ladies and the clumps of gentlemen slowed him and caused him to lose the servant.

His eyes darted this way and that until he was locked on his target once more. Sam pursued. The peacock was leaning against a pillar, charming a gaggle of cheetahs with his expanded fan of feathers.

The servant was only steps away.

Sam darted toward the king. He was deaf to the disgusted, disapproving noises from the people he pushed past and through. None of them mattered.

The servant reached the king.

The servant bowed to Herod, who accepted the glass without any reservation.

The glass rose to the king's lips.

"NO! Your Majesty!" Sam commanded, batting the glass out of the king's hand.

The glass shattered on the floor.

The ballroom dancers stopped swirling, and the orchestra clumped to a sloppy stop.

The servant dropped the tray to the floor, where it landed with a reverberating clang and the noise of shattering glass.

The man ran.

Sam grabbed the silver platter from the ground and hurled it with all his might at the perpetrator's back.

The tray struck the man's shoulder, sending him falling onto the cold, hard dance floor, right at Gertrude's and Breyton's feet.

Two of the king's men apprehended the fiend and dragged him over to the king.

The servant glared at Sam. His face alone proclaimed his guilt, but the empty finger-sized vial Mr. Maison plucked from his pocket was the end-all facet of condemnation.

Sam handed the little bottle to Herod.

The king could hardly believe this. An actual assassination attempt on his life at his party, and he was only aware of it because a Maison had saved his life.

"Well done, Sam," the king humbly said. Reassuming his confidence, Herod then growled to his would-be assailant, "As for you, I'll make sure you never see the light of day again. Away with him." Herod waved his hand, and the king's men dragged off the man, who screamed violent curses at the high-borns.

Breyton stood before Gertrude as the perpetrator was pulled past them.

"Talk to him!" the man screamed to Gertrude. The desperation in his eyes pierced her heart. "You *know* the truth. Tell him, or we'll kill him!"

Gertrude trembled.

Now, *will he believe me?* She wondered, watching the young man be dragged away. Shutting her eyes, she made a silent prayer, begging the heavens that this would be the turning point for their nation that might finally shake things to right.

Gertrude turned her eyes to see Herod hold out his hand to shake Sam's.

"Thank you, Sam, truly," Herod said. He was trying to hide how shaken he was, but, in their moment of contact, Sam could feel his fingers trembling.

"Of course, Sire," Sam said, not knowing what else to say. It had all transpired so quickly. *Maybe now you'll start listening to Gertrude that I'm not the bad guy,* Sam thought as he released the hand of the king.

"Let it be known," the king's voice boomed throughout the whole ballroom, "yes, let it be known that Samuel Maison of Legrette and his kin are forever pardoned of all sins they may have ever committed against the state."

Gertrude touched her heart. She could not believe that only yesterday, Sam's family was considered traitorous and that Sam was hardly tolerated in the presence of the king. Now he was being granted a total reprieve.

The remaining guests could not wait to share their accounts of the scene.

~*~*~

Herod left the ballroom with his head held high, even though his fingers were trembling.

Seizing this opportunity, Gertrude found her chance to inform the king of the morrow's potential threat. She left Breyton's side abruptly, much to his sorrow. She did not give him the opportunity to argue, rushing after Herod with a quick signal to Sam to follow.

The words that she spoke of Donovan's conversation with her, the doubts she held of his sincerity—none of them seemed to be registering with Herod as they hastily walked through the halls.

"Your Majesty, please," Gertrude begged, following the king into the chambers preceding his bedroom. She jumped on this chance to talk to Herod. The entourage of extra soldiers left outside the door gifted her this quasi-intimate moment. Sam and Aleksie would not interrupt her present course, and yet, as the words left her mouth, she distantly thought on how many times she had already sung this tune. Upon hearing the door close behind their small group, Gertrude decided to dig into a different chorus: "You must enact monarchal privilege tomorrow before any vote is cast against you."

Herod threw his head back. He was grateful to have Gertrude and Aleksie here with him at this moment, but all he wanted was to have silence and peace. Turning to face her, he heavily sighed and asked, "And what difference would it make if it was before or after? Monarchal privilege is absolute, no?"

Though in one sense, she was glad to hear him pose a question that was relevant to their current conversation, she could see that his hands were still shaking. *I will not let your shock get in the way of this conversation.* She closed the distance between them and took his trembling fingers. Herod looked at her. "It will show any who doubt you or your resolve that you are far stronger than they believe." She looked to Aleksie and prayed that he would support her argument to Herod later. "You must do this, Your Majesty." She knelt before him, something that she had not done in memory. "I beg of you, Sire. If you do not stand up tomorrow, the Council may vote you out, and the people will come for your blood."

Herod felt his heart catch in his throat. He felt ill. "My dear, they've just done so." He tried to swallow, but he felt like he was choking. "What will stop them now?"

Gertrude squeezed his hand. "Prove to the people that the Council will not control you. Show them that you are trying to be *their* king." She felt her eyes line with tears and decided to let them flow. As one drop ran down her cheek, she continued to implore her king. "Herod, you are a good man. Please, *please* show them, the people, the Council, everyone, who you are." She drew his knuckles to her lips and kissed them. "Please, my king." She raised her eyes to his.

Herod did not know what to say. He turned his eyes to Aleksie and gently slipped his hand from hers.

The other three in the room watched Herod walk toward the door that led to his bedroom as a man condemned.

"Thank you, Gertrude," Herod said quietly over his shoulder. "And to you, Sam—to both of you, truly." He did not turn to look back at them as he spoke. "I must ask you to leave now. I have had a bit of a trying evening and have much to think about." Without another look, gesture, or word, the king excused himself and disappeared into the room beyond.

Staring through the darkness, Gertrude remained on the floor. She heard Aleksie and Sam frame her sides and felt them help her up to her feet. It wasn't until Aleksie began to speak that she regained comprehension of the moment around her.

"I will talk to him," he said to her.

Gertrude had never before had a conversation with Aleksie, where he was not trying to push her away. Both she and Sam stared dubiously at him.

He leaned closer and whispered, "He's pretty shaken up right now; this may be our chance." He rested a reassuring hand on Gertrude's shoulder and gently encouraged them to follow the orders of their king.

In dumbfounded silence, Gertrude and Sam exited.

Halfway down the hall that Sam thought, *What a fucking week.*

~*~*~

He wanted to run his hands down her sides, to pull her lips to his. He tried to stop thinking about how close Herod had been to being murdered before their eyes. Of how it would have happened if he had just looked away for a moment. He wanted to do anything but stare out the window in her bedroom, wondering what would happen next.

Sam looked to Gertrude, who also gazed into the darkness. He could see her mind racing back and forth in a silent attempt to analyze all that had transpired tonight.

Her mind was leaping from Luda to the fear and desperation in the eyes of the young man who surely would be martyred for the cause.

Silence. There was so much happening, and yet, right now, there was only silence.

"I don't understand, Sam," Gertrude said to break it.

He looked at her, grateful for at least some relief from the thoughts they were facing together and alone.

"I don't understand," she continued, "how even after all of this...Herod still..." She couldn't finish her thoughts.

Sam sighed. "We don't know that." He turned his back to the window and took her hand. "Aleksie is talking to him. He has the potential to be the greatest voice in his ear of all." He could see that his words were passing around her, but he continued more for himself at this point. "Herod was probably shaken to life by that attempt on his tonight, which I more than understand. Hell, I've seen men slain before me, and I still feel shaken. If I had just blinked...And, for all we know, Gertrude, Donovan could have been lying. I agree it was right to warn the king either way."

Gertrude remained still, staring out into the night.

"Gertrude," Sam whispered. He drew himself around her and kissed her shoulder. "Let it go." Her shoulders began to relax ever so slightly. "You got through to Aleksie; that *has* to count for something."

This was true, but there was more to the evening that they'd just endured that worried Gertrude. However, she listened to Sam's soothing voice as she stared out the open window of her bedroom. The late-night air was refreshing after being locked up in that stuffy ballroom with so many different perfumes, the cigar smoke, and all those sweaty moving bodies. She was tired, so being undressed by another saved her the energy of performing that chore. She let Sam pull off her outer-layer dress while she stood with her back to him. As Sam pulled off his outer layers, Gertrude thought of the other night when last they made love. She promised herself that she would be more attentive to Sam's needs this time like she used to be when their romance was young. She longed to be enveloped in a truly passionate and carefree embrace, but, after so much time apart from him, something felt off. Different. She did still love him, and yet, the desire that she'd had for him before felt like it had ebbed.

No, she thought. *I love this man.* She turned around in his arms and pressed her lips to his.

Yet, just as the enthusiasm of the moment started to escalate, nearly the moment after Sam pulled Gertrude one suggestive step closer to the bed, a revelation popped into the lady's mind. "I think I may have figured out why Herod always listens to Absalom and is so protective of him," Gertrude muttered as she took a step back toward the window, leaning her rump on the sill.

"Now?" Sam questioned, agitated by the lady's sudden retreat, as his mind was currently nowhere near the political spectrum. However, after scratching his chin and rolling his head back, he motioned her to continue, wishing that she had saved this for later. Sam sat down on the edge of the bed.

Touching her fingers to her brow, Gertrude organized her thoughts. "When Herod was a child, his father was already nearly my father's age, so I doubt that the last king had much time or energy to advise his youngest son. As it was, the former king, so I've heard, spent most of his time doting on and spoiling his second wife, answering to her every whiff and whim.

"From what I have been told, and this is hearsay and guessing..." Gertrude disclaimed as she started to pace slowly. She did this absentmindedly in her silky, white underclothes, missing Sam's rising interest. "Absalom became a sort of a surrogate father-type to Herod, which might explain why our king is so naïve and so willing to trust him blindly."

Sam crossed his arms over his chest and shrugged. "That makes sense, huh," he chuckled with a smile. "In a sick sort of way that almost makes you and Herod kin, if you think that the Bloody Prime played papa to the 'little prince.'"

Shuddering, repulsed by the thought, Gertrude feigned gagging. "Perhaps, but since neither of us looks a thing like Absalom, I have my doubts." Looking at her lover who sat so patiently listening to her, Gertrude felt a wave of guilt hit her. "Forgive me for this distraction, which does absolutely nothing for either of us."

"I will forgive you, only if you do me one favor," Sam suggested as he stood from the bed and pulled Gertrude's body against his.

"Oh, aye? Do I dare to ask?" Gertrude whispered while kissing her lover's heart.

Sam gently pulled the pin from Gertrude's bun. Her hair fell across her shoulders. He pushed a gathering of her locks behind her ear and whispered with his cheek pressed to hers, "For the night, let it go."

Down onto the bed, they went.

Sliding himself on top of her, Sam kissed Gertrude as he began to pull the strings that kept her bloomers to her waist. However, after skimming his hand down the soft skin of her stomach, Sam quickly sat back and stared off into the distance, his eyes scanning madly as his head connected the dots of the day. The thoughts were pouring in so rapidly that the irony of his political distraction at such a time was lost on him.

"Sam? What is it?" Gertrude asked, frightened that he felt cause for such alarm. "What's wrong?"

Another moment passed before Sam darted his eyes back to

Gertrude. He said, "I think the prime minister and Donovan may be the masterminds behind the assassination attempt tonight."

"Excuse me?" Gertrude asked incredulously.

"No, really—think about it," Sam quickly explained with such ardor that Gertrude had no choice otherwise. "Their meeting in that alley yesterday—they must have planned the rendezvous so that Donovan could somehow pass the poison-filled vial to Absalom without being seen by someone in the castle. That glass container would have fit perfectly in that pouch. It all makes sense; Donovan is next in line. If Herod died tonight, tomorrow the duke would be king. Maybe he told you about your father's intent to distract you from his own."

"*That* I would be willing to believe," Gertrude confirmed after a moment of reflection. "After all, Donovan hates—absolutely *loathes*—everything about his brothers, so I would easily accept the notion that he would be guilty of conniving such a scheme, but Absalom has no direct access to the crown. Our constitution states that if the king were to die without leaving an heir, the king could choose his successor."

"Isn't that how Herod became king?" Sam asked.

"Essentially. Herod's father had a firmer grip on the Council and was able to bend the rules a bit more than Herod would be able to. If, *if* Herod has been smart enough to choose another heir over the delineation of his throne to Donovan, which I *highly* doubt he's done, then we don't have to be concerned about Donovan seeking power. However, if the Council determines that Vitenka should become a republic, without a single leader, then there could be a glimmer of hope for Donovan to snake his way into power. He could become a council member himself, or, he could convince the Council to make him king. So, Mr. Maison, what would Absalom have to gain from any of this?"

"Absalom may think he's losing his grip on Herod," Sam answered.

"After you convinced Herod to approve the divorce, which stripped him of *his* lands, it probably made him realize the power that *you* have or possibly could have over Herod."

Gertrude wished that she could be able to prove Sam's theory right. She wanted to have her father taken out of the scene once and for all. However, reason told her that there would be more to it than just locking a door and throwing away a key based on speculation from a bodyguard, no matter how intelligent the bodyguard or the evidence he had. "Sam, these are serious accusations. Treason. An attempt at murder most foul. Even with their history, which is indeed black, I doubt that any court, especially the Council, would have an easy time believing or admitting to the idea that Donovan could kill his brother."

"But *he* won't, and *he* didn't," Sam pointed out, thrilled by his hypothesis. "Not directly at least. He sent a lackey to do it for him. These men are not stupid; they've probably been planning this for years. They probably decided to do the exchange of the poison themselves because there was too much to risk entrusting that task to others…men like that want to maintain as much control as they can. With the way everything is right now, whoever kills Herod, God forbid, would undoubtedly win the instant favor of the people. Maybe that's what your father has to gain."

"What? Good standing with peasants? The man has spent years perfecting his seething disgust toward anyone and everyone who does not have lordship attached to their name."

"That doesn't matter," Sam said, shaking his head. "We are on the brink of a revolution; there is no doubt about that. Our government cannot control what's happening or even provide for the people who need saving the most. Everyone who is connected to the politics of this country is at risk of being subjugated to the people's will, whatever that may be. The prime minister is the king of cowards; if he could find any way to make his way out of something, he would. And, Gertrude, believe it or not, I think that he has found his ace in the game here."

The past few days had been too weighty for Gertrude. She could no longer think. "Sam, I would love to believe you, and I probably will in the morning, but I'm so tired now I can barely think straight," Gertrude solemnly confessed. She did want to pursue the subject, but she just could not at this time. "Could we talk about it in the morning? Or on the road home?"

Sam looked away from Gertrude. He did not know what else there was to say. This was a difficult situation, something that was beyond control, perhaps, especially because of who they were. He could continue to grind this information into Gertrude's head until the morning light, but if she tried to pass it on, who would even care? No one would listen to a woman whose source was a bodyguard and former peasant who'd only just established good standing with the king. Sighing, discouraged by the truth and the pathetic reality that they had to face, Sam settled beside Gertrude. She tucked herself close to him.

They let it rest for the night, but neither could fall asleep. Sam stared up into the darkness, listening for any sound or movement beyond their door or in the bailey below. If anything was stirring tonight, he wanted to ensure that he would be the first to know.

Beside him, Gertrude lay still, but awake.

Her world was falling apart.

The past few days, hours, were positively exhausting, but she could not shut her eyes to welcome dreams. She should have passed out the moment she grew still in bed, yet her tenacious mind mulled over everything.

Herod had assured her that he would have extra guards on hand if the Council turned on him. On their way to his chambers, she had explained everything that Donovan had told her, but he expressed substantial doubt that Absalom would have any hand in anything foul against the crown. A life's exposure to him alone was enough for her conviction that Absalom would be the one to start the coup. She wanted to think that Herod was only unwilling to believe her because of her hatred toward Absalom. It did make her biased against him, but the facts were in her favor.

Sighing angrily, Gertrude acknowledged that for now, she had done all she could to make the possibilities of the morrow less miserable. While she rotated her shoulder, still sore from Absalom's abuse the other day, Gertrude reflected on the king's hesitation to believe her fully after all her years of unrelenting loyalty. *It isn't fair!* She thought. *If that blasted king is willing to ask me to marry him, he has to be ready to listen to me first! How can I possibly have any power with the crown on my brow if this is how he's acting now?*

She sighed heavily.

There would be no real benefit in marrying Herod, but how do I turn down his proposal?

And Breyton. Will that develop? Not just from him to me, but for me to him? She rolled over and looked at Sam.

If I say that I'm already involved with Herod's brother, could that be enough of an excuse? She tucked herself close to Sam. *Oh, Sam...if only you weren't married.*

It was possible that she could open her heart to Breyton, for he seemed to be a charming, amiable, and honorable man. He would show her great respect that she already knew, and of his loyalty to his late wife, she had only heard wonderful things. Gertrude drew herself closer into Sam's side. He pulled her in close.

She knew the day was approaching when they would share their last dawn, be it by the conflict ready to boil over into their lives or her impending intimate involvement with the Malleuses. She stretched her legs and kissed the crown of Sam's soft black hair.

But it is not this dawn.

14

The Fountain

Absolutely no women were allowed in the Council Gatherings.

Especially Gertrude.

To this point, she and several other women before her had protested, but to no avail. On all occasions following the umpteenth time the doors of the building slammed in her face, she'd sent in Sam to take notes so she could later analyze the occurrences within. The doors would open for any man. The patriarchal society may have kept her grounded on the bench outside the hall, but her little loophole let her inside.

An unprecedented number of men had gathered to see the three brothers together again. The possibilities of what could happen were endless, which only made Gertrude all the more frustrated that she could not be in the hall to witness whatever came about.

"You're rather quiet," Sam observed of Gertrude as he strolled beside her en route to the hall where the Gatherers conducted their business.

Exhaling dramatically, Gertrude looked up at Sam, holding her hand above her eyes to dim the intensity of the summer's sun. "I'm lost in thought," she answered.

The pair strolled across the lowest tier in the three-and-a-half-level bailey in the heart of the castle. The curtain walls shaded most of their path in the afternoon, but the sun was hanging directly over Sam's head.

"Anything in particular?" Sam inquired, hoping that he could help to clear her thoughts.

Fiddling with her class ring, Gertrude nodded and replied, "Yes. I can't understand why the king would put more trust in a man who is incontrovertibly evil over in me."

Looking at a maple tree, lonely in its stance out on the court's edge, Sam answered, "He probably doesn't put stock in your words against Absalom because, as you said, he's the only father figure Herod has ever known. Even if he fully believed in every word that you said, do you think you would ever expose the full extent of Absalom's brutality to you and your family?"

"No," she succinctly and firmly responded. "It's not appropriate or necessary for many reasons. It would reflect poorly on my family and me, I mean my politics; I would look like a mud-slinging father betrayer or something primitive like that." Gertrude sighed. "I often think about how my mother might still be trapped in her marriage with Absalom if it weren't for my relationship with Herod. Having his ear granted her the divorce." Gertrude chuckled. "Herod didn't even ask any questions because he adores my mother." She looked mournfully to Sam, wishing that their situation could be so easy.

Resuming their walk, a delicate smile spread on Sam's face, but before he shared what was on his mind, he checked their immediate surroundings to ensure that no one was around to listen in on their conversation. He asked in Heltkor, the neighboring country's language, which he had learned years ago, "Do you know why I love you?"

Chuckling at the sudden change of subject, Gertrude, too, smiled and looked at him expectantly.

He looked ahead and behind him, then leaned close to her ear to confess, "I love you, aside from the other million reasons, because of your ability to be so uncommonly kind."

Gertrude scoffed, "Huh, not me and my stinging tongue."

Shrugging and shaking his head, Sam continued, "You're blunt, Gertrude. You tell it like it is, and it takes guts to tell the truth, especially to a king. Hmm...if God himself gave you the means to kill your father for what he did to you and your family, if He flat-out guaranteed to you that you would emerge from it without a mark against you, you still would not do it."

At the bottom of a curved stone stairway, Gertrude and Sam paused their walk. Looking up to the eyes of her lover, the lady gave a curt nod and affirmed, "You're right. I wouldn't. Not from squeamishness, but because I hold no position that would give me that right. What right would I have to be the judge of his sins against my family? He's a frightened little man whose only way to feel powerful like he was in control, was to terrorize us."

Nodding his head, Sam said, "It's a God-given grace you have, Gertrude. To forgive your enemies and let them be, that's truly something to be admired." For the quickest second, Sam grabbed hold of his lady's hand and gave it a loving squeeze. They had never held hands in public before on account of the apparent repercussions that could emerge. It was Gertrude's most repeated wish to be able to lock her fingers with his for all eyes to see.

Sam quickly released her hand.

"However," Gertrude began; her tone had changed entirely, removing them both from the precious brief moment they had shared. There was power behind her word, and it surprised Sam. "For Absalom's crimes against our people, ...*that* is another story entirely." The pair ascended the last of the stairs. "For that, Sam, someday...I'd like to see him hanged."

The lone, gray stone building set away from the rest of the castle was where four generations of Gatherers convened over the years. A statue of white stone, settled in a pool of water, stood several strides before the edifice. Carved long ago from a solid block were three levels of scenery, all turned toward a crested middle piece. On the bottom rung were the figures of the lower class on their feet, looking up to the next landing as though they were speaking to the figures. The middle level was composed of twelve figures of men; these men were meant to represent the Gatherers, who were the supposed voices of the people. The demeanor of each figure was designed as though the Gatherers genuinely cared for the qualms of the people and meant to share their every concern with the king. The crowning piece of this not-flowing fountain was the carving of the king. This figure, with sword unsheathed and hand over his heart, knelt as though humbled by the words of his people. This fountain was built by the current crown's great-grandfather as a reminder to the kings and Gatherers to follow to be mindful of their place in the game. The only problem with the fountain was that the water did not circulate anymore. The pool was stagnant and rank with a green belt of mold. It was crawling with mosquito larva.

"I wish someone would clean that," Gertrude commented as she and Sam passed the fountain's spot. With her hand wedged under her nose, she added, "The smell is foul."

The smell was terrible, but Sam failed to notice. He was distracted by something else. "Looks like Absalom is getting ready to travel." Sam pointed to a horrible-looking creature, one that Gertrude knew too well.

The skulga was a foreign and, as such, an expensive alternative method of transportation from the everyday horse. Native to lands far from this part of the world, skulgas had circuitous cone horns that grew from the ridge above their eyes. Their muscular built and bat-like wings made them powerful beasts. The alien horse drew much attention from the rest of the men who came to attend today's event, but none were comfortable getting too close to this steed.

Licking her lips, dry from the warm summer day, Gertrude wondered aloud, "That skulga would be a convenient means for getting away quickly. There is nothing else in our country that could escape a pursuit. Your theory and Donovan's warning may pan out after all."

A man emerged from inside the building to announce that the meeting would start soon. The men standing under the building's awning shuffled to the small hall.

Gertrude watched them enter, envying every one of them regardless of their placement on the social ladder. They all had the opportunity to be listened to and not ignored simply because of their sex.

"I'll see you soon, Gertrude," Sam said quietly, lightly touching his hand to her shoulder to catch her attention.

She responded with a click of her tongue, and her finger pointed at Sam. "I'll just wait here, then," she said, planting her rump on the hard wooden bench.

With a heavy heart, Gertrude watched Sam file into the line of men flowing into the building. She was surprised to see the large crowd that came today. Interest in the Gatherings had grown low among spectators lately. She thought, *They're probably only here for the entertainment factor. After last night, and the three Malleus brothers in one sitting, it's bound to be something of a show...and I'm going to miss it.*

Behind the last man, the heavy doors closed with a loud, reverberating thud. Two fully foiled soldiers stood guard at the door. This was the first time such armored men had been posted at the Gatherings. These were the men that Herod had requested to be on guard in case anything went awry. Seeing them up close made Gertrude whisper to herself, "Shit."

These were not guards of the king. The emblem of a torch over their hearts marked them as the prime minister's men, not the king's.

15

The Council

The small hall was uncomfortably packed for such a warm summer's day. As soon as the meeting came to order, the men would take their seats on the benches. Sam slowly moved about the floor, listening in on various conversations, as instructed by Gertrude, as he made his way toward a bench. The twelve-seat table in the center of the room and the decorative chair that the king sat upon were not yet visible to Sam as he walked by, for far too many men hovered around them. Sam walked behind Herod and Aleksie, both too engaged in a conversation reliving last night's assassination attempt to have noticed the hero of the very same occasion.

Already seated on the higher of the paired long benches on what eventually would be the right hand of the king, Breyton spotted Sam and waved him over. The bodyguard thought it odd that this prince, even though he was technically a former, would not be seated on the central stage with his brothers.

Breyton smiled at Sam and stood at his arrival. "How are you, Sam?" Breyton asked, shaking his friend's hand.

They both sat.

Unbuttoning the top of his restricting white shirt in the hope of alleviating some of the stress from the heat, Breyton said, "It's hell in here. How's Gertrude?"

Sam chuckled. "She's never exactly happy on the days of the Gatherings, and I can't blame her. All she wants is to be treated like an equal, but these men don't give a damn."

Nodding, Breyton stroked his short beard. "It can't be easy. How is she supposed to be an advisor to the king if the rest of these buffoons won't let her in here?"

"They know that if she is in here, she'll tear them apart." Sam sighed. "Why aren't you down there, Breyton? Shouldn't you be sitting on the opposite side of Donovan with Herod in the middle or something?"

Though the question was posed under the innocent surge of curiosity, Breyton could not help but feel small. Sighing heavily, he answered, "I'm afraid it wouldn't matter if I was down there or not. The Council has become a mockery of our democracy. It's nothing more than a show. The Council members gather to present their, not their people's, ideas and qualms to the king and the prime minister decides for him. Herod is a figurehead, and he doesn't recognize it. Here before us, the king talks with the men, not realizing that they are talking for him. It's the dualistic nature of the Gatherers that puts me on this bench instead of down there with my brothers. I am not down there because Donovan and many of the Gatherers do not believe that I am capable of having a political view."

"Not capable of?" Sam found this difficult to believe.

Breyton clenched his hands. The decision that he had once been so proud of making was beginning to burn him more and more each day. "It's as if I relinquished my rights as a lord when I stepped down from the crown. This is the first time I have ever been invited to these Gatherings. I don't even know why Herod asked me here when he knew full well that I would not be allowed to have any say in this game."

"Maybe he asked you here as a source of strength?" Sam offered in theory. "His mother passed away not too long ago, so you're the only true family the king has left." Sam leaned in and quietly added, "Donovan's by far more an enemy to him than a brother."

Lord Philemon's face emerged from the crowd of men on the floor headed for Breyton. However, as soon as Yuri saw the company that Breyton shared, he merely waved to his friend, then proceeded to take a seat on the opposite wall.

"Well, that was odd." Breyton could not understand what would drive away his friend. "I thought Yuri was going to sit with us. It certainly looked that way, didn't it?"

Sam did not find Yuri's behavior odd at all. Like Gertrude, Sam was not one who enjoyed sharing personal grievances, but he thought it prudent that Breyton be provided insight into the situation. "I'm sure he would have sat with you, Breyton, if you were not already sitting with me," he confessed. "There is tension, shall we call it, between him and me."

Finding the whole Sam and Yuri situation to be puzzling, Breyton inquired, "Why? What happened that you two should be so hostile?" He knew both men to be amiable and lighthearted souls. It did not make sense to Breyton that such a divide could exist between such similar beings.

Sam was surprised that Breyton would have been kept in the dark from this event, but before he could answer, Absalom rang a bell and knocked the gavel to the table, calling the men to settle themselves.

"Breyton, it's a long and complicated story," Samuel said as the men quickly found their seats and as the Council members gathered around their own. "To do it justice, I'll tell you about it some other time, preferably with a large glass of wine."

When the guests of the Gatherers took their seats, the men on the center stage took theirs, but one remained empty: Deo Aspiruth's former chair. At the head of the table, Herod sat with Aleksie standing right behind him. Donovan sat, as a guest, to his brother's left, staring straight at the man on the far opposite side of the table. This man, who remained standing, his seat back to the door, was the well-aged prime minister. Absalom put his round spectacles on the bridge of his hooked nose. He held the list of items to be discussed.

In his deep voice, Lord Kemen read off the list: "Gentlemen, Your Majesty, Duke, and other guests. Today's order of business includes that which our Council has not done in three years. As you all see, one of our members is still missing; Lord Deo Aspiruth will no longer be fit to take a seat amongst us due to his deteriorating health. Today we must nominate a new member of the Council. Following that, His Majesty, King Herod, would like to award Mr. Samuel Maison the Silver Star for his patriotic duty."

This surprised Sam. *Me? Awarded by the king?*

Absalom continued, "The king also has requested that we have an open discussion about the scenes he witnessed on his journey 'round the country. Your Majesty, let me say welcome back; your presence was missed." Absalom bowed his head to the king, who received the gesture dryly.

Herod was starting to realize the irony of the speaker's words.

Throwing the pile of paper down in front of him, Absalom looked up to the surprisingly large number of men in the hall. Their eyes bore down on him, making his palms sweat more than the room's heat. He was already nervous enough as it was without the staring eyes of so many men upon him. The prime minister cleared his throat. "As I asked you all at our last meeting to consider the names of the candidates with your people, I will assume that you know the man your people chose to fill Deo Aspiruth's position."

Several of the Gatherers nodded their heads, but few of them knew who it was their people would have chosen. Familiar with the procedure, the men at the table pulled out from their pockets the cards with the name of the candidate their people may or may not have voted for. The cards were passed to the prime minister to be counted. Absalom took every card and made notes on his pad to keep tally. A brief collection of minutes passed before Lord Kemen had the results of the election.

Standing up properly, Lord Kemen, pad in hand, read off the electoral numbers. "Well, I'm astonished; we have a tie."

On the other side of the room, Sam saw that Yuri looked rather sweatier than the rest of the men, undoubtedly from nerves.

"As you all know, should we come to such results, the king makes the parting decision between the two." Absalom looked straight at the king. "Your Majesty, as prime minister, I am asked to present to you the choice between Lord Magnes Dawes, who is unfortunately absent today," Absalom briefly scanned the faces of the men in the room to verify his statement ere continuing, "and Lord Yuri Philemon."

Gertrude was right, Breyton thought.

King Herod licked his lips nervously and pulled on the bright yellow collar of his suit. He was not comfortable making this decision without first consulting Gertrude, but somewhere deep inside, her words in favor of Lord Philemon rang clear. Clearing his throat, Herod continued, "Council Members, gentlemen, considering the present circumstances of the country, I believe it necessary that we include in this collaboration of individuals a man who has deep ties amongst the people, that is, someone whom they trust. It is thus that I say that my vote goes to Lord Philemon."

Yuri looked struck. He'd never dreamt that he would be picked by the king as an important piece to keep the puzzle from falling apart. From the encouraging words of some of the members of Council, Yuri was invited to fill in the empty seat in their circle.

"Welcome to our society, indeed," Absalom dryly greeted as Yuri took his new seat at the table. He, too, knew that his daughter favored this man, which made him nervous. "Later today, Lord Sanford," the prime minister gestured to a man on his right at the table, "will instruct you on your specific duties to the crown, to this order, and to the people. Before we forget, just for the record, do you, Lord Philemon, accept this seat and this honor as your public and patriotic service?"

Nodding and smiling enthusiastically, Yuri answered, "Yes, sir, certainly."

Absalom made a grunting noise—a cross between stern disapproval and acknowledgment. "Right. Well, Your Majesty, I hand the floor to you to award Mr. Maison his trinket."

Though Herod missed the intent in Lord Kemen's choice of words, Sam and Breyton did not. The Silver Star was something so much more than any old trinket. It was a high symbol of honor, one that deserved respect.

From the brandy-colored box supplied by Aleksie, Herod retrieved the Silver Star with its thick purple ribbon. "This man, Samuel Maison of Legrette, saved my life last night," the king said as he held the star proudly. "I owe him my eternal gratitude. Mr. Maison, wear this to show all members of this country the thanks their crown owes you. This award, as many of you know, marks this man as a hero to the crown. Without him, I would be lost." The king pinned the shimmering star onto Sam's vest over his heart. Herod patted Sam's shoulder and thanked him once more.

As there was scattered and dry applause from the men in the room, the king whispered to Sam, "I hope, too, Sam, that someday you can forgive me for my unwillingness to trust you?"

Initially shocked by the award and this apology, Sam stood like a wall. Eventually, he nodded his head and said, "Thank you, Sire."

Though he tried to stay focused, Herod remained distracted by the threat of what could still happen.

There was no grandiose ceremony for the hero of the hour. He knew that there would never be, and he did not care. Samuel rejoined Breyton on the bench. He could not help but notice how Breyton stared at Donovan and occasionally at Absalom. Sam could only begin to wonder what cogs were turning in Breyton's analytical mind.

"Lord Prime Minister." Herod remained standing. "If I may, I would like to open discussion now."

"Please, sir, the floor belongs to you," Absalom said, settling his old body comfortably in his chair.

The king caught the sarcastic tone that Lord Kemen used. Herod was unnerved by this comment, and he was sensing the animosity about which Gertrude long ago had warned him to mark. Herod felt as though his tongue was sandpaper, and his throat was full of ash. Regardless, the king spoke to his Council with great dignity. "Gentlemen, as you know, for the past few months, I toured the country to absorb and observe the complaints and trials of our people. On the surface, I thought that all I found were peasants who complained and moaned endlessly, dull to the fact that the land was abundant." Looking down, Herod let the wisdom of Gertrude and everything he saw on his journey finally apply to his politics. Even though she had thought him blind, there were many things that he had seen. "I was wrong. Gentlemen, our people are angry because they do not believe I, their king, care about them, and they think that because the men who are supposed to be rallying their words to me are failing to listen from the start. Why is that? Why are some of you betraying your people by not adhering to the governance of this Council?"

None of the men had been expecting a direct question from the king. The men in the crowd were duly shocked.

A soft, small smile showed itself on Breyton's face. *Well done, brother,* Breyton proudly thought.

Lord Istanov was the first at the table to speak. "Your Majesty, we can only report to you what the people choose to report to us."

"Are you saying that they would withhold their most dire expressions from the men who could bring them almost immediate action?" Herod queried.

Several of the twelve nodded their heads, but Yuri did not see the truth in this. "And why do you think, Lord Istanov, that the people would choose not to come to you?" Yuri bravely asked. "My people come to me, and they tell me like it is. Perhaps you may have given them a reason to be wary of approaching you?"

"Now see here, lad!" The eldest member of the Council pointed an angry arthritis-bent finger at Lord Philemon. Lord Rada, a gatherer for forty-some years, smacked his lips together and rattled, "How dare you take that tone with these men! You've only just joined, and you're already out to cause trouble."

"No," Herod sternly said. "Lord Philemon has raised the precise point that I intended to examine. Why are the people not sharing their doubts with you? These people used to trust you and communicate freely with you. How has this bond been broken? What can we do to fix it? It must be done expediently before it escalates to something out of our hands to control."

"Tell me, brother," Donovan loudly chimed. "Why is it that you so readily accuse these men, your lords, of betraying the trust of the public? Hasn't history shown that it's the people who usually start mobs and messes? Aren't they the ones who first betray the king?"

"I suppose you are the most adept and well-learned expert on betrayal, Donovan, aren't you?" Breyton cut in. He stood, too consumed by his anger toward Donovan to care about making a scene. "After all, you have had so much experience in doing it yourself."

This was what the men in the crowd had been waiting for.

A highly tense moment passed before Donovan made a response:

"If there is anyone to be accusing, Herod, it is the men like our dear brother who are so deluded by their hope to believe in the goodness of men that they are blind to the ones actually picking their pockets."

"Then, it's your hands that ought to be checked for the missing goods of this country!" Breyton yelled, his face a bright crimson. "It's your ilk that's been telling the people to turn on their lords and to lose faith in their king!"

Donovan was not so quick to respond, and certainly, no one in this hall was about to touch this boiling pot with their bare hands. Years of festering anger and doubt were turning in Donovan's core, but he knew that he needed to bottle his temper for a bit longer. He knew that very soon, Breyton would get all that he deserved. Calmly, he smiled and said, "Oh yes, Breyton, I have turned all the people in this country against our brother so that I could be king. Is that what you think? In your quest here for righteousness, you've failed to mention that were the people to throw their little revolution, you and I both would be the top targets on their hit list after the king!"

"Enough!" Herod ordered, slapping his hand loudly on the table. "We're losing sight of the issue, and I'll not let the severed tie between the three of us interfere with the importance of this meeting."

"My king, with all respect," Lord Montgerovich piped in, "the strength of your family reflects the strength of your kingship."

Were this gentleman a year younger, the king would have challenged him to a duel for insulting his family. Instead, his actions proved another example of his weak command as king. He sank into the back of his chair.

Lord Kemen stood, his enormous domineering body standing as tall and as proud as his tired bones could allow.

Seeing Absalom rise, Breyton lowered his body to the top of the bench behind him to draw attention away from himself and center his own upon the prime minister.

"Your Majesty, to that note, *my* people have had a say," Absalom announced.

"Really?" Herod asked, sinking into his chair even farther from the fear of Gertrude being right. "Go on, then," the king encouraged as his bodyguard instinctively drew closer to him.

After swallowing hard, the prime minister started, "Your Majesty, it has come to the attention of the people and of the lords in this room that the current body of politics are no longer appropriate for these times."

"What are you getting at, Lord Prime Minister?" Yuri asked. Many in the room held the same questions in their heart.

Looking at the faces seated at the table, Breyton saw many men exchanging nervous glances with one another.

Sam's stomach clenched. He held his breath. *Was what Donovan told Gertrude not a lie? Absalom must have a death wish.*

Standing tall, the prime minister continued, "Your Majesty, it is with a heavy heart that I must act to protect the sanctity of this country and to obey the words of the people I represent. Your Majesty, gentlemen, I move to have the figurehead of monarchy removed from our constitution, our Council, and quite frankly, from our country."

A sound of shock echoed throughout the room.

"Vote out the monarchy?" one man among the crowd loudly asked.

"Can you do that?" another followed.

Absalom did not wait for the looks of shock around the room to manifest into further questions, but his control was slipping. More and more voices were arising. Absalom banged his fist on the table and shouted, "This is a democracy, and we will vote on this matter brought before us. All in favor of removing the king, say 'aye'!"

Several men began to holler, including Breyton: "You can't do that! It's not within the constitution!"

Several "ayes" snaked out and around the growing number of voices filling the hall.

From the risers, men took to their feet, loudly expressing their opinions for or against the king.

The room erupted with movement and sound.

Herod's heart raced. Sweat ran down his brow. Though Aleksi stood firm beside him, many, far more than he had imagined, were calling for his end. He looked to his brother Breyton. The eldest of the Malleus kin was yelling to the men around him, what he was saying, Herod could only guess, but it looked like Breyton was rallying them to support their king. Herod's heart dropped as he thought, *That is the man that should have been king.*

The room was a cacophony, but the voices of those who supported the crown grew stronger.

Those who would have cast their votes with Absalom began to recede. They wouldn't so much as look at him. Absalom sent a panicked glare to Donovan, but the duke would not meet his gaze.

Those loyal to the crown called louder and stronger than the shrill voices of the betrayers.

"Traitor!"

"Down with Absalom!"

"Treason!"

"Arrest the Prime Minister!"

The hodge-podge of noise deafened Absalom, who could only see the mesh of angry men around him. Though this turmoil had been a part of the plan, the role of having more loyal to him emerging at this moment had failed.

Panicked, Absalom's dark eyes sought the enclosing walls around him for any hope toward his cause, but all he could see was Herod on his feet, arm and hand outstretched, pointing at him, and Aleksie charging forward.

"Fools!" Absalom shouted. "Damned be the lot that sides with the king!" Whipping out his sword and shouting, "Out of my way!" Absalom ran for the door.

16

Exodus

Bursting into the outer world, blinded temporarily by the brightness of the sun, Absalom failed to see Gertrude leap up from the bench onto her feet.

"To me, you fools!" the prime minister shouted as he ran toward the men holding the reins of his skulga.

Running out with a few other men, Sam came rushing to Gertrude's side. The small crowd outside the Council's meeting place saw Lord Kemen mount the ferocious steed. Gertrude, Sam, and the others outside watched helplessly as the prime minister brought his horse from canter to gallop, and, with its great wings pounding the earth, to flight.

With an eerie elegance, the skulga and its master escaped, shrinking in the mountainous horizon until they disappeared.

Gertrude sighed heavily, unable to immediately comprehend what she'd witnessed. Before she could say anything, the cacophony from the hall behind them faded to silence, save for two distinct voices shouting brutal curses at one another. Sam, Gertrude, and most others outside rushed to the doors of the hall to see the duel of the brothers.

Inside the hall, Donovan and Breyton argued ferociously.

"You who are such a coward that you would turn down the crown keep trying to play king! You're a bastard hypocrite, Breyton!" Donovan screamed. "The people don't give a damn about you. You disgust me, you shameless pig!" Donovan spat on Breyton's boots.

"You're the one who ripped apart the honor of our family name!" Breyton shouted. "It was you who drove Mother to an early grave! The devolution skipped you for a reason, Donovan. The best decision our father ever made was to renounce your right to the crown!"

"Bastard!" Donovan bellowed, reaching for the tang of his sword. Breyton reached for his.

"NO!" Herod commanded, jumping between his brothers. "Let no blood be spilled in the house of the common good! Donovan, I've had enough! Leave this place and do not count on any chance for your return."

The crowd was mute.

Donovan took a threatening step toward Herod. His bright blue eyes looked so inhumanly cold that the temperature of the room seemed to drop.

With his naked sword in hand, Aleksie said to Donovan, "Move along, sir."

The denounced prince lowered his sword. He turned to Breyton.

Many of the people in the hall thought that they were about to witness Donovan kill Breyton right there, and then he did something that none of the onlookers expected.

Donovan sheathed the blade then held out his hand to his brother. "It looks as though this is where our paths permanently part. If that be the case, ...goodbye, brother."

Breyton was furious, and this extremely sudden change in Donovan did little to set his rage at ease. However, he recognized the significance of this moment. Taking a deep breath, Breyton shook hands with his brother. "Goodbye, Don."

With a curt bow of his head, Donovan turned. He did not so much as look at Gertrude and Sam as he walked calmly out from the hall. This man of great evil left thinking comfortably to himself, *Someday, I will return, and I will be king.*

~*~*~

The prime minister was gone. News carriers and criers all across the city were spreading the gossip faster than any plague had spread. The far side of the country would know of the disaster before the morrow's dawn.

The words *I would like to review those plans of yours, Gertrude,* were the most beautiful that the king had ever said to her. Laying out the plans before Yuri and Herod in the king's study filled Gertrude with a high that she had never known.

"How will we pay for all of this?" Yuri asked. "The funds needed for these projects will be astronomical, and I doubt that the high-borns will be willing to sponsor any of them out of the goodness of their hearts."

Gertrude had an answer. "With the prime minister gone, we will redirect the taxes that he and his lot have been stealing to be invested in the people as originally intended. The projects will be slow to start as we rebuild those funds, but they must start."

"And they will," Herod proclaimed.

Gertrude looked to Aleksie and smiled. He did not return the expression, but at least the coldness in his eyes toward her was gone.

"You have all of the contacts for starting these projects already, don't you?" Herod asked. He peered down at the journal that Gertrude had handed over to him.

"I do," she answered. "Their names and locations are underlined."

Yuri leaned back in his chair. This meeting had been both exhausting and exhilarating. "This will make tremendous changes, Sire."

Herod nodded. He looked up to Gertrude. "While I'm not happy that you are leaving, the lords and experts around the country will indeed be more accessible to you at your mother's home."

Gertrude agreed. However, before she could respond, a knock came at the door.

With the king's approval, Sam opened it.

A servant entered and said, "Lord Malleus has left, Your Majesty."

"Good," Herod said, a scowl on his face. "May Donovan never step foot on these grounds again."

"Forgive me, Sire," the messenger clarified. "Not the duke, though yes, he is being escorted off the grounds as we speak. It is your other brother, Lord *Breyton* Malleus, who has left."

Silence overtook the room.

"Breyton?" Gertrude asked. Her stomach clenched. "Why?"

The messenger responded, "I'm sorry, my lady. He did not say a word beyond that he was going home."

Herod fell slowly into his chair.

The servant saw the heaviness in the room. He bowed his head and dismissed himself.

Once the messenger had left, Herod turned to Yuri and said, "Yuri, you've been Breyton's friend as long as I can recall. Try to catch him. Tell him that *I* need him here now more than ever."

Yuri nodded and began to stand.

"Tell him," Herod continued, "That I am asking him as his brother, *not* as his king."

Yuri nodded once more, then left the room.

Why didn't he tell me? Gertrude wondered. Immediately after, she rolled her eyes and realized, *He barely knows me; that's why.*

"I don't understand why Breyton would leave," Herod mumbled, sitting at his desk and rubbing his aching forehead.

Breyton's departure was one Gertrude did not want to think about at this moment. Clearing her throat, she answered the king's question as delicately as she could. "Well, Your Majesty, er, he probably feels betrayed by his family? Donovan did just call him a coward, among other things, in front of a crowd of fifty men. It's a bit embarrassing, belittling, to say the least." She wanted to add, *and you did relatively nothing to assuage his poisonous tongue even though you have the power to do anything,* but this was not the appropriate time for her to be blunt.

"Must you also leave today?'" Herod asked Gertrude.

"Yes, Your Majesty, I must," Gertrude firmly answered. "If we can get ahead of the confusion and the assumptions that may be made by the people about the reasons for Absalom's departure, we may have a strong chance of turning favor back to our side." Her original intent of escaping to her mother's had been replaced with this sense of duty to her fellow countrymen. "You're a brilliant man, my king, and you proved yourself beautifully today to the court by not standing for Absalom's shit. You'll be fine without me for a few months. It's the people who need me now."

Rubbing his temple in deep circles, the king contemplated sharing something most sensitive with Gertrude and Sam that he would have to tell her eventually, especially if they were to marry. Family secrets did not dwell well in relationships between husband and wife. "Gertrude, Sam, there's something I think I ought to tell you," Herod admitted quietly. "Sam, you may know this already, but I'm fairly certain that you, Gertrude, do not."

Gertrude stared out the nearby window and sighed. The clouds were beginning to absorb the hues of what was sure to be a brilliant sunset. She wanted to leave before the clouds rolled in from the ocean to smite the sun, but she doubted that would happen now. Putting aside any regret, she encouraged the king to tell his story.

Sitting up straight, Herod began. "About six years ago now, my father grew ill. We all knew he was not going to pull through. I had never left the castle to live elsewhere like the rest of my siblings, and I had not seen my brothers in so long. They came, both of them. Brey brought his beautiful wife, Inya, whom he'd been married to for some time then. They had borne no child, but they were still wonderfully happy together. Donovan did not bring anyone or anything. He only came so that he could be declared king. Donovan and Breyton arrived on different days. They avoided one another as they had done for some time, but Donovan took an interest in Inya. He saw her beauty, and I'm sure he immediately coveted her. He pretended to be disgusted that his brother would marry a peasant, even though he had bedded who knows how many."

Herod hesitated a long moment before he continued. The scene he was about to divulge had been seared into his mind's eye. "About two days after their arrival, I accidentally walked in on Donovan, forcing himself upon poor Inya." The king paused. To this day, the memory made him shiver. "Don stormed out of the room without a word. Inya was a mess. It was awful. I'll never forget the terror in her eyes. I took her hand, and we found Breyton together. He was with our father and my mother. Even on his deathbed, my father was furious, as was Breyton. Father was so disgusted by Donovan that he changed his last will that night. He made it so that the devolution of the crown would pass to me when he died, not Donovan. I can't tell you the shock that swept through the room. I never expected to be named the heir to the throne, being the youngest and born of a different mother than my brothers." The king paused and briefly thought of his mother, whom he loved dearly, though he was never so lucky as Breyton and Donovan, whose attentive mother genuinely loved them. "The next morning, Breyton and I were in the courtyard when Donovan came out in a torrential rage. Breyton had barely turned his head to see him when Donovan delivered a brutal blow to the side of his head. I reached for my sword—I'm still not sure what I thought I was going to do with it—but Donovan whipped out his dagger first and sliced my forearm, deterring me from doing anything. Breyton punched Don, even though his world was spinning and ringing from the pain in his ear. After the blow, Brey fell to the ground, clinging to the side of his head. Donovan drew his sword. I was scared to death. I thought that I was going to witness Donovan behead our very own brother. I truly believe that if Aleksie had not stepped in and broken up the situation, Donovan would have killed Breyton right there." Herod gave a grateful look to his dearest friend. Aleksie was proud to receive this recognition, but it broke his heart to see his king's family so broken.

"But why?" Gertrude asked as she watched the ball of fire disappear beyond the thick blanket of coastal clouds. "Why would Donovan target Breyton, when technically he should have come for you?"

"Because Breyton willingly gave up that which he could then never have," Sam answered. He vividly remembered hearing about this event six years ago—news of its happening whisked across Vitenka with aggressive force. "He feels that Breyton did a greater crime against him. He blames Breyton for everything." Sam thought about the conversations that he and Breyton had shared in their days in the military. "In Donovan's eyes, Breyton has been the cause of every wrong in his life."

Nodding, Herod agreed. "Yes, that is true. What's more, if I should die, according to my father's will, before I seed a legitimate heir, my crown, my country—everything—falls, irrevocably, to Donovan."

17

The Toll

I n a humble coach, they rattled through the twisting streets of the capital. Sam insisted that Gertrude keep the curtains closed, but she wanted to see the state of the city. From the split in the drapes dirtied by passengers before her, she saw the messages painted on the walls. Though each was different, the unifying theme was calling for the blood of the king. There were more beggars than she could ever remember dotted across the streets. Lines for bowls of watery stew offered by the churches snaked their way down several blocks. Sallow faced children with sunken eyes looked up to the skies with no traces of hope in their gazes.

As their departure from the city led them toward the suburbs away from the scenes of extreme poverty, Gertrude prayed and prayed, *Please,* please *let us not be too late.*

The distance to her mother's home was relatively short, but it felt longer than usual, marred by the fact that they were taking roads less traveled in their humble, slow-moving coach.

"Do you suppose we'll ever get there?" Gertrude asked toward the end of their first day of travel. She had been silent and lost in thought for close to two hours.

Sam was fine with the silence. It allowed him to concentrate on their surroundings. He did not much care for being cooped up in the carriage, feeling like he had no control over their stops or of who could also pop in. Drawn from his alertness, Sam looked to her from across the coach and said, "Of course. I think we're rolling into the town where we were hoping to stay for the night."

Gertrude pressed her forehead to the thin glass that separated her from the outside world to look ahead. Beyond the rolling fields of farmland, she could see the town ahead.

"Are you certain you don't want to stay at the house of the Posonovs?" Sam asked though it sounded more like he was begging. "They're just another hour that way." He pointed to his right.

Gertrude clutched the worn velvet padding beneath her and shook her head. "I'm sure." Her stomach was churning, but she knew that this was something they had to do. "We must stay at their local inn to prove to the people that we are one of them, that we—*I*—still trust them and that I am their champion. How poorly would it look if I slept and dined in a high-born house and still called myself their champion? Now, do I think that either of us will feel comfortable enough to have a wink of sleep at the inn tonight? No, but this must be done."

Sam knew that he could not argue with this, but he sure wished he could.

Staying at the inn may seem like a luxury, Sam thought as they passed the houses on the outer periphery that looked to be made of little more than branches. *How many of these people will survive winter living in those shacks?*

Their carriage rolled into the gray-stoned-faced town.

The people look as gray as the buildings, Gertrude thought, seeing the inhabitants of the town milling about. There was no work to occupy them, no projects passed by their lord, so they had nothing to do but sit and drink, for those who could afford it. The rest simply starved.

Realizing that the inn was but a few buildings away, Sam leaned forward and said, "I'm not so certain that we shouldn't reconsider staying at the Posonovs.'"

Gertrude leaned forward and quietly said, "Sam, we've just been through this."

"Every instinct in my being is telling me that we are going to die here." Sam had rarely felt more strongly about anything. "If you intend to continue with this, you need to hide your jewelry *now*."

"Shit," Gertrude hissed. They had always been so good about this before; she had even remembered to wear one of her more unadorned dresses, but here she was with rings and earrings on. "Couldn't you have thought of this earlier, Sam?" she asked, frustrated with so many things.

Sam resisted rolling his eyes.

She pulled off her university ring and the other two decorative bands that she wore and fussed to remove the pearls dangling from her ears. "How stupid of me," she muttered, knowing full well that this was her fault.

Sam pulled from his pocket a handkerchief that he ripped in half. "Here." He reached for her jewelry. "We'll put your earrings in this and your rings in the other." He scrambled to tuck her items into their cloth trappings. "You need to shove these in your boots. They'll be less likely to harass or try to pickpocket you, their champion than they will me."

Gertrude took the little packages and pulled up her skirt to her knees to shove them in her boots. She was glad that her tobacco and pipe were in the boot of the cart, which left plenty of room for these new items. "Let's just hope that I am still their champion, or we may need to grab these as bargaining chips."

Sam didn't say it, but he thought, *I hope they'd be enough.*

The carriage slowed and then pulled to a stop.

Both of the passengers looked to one another intently.

The driver announced that they had arrived with three bangs of his fist to the side of the cart.

Holding his breath, Sam stood and prepared to leave the cart.

"It'll be fine, Sam," Gertrude assured him, not sure where this dose of courage was coming from. "We will be fine."

Sam nodded. He sharply exhaled, then opened the door.

He stepped out of the carriage onto the dirt road. His eyes scanned their surroundings with a casual look upon his face. He did not want to appear unnerved in the slightest, though his heart was racing.

A small crowd of women stopped to stare at him. While curiosity to see strangers arriving in a cart was not anything unusual, their stern expressions and arms crossed over their chests were less than inviting.

Gertrude is right; everything will be fine. Without completely turning his back to the growing group of watchers, he reached back into the cart for Gertrude.

She placed her hand in his and leaned heavily into his grasp to step out of the carriage. She, too, saw the women and now men standing just beside the entryway of the inn. *Alright*, she thought, her palms beginning to sweat. *Let's begin.* She smiled at them and kindly said, "Good afternoon."

Silence.

Sam wanted to throw Gertrude back into the cart, but he knew that that would solve nothing.

The driver was beginning to unbuckle Gertrude's trunk from the cart's boot. Though she was traveling with only a handful of items, many eyes in the crowd locked on it with interest.

"What's in the trunk?" one of the villagers asked.

Gertrude began to proceed toward the door of the inn calmly. "A second dress and my bloomers, I believe."

A woman positioned herself to stand in the path of the driver, blocking him from entering the inn. "Let's see it," she demanded.

Sam took a short glance behind them. More people had gathered on the other side of the entryway, enclosing the distance between the building and the cart.

They were trapped.

Gertrude smiled warmly and asked, "See it?"

"What you got in that trunk?" the woman persisted. She placed her hands on her hips. "I'd like to see what else you got in there."

"How would seeing the items in there improve your day?" Gertrude returned. She remained calm, her voice measured. She only hoped that the driver would be able to stay calm as well.

The woman wrinkled her brow. She had not been expecting this woman she was trying to intimidate to ask questions. "Won't improve my day none, but we here have a toll to use our road, and I'd like to make sure that you can pay."

"A toll?" Gertrude continued. "Does that mean you are the toll collector?"

"It's none of your business what I am or am not." The woman wanted to beat this newcomer, but *she* felt slightly intimidated like she was trying to attack her mother and not a high-born.

"I'm so sorry," Gertrude apologized, touching her heart. "Where are my manners? You all surely think that I am just some horrible, lost high-born. Let me start over: my name is Gertrude, daughter of Galina Galiova, and I would very much like to stay at this inn tonight."

"Galina's daughter," many people began to whisper.

"This is the advisor to the king!" others exclaimed.

"She's the one who fights for us!" another shouted.

The temperature and intensity of the crowd dropped, making the heat of the day suddenly so much more tolerable.

Sam felt like he could breathe again.

Gertrude smiled. "I am on my way to my mother's home, where I intend to have meetings with several people from around Vitenka to see how we may talk with the king now that the prime minister is gone." Gertrude had not exactly planned on using Absalom as a scapegoat for all that had occurred, but she was not opposed to it. "How would you all like to join me for a drink or two in the inn, my treat, so that we may talk about what is happening here?"

The woman who had been blocking the driver's path smiled. She stepped back and said, "Sure hope the keep's got enough barrels for the lot of us and that you have enough coin on you to pay for it. We're thirsty, and we have a lot to talk about."

~*~*~

Throughout the night, Gertrude listened and explained to the people the initiatives that she and the king were implementing. The people listened to her proposals, from working with experts from around the world, to develop proper sewers in their cities to create a standardized educational system for their children. Many drinks passed among them, and the next morning, when they left, regardless of her headache, she felt like she had done some good.

"That's one town," Sam said on the back of a yawn. "Only about two thousand more to go?"

Gertrude's head dropped to the back of the bench. "Please don't remind me of that. Hopefully, word will start to spread that their high-born champion is trying. If only Herod had already done this when we were on our tour, how many lives could we have saved?"

Sam sighed heavily and looked out the window.

There were many miles yet to go.

18

Her Mother's Garden

T he dogs of Forsythia Valley Manor came rolling out from the side of the house in a loud, tumultuous wave, to greet their favorite lady. Gertrude had hardly stepped a foot out from the cart before the furry, slobbering faces of her mother's dogs jumped up to lick and lap at any and every inch of skin they could reach. The lady knelt to stroke and pet the half dozen dogs she loved so much. A particularly excited pup, whose golden body waved madly as its little tail wagged, was plucked from the ground and delightedly held against Gertrude's body.

Quietly, with a smile, Sam followed Gertrude into her mother's home. Gertrude glowed when she was home. He loved to see her radiating brightly once more.

The visits from the daughter to her mother had of late become less and less expected. There was a time right after Gertrude graduated from the university when she would visit home regularly, but now her life on the coast grounded her wings from seeking a peaceful sanctuary.

The heels of Gertrude's boots tapped on the mosaic floor of the inner parlor in the light of the midday sun. As she stood over the tiled faces of mosaic angels, an elder servant dressed in elegant white and black clothes approached, greeting them warmly. "Welcome home, my lady," the gentle-servant said, "I pray you enjoyed a pleasant trip?"

"Yes, Franklin, we did," Gertrude answered with a smile. "Tell me, is Mother around?"

Nodding, Franklin turned and pointed toward the hall that led to the back porch. "Yes, child," he responded, "I believe she's out in the gardens."

Gertrude thanked Franklin, then proceeded down the well-lit hall warmed by the summer's sun. She was much too excited to see her mother to wait for Sam.

Gertrude walked out of the house into the cool shade of the enclosed back porch, where she set her dog down. A summer breeze enveloped her in a sweet jasmine embrace from the verdurous garden to officially welcome her home. The little golden pup wobbled along next to Gertrude as she always did when her lady was home. Gertrude stood on the shaded porch, trying to spot her mother over the large, green-leafed forsythias, but she was not there. She hopped off the porch and walked down the steps to the dirt path toward the next patch of flowers, blooming verbena, her favorite. Their citrus-like smell was divine. The trail wound to the left toward a row of cherry trees. Through the multihued roses of damask, red, and white, the yellow daisies, daffodils, and tulips, Gertrude and her pup walked. The pair nearly searched the whole garden, which was no small feat, until finally, she found her mother in the gated area nurturing her most prized collection of herbs.

"Mata!" Gertrude hollered for her mother from the edge of the poppies.

The green-eyed Galina Galiova, the former Lady Kemen, turned slowly, unable to believe that it was her daughter calling and not some trick of the summer sun. She screamed delightedly when her eyes found her daughter. "Oh! Gertrude, sweetie!" She popped up from the ground with her hands still coated in a fresh smudge of earth. Gertrude received her mother with a love-filled hug and a whirl of laughter. "Oh, my baby girl!" Galina said as she kissed her daughter on the cheek and held her tightly. She kept her hands bent away from Gertrude's dress, mindful of the fact that her digits were covered in soil.

Coming out of the house, Sam was guided toward the women by their laughter. He, like Gertrude, was highly impressed by the garden and surrounding orchard, for it was brighter and lusher than he had ever seen it before. When Sam came upon the women, he stopped a few feet away to respect their moment. He could not help but notice how much Gertrude looked like her mother, save for the hue of their eyes, though both had a beautiful pair. The women shared the same gentle features, the same intense stare, and the same rich laughter. It was not long ago when Galina held the title of the most beautiful lady in the valley, and now it seemed that she'd passed down that crown to her daughter.

"Mata, I've missed you so!" Gertrude confessed while holding onto her tight. Letting go seemed like such a foolish thing to consider.

"I've missed you too, baby," Galina said with tears lining her eyes. Her sons had left so long ago now that she could hardly remember the sounds of their voices. Gertrude was all she had, her only family aside from an all-too-far-away twin sister. She treasured her daughter more than her newly gained freedom from Absalom. "Oh, Sam!" Galina shouted, seeing the gentleman standing not so far away. Holding out her hand, Galina called him over. He, too, received a long hug and a kiss on the cheek. "How's our Sawsha?"

"Brilliant, absolutely brilliant," Sam answered proudly. "He wishes that he could have stayed longer on our last visit, though."

Waving her hand, Galina arched her shoulders. "Sam, you know that you and your precious boy are always welcome here," she said as she wiped her hands off on her well-used apron.

Sam smiled gratefully at his employer and wished that he could grant his son's other wish. The boy wanted to become a permanent resident of Forsythia Manor. In truth, Sam and his son practically did live there, so much so that Sawsha addressed Galina as his *babu*, his grandmother.

"I can't believe you two are here!" Galina exclaimed. "You will be staying with us for a while, won't you, Sam? I'll not be letting either of you slip away so easily. Or do you mean to go and fetch your boy?"

Shaking his head, Sam confessed, "I'm afraid I can't stay long. I have to leave on Sunday to be back home in time for my wife's ceremony."

Galina made a snorting noise. Like her daughter, she was not a particular fan of Mildred. "Pity that but you will stay with us at least for church, Sam, yes?" she asked with the same sort of pleading he often saw in Gertrude's eyes whenever she wanted something of him.

"Of course," Sam answered with a wink and a smile. "Wouldn't miss it for the world."

With the golden dog, Buttercup, at their feet, the three headed toward the porch, and Galina offered them both something to drink. Walking back through the gardens at a much slower speed, Gertrude was able to fully appreciate the glory of their floral scents and visual pleasantries. "Mata, I've never seen your gardens looking so beautiful."

Laughing proudly, Galina responded, "Yes, I know, it's brilliant, is it not? Since my divorce, I have finally been able to devote my days to this garden, and it's never been brighter."

"How long has it been?" Sam asked, "Your divorce, I mean."

Reaching the shaded porch, Sam, Gertrude, and Galina sat around the wooden table faded by the touch of the sun. The matron sighed, exhausted from her day's toil. She answered, "With the prodding from the king, which I know I have you to thank for, Gertrude, Absalom finally realized that I was more trouble than I was worth and signed the paper on April fourth, so I suppose it's been nearly five months now." A beautiful and delighted smile erupted on Galina's face. She had never looked more at peace to Gertrude or Sam. "We were married for twenty-seven years," she added as she waved down a servant-girl from inside the house and asked her to bring out three glasses of a regional favorite, chilled mint-infused vodka. "That was the last time you were here, wasn't it?" she asked her daughter.

Nodding, Gertrude waved her hand in front of her face in an attempt to generate a breeze. "Yes, I stayed for about two weeks and left just before the Midnight Sun began, or something like that. I'm sorry, Mother, that I haven't been by more, but Herod insists on keeping me rather busy."

"Don't worry," Galina said with a wave of acquittal from her hand, "Sam and Sawsha have been here to fill your absence and have been keeping me company well enough. Oh! You should see Sawsha, sweetheart. He's getting so big!" She spoke as though she were the grandmother of Sam's son. "When was the last time you saw him?"

"Not long ago at all, actually," Gertrude admitted while flicking a pestering mosquito from her forearm. "I accidentally ran into Mrs. Maison and her son when they were visiting her brother in Caldbluthe about four weeks ago. He had his first wiggly tooth then, and he told me all about it, but Mildred was not so anxious to talk, so our visit was rather short." Gertrude smiled awkwardly. She loved Sawsha with all her heart, but she could never be his mother, no matter how much or how hard she wished. Her stomach began to tighten. She wondered, *How much longer can we put him through this?*

To clear the humid and mildly awkward air, Galina asked excitedly, "So, what's the latest gossip from the castle by the sea? Is it true what they're saying? Did all three of the Malleus brothers convene?"

Sam and Gertrude exchanged ominous looks. As their drinks were served and sipped, the two regaled Galina with all the details of the past week.

"He just flew off?" Galina asked concerning the departure of her ex. "Oh! I can see him now, the coward. He's probably hiding out at one of his henchmen's houses if I know him."

"You don't think he would come here, do you?" Sam asked.

"No, not at all," Galina assured him. "No, Absalom knows that were he to come here I would show him no loyalty and that I would find a way to hand him over at once. Has Herod declared him a traitor?"

"Yes," Gertrude answered. "As we speak, notifications are being posted all over the country with a tremendous award for his capture or information on his whereabouts." Gertrude took a sip from her glass and added, "He will be caught, and finally, true justice will be served."

"What justice is it that you think awaits him?" Galina asked, curious as to what her daughter, who suffered the most abuse from Absalom, would say.

Gertrude confessed what Herod told her: "The king has proclaimed that if Absalom is caught, he is to receive the full sentence for a traitor. Herod believes, thanks to very credible information," she looked to Sam and smiled at him, "that he was connected to the assassination attempt. If Absalom is caught at this point, well, he will be hanged."

~*~*~

Falling flat on her back onto the soft mattress of her bed, Gertrude made a loud grunt before admitting the obvious: "I'm tired." It was well after seven in the evening, but the summer sun remained high in the sky.

After sneaking into her bedroom through a hidden door, Sam crawled onto the bed, lay atop Gertrude. "Me too," Sam playfully said as he kissed her chest.

"This isn't exactly what I meant," she said with a smirk. That twisting feeling in her stomach returned. She wanted to enjoy his kisses, to dive in as she had on countless occasions before, but she could not shake the guilt in the way that she used to before this summer away from Sam.

When his lips trailed to hers, Gertrude slid her fingers to touch his jacketless shoulders. She whispered as he kissed her forehead, "I hope that I can be half as strong as my mother someday, Sam."

Chuckling, Sam kissed Gertrude's shoulder and affirmed, "You are. I assure you that you are." He ran his fingers down her neck.

Not sure where this desire was coming from, she gently pushed him back and asked, "Will you come on a walk with me?"

He had been hoping for an activity that would lead into a nap, but the gentleman nodded and answered, "Of course." Walks usually meant in-depth talks, which, after the long spans of silence they had shared on the road, he was happy to indulge. Sam stood and walked to the window. He pulled open the floral-patterned curtains to admire the glorious summer evening.

A cool breeze came in from the window. It felt so refreshing, and it smelled of her mother's gardens. Gertrude stared at Sam, peering out into the day and tried to imagine how she would tell him what was on her mind. They had been to the lake for private talks countless times. Being back at her mother's home allowed her to imagine what scenes from their married life would look like. The thought warmed her heart before guilt froze it cold.

19

Sensing Summer's End

As they walked over the hill toward the lake, Gertrude reflected on all the talks she and Sam had shared on these grounds. She thought of that time when she told him she loved him, and the other more recent time when she told him she was pregnant. What a frightening fall that had been! She remembered how wonderfully Sam received the news when first she told him. He was not angry or panicked at the notion that his lover was going to have his child. He was fully prepared to accept all the responsibilities of having impregnated the prime minister's daughter and to be the supportive and attendant father of their child. It was almost like a dream come true. She would have proudly had the baby, and she would have loved the child with every beat of her heart, but she miscarried just after she started to show. Her mother never knew, nor did any soul other than Sam. Gertrude remembered how dreadfully miserable she felt emotionally and physically when and after it happened. Sam, too, was struck with depression when she came crying to him one morning to tell him of the loss. Those days were extremely stressful for them both, some of the most difficult of their lives.

A gaggle of birds chirped madly in the trees by the lake. A wavering breeze shimmered through the leaves. The sun was starting to make its descent over the mountains in the not-so-far west when Sam and Gertrude made it to the lake's edge. It was more humid here, but the beauty of the sun radiating against the water's surface was compensation enough for the small inconvenience of the air being a bit thicker.

Gertrude sat on the grass, and Sam followed her lead. She sighed into the gentle late-afternoon wind, hoping that nature's arms would take her burdens away. Tilting her head far back so she could see out from under her hat, Gertrude confessed with a tone too serious for Sam's liking, "Sam, there's something I want to talk to you about."

To lighten the moment, Sam pushed the hat's rim up a little so that he could better see her eyes.

She smiled at the gesture and shared, "Sweetheart, the night of the ball...Herod, well, um..." She cleared her throat and broke a long, thin stick in half that she picked up from the ground. "Herod asked me to marry him."

"What?!"

Gertrude already hated saying it, but she knew she had to elaborate. "Herod asked me to be his wife, his queen."

Sam held his breath. He stared off to the lake.

Gertrude closed her eyes. "I realize how ridiculous it sounds, trust me, but I need your help, alright? I need to figure a way out of this."

"Why?" Sam asked, turning to face her. His question surprised her. "You'd be queen."

"It's not that simple, Sam," Gertrude explained. "Not only do I *not* want to marry Herod and produce heirs for him, but have you ever heard of a queen who can go to local inns to share drinks with the people? What would the people think? Would they think me doing this is to try to buy power on their behalf? Or if Herod doesn't end up enacting the plans I've suggested, they'll hate me, and I'll be the ultimate betrayer." She shook her head. "I don't like the idea at all, Sam. I have to find a way to tell him no."

Staring at Gertrude, Sam had to hold a fist up to his mouth to hide his smile. It was just too funny for him to know that their king believed himself brave enough for Gertrude. However, Gertrude did raise a very valid point, so clearing his throat and shaking his arms to rid himself of the humor, Sam was able to talk in a more composed manner. "Gertrude, just say the word, and I'll do anything you command. But remember that I'm rather limited in my ability to give you a way to say no to the king, I'm afraid."

"I know," Gertrude said shamefully. "You can't marry me because you are already married." She sat quietly for a moment, watching the birds in the trees hopping from branch to branch and dive-bombing to capture snacks from the ground and the lake's surface. "If I were to marry Herod, I know that you and I could continue our relationship."

Sam sent a look of disbelief to Gertrude as he played with a long whip of wild oat that he plucked from the ground. "How do you figure?" he asked.

A dragonfly buzzed past Sam and Gertrude before she answered, "Can you honestly believe that Herod is going to be faithful to me? While queens have lost their heads when their kings questioned their loyalty, I expect, with Herod, that he wouldn't expect me not to sleep with other men if he is also sleeping with—"

"Other men?" Sam offered a half-smile.

She hit him gently with her forearm. "You and I are not exactly the best to judge other people for who they love, now, are we?"

"I guess that's true," Sam said. He sighed heavily. "Gertrude, maybe Herod's looking to make you his queen in an attempt at a peace offering to the people? Offering you the crown may also be his way of giving you more power."

Sighing, Gertrude was slightly agitated, but not at all toward Sam.

"Who knows, Sam." In her hours of silence on their journey to her mother's home, Gertrude had begun to wonder about the other option she had—one that, though it killed her to think of it, would legitimately give her cause to say no to the king, but would also permanently remove her from Sam.

He watched a pair of dragonflies fly by and disappear over the slow-moving waters of the lake. Sam cleared his throat and threw the oat blade to the ground. He sighed and offered something he did not want to say. "There is another option. I know that you know what it is."

Gertrude looked away from Sam and swallowed hard. That heavy feeling in her stomach turned to stone. "What do you mean?" She hoped he would say it so she would not have to. Blunt as she was, there was too much between them for her to say this aloud just yet.

With his eyes straight down, Sam quietly said, "I happen to know of a man who is available and who would have the ability to overrule the king."

Gertrude hung down her head. "Let's not think of this for right now, Sam." She did not want to think about what she would have to do, and the short time that she would have to do it in, to convince Breyton to marry her if indeed she decided that she did not want to be queen.

The pair sat quietly together for a long time before Gertrude pulled up the nerve to say, "Sam, I fear that any way we look at it, our extended summer romance is nearing an end."

~*~*~

From the open window of Gertrude's room, rays from the mid-morning sun trickled across the cream-colored sheets that lay gently thrown over her and her Sam. The lady lay asleep, swimming in the pool between dreams and awake, while the gentleman locked his arms protectively and lovingly around her. Being the early riser, Sam had been awake for some time, but he was not at all tempted to rise. He was much too comfortable in bed with his lover and the sensation of the sun warming his legs. Forsythia Manor was their sanctuary, the place where they could stay in bed together all day if they wished. With the threat of Absalom gone, no one here now would question their absence or the appropriateness of their relationship. Unlike the castle by the sea, Forsythia Manor had no nosey maids that would come into the rooms in the morning to prepare the sleeper for the day. The threat of an intruder disturbing their mornings was happily left behind at the coast.

For about an hour, Sam had been awake now, occasionally kissing and stroking his lady's face. He did not wish to rouse her from sleep. She was so beautiful. It nearly brought him to tears as he thought about how special his dear one was and how blessed he was to have her in his life. She completed him. He did not know what he would do without her.

She began to stir in his arms. He kissed Gertrude's cheek. "Good morning," he whispered. "Did you sleep well?"

"I always do when I'm in your arms," she said drowsily, though the answer did not feel as genuine as it used to. Gertrude rubbed her eyes and sat up a little. She felt the weight of something other than Sam sleeping on her feet and saw that it was Buttercup. "When did she get here?"

Clearing his throat, Sam answered, "She followed me in when I came through the entrance from my room to yours."

Sitting up properly and pulling up the sheet to cover her chest, Gertrude sighed, reflecting on her dream-memory. "I just remembered something. When we made love that first time, that day on the island, I said something along the lines of 'we had better make sure our affair is worth the prospect of an eternity in hell.' Well, do you think it has been?" she asked, now looking down at Sam.

This was a big question for a first-thing-in-the-morning conversation, but this was Gertrude. Sam assured her as he gently pulled her back flat on the bed, "There's not a day of our romance that I would trade for anything." Hell was a daunting place, but an eternity of damnation in their eyes was worth the love of a single lifetime.

Gertrude smiled for a moment, but her smile quickly faded as she asked, "Must you go today, Sam?"

"You know I have to," Sam answered firmly. "It's only once a year that my wife asks me to come home, and yes, her reasoning is a little odd, but I've still the obligation to go to her...She is my wife."

"A little odd?" Gertrude questioned. "I mean, I understand that she is your wife, Sam, but 'a little odd' does not cut it; it's been what, ten, eleven years? And she's still celebrating what would have been the birthday of the child that she miscarried? I miscarried only a few years ago, and I love you." Gertrude paused to see if Sam had anything to say, but since he did not, she continued. "And your poor son is being forgotten by your mother, pushed aside by the memory of a sibling that never was when I would die to call your boy my son."

"You practically do," Sam muttered during Gertrude's pause for breath as he fiddled with a corner of the sheet. He felt small. It pained him that he could not make his family and the love of his life happy in the way they deserved.

Combing her fingers through her hair, Gertrude licked her lips and added morosely, "For the life of me, Sam, I'll never understand why you married her."

Frustrated, Sam rolled onto his back, rubbing his forehead and staring blankly at the ceiling above. "You know that Mildred and I were arranged in marriage. I had no choice."

Silence passed between them as they allowed the flare-up of their quick spat to simmer down.

~*~*~

For Galina's comfort, a carriage transported them to the chapel on the hill that was a league away. Many of the people greeted Gertrude, but hardly anyone noticed Sam. To these parishioners, he was nothing more than a servant. Even these people of the country held their class-based prejudices. Nor did they care for or notice the Silver Star he wore. He felt ridiculous wearing it out and about anyway, but Galina insisted that he do so as she pinned it onto his vest. She was so proud of the man she had hired to protect her daughter—she wanted the world to know that he had saved the king. Neither Sam nor Gertrude believed that too many people would be excited to hear that he had saved the man most people currently despised, but denying Lady Galiova was much like denying his mother.

The service passed in a flash, and her fellow parishioners flocked to Gertrude for another two hours. While Gertrude listened to the concerns of the people in the central region, Galina bragged on and on about how her daughter was the loudest voice of the people.

"Not to worry," she assured the group of men and women, "my daughter is nothing like my ex-husband. She is doing everything in her power to protect the people's rights. I assure you that she will help to make everything fine again."

When Gertrude would hear this and similar comments from her mother, all she could do was pray that she would be able to prove her mother right.

~*~*~

"I'm so sad to see you leave, Sam," Galina said as she stood out on the front porch with her daughter. "I know you think me paranoid, but I do fear for you leaving so late in the day, Sam—take Chester, here, with you." She handed him the long leash of a red hound. "I don't know if he'll do much good as far as protecting you goes, but maybe he'll hear or smell something you wouldn't." Sam obediently tied the leash to his saddle's canter. He would be glad for the company. After patting the dog's brow, he turned back to hear from Lady Galiova,

"You will bring your boy back, yes?"

"Of course," Sam agreed with a smile as he put his hat on his head. He walked to the bottom of the steps on which Gertrude stood. His eyes said, "I love you," but his voice said, "Goodbye."

Gertrude said, "No, for goodbyes imply that we may never be together again, so to you, sir, I will say as they do in the common tongue, 'ta-ra' for it is by far more appropriate for the situation."

"Ta-ra it is then, I—" He caught himself from ending the statement with "love." For a moment, he considered kissing Gertrude on the cheek, but with her mother right there, he decided that it probably was not the best of ideas. With a somber demeanor, he mounted his horse. The horse, the hound, and the man with the heavy heart turned down the road, away from the love of his life to return to his wife.

After Sam left, Gertrude and her mother changed from their Sunday dresses into clothes appropriate for gardening. They spent the rest of the afternoon outside in the sunlight of summer's end.

The pair paid particular attention to the herbs that grew wildly around and within the garden. What most would excuse or condemn as weeds, Galina saw as precious gifts to be nurtured. Galina was what the locals called an herbal healer, and she was well skilled at all medical aspects. There was not one household within six hours of hard riding that had not at least once come to her for help.

As the sun began its slow descent over the horizon, they headed to the upstairs tearoom, where they lounged with books and minted vodkas in hand.

However, an eruptive thud resounded from the entrance of their home, ripping the women from their peaceful evening.

20

Unexpected Company

A trumpet of fear sounded in Gertrude's heart.

Galina shot up to her feet and dove into action. For her, this was business as usual.

"HELP!" an all too familiar voice sounded.

To the tune of that cry, following the steps of her mother, Gertrude bolted out of the room and down the stairs to the entrance parlor, where they found servants fussing over two men. The ladies of the house pushed through the gathering to see what captured such attention.

To their shock and horror, Sam and Breyton were the pair on the mosaic floor.

Blood splattered across the tiled angel's face was the first thing that Gertrude saw and the sight of it made her weak. A muffled silence entrapped her as she saw Sam kneeling over the wounded and pale-gray prince he had carried into the house. Gertrude barely heard her mother holler orders to prepare a room for Breyton. The haggard prince already seemed so lost. His brow was filthy and bruised, his skin colorless. His clothes were streaked with grime, sweat, and large sanguine stains.

"What happened?" Gertrude asked Sam as three male servants helped to carry Breyton. The crowd followed Galina to the nearest room on the first landing. The medical ward was too far a distance to carry this wounded man.

Sam struggled up from the ground, keeping his eyes on the barely conscious prince. He nudged Gertrude to follow with his elbow, for his hands were painted red. "I was halfway into my trip when I found him," Sam said as he and Gertrude trailed after the parade of people down the hall. "Chester started to whimper and bark as though there was something off the edge of the path. I figured that it wasn't a raccoon by the way the dog was acting, so I let him follow the scent. That's when we found Breyton with an arrow in his chest, but I-I don't think it was shot, I think it was stabbed in him."

"Who would do such a thing?" Gertrude whispered to Sam as they entered the room full of chaos and a burble of noise that Lady Galiova was shouting orders over.

"Get out! Half of you, get out!" Galina yelled over the mess.

A crowd of people left the room, leaving behind Galina's apprentice, two men, Sam, and Gertrude to tend to the prince.

"He's burning up," Galina muttered as she unfolded the cloth belt that held the tools of her trade. "We have to cool him. Infection, not the arrow's head, will kill him."

From the opposite side of the bed, Galina issued orders as she received her full kit from her young apprentice, Karine. Galina shouted after Karine to return with a clean linen bundle from the medical ward. "Sam, wash up quickly, then go to my apothecary and grab me two bottles labeled anticeptic acid—they are on the top shelf, clear, large bottles. Go." Sam nodded curtly, then ran out of the room. "Lev, Simon," she continued, addressing the other two men, "go to the buttery and grab two satchels of ice each. Bring those back as if the devil were on your heels!" The two men darted out of the room to fulfill their orders. Now that Galina and Gertrude were the only two left in the room, the latter looked down and saw that she was holding Breyton's hand.

"Gertrude," her mother called. "I need you to help me remove his clothes."

"What?" Gertrude quickly asked.

"His clothes, girl!" Galina shouted. "Help me get 'em off! He can't be stuck in these! They're filthy and we have to cool his skin." In one quick motion, Galina used a knife to slit Breyton's shirt, peeling the sticky fabric from his skin, careful not to disturb the area immediately surrounding the arrow.

"Gertrude!" Galina snapped. "Take off his shoes!"

Removed from her state of shock, Gertrude popped into action. She scurried down to the foot of the bed and started to unlace Breyton's mud-covered boots.

Galina reached back into her kit and procured a bottle of a clear liquid that she poured over the remaining fabric, including the improvised dressing Sam had made, encircling his wound.

Breyton made a dreadful cry as Galina delicately pulled the now wet fabric from around the arrow.

Gertrude looked up and felt sick the moment she saw the worst of his wounds. From below his ribs, the broken staff of an arrow stood. The young lady looked away and swallowed hard, finishing her task of removing Breyton's shoes. "Why is it broken?" she asked her mother as the sound of running footfalls drew closer.

Karine returned to the room with a bundle of white linens in her arms. She had assisted Galina in enough procedures at this point to know what to do without direction. She unwrapped the outer sheet, set it above Breyton's head on the bed, then laid out a thick row of white towels on the bed stand closest to Galina.

Distantly, Galina answered her daughter as Lev and Simon came into the room, "Sam probably broke it so he wouldn't knock it about when he brought Breyton here, but I imagine being carried on a horse as opposed to being laid out flat did him no good. Simon, Lev," Galina said more loudly to the men who brought in the heavy, cold, and cumbersome satchels of ice. "Put those down a moment. Let's lift him onto this sheet." The two men raced around to either side of the bed, rushing past Gertrude in a silent but well-coordinated dance. Without hesitation, the men, with the assistance of Galina, lifted Breyton enough so that Karine could swiftly slide the sheet completely under him. From the foot of the bed, Gertrude thought the poor man was beginning to look like a martyr with the halo of white now surrounding him.

"Start packing the ice around whatever skin you see," Galina ordered the men. The apprentice ran to the opposite side of the room to crack open windows to allow air circulation inside. She then swept up Breyton's clothes that had been removed and whisked them out from the area to lay them by the door.

While the men began to shovel ice around Breyton's head, neck, and bare shoulders, Galina dug through her bag and pulled out a ribbed, green glass bottle. Carefully, she removed a dropper's worth of the liquid. She pinched open Breyton's jaw and emptied the opiate sedative into his mouth, pinching his nose to help it down. The prince made a brief face of disgust followed by a resurgence of his grimaces.

Galina went to unfasten Breyton's belt. Sam came rushing back into the room with the two bottles of disinfectants. "There you are, Sam," Galina muttered as she undid the clasp on Breyton's pants. "Put those bottles there on the nightstand. Gertrude, pull down his trousers."

Gertrude sent a look of shock and disbelief to her mother.

"NOW!" Galina hollered.

Gertrude did as she was told.

"His leg is bleeding, too," Gertrude said in a panic when she saw the large scrape and bruised shin of the prince.

"Is it bleeding or is it just bloody?" Galina asked as she methodically poured the disinfectants onto the rags and surgical tools. She laid out each cleaned tool in a straight line on one of the towels as Gertrude took a closer look at Breyton's leg.

"It's just bloody," Gertrude said with relief.

"Can't worry about it now," Galina snapped, continuing to lay out the tools in straight lines. "Both of you, help line him with ice. I have to sterilize the wound."

Sam and Gertrude joined the assembly of people packing Breyton with ice. Gertrude had seen her mother utilize this technique once before on her older brother when what was believed to have been a harmless scrape turned out to be a struggle for the boy's life. By surrounding and covering him in ice, Galina managed to calm her son's fever so that she could attack the infection with her medicines effectively. This was precisely what she intended to replicate with Breyton.

The sedative Galina dumped into the prince's mouth was already beginning to calm him, settling down his squirming about. His fidgeting and his breaths, though still laborious, were no longer as violent.

The group finished their task and Galina was ready to proceed.

"Gertrude, I want you to talk to him, let him know that you are here. Keep him distracted, because this is really going to hurt." Galina brought one of the bottles of disinfectant over Breyton.

The apprentice rushed over to help. She surrounded Breyton's wound area with a circle of towels that she held in place. Galina uncorked the bottle, the misleadingly sweet smell immediately striking all of their noses.

"Sam, Simon, Lev, hold him." The men took their positions, Sam at Breyton's feet, holding down his legs, while Simon and Lev held his arms.

Gertrude wedged herself as close as she could to the headboard and leaned her upper body down on the bed to speak to Breyton. She spoke sweetly, gently, with a dire tenderness. "Breyton? Breyton, dear, this is Gertrude. You are here in my mother's home in Forsythia Valley. My mother is a healer, Breyton, and she is going to take very good care of you."

Galina parted the severed skin around the arrow with her fingers and poured the disinfectant straight into the wound.

Breyton's face erupted in agony as the anticeptic acid stung, punched, and ripped through his nerves. His body lurched and retched. The men held him tight so that the women would not be accidentally struck.

The apprentice removed the ring of towels and handed Galina a fresh one. Galina tenderly cleaned the blood, dirt, and liquid from the surrounding area of the wound. "Keep talking to him," she encouraged under her breath as she analyzed the severity of the gash, judging how deep she would have to reach to remove the arrowhead safely.

After a deep inhale, Gertrude slowly released her breath and continued to talk to Breyton. "Breyton, don't you worry now, you're really in the best hands this country can provide. My mother is the best around. She won't let anything bad happen. You see, good ol' Sam found you and brought you to us. That in itself is a miracle. God is clearly on your side." Gertrude paused to watch the apprentice hold up a light for Galina to see properly. The look on the healer's face was less than comforting.

Galina licked her lips and looked pleadingly to her daughter. "You're not going to like this," she warned, a disclosure that certainly did not put Gertrude's heart at ease. "The arrowhead is in there in such a way that it's not terribly deep, but that's not the issue. The problem is there's a bit of muscle tissue that has folded over the blunt extension of the arrowhead and it's going to take more than one pair of hands to convince it out." Galina paused to allow her daughter the chance to figure out what she was asking, but the petrified look on Gertrude's face forced her to elaborate. "Gertrude, I know you're squeamish, but you have to do what I ask of you or Breyton will die. I can't ask Karine to do this, as she's the only one here who's familiar with the tools I'll need her to hand to me immediately. In fact, Karine, prepare a needle and thread for me now and have the *achillea millefolium* ready." Karine immediately set off to work. "Gertrude, I'm going to hold open the gap in his skin wide enough so that you can see what you are doing, and then I need you to reach in, gently scoot the muscle off the arrowhead, and then carefully pull out the arrow while still holding back the muscle."

Gertrude looked just a shade brighter than Breyton. "You want me to stick my fingers...*in* him," Gertrude restated.

Galina nodded slowly. "As soon as that arrow's out, he will begin bleeding, and I will need to immediately address the bleeding and the wound. You will have to get out of the way as quickly as possible."

Gertrude desperately looked around to the others to see if she could possibly switch places with anyone, but she wouldn't know what tools to grab for her mother next, she had no idea what an *achillea millefolium* was, and she would not be able to hold down the strong prince. There really was not much choice in the matter.

"Right then," Gertrude quietly said. She positioned herself on the other side of the bed, leaning over the arrow.

"Karine," Galina whispered, "watch, dear, how this is done and hold the light steady and close. "Gertrude, if you should feel the need to vomit, it is okay, but it's not okay if you do it on Breyton, so if you have to, please, turn away." Galina leaned forward, over Breyton's body, ready to do her part. "One last thing," she added. "Gertrude, don't take the time to think about what I'm telling you. Just do it."

Galina rested the fingers of both her hands on either side of the wound and delicately pulled it open ever so slightly.

From the direction of her mother's words, Gertrude took a deep breath and with two fingers, she entered the wound.

21

Stitches

I t felt like warm, raw meat.

Her body quivered. Her heart beat madly.

She slid her fingers down by the side of the arrow's stock. She stopped as her mother told her when she felt the slightest bit of resistance.

"Do you feel it?" Galina anxiously asked when she saw her daughter's hand stop. Gertrude nodded. After pausing for a deep breath, Galina told her what next to do: "Now, as carefully as you can and with only one finger, push the tissue to your right."

The tissue she moved was thin, light, like a slim slice of salmon. Gertrude felt sick, but she knew that she was already halfway done. She knew she had to get through this for Breyton's sake. The tip of her trailing finger could feel the sharp steel bottom of the arrowhead. When she slid the muscle over as far as the wound would let her, she told her mother that this step was done.

Galina responded, "Excellent—you're doing great, love, you're almost done. Here's the last bit: keep pushing back the muscle with your finger, and with your other hand, you must pull the arrow out delicately. Wait to remove your finger until the arrow has cleared the wound. Do you understand?"

Gertrude nodded and leaned down to look directly into the gash in Breyton's abdomen. What should have been pink and healthy flesh was raw and dark from the arrow's ungodly abuse. With the help of the light, Gertrude could barely see the gray of the arrow. Swallowing back the building acid in her stomach, Gertrude took hold of the arrow's smooth stem, though there was not much to hold. Those around the bed watched as she convinced the arrow from his flesh. When the head met her finger's tip, Gertrude did as she was told and let the muscle go. In one smooth sweep, her fingers and the invasive arrow were free.

A great breath of relief escaped from all in the room.

Galina smiled and said, "Well done!" to her girl before taking a closer look into the afflicted area for further examination. The wound was beginning to bleed as expected.

Gertrude did not hear what her mother said to Karine, nor did she see her mother make the next steps to stop the bleeding. She was far too focused on the blood on her fingers and the arrow in her hand. Gertrude slowly backed away from the bed. Steps before her back hit the wall, Gertrude could hold it back no longer. She fell to her knees and vomited on the floor.

Galina rolled her eyes, but she was grateful that her daughter retched away from, instead of on, Breyton.

"That's remarkable self-control your daughter has," Sam said to lighten the moment.

"I knew that if I gave her a job that intently kept her focus, we'd have at least a gap of time before she retched," Galina responded, removing her fingers from Breyton's abdomen, now covered in the powdered herb that would help to stop the bleeding. Standing straight and rubbing her forehead with the inside of her wrist, Lady Galiova scoffed and said, "Well, all, we have here the luckiest man on earth.

He is bleeding, but a pinch deeper and that arrow would have pierced his organs, and no medicine of mine could have saved him."

"He's going to be okay?" Gertrude croaked, shamefully wiping her mouth with her forearm, still clutching the arrow.

"Karine, hand me the cotton and some more of the powdered yarrow," Galina requested. While Karine held the lantern and fetched the cotton from the linens on the nightstand, Galina once again used the disinfectant around the area of Breyton's wound, before quickly patting the area dry with a fresh towel. With one hand, Karine sprinkled a second healthy amount of the requested yarrow powder, the *achillea millefolium*, onto the cotton before handing it over to Galina. Galina packed the wound with the treated cloth and answered Gertrude, "Yes, but only if I can get him to stop bleeding and clear the infection, which may take a while. Karine, at first sunlight, it's a bit early in the season, but I want you to go to the forest and harvest some of the more robust goldenseal. If we're to ensure he has no internal bleeding, he's going to need an awful lot of tea. How are our stores on comfrey?"

Karine thought a moment, recalling the hundreds of herbs, she helped Galina to gather, store, and prepare. "If that's the knit-bone, then we should be fine. Comfrey is also known as knit bone, yes?" she asked hesitantly to confirm.

Nodding, Galina answered, "Exactly, dear. Comfrey stimulates our body to heal faster, and it is one of many herbs we will use to help his body fight the infection." Looking back down to the pile of cotton on her patient's stomach, Galina came to a quick decision. "Sam, in your military days, you had experience doing field dressings, yes? Sewing up wounds?"

Sam nodded, and without a word or any fuss, Galina handed him a needle and suture thread from her kit and then proceeded to address the wound on Breyton's leg. Using a similar application of disinfectant and powdered yarrow, Galina tended to the injury.

In slow, methodical movements, Sam began to dip the needle into Breyton's skin, making his continuous suture pattern with the silk thread.

"There," Galina said approvingly of the work they had performed. "We'll remove the ice in a few minutes." Karine handed Galina a clean towel that she had soaked in the bucket of water so Galina could rinse the blood from her hands. Karine kindly gave Gertrude a moistened cloth so that she could do the same.

"Thank you, all," Galina said graciously. She asked them to stay at the ready and nearby, just in case. She instructed Karine to take the soiled equipment to the medical ward and to return to clean up the rest of the room as soon as she was able. The men, except Sam, were excused. All three left without a word, happy that they could be of help. Turning to the corner of the room where Gertrude remained, looking slightly sick still, Galina spoke to her daughter. "How are you faring? Come back over, love—I need you to hold the light. I'd like us to have one more look over him."

Removing herself from the floor, Gertrude felt humiliated. She had felt useless cowering in the corner with blood-soaked hands while this incredible show of heroic medical work happened before her. She dragged herself to Breyton's bedside. "What about the mess?" she asked her mother as she put the arrow on the nightstand. "Shouldn't I clean it up?"

"No," Galina answered while using a fresh towel to clean some of Breyton's more minor wounds. The sight of which made Gertrude want to retch again. "Karine will return to clean up." Gertrude held the lantern above Breyton and looked down at his face. Galina continued, "I need to collect the tinctures that will fight this infection right away. Stay here with Sam and watch over him." She hesitated a moment to see how her daughter was peering at the injured prince. For the quickest of moments, she looked from Gertrude to Breyton and then to Sam, but she realized that time was of the essence. Shaking her head, Galina scurried out of the room, headed for the apothecary in the medical ward where all her chemicals, medicines, and herbs were stored.

Sam and Gertrude did their parts quietly for the first few moments. As Karine worked to disinfect the entire floor, a regular chore in the medical ward, Gertrude said to Sam in Heltkor, "Thank God you were there, Sam. You saved his life. Not Mother or any of us. Now two-thirds of the Malleus men owe you your life."

Smiling shyly, Sam kept his eyes focused on his task of sewing, though he was nearly done. Quietly, he returned in the same language, "Although I'll give most of the credit to the dog. Maybe the Malleuses will give me another star, but I'd settle if they made me heir to their throne."

Chuckling, Gertrude added, "Would you have a preference, sir?"

Sam sent a warm look to Gertrude, subconsciously relieved that she was interested in him at the moment. He returned the banter. "Well, I already have a star, so I guess the throne would be alright."

Sighing, Gertrude looked up and asked Karine, "How long will his stitches have to stay in?"

"Just a few days," Karine responded. "Your mother will keep an eye on them to ensure no infection starts, but if all goes well, we'll take them out in no time." From the floor where she scrubbed, Karine asked, "If you'd like to help, my lady, feel free to dab the cut on his eyebrow with that cloth and the oil *lavandula officinalis*, lavender; it's the small glass vial on the nightstand."

While Gertrude did as directed, she stared at Breyton. His face was a mess like the rest of his body. It was all rather strange, really, seeing a beaten-up and filthy prince lying surrounded by the gleaming halo of an ice-filled sheet.

"At least he's not conscious enough to know how ridiculous he looks," Sam dryly joked, seeing her stare.

Gertrude smiled blandly. After a moment more, she asked, "So now what do we do?"

Sam shrugged as he continued his chore.

Karine said as she moved quickly across the floor with her brush and bucket, "Let's remove the ice, and then you could continue to clean him up if you're willing. Wash his hands, skin, and face a bit to get off as much of the dirt as possible. Mr. Maison, you could follow suit with that same cloth and address his other minor cuts. My lady, your mother believes that a clean patient and a clean room are as important as the medicine she makes."

It made sense. Sam and Gertrude took the last of the towels from the stand, and as they worked, Sam said, "Then we do all we can do; we wait and pray."

An hour later, when Lady Galiova returned with fresh bandages and the tincture needed, she was delighted to see the mass improvements made to Breyton in her absence and that the ice had been removed from his side. She was not surprised to find Sam and her daughter half asleep by Breyton's bedside. It was late, and it had been a trying evening. Sam's head bobbed up and down, leaning as far back as the chair would permit, and Gertrude rested her head and bent arms directly on the mattress only about a hand's distance away from the prince's side.

Galina dumped the first serving of the thick, brown, bitter medicine down Breyton's throat. He did not receive it well, but it had to be done. Quietly, Galina woke Sam and sent him off to have something to eat and to go to bed. He deserved to rest. While Sam obeyed his employer, Galina and Gertrude stayed by Breyton's bedside all night to monitor him and to give him the tablespoon of medicine that had to be administered once every few hours.

The night passed in a hub of tense silence as the women prayed for Breyton to wake.

22

The Apothecary

Sam left that following afternoon. He had no other choice. As it was, his wife would be furious that he'd missed the day he was supposed to spend at home regardless of circumstance. Galina would not let Sam leave without the escort of her horseman Braum. Sam was reluctant to take another man with him, and he only agreed to because Gertrude begged him not to go alone.

By nightfall, Breyton's fever was all but gone. The ice regimen had continued throughout the day—twenty minutes on, two hours off. Galina believed the sudden decrease in his exterior temperature would help to calm the infection in his blood, paired with the powerful fighting force of her medicines. Though he remained unconscious, he was resting comfortably beneath a coverlet, no longer with the aid of Galina's sedatives.

Galina was heavily occupied with a new patient who'd arrived that day with a broken wrist. Gertrude took over administering to Breyton a tincture her mother drafted. Though the drug only needed to be administered every few hours, Gertrude remained by his side. She tried to write letters to various town leaders throughout Vitenka, but her gaze never strayed far from his face.

When the sun made its descent, Gertrude ate a small meal of sausage and black bread, feeling guilty about eating when Breyton could not. She was so worried about Breyton she hardly cared about her health. The prayers that she sent to heaven were riddled with his name and the hope that he would wake at any moment.

A noise somewhere between a grunt and a moan escaped from Lord Malleus, sending Gertrude's tired eyes to perk up from the note she was drafting.

Though affected by the passing fever, the trauma, and the heaviness of the drugs he was on, Breyton's eyes cracked open. His vision was dazed and unfocused as he peered around the room.

Gertrude removed herself from the chair and knelt by his bedside. Noticing the movement in his peripherals, Breyton slowly turned his head to see what caused the shadow. At first, he saw nothing but darkness, but after a few seconds, the first thing he saw was the eyes of what he had deemed not so long ago to be a swan.

Her hand softly held his, and her voice gently said, "Hello, Breyton." She leaned far forward, as close to Breyton as she could, knowing that she was on the side where his hearing was compromised.

Breyton released a sigh of relief. He was so happy to hear the sound of her voice after all he had been through. It felt like a dream. "I remember you," he whispered, unable to make much noise. The prince made a face of discomfort, and his hand reached for his throat. His mouth was so dry.

On the bedside's nightstand, there was a bottle of mulled wine Galina had left for Breyton, knowing he would be parched. Gertrude poured him a half cup of the liquid. "Here, dear," she said, sitting on the side of the bed. "Do you think you can sit up? I don't want to pour this all down on you."

The twinging pain in his stomach told him that he probably could not sit properly. So he instead pulled his head up as high as he could from the pillow. Gertrude used her other hand to cradle the back of his head as she helped him drink his fill. The thick wine filled him with replenishing warmth, but the taste was less than satisfying. He made a face, to which Gertrude replied, "Mata warned that this might not taste that splendid; she said you're probably tasting the myrrh. It's a bit gritty, but she said it has powerful healing properties and that it will help you to press through this." Gertrude didn't think that using her mother's phrase, 'It'll give him the clairvoyance to understand life's bitterness,' as the most appropriate sentence at the moment. She was not even sure if Breyton was comprehending what she was currently saying.

When Breyton was through drinking, she wiped the corners of his mouth with a cloth.

When the prince flattened himself again, a loud, long breath of relief came from his chest though his entire body ached. Every joint, muscle, and inch of his skin burned. Looking at Gertrude, Breyton asked, "What the hell happened to me?"

"What do you remember?" she asked. "Did Yuri ever catch up to you in the capital?"

Breyton licked his lips and answered as best he could. "No, I didn't see Yuri before I left. Wish I had—might have avoided this mess. Last I can recall, I was riding over by Bridgewater. I was about a day and a half away from home when three or four men charged me; they were all masked. Huh, I seem to remember being hit in the head. The rest are just flashes of intense pain." He sat still a moment, then thought about his horse. "Those bastards took one of my best steeds. They better treat him well."

Knowing Breyton's love for riding, she let him have a moment to pray for the safety of his horse before asking, "It wasn't a random robbery, then, was it?" She took hold of Breyton's hand once more.

The prince looked at the gentle grip Gertrude held upon his hand,

and his pain numbed. Nodding, Breyton responded, "Well, it could have been. I've always been a friend of the public, regardless of what Donovan said. I don't understand why I would be a target if this was politically based."

"You're a Malleus," Gertrude said with a shrug. "That seems to be cause enough these days. I've been receiving letters that people are noticing that you're missing, but I've been responding to them that you're fine and just took a detour to our home. The fact that you're a guest of my mother's, and not merely as one of her patients, should help to tone down ill-sentiment against you, but who knows. Perhaps if I had been on the road alone, I might have been struck down too because of the associations of my last name."

"God forbid," Breyton quickly said. He licked his lips and took a couple of deep breaths. "I never should have left alone. I am so sorry I left without saying goodbye to you. I might never have…" Breyton paused. "As you said if it hadn't been for Sam finding me…"

"Shh…" Gertrude comforted Breyton, leaning down close and giving his hand a reassuring stroke. "Let's not think about that now. You survived, Breyton—that's all that matters. You'll be up and out of bed in no time, too, I bet. A strong man like you? You'll be out with the rest of them racing horses again soon."

Her smile was so beautiful, so intoxicating, it fogged Breyton's thoughts and chased the grievances of his body away.

Gertrude saw how the prince looked at her. She was instantly reminded of the way Sam would look at her after their most intimate moments. She was not disturbed or discomforted by this. On the contrary, her cheeks grew warm, and she felt the butterflies in her stomach come to life. She softly rubbed Breyton's shoulder and asked, "Are you hungry?"

Breyton nodded with a smile. He was impressed by how attentive she was to him.

"Well, in that case, I'll go get you something warm to fill your stomach." Gertrude started to slide herself off the bed, but Breyton tightened his grasp on her hand.

"Just a minute, Gertrude," Breyton said a tad more enthusiastically than his sore body would have preferred. "Just one last thing."

The lady sat back on the bed, and having seen the pain in Breyton's composure when he spoke, she leaned down close to him so that he would not have to exert more energy than necessary.

Much to Gertrude's shock, the prince gently pulled her face closer and pressed his lips to hers. It was brief and followed by a whispered, "Thank you for staying with me, Gertrude."

~* ~*~

"I have a problem," Gertrude said the moment she plopped herself into the open chair in her mother's apothecary.

The workroom below the house was perpetually cool. This was where Galina dried and stored her herbs and crafted her medicines. The walls were lined with colorful glass bottles of all shapes and sizes. The most dangerous of concoctions were contained in a locked glass cabinet behind Galina's desk. Gertrude always thought her mother looked like a queen of botany, as she sat before that wall, surrounded by the bright array of ribbed glass bottles. This room had been Galina's escape from Absalom. Galina spent hours in this room away from the abuse of her husband, to make her bit of good for the world.

Reconsidering her initial statement, Gertrude quickly corrected, "Well, I have multiple issues, but right now, I have a serious problem."

Galina removed her half-rimmed glasses and placed a marker in the stained, crinkled, and well-used reference journal to later recall her place. She sat behind her desk with a calm but entertained expression. When earlier Lady Galiova had gone to check in on Breyton, she found Gertrude helping him consume a cup of broth. There seemed to be something between the pair, something awkward but enjoyed.

Before Galina could say anything, Gertrude added, "He kissed me, tonight, I mean."

Galina tensed. The idea of a Malleus kissing her daughter made her exceedingly uncomfortable. "I realize that you've only known Breyton a short time, but what is your instinct telling you about this? Also, please keep in mind that tonight may have been a result of his fever."

Shaking her head, Gertrude disagreed. "I'm not so sure. We did have a bit of a spark when we were in Maltoro."

"There's also the opiate-based pain medicines I've been administering to him since his arrival." Galina was hoping to find a way of dismissing the kiss, but the expression of her daughter told her this task wouldn't be so easy. "Do you intend to pursue Breyton? Have you already discovered that you have much in common? I'm not certain how I feel about you two as a pair. How different would it be marrying him over Herod? Are you sure it wasn't the drugs?"

"No, it *wasn't* the drugs." Gertrude stared down at her class ring, slowly realizing the many things she did have in common with Breyton. "I sort of got him to confess that he had a fancy for me a week ago. The thing is, I don't want to break things off with Sam, but he is married, and I think that it's time that I start respecting his ring…that I get my head out of the clouds. He is my everything, my whole world. I would die for him…but I've been feeling so guilty for *so* long. I think that the best thing I can do for all of our sakes is to pursue something deeper than friendship with Breyton."

Galina never felt more terrible for her girl than she did now. With everything that had happened to her daughter, it seemed cruel of fate to keep from her the man who loved her. "I know that it is hard to part from the ones we love when we feel that our destiny is with them, but circumstance tells us otherwise," Galina sorrowfully acknowledged, staring blankly into the distance. Her skeletons seemed to dance before her eyes, brought back to life by her daughter's situation. Shrugging off the past and reminding the skeletons to go back to the closet where they belonged, Galina looked at her daughter. "I think that for the time being, it is a good idea to pursue stronger ties with Breyton," the mother advised, patting the desk lightly with her palm. "I am concerned about what might happen to him due to the ties of his name but other than that, Breyton seems to be a good man. He was wild in his youth, an unnecessary risk-taker, but I understand that his late wife tamed his spirit greatly. He could make a wonderful husband for you. He is and always has been charming, intelligent, and he's the most handsome of the Malleus men if I do say so myself, but be careful, Gertrude. Think. Remember, Breyton is still a Malleus, and right now, their name is held to the same regard as shit."

23

Healing

O ver the next three days, Breyton recovered little by little. Gertrude spent much of that time at his side.

On the third day, Gertrude convinced Breyton to get out of bed. It had been four days since he arrived at the manor, and he could walk now with assistance from a cane. The lady wanted to show the guest her home. Out on the patio, the air was still warm, but the looming cool breath of fall played in the breeze. It would not be long before the wonderful weather of summer drew to an end.

The pair sat on the deck chairs and gazed at the beauty of her mother's gardens. For a while, Breyton and Gertrude were quiet, enjoying the chattering birds and the occasional distant horse's whinny, but the lady with the small golden dog on her lap held a question in her heart that would not grant her peace.

Breyton slowly sipped a thick medicinal tea that Galina's apprentice, Karine, had prepared for him. "This tastes fantastic," he said aloud. Gertrude's raised brow encouraged him to say, "I have found that if I speak while I drink it, it helps to keep me from gagging."

Gertrude chuckled. "Judging by the smell of it, I'd wager anything you could do to keep you from gagging would be acceptable." She looked at him. *He is the most handsome of the Malleus men,* she thought, *and certainly the kindest.* Though rocks were forming in her stomach, she decided it to be the moment to begin this awkward conversation. "Breyton," she softly said, hoping to roll into the conversation gently. "How do you feel after your latest ice bath?"

Breyton shivered from the memory. "I must say, grateful that I am for her art; your mother's treatments ought to be added to the banned list of torture. I've had more tea and bitter green leaves than I've consumed in my life. I've been thrashed mercilessly with stinging nettles, and I've been subjected to those awful baths more times than I'd ever like to recall." He shook his head at the thought of his sixth conscious treatment of being wrapped in soaked, wet sheets and having ice-cold water dumped down the back of his neck. It was radical, horrible, but he was feeling better with every treatment, even from those nasty stinging nettles. "But, if it works...it's worth it, no?" he said.

"It does," Gertrude assured him. "I was subject to those baths when I was struck with influenza that nearly killed me when I was a student in Viramont. The doctors and medical professionals over there thought her treatments to be heretical, but to the best of my knowledge, they're still using them to this day." Gertrude sighed. She wondered as she had numerous times before, if she had not gone to Viramont, she would have become her mother's apprentice instead of or alongside the young Karine. She thought that maybe it would not be such a wrong way of life, as she'd be helping her mother to save lives. "My mother has done so much good for this world, she and her bag of tricks."

Feeling herself falling from the intensity of the stare, Gertrude quickly decided to drive her earlier thought forward. "May I ask you a personal question?"

Over the past few days, it had not been like Gertrude to ask permission to pose a question, most of which were rather blunt, so Breyton took her statement as an explicit disclaimer. He nodded with a smile, and she asked timidly, "Why did you leave, Breyton? Truly. Why did you leave Maltoro so quickly after the Council Gathering?" Breyton leaned back in his chair slowly. This was not the question he had been expecting, nor was it one he wanted to answer. He shut his eyes. *If there is anyone to explain this to,* he thought, *it's Gertrude.*

Opening his eyes, Breton looked down and said, "The easiest answer is that it's that male arrogance you mentioned when we first met." He smiled fondly at her and then continued, "I've actually been wondering that a lot myself. It used to be that I considered myself rather brave and very wise, not so humbly so, but there you have it. I thought I made the right choices for myself; I saw what power did to people, saw how it corrupted their souls. I did not want that for myself, so, as you know, I declined the throne. What does that have to do with my leaving?" Breyton gave a deep sigh and looked at Gertrude. "Well…for the first time in my adult life, I wanted it."

Gertrude's brow raised. *What would happen if Breyton became king?* Her stomach clenched. *No, Herod will not step down. Wishing for Breyton to be king, removing Herod from the throne…how different would that make me from Absalom?* Gertrude looked down but motioned for Breyton to continue.

"I wanted to be king. There were so many things in that meeting alone that I would have done differently, but had no power to. I wanted to indict Absalom, start an investigation committee to see how deeply he thought his influence in that room ran, to weed out those spurring the rebellion within that room, but I am not king. And I let Donovan get to me. Struck me like I was a child, and like a child, I ran, shirking from the responsibility like I was a dumb boy all over again." He looked out to the gardens, hoping to find any other truth. "Turns out, I'm not wise or brave at all…just a damn selfish fool who doesn't have a bone of bravery in his body."

"That's not true." Gertrude rested her hand on his forearm. She squeezed his arm and shared, "I find myself in...not the same position, but a similar bind to the one you encountered, facing tremendous responsibility, and I'd..." She hesitated, but she felt like there was no going back at this point. "I'd appreciate some insight from you to help me figure it all out."

Breyton drew his eyes to hers. Her touch on his arm drew him out from his thoughts and to a place of comfort. "Anything, Gertrude."

His words were so genuine, the care in his eyes radiant. She did not want to tell Breyton about Herod's proposal yet.

I don't want to sound like I'm using him. Oh, God, I am using him. But, there really is something between us that I would like to explore. Maybe we can talk it out a bit more first? She wondered. *I know that my time with Sam is essentially at its end, but perhaps he can help me to either accept Herod as my fate or save me from it.*

Slipping her hand from Breyton's arm, she explained, "Breyton, you may be the best authority to ask this: how...how influential, rather, how much power or control did your mother have over your father?"

His brow creased. This was a second question he did not expect.

"My mother?" Breyton shook his head. "My mother had *no* power over my father. She was a good mother and a good wife, regardless of the horrible man that she was married to, but she had no influence over anything that he did. Now, my stepmother, Herod's mother, *she* was the exact opposite of my mother in *every* regard. My father married that woman only a few months after my mother passed. She wasn't yet cold in the ground. There was wide speculation that she was pregnant with Herod at my mother's funeral." Breyton reached over and gave Gertrude's hand a gentle squeeze as he shook his head in disgust for his father's only too truthful reputation with women. "That father of mine was sleeping with that woman while my mother was dying. Young as we were, Donovan and I both knew that she was having an affair with our father while our mother's health was rapidly declining, but what could we have done about it? We were just children at that time.

"At any rate, Herod's mother had a profound influence over my father. I suspect that she was the one who helped influence Absalom's rise to power. I also hold her responsible for many of the tensions among the classes. She believed that if you were born into a class, that's where you stayed." Breyton shut his eyes as a thousand memories of this woman arose. "She *hated* my late wife; Inya had been born into one of the vile classes, as my stepmother would have said. She came to my wife's funeral, and I wish she hadn't. It would have spared the memory of my wife, the humiliation. Herod's mother openly stated that it was my wife's 'filthy peasant blood,' which condemned her in the first place, *not* her fever. Her death was just God's way of sorting things right again or something like that. I was furious. If Yuri had not been there to be a sense of reason to me at that time, I can't begin to imagine what I might have done to her. The humiliation to my mother aside, she greatly bled our country with any frivolous fancy that delighted her. The one thing that Donovan and I agreed upon in our lives was that she was nothing more than a snake in queen's gowns."

His answer, though genuine, did not help her conundrum.

Breyton studied her silence for a moment. He had an inkling as to where this question was headed, but before he could inquire, a small voice from behind them called out, "Auntie!"

24

A Look Back

To Breyton, the little boy with the dimples in his cheeks sprinting toward Gertrude was just some local kid, but to Gertrude this was the boy whom she wished to call her son. "Sawsha!" She stood and quickly fell to her knees, wrapping her arms around Sam's little boy. "I've missed you! Let me look at you!" Gertrude pushed the lad to arm's length and took a good look at the boy who was the spitting image of his father. "Your hair is getting so long." Gertrude fussed as she ruffled little Alekzandre's thick black hair. "Are you hungry? You look so thin! Let's get you a snack. Where's your father?"

The sweet-motherly babbling led Breyton to guess that this was Samuel Maison's child. Breyton was amazed to see the way Gertrude plucked the boy from the ground with a gentleness that would suggest she actually was his mother.

Holding the tall, skinny lad up proudly, Gertrude started to introduce him to her friend, but the boy had something much more important to say. "Auntie, look!" He pointed at the large gap between his teeth. "I pulled on my tooth and it came out!"

Gertrude playfully said back, "Oh! You're going to be all grown up before we know it." She plucked some fluff from Sawsha's shoulder.

He poked his finger at the smooth face of the jade jeweled necklace she wore, but did not respond to her comment as he now noticed the stranger standing next to his auntie.

Gertrude looked at Breyton and smiled warmly. She locked her grip around the boy and bounced him up higher on her hip. "Oh, love, no need to be shy. This is Lord Breyton Malleus; he is a very good friend of your father's and mine." Gertrude paused to see if the beady-eyed boy would say anything, but he continued to quietly stare as children tend to do at first meetings. Gertrude rolled her eyes and said to Breyton, "Let me tell you, this boy is anything but shy. He's probably just tired from the ride here. Breyton, this is Alekzandre Maisonov, more commonly known as Sawsha, his father's pride and glory."

"It's a pleasure to meet you, sir," Breyton said with a friendly bow even though his stitches burned something fierce.

The boy liked that. No one had ever bowed to him before.

Standing up properly again, rather stiffly, for his stitches were still twinging, Breyton asked Sawsha, "Did you know, lad, that your father saved my life?"

Sawsha looked to Gertrude with his brows raised, struck with curiosity. "It's true," Gertrude verified.

The boy looked back to Breyton with an excited look of inquiry and asked, "How?"

As Breyton embellished the already incredible story of how Alekzandre's father saved him, down the hall came Mr. Maison himself on the arm of the lady of the house. They were chatting about the steady progression of health Breyton was making. Sam had been very interested when the conversation started, but now that his lady holding his son was in sight, he could not help but feel a great blend of love for Gertrude and great jealousy toward Breyton.

"Papa!" Sawsha shouted excitedly down the hall. "You saved a prince?!"

"And a king," Breyton and Gertrude added together. They looked at each other and smiled like teenagers who could sense an infatuation growing between them.

Seeing the look, Sam stiffened and tried to focus on his boy alone.

Sawsha smiled so big that his face looked as though it would burst. "And a king?" he shouted once more as his father and unofficial babushka came up to the group.

Sam smiled shyly, then answered his son, "I did. That's how I got that star I showed you. Come on down from Gertrude's arms, Sawsha—you'll break her back." Sam reached for the boy, seeing that the lady was struggling. "You're not as small as you think you are, little man."

"Actually, Sam, let me have him," Lady Galiova said as she reached for the boy. "You all go along and have some lunch on the porch. Come on, Sawsha, let's get you something to eat." Without waiting for a response, Galina took the boy's hand and led him down the hall from where they came. On their way out, Sawsha waved to his hero father, the saved prince, and his auntie, who was more than worthy of royalty in his young eyes.

Sam began a conversation with Breyton about how he was healing, but Gertrude heard none of it. As they returned to the porch, with Sam on one side of her and Breyton on the other, Gertrude thought to herself, *Thus far, this is probably the most awkward and uncomfortable walk of my life.*

Out on the porch, Breyton cheerfully mocked, "So, Auntie," having no intention of saying anything else.

"Don't poke fun at that," Gertrude mumbled with a repressed smile. "As Sawsha was first learning to talk he couldn't say the 'Ger' part of my name, so he called me 'Udie' for a while, and that eventually just became Auntie."

"He also called you 'Ma-tee' for a while as well," Sam added with a glow of pride as he remembered how angry that term used to make his wife, as it was a bit too close to "Mata" for her taste.

Gertrude confirmed this with a slow nod. Breyton asked what that came from, and she answered while chuckling, "Well, Sawsha started calling me 'Ma,' which angered Mrs. Maison, rightfully so, and he couldn't quite understand the aunt concept, so I just became Ma-tee...which also angered Mrs. Maison because it is like the word *mata* in Heltkor, which is a term of endearment for 'mother'...though it's slang here, but here we've arrived at Auntie, and that seems to be the best middle ground."

A servant quietly came onto the porch carrying two letters for the young lady of the house. After handing over the letters, the servant excused himself as quickly as he came. Gertrude's eyes grew wide. She broke the seal of the first envelope, a seal with the face of a mountain, a sign that she had not seen in at least a year. "It's from Albert!" She tossed the second letter onto the table.

"Who?" Breyton quietly asked Sam as they both watched Gertrude read her letter.

"The oldest of her brothers," Sam informed him, pleased to know that he still held the better hand of Gertrude's personal information over Breyton. "Albert left a few years ago after Lord Kemen nearly killed him."

"What?" Breyton asked, searching for some grasp of the former prime minister's domestic practices.

Gertrude heard the question and looked up from her letter. "Absalom nearly beat him to death when he declared that he was marrying outside of our class. Probably not surprisingly, he and his now wife packed up and moved to Viramont." She smiled reverentially at the note, happy to have received a piece of good news. "And they are now expecting their third child. Mother will be so glad about this." She sighed and put the letter down. As she reached for the second, she added, "I can't imagine what my mother has been through; we still haven't heard from Camden in quite some time."

"Your other brother?" Breyton pieced together. "What happened to him?"

Gertrude looked to Sam for guidance. He gave her an encouraging nod. Turning back to Breyton, she answered, "Do you remember asking me how I convinced Absalom to let me go to school? Well, Camden and I are barely a year apart. My poor mother. I am the elder, even though Absalom seems to think that I came last...Absalom always wanted one of his sons to follow in his footsteps, that is, go to the Northern University and then eventually become prime minister, and whatever else. Albert evaded the plan when he left, but Absalom still had Camden. My younger brother wanted absolutely nothing to do with anything that Absalom touched, especially politics. My brother wanted to draw, write, and to see the world. He wanted to be a poet who lived on the sea. Absalom would not hear of it because he wanted Camden to go to school, and like a fool, when Camden turned seventeen my father sent a year's worth of tuition to the Northern and they gladly accepted.

"The week before Camden was supposed to go, he begged our mother to find a way to save him from that fate. I will never forget the way Mother looked at me. She knew that I would have given anything to have a chance to go to secondary school, let alone the Northern. She told Camden that if he was willing, she would give him enough money to escape and make it to the sea, and all she asked of him in return was to allow me to go to the university in his place; she swore to me that she would find a way to fund my entire tuition. Camden and I were ecstatic. Our mother's love let us pursue the horizons of our dreams." She sighed heavily. Though it had been the best moment in either of their lives, it divided her from her brother, whom she loved dearly. "Last I saw or heard of Camden was the week I left for Viramont. He was going to take to the seas, Southern Half bound." Gertrude sighed again and stroked the edge of her glass. "I only wish I knew what happened to him."

The late lunch intended for the small group on the porch was placed onto the round table. At Gertrude's feet, Buttercup sat up, her little eyes pleadingly watching the warm and incredible-smelling plate of pork sandwiches. The men and Gertrude each took a triangle sandwich. Before taking a bite, Gertrude plucked a small bit of meat for her baby-dog.

Breyton referenced the second letter. "Is that Yuri's seal?"

Gertrude hastily threw her sandwich back on her plate to pick the letter up. "I can't believe I missed that." She tore the red wax seal and unfolded the parchment.

The two men watched her intently, seeing her eyes quickly run across the contents of the note.

She read it through a second time before leaning back.

"Everything alright?" Breyton asked.

Gertrude answered, "Not particularly. The king and Yuri are attempting to implement many of the measures outlined in my plan, specifically to organize the lords of the Council, but," she looked again at the letter to ensure she was interpreting it correctly, "it sounds like many of the Council members have left."

"Left?" Sam and Breyton asked in unison.

She nodded. "I'm willing to bet that they were—are—afraid that they'll be connected with Absalom's stunt. There's apparently a lot of confusion in the city…People are…" Gertrude looked away. "Are blaming the king." She licked her lips and placed the letter back down on the table gently. "There've been a number of demonstrations around the city that have turned violent. Yuri fears that…we may have started too late."

Frustrated by this whole mess, Sam offered, "Let's write to your other contacts in the city; I'll also write to my sister. Let's verify this story. For all we know, Yuri could be saying this to make you feel guilty for not being there."

In the instant that Sam looked away, disgusted by anything to do with Yuri, Breyton leaned forward to ask about the rift between his two friends, but Gertrude caught him. She placed her hand warningly on his knee.

"Not now," she mouthed, knowing precisely where Breyton was headed. Slipping her fingers off Breyton's leg, Gertrude unintentionally lit the sudden want within the man to be alone with her.

Taking a bite from his sandwich, Breyton stayed himself and focused on his chewing.

"That's a good idea, Sam," Gertrude agreed. "I'll start sending out letters in just a bit. Try to get as many done as possible before my meeting this afternoon. I have a priest from the far eastern side of the valley coming in this afternoon to talk about the major issues facing his parish."

"Meetings on your birthday?" Sam asked playfully. He knew he sounded childish, but he hoped that this distraction would make her smile.

Breyton nearly fell out of his chair. "It's your birthday?" he asked. "Why didn't you say anything?"

Sam kept himself from smiling, pleased to see that he had yet another intimate detail about Gertrude that Breyton did not.

The lady nodded and shrugged, still rather preoccupied by the letter. "Compared to everything that's happening, it's truly not that serious," she answered. "Just another year."

"Here they are, Sawsha," Galina said as she approached, exhausted from the heat while holding on to the little boy's hand.

In his other hand, Sawsha carried a slice of bread with cheese. He immediately ran to his Auntie to pet the dog at her feet.

"My, it's a warm day," Galina said while wiping the sweat from her brow. "Best enjoy it while we still may, though."

Gertrude picked up the letter from her brother, refolded it, and offered it to her mother. "Mata, this is more for you than it is for me." As her mother reached across the table, Gertrude added, "I recommend you read it as soon as you're able."

Galina nodded, albeit she was too focused on her present task, and tucked the letter into the pocket of her canvas apron.

Gertrude said, "Mata, won't you sit down and have a drink with us?"

"No, thank you," Galina said, waving off the invitation. "Actually, Lord Malleus and I have a date. Will you join me, Breyton? I know you won't like me after this, but I have to remove your stitches today."

Breyton really did not like the sound of having stitches removed, nor did he wish to leave Gertrude's company, especially with Sam back at her side. However, he knew he had to go for the sake of his health. The cane leaning against the table was firmly grasped in Breyton's hand as he stood. Sam helped him up and led him to Galina. "Wish me luck," Breyton said. After thanking Sam, Breyton left with Galina, with the hope that being with her alone, maybe he could gain some insight into Gertrude.

25

A Glimpse Forward

"Oh, Gertrude." Breyton yawned as he woke from his medicine-induced nap. "I didn't expect to see you." He sat up in bed, but a new strum of pain deterred him from going any further. "Forgive me for not standing," he apologized, looking down at the bandages wrapped around his bare midsection.

"It's quite alright," Gertrude said, she was also looking at his abdomen, but more at the masculinity of his exposed chest rather than the bandages.

Breyton blushed, but he did not mind. He was flattered to have caught a lady in the act of sweeping her eyes over him. "What time is it?" he asked, seeing that the daylight hours were gone.

"It's half-past nine," Gertrude answered as she brought the tray of cheese and buttered toast with a glass of sweet kompot to the prince. "Mother said that you would be waking soon, so she sent me with this." The lady sat on the side of the bed. She offered the tray to Breyton, using her lap as a table. "She said the sweet fruit drink would help you to swallow the same medicine she gave you earlier, just in case you need more tonight."

Being that he was trying to impress her, Breyton refrained from asking for the bitter painkiller or the kompot to wash it down, even though the pain in his stomach was killing him. He thought for a moment as he popped a bite of bread into his mouth. Quietly, he said, "Is there any way you could leave it in case I need it later? I mean, it knocked me out earlier. I didn't feel anything, and it successfully cut me out from the conversation, so if that is the intended effect, then, by all means, let's have it."

Gertrude chuckled and said, "It is not, I assure you." From the core of his beautiful, round blue eyes, Gertrude saw that while he was joking, he was in a considerable amount of discomfort. She placed the small bottle of red-hued medicine on his dresser alongside the syrupy drink, respecting his wish. "Don't take any more than a spoonful, alright? I wouldn't want you accidentally getting yourself into more trouble, my mischief-maker."

With a smile, Breyton said, "What can I say? It's hard to break away from a lifelong ride of rebellion." He chuckled, then shamefully asked with a bite of toast, "Miss your birthday dinner, did I? Oh! Did you get those letters out? How was your meeting with the priest?"

Gertrude tried not to laugh at his rapid series of inquiries. "I was able to send a few notes today to try to get the real story of what's happening in the capital, so we'll see what's going on. If what Yuri says is true, I suspect we'll start hearing things on the good old rumor line tomorrow. The meeting with the priest went about as expected. He's staying the night in one of the extra rooms, and we'll likely continue our conversation in the morning. The issues facing his parish are about the same as everyone else's, but everyone deserves to be heard, no?"

Breyton nodded. "I'm sure the people you're meeting appreciate you taking the time to see them. It's been quite a day for you. I am sorry too, Gertrude, if I missed any celebration for you."

"No, please, don't be, really," she answered quickly. "The only special thing we did was serve my favorite dessert, but that was about the grandeur of the ordeal. I barely felt right, even doing that. My mother and Sam are the only ones who persist in making a big deal out of it."

"Where are Sam and his son, by the way?" Breyton asked. "And, if it's not too much for me to ask, can you tell me what happened between Yuri and Sam?"

She exhaled slowly, hoping to evade addressing the second statement by answering the first alone. "Sam is putting Sawsha to bed now. The lad's had a long day. The ride from Legrette to Forsythia is no small feat for a pony and his master. I'm sure Sawsha is exhausted from playing with a kite, chasing dragonflies, playing fetch with my dogs, and all the other things we did while Mata was treating you." Gertrude paused, hoping that Breyton might have forgotten his other question.

However, Breyton was an attentive man. He had not forgotten his question, but he could also see that this would not be an easy subject for her to broach. "Gertrude, forgive me, I shouldn't have asked that other question; it's really none of my business."

Gertrude shook her head and lightly touched her hand to his arm. "It's not exactly a secret…it's just not a particularly easy topic to talk about, but…" Gertrude paused to look at Breyton. "I trust you and gaining my trust is no easy task, sir, so good for you, I suppose." Swallowing hard, Gertrude started her tale. "I don't know if you know or knew about Sam's younger brother Brody, but, um, he was, oh, how can I say this…he was challenged mentally, and he was affected socially by his handicap. I mean, he could function reasonably well, but he did require supervision all his life.

"When Sam's parents passed away, Sam retired from the military so he and his wife could be the support Brody required. Brody did have a difficult time interacting with people, looking them in the eye and having coherent conversations, but when he was with Sam, he was reasonably functional.

"But, he, um, he did not handle change in his surroundings well, so when Mrs. Maison became visibly pregnant with Sawsha, and the house started to change with the prospect of a baby, he became irritable and agitated. Brody had never been violent, but he would occasionally throw tantrums when he became angry or confused. On one such occasion, he broke a mirror and scared Mrs. Maison and Sam. Though they knew that Brody never meant any harm in anything that he did, the threat of him accidentally doing something unwanted to their baby was quite real. Sam's sister and her husband's children were older, and the parents knew that their girls could handle themselves, so they offered to take on Brody. Sam was hesitant, but as the pregnancy progressed, his wife convinced him that something needed to happen. Mildred held off as long as she could, but there came a point when her motherly instinct did supersede all others.

"I was at the university during most of this, but I was home during the transition, and I remember how sad Brody and Sam were. It was awful. Everything eventually did work out until exactly two years ago. We were celebrating my birthday when a post rider was sent from Sam's sister, Beth. Because we know that's quite the long ride, we immediately knew that something was very wrong. We were more right than we could have imagined—Brody had vanished. Gone. He took nothing with him—no bags, no belongings. Sam was devastated. It was such a shock. Brody had never threatened to run away; he had never even tried it before. He didn't like leaving his room, let alone the house! So, Sam and many others searched every inch of the western country for weeks, more than a full month even, but there was no sign of Brody. It wasn't until late November when the prayers turned from 'I hope we find him' to 'may he rest in peace.'

"In my years of knowing him, I've never known Sam to succumb to such inward agony. He was quiet, dreadfully quiet for weeks, and at that time, I was freshly back from my schooling in Viramont, my career was taking off in the political world, and he and I were spending a lot of time at Maltoro. Due to the weightiness of the months before, we decided to come back to Forsythia for Christmas for a bit of peace. Mildred and her son were to meet us at my mother's home, and it sounded as though we were going to have a reasonably nice holiday.

"Instead, we were met on our journey with a terrible snowstorm, so Sam and I had to stop at a cabin not too far from here for shelter. In the middle of the night—I'll never forget it—the husband and wife, our hosts, were arguing; there was some strange bloke in their barn. The wife wanted her husband to kill him because he was a 'frightening, raving lunatic,' but the man did not think it humane to murder a 'half-wit,' who was just seeking shelter from the storm. After hearing all of this, Sam rushed out to the barn. I was only a few strides behind him.

"Neither of us could believe what we saw. Curled up in a ball, crying and covered in filth, was Sam's brother." Gertrude pressed her fist to her mouth as her jaw quivered, and her eyes watered upon the recollection of seeing poor Brody in such a state. "Brody was a disaster. He wouldn't let anyone near him for a long time until he finally recognized Sam. It was so sad. God, I remember it so clearly. Brody looked up at Sam with a glare that I'm sure has been seared into Sam's heart. There was this twisted duality to his stare; on the one hand, Brody was grateful to see his older brother, but on the other hand, he hated us. Hated everyone. Sam, me, the farmer, his wife—all of us for whatever happened to him because we weren't there to protect him from whatever demons had tortured him." Gertrude snuffled hard and quickly wiped a tear from her eye. "Sam and I quickly took him out of there and brought him here, but we were scared that the farmer and his wife were going to tell someone because Brody kept repeating 'the blood and the crown,' over and over, which was unnerving. I gave the couple what was a handsome bribe to keep them quiet.

"He would not stop repeating 'the blood and the crown.' Men from Absalom's guard arrived to arrest Brody on Christmas Day; they believed that my mother was aiding a suspected traitor to the throne. By the time they pushed past my mother, Sam and Brody were gone. They snuck out the back. Sam did not know what to do. He could not take Brody to his home because that would be the first place the men would check, so he went to his neighbor, Yuri Philemon. Sam asked if he and his brother could be boarders for a few days. Yuri was fine with this, so Sam and Brody went to his friend's home. Brody was scared, but Sam had to leave him to find out more about the situation and to figure out what he could do.

"Sam returned to Forsythia for advice from my mother. He came back to beg her to talk reason to Absalom, to tell him that Brody was incapable of such things. My mother tried, but Brody and Sam's secrecy was betrayed. Brody was apprehended. We would not have known that it was Yuri who betrayed us if my mother hadn't overheard him talking about a 'half-wit' traitor he expelled from his lands to keep his hands clean of this ever-forming conspiracy against the king.

"We raced to the castle to beg for asylum for the man who needed help, not a jail cell, but none of us had any sort of political standing then, not really, so we were muted by the multitude. My father, the judge and prime minister swore before the Council that Brody was a raving, bloodthirsty killer who would stop at nothing until the king was dead. As you can imagine, that testimony was brought upon examination of Brody, who said nothing but 'the blood and the crown.'

"With Herod's uneducated decision and his signature...Brody was hanged. That is why your brother was always wary around Sam. That is why Yuri and Sam despise each other—Sam for the betrayal and Yuri for thinking that Sam was maliciously trying to get him involved. It breaks my heart to think that poor, innocent Brody was being treated like a mongrel of a man just because he was disabled." She snuffled hard, then added, "Brody used to collect toy soldiers. He carried a bag of little tin soldiers with him always. They were his guardians, but they were left behind the day he disappeared..." Her voice faded as her sorrow thickened.

"I just," she looked to the ceiling, "I've been trying for years to be heard, so to correct, or to avenge Brody's memory. I failed him, and now I feel like I'm failing the people as well. I've fought *so hard* for the people for so long now, but...even after catching the king's ear, at last, I still feel like the people who will be the ones to make change still aren't hearing me."

The idea chilled him. *How many innocent people have been slain for Absalom's political gain? How many could have been saved if the monsters in that court had only listened to her?*

Watching Gertrude quickly wipe away her tears, he knew there was little to do to make her feel better, but he still wanted to try. "Gertrude," Breyton sweetly said.

She looked up to him with eyes red and cheeks wet. "Forgive me; I must look a mess."

With smooth, gentle strokes, Breyton wiped away Gertrude's tears and then held her face. "You still look lovely. You always look lovely. You mustn't blame yourself for what happened. There is nothing that you could have done that would have prevented what happened. I truly believe that Herod has seen the stupidity of his action. I think he may have apologized in some form for what happened when he awarded Sam the Silver Star, but Gertrude..." Breyton sat up as straight as he could. He felt Gertrude tremble as he moved closer to her. "Don't ever think that you are voiceless in this country. You have come so far, and you are *so* strong. You alone could lead a revolution, I'd wager. I know I would follow you, whatever your platform, to the end of the world and back again. You've bewitched me, Gertrude, and

I can't imagine life without your spell." Breyton could not stand for it any longer. He gently took hold of her face and pulled her forward to meet her lips.

The kiss startled her at first. Her initial instinct was to push Breyton away, but she knew that this was the man that she needed to pursue. And, she realized as well, his kiss felt *so* right.

She leaned into the kiss, held his face to hers.

They kissed ever more passionately, like lovers destined to be.

But wait. What's this? A man dying at the doorway, dying from heartbreak? Sam's worst fears were being consummated right before his eyes. He could watch no longer. His desire to see how Breyton was feeling was shattered by the sight of that man's hand slipping down his girl's back.

Sam could not stand. He whipped himself out from the room and melted down the wall that held the door's frame. Even though he firmly knew that this would happen, nothing in the world could have prepared him to see it.

His whole world was collapsing. Everything was falling apart, but he knew he could not dare to remain in this spot. He gathered from the reserves in his body the strength he needed to stand. With his heartbroken, he used the walls as his canes to help him walk to where or to what he did not know. He had no plan. He just had to escape.

Gertrude gently pulled away and softly pushed Breyton back. They were in a quiet state of shock and reflection as they realized how dearly they cared for one another and how great a future there could be between them. The lady ran her hand down the side of Breyton's face. "Breyton...does this mean that we are something more than friends?" she asked with hope, though her stomach was twisting in knots.

She indeed was drawn to his spirit, his humor, his body, just like she was with Sam. However, she presently felt ill. *How can I abandon*

Sam like this?

The gentleman smiled. His face was a delightful shade of pink. "It certainly seems that way. I mean, friends don't typically kiss in that manner, but we're not quite lovers…yet, and I certainly hope that road isn't too far—I mean, if it is—if it's not too bold of me." He quickly coughed, hoping to stop his nervous babbling.

"How ungentlemanly of you," Gertrude said with a smile as she slipped herself off the bed. She gave his hand a loving stroke and added, "If you'll excuse me, sir, I need to take this dish back to the kitchen, then I think I'm going to scoot off to bed."

"I hate to see you go, but if you must," Breyton responded, still glowing from the kiss.

"I must. Good night, Breyton." She slipped out the door. As her feet reached the hall, she wondered, *How will I tell Sam?*

26

Desperate Men

With the razor properly sharpened, Sam put it to his flesh. He dragged the blade over the stubble that was growing on his cheeks. He wanted to look sharp for Gertrude. In the oval mirror, he glared at himself shamefully. He prayed that the red in his eyes and his snuffling nose would clear up before his, no, before the lady came in through the door of her room. His hand with the razor had a difficult time maneuvering over the round in his neck as he kept swallowing hard to choke back his sorrow.

He decided that he could not let Gertrude know that he'd witnessed her act with that other man. He knew that he would be considered wretched were he to confront her about the image that was still burning his eyes. It would not be fair of him to say a word when she, for the most part, never asked of his relations with his wife, nor had she ever complained a word to him when she saw Mildred. Now he knew exactly what she felt on those occasions when she saw Mrs. Maison kiss him. He never knew that anything could hurt like this. Even after all the troubles and bruises he'd received and survived, this by far was the most cataclysmic.

The towel he used to wipe his face of the shaving cream was neatly folded and returned to its spot beside the wide-rimmed porcelain water bowl. On top of the towel, Sam gently placed his razor down like a mother rests a babe on a pillow. He put on his Sunday jacket and the fancy green cravat Gertrude gave him on his birthday last December. He combed his fluffy black hair, parting it on the left like he always did. With one last look in the mirror, Sam straightened out his coat and took a deep breath.

She would be here soon.

Of course, it'd be Breyton, he thought bitterly.

The silence of the room was driving Sam mad as he sat still on the edge of Gertrude's bed.

Why isn't she here yet? Where is she? Sam shivered and clutched the edge of the bed as he dared to wonder if perhaps she would not come.

Sam hung down his head.

"Is there no other way?" he asked the empty room. "I'm not ready to let her go."

In through the door pushed Buttercup. She was also expecting Gertrude. The happy little pup wobbled her way over to Sam to nudge his calf with her nose, for this was her way of asking to be picked up. Sam smiled softly and plucked the pup from the ground, placing her next to him on the bed. Buttercup scooted herself onto Sam's lap. She could tell that her lady's man was sad, even though she could not understand why, so she nestled herself comfortably on top of his thighs and convinced the man to forget his problems for a moment to pet her.

"Looks like it's just going to be you and me tonight, kid," Sam said solemnly to the panting dog, who was content so long as she was stroked.

At that moment the door opened wide and in came Gertrude. "Oh, hello, Sam," she greeted. Her voice did not betray that her stomach was in knots.

Sam pushed the pup off from his lap to stand and to greet the lady. "You look beautiful," Sam uttered as he gazed at the grace Gertrude emanated as she entered. It was all he could do not to lose himself to emotion and beg her not to leave him.

She approached him and reached out her hands.

For the briefest of moments, he hesitated. He was momentarily disgusted by the notion that Breyton had not a half-hour ago been kissing her, but then the awful thought ran away. Sam pulled Gertrude to him.

Tucked closely together, they both independently knew that tonight would be their last night with one another.

Gertrude brought Sam's hands up close to her heart, though it was heavy with guilt. "Come with me?"

Having not expected to go out, Sam took a moment to process her request before agreeing, "Oh, um, alright, but where are we going?"

Ignoring Sam's question for the moment, Gertrude called Buttercup. The pup followed obediently as her mistress pushed the man through the secret door, so it would look as though they'd met in the hall and not in her room. It was more of a habit than anything else at this point. "Come lie out beneath the stars with me. Let us stare back at heaven's eyes tonight."

~*~*~

It was chilly out. The warm touch of summer's nights had faded.

At the peak of the first hill toward the lake, Sam, Gertrude, and the pup halted abruptly, stunned by the sight. A thousand fireflies flickered in the night. Their blinks of light shone in the darkness like a far-off festival's lanterns aglow. This moment was sacred, Gertrude and Sam decided, for never had either seen so many before this late in the season.

The last of the fireflies, Gertrude mournfully thought.

Strongest and brightest on their last stand, Sam's thoughts followed.

On the top of this enchanted hill, Sam, Gertrude, and Buttercup settled. For only a few moments, Gertrude remained erect as she watched the incredible insects bobble slowly up and down on an indifferent breeze before she lay flat on the grass. She looked up to the heavens, searching for an answer that she already knew. However, determined she was presently to forget the kiss with Breyton in respect for Sam, she could not help but recall the taste, the touch, the energy. The energy that once she and Sam enjoyed had faded as her guilt for what she was doing to his wife grew over their months apart this past summer.

Her heavy sigh and silence brought Sam to look away from the dance of the flying, lighted ones to see what troubled the lady. He stared at Gertrude's mismatched eyes, a pair that he could always read. He quickly knew what baffled and concerned her thoughts because it troubled him too, but he could not stand for this.

Sam stroked her face.

Beneath heaven's eyes, they refrained from the full physical expression of their emotions, but beneath the stars, they lay silently together, hand in hand.

~*~*~

"What's the update?" Gertrude asked, grabbing the arm of a young man on the staff who had been running by.

"Still no news, ma'am," he answered, looking between her and Sam. He wiped the sweat from his brow, further smearing ash across his face. "Stay in there. We'll let you know when we hear anything." The young man nodded his head to her and resumed his race down the hall.

Gertrude and Sam said nothing to one another as they continued to the porch where they could see what was happening.

"We really should stay in the house, Gertrude," Sam insisted.

"No," Gertrude answered immediately. "I want to see it."

First, the smoke came into view, then the flames. They licked and reached toward the sky as they consumed the shed beside the stables where Galina's gardening tools and the tack for the horses were stored. A long line of men was passing buckets of water to one another to douse the flames.

"This is a nightmare," Gertrude whispered as she watched more hands show up to get the horses out of the stables before that building, too, set ablaze. "We should go help them, Sam." Her eyes were wide, staring into the fires consuming a piece of her mother's home.

"Absolutely not," Sam refused. "Knowing that Absalom and his supporters did this in the last however many minutes, we are not stepping out there, and I am *not* leaving your side. I was initially hired to protect you from *him*."

"I need no reminder, Sam." Gertrude slowly sank into the chair and leaned back. She'd barely caught a few hours of sleep, having been out so late with Sam the night before. It was still so early. The pale gray of dawn had not even begun to replace the shades of night. "Just think," she began, her eyes transfixed on the flames, "while we were out there last night, Absalom was closing in. It's a damn miracle our paths didn't cross."

"It's a damn shame; I would have liked to have killed him myself," Sam said, keeping his eyes moving to ensure their security on the porch. "I hate the idea of him stalking the grounds, targeting your mother."

"He's won no sympathizers in doing this," Gertrude said.

"Then why would he do this?" Sam asked.

Gertrude watched the horses set loose from the stables. The beasts pounded the earth with their hooves, fleeing from the flames. They ran right by the porch, trampling through Galina's beautiful garden.

Gertrude shut her eyes. "Men do desperate things when they sense their end."

27

From the Ashes

The pale rays of morning streaked across her mother's lands. The dew of the night still clung to the leafy branches of the trees. A cool breeze blew. Gertrude drew the blanket she had draped over her shoulders more tightly around her as she drifted in and out of uneasy sleep. The sun's warming presence did not yet touch the gardens. It was chilly on this side of her mother's home. Even amid the chaos and the destruction, it all seemed so beautiful.

The silent peace that overtook the lands was a stark contrast to the fire that had raged not more than two hours before. The men had defeated the blaze and managed to save the barn. It was now a matter of collecting the horses and cleaning up the devastation left behind of the shed.

The smell of the fire remained heavy on the air as Breyton emerged from the house. Before he approached Sam, who stood protectively behind Gertrude, Breyton peered out across the field to the still smoking pile of rubble. Many hands were raking over and picking through the mess, their faces partially covered with scarves or handkerchiefs. They worked quietly, orchestrated by the lady of the house herself.

Breyton sighed.

Sam whipped around, startled by the sudden sound.

Breyton held up his hands. "It's just me, Sam."

Sam's instinct to defend Gertrude faded only slightly. He closed the distance between them. Every step forward drove his desire to send his fist into Breyton's face, but every breath steadied his pounding heart. Pushing his feelings aside, Sam whispered, "She's asleep." He motioned to Gertrude, who sat in the chair, her head drooped slightly to the left. "It's been a long night."

"I can see that," Breyton said, looking out at the mess. He took a moment to ponder the unwelcoming approach this man whom he considered a good friend made toward him. "What happened?" Breyton asked in a calm voice.

Sam clenched his jaw. *Right now, I'd far rather see Absalom standing before me than you. At least I'd be justified for striking him.*

Breyton waited patiently. The reasons behind Sam's turn of affection away from him were coming together quite clearly.

Sam drew in a deep breath and closed his eyes. *You're better than this.* He turned his gaze to Breyton. This man before him was one of the best that he had ever known. Sam cleared his throat and apologized, "Forgive me. I'd like to reemphasize that it's been a long night. Absalom was spotted within the valley. We believe that he and his supporters tried to burn down the house this morning."

Breyton tensed. *Was this because I'm here?*

"This fire," Sam motioned with his brow, "took. The others did not. Galina's community has found several arrows sticking out of various parts of the house that smoldered, but didn't catch."

Breyton shook his head. "That's concerning, but it does tell me this: Absalom's supporters aren't military men. Sounds like they wouldn't know the right side of an arrow from the tip of their lance."

Sam chuckled. "I figured that too. They were likely too far, trying to stay out of sight, and likely also couldn't hit the eye of a target if it was three feet in front of them." Sam looked off. His reasons for not wanting to talk to Breyton began to creep in around his heart once more. He swallowed hard.

The men held their breaths and stared at one another.

Breyton looked away. He did not want to poke at this man who was his friend and who was hurting. However, hearing all of this, he had to talk to Gertrude. Standing as straight as his healing wounds would allow, Breyton asked gently, "May I speak with her, Sam?"

No, Sam answered in his thoughts. His throat felt try, and his heart was beginning to escalate once again. Sam inhaled deeply. "It may be better later, Breyton. She's sleeping."

Breyton looked over Sam's shoulder.

Sam knew without looking. He could hear Gertrude shifting in her chair.

She stretched her arms wide, the peace of sleep shifting back and forth from blissful ignorance to the memories of the blaze.

Was I dreaming? She sent her half-opened eyes across the field of the trampled crop to the mess in the not-so-far distance and quickly realized, *Damn. It wasn't a dream.*

"Good morning, Gertrude," Breyton said.

The sudden voice shattered her thoughts. She jumped. "God, Breyton!" Gertrude said, grasping her heart. "You startled me."

"Couldn't let you get too comfortable out here," he said while smiling. He gave a nod to Sam.

Sam did not want to give them privacy, as Breyton had asked. *If I stand just beyond the door, will that be far enough?* Sam thought as he slowly left the porch and returned to the interior of the house. *I'll stand here within earshot and then—*

"Papa!" Sawsha called, breaking his thoughts. The boy ran to clutch onto his father's knee.

Sam picked up his son and held him close. He looked back to the door that he had let close behind him. Pulling his son tightly to him, he kissed his brow. "Come, Sawsha." Sam, still holding his boy close, began to walk away from the mess on the other side of the doors. "Let's find you some breakfast."

On the porch, Breyton asked Gertrude, "Do you mind if I join you?" He pointed to the chair, tired from his walk through the disturbingly empty house.

"No, not at all," Gertrude said. She looked behind her to invite Sam to join them as well. Her eyes looked this way and that on the porch, unable to find him. "Was Sam here when you came out?"

"Yes," Breyton assured her. He took his seat and continued, "I asked if I could speak to you privately, and he respectfully agreed. I can't imagine he's more than a room or two away if we should need him. I will say, though," he patted his cane, "I may be injured, but I think I could still fend off any threat with this as if it was my sword."

"Ha," Gertrude teased. "I'm sure you could." She sighed and turned her gaze out to the cleanup operation.

They sat quietly a moment, taking in the status of the morning.

Eventually, Breyton said while still looking away from her, "May I ask you a bold question?"

She nodded. "How many times have I been bold with you?"

Breyton chuckled, and, keeping his gaze toward the gardens, said, "I'm a little surprised that you're not out there."

"It's killing me not to be." Gertrude looked at him. "My mother and Sam have both forbidden me from stepping a foot off of this porch until the horses are rounded and Absalom is found." Gertrude leaned back in her wooden chair. "Did Sam or someone else tell you what happened?"

"Yes," Breyton answered. "One of the staff woke me, and Sam filled me in on what happened with the fire and that Absalom was spotted in the valley."

The gentlelady stared at the table for a moment, then dryly informed him, "Absalom was seen at a town not so far from here. We have people patrolling the borders of the estate to make sure he doesn't make any further attempts to come here. He's lost likely any ally that he may have had in this valley, coming after my mother like that."

Breyton looked down. "Do you think he was targeting your mother?" He turned his gaze to Gertrude.

She stared at him a moment before answering, "No. I don't think my mother was the *only* target." While roll-tapping her fingers on the arms of the chair, she continued, "This would have been the trifecta of targets. My mother, myself, and a Malleus. It would not have served the people's agenda any, but it certainly would have played to the agenda that Absalom serves."

"You don't think he's the mastermind?" Breyton asked.

Shaking her head, Gertrude answered, "No. Absalom is a coward, and he had a fairly comfortable spot as prime minister. He would only have chanced this if he felt his grip over Herod was slipping, which I'm happy to take full credit for making happen, and if someone else was offering him a better deal."

"And who do you think that was?" Breyton asked. He leaned closer to her in his chair.

"The same who ordered you dead," Gertrude said simply. She wasn't prepared to tell Breyton that she suspected these vile acts to be spawning from one of his brothers. "This," she pointed to the field, "I believe was also for you. Mother and I would have just been bonuses to whoever gave the order."

Breyton looked down. "I agree." He sighed heavily. "Gertrude, I...I don't want this, but I think it may be for the best." He turned his eyes back to her. "I think I should leave. The longer I stay here, the longer I am endangering you and your mother. What a terrible houseguest I would be if I ended up getting you both killed."

Gertrude shook her head. "No." She rubbed her face with her hands. This was all far too much to be taking in before tea. "No. I forbid it. You are not allowed to leave. What are you smiling at?"

He chuckled. "Oh, Gertrude." He shook his head. "Are you sure you don't want to marry Herod?"

"How on earth could you think that now? What do you mean?"

Did I tell him that? She wondered, unable to recall that conversation.

"Your mother told me." Breyton shrugged and smiled.

"Oh, did she?" Gertrude said. Her cheeks flushed. *There goes any chance I might have had at making our relationship grow naturally, if at all.*

"It's quite alright," Breyton responded. "I'm glad she did." The sun streaked shadows of light across the lady's turned face, allowing Breyton to admire every detail of her beauty. *Stunning* was the only word for her. He reached out his hand to take her fingers gently into his palm. "You would make one hell of a queen, you know."

Gertrude laughed. "I think Mother does have you on too strong a dose of opioids. Please, let's forget that for a moment. I cannot stand the thought of you leaving. I want you to stay, Breyton." She tightened her fingers around his. Her heart felt heavy for what she was about to suggest, but she knew that it had to be done. "I *need* you to stay."

Breyton's face erupted with a smile as he embraced the thrill of emotions he was experiencing. "Gertrude, I have to say that I'm glad to hear that." He looked down at their hands. "So, you're absolutely sure you don't want the crown?"

Gertrude leaned forward, looked him in the eyes, and said, "Yes. I'm *quite* sure."

He chuckled. "In that case, I have a bit of a confession...You're all I ever think about. Your smile, your laugh, your kiss..." Breyton paused a moment as his cheeks turned pink. "I was up all night thinking about you. I guess, I mean, what I'm trying to say is, er, I...I can't imagine spending another day of my life without you."

It took a while for Gertrude to build anything to say. It was as if a part of her soul was dying while another was bursting into life.

"Breyton," she said. He could see the stars glowing from her eyes. "I think I am falling quite fast for you too."

He was elated to hear this confirmation. He was surprised as well, on account that he was afraid her heart would be too contently situated elsewhere for her to have reciprocated the emotion. "Gertrude, I'm so...I'm not going to waste a moment with you. With everything happening, it would be foolish to let a single instant slip away. Gertrude..." As best he could, Breyton jumped on the wave of the moment, tenderly lowering himself to kneel.

He kissed her knuckles.

She could not find her breath.

"Gertrude, in a gentlemanly effort to spare you from marrying my younger brother and, well, you know, to allow you to spend your life with a man who *will* hear you when you speak, would you marry me? I know that this is unbelievably fast, but I learned long ago that if something good comes into your life, you have to hold it dearly before something takes that light away."

A million thoughts were screeching in Gertrude's mind. She ignored a great many of them, for this was her chance to escape marrying Herod and to be openly loved.

"Yes," she finally said, overcome with tears. "Yes, I'll marry you, Breyton."

Against the pain and weakness in his body, Breyton jumped from the ground and held Gertrude in his arms. They held each other close.

Breyton kissed Gertrude's brow tenderly.

However, a shadow fell across her thoughts, and she pushed him away.

"Gertrude, what's the matter?"

She did not look at him. She was not sure if she could. There was something she needed to say before another minute fell. "Breyton, there's something I ought to tell you, something you need to know before we go an instant farther."

"Well, you aren't secretly a man or anything like that, are you?" Breyton jested with an adorable smile.

Though appreciating his joke, Gertrude only gave a half-smile in response. "No," she succinctly answered. "Breyton...I, hmm, for some time I, I haven't been, well, pure... You would not be my first lover, which, as our church commands of a lady, is not...a decent precedent for marriage."

Breyton had already guessed that bit of information. As long as it was not Herod or Donovan, she gave her innocence to, he could live with this idea. "That's fine, Gertrude," Breyton gladly admitted. On a whisper, he added as though it were a great secret, "You know, you would not be my first either."

The gentleman's adoring smile did nothing to comfort her, even though she was relieved to know that he still wanted her. "There's something else," she continued, and this time, Breyton expected what he would hear. "I haven't been pious in general. The man who took my virginity was married. I loved him very much, and I know he loves...loved me. It's going to take me time to heal from that completely, but I *do* want to make a life with you, Breyton...have children with you, rear horses, become old toads in the country together; I just want you to know that my heart has had a rough ride these past few years because my first love and I could just never be together, not really. So if ever I am to seem hesitant with you, please, please know it's not you."

"Gertrude," Breyton said, "I know that you and Sam have had an affair."

Her heart dropped.

"I've suspected by the little things you two do for each other. By how protective Sam is of you...the way he looks at you. I can't say that I am terribly comfortable with the idea of you two remaining in such close proximity with one another, I'm not sure if that's healthy for any of us, but no matter what, I want you to know that I will be there for you every time you cry and for every hour, the miserable and the glorious, of your life.

"All that I ask from you, Gertrude, is that you do not say that you will marry me unless you are truly over Sam, meaning, once we say our vows they are binding, that you are completely willing, and completely mine, as I will be yours. At the same time, I don't want to be responsible for making your heart grieve any sooner or longer than needs be, so if you want to wait to get married, I'll wait however long it takes."

Never could she have expected to find a man as wonderful as Sam, and yet here he stood before her. She pulled Breyton into a kiss, then said, "I can assure you that I mean it when I say I want to marry you, I do. Sam's and my romance has run its course. We've both known for some time that things were rolling to an end. I'll not lie to you, Breyton. As hesitant as I am to admit it, I have been selfishly jeopardizing his marriage and our reputation for years. I've hated myself for loving him. His son has thought that I am his mother far too often. I've unintentionally misconstrued and complicated that little lad's life. It's a very selfish love Sam and I have carried. We've risked so much with little regard for how it would affect others, should we have been discovered." She realized the contradictory nature of her upcoming statement to the one she just made, but these words could not be saved. "Breyton, you are the best thing that has ever happened in my life. You're a stable and brilliantly wonderful man whose hand I can openly hold in the sunlight."

Gertrude kissed Breyton's knuckles, then held his hands tightly to her heart. "I don't mean that I'm running to marry you for sanctuary, no. You are my hope that I can prove myself as a true and loving wife to the whole wide world, for everyone's eyes to see." Breyton stared at Gertrude. She saw the ambiguity in his eyes and sighed. "I'll turn the question to you then, seeing as you already have my answer. Do you, Lord Breyton Malleus, wish to marry complicated little me with all the bells and whistles that follow my name? Do you truly think you can handle all that?"

Breyton laughed and pressed his body flat against Gertrude's. With a confident smile and a charming twinkle in his eyes, Breyton answered, "You bet I can."

28

Mother's Love

Sawsha listened with an extra special gleam in his eyes as Breyton and Galina regaled him with stories of his father. Gertrude also listened intently to her mother and Breyton speak. It did her heart well to hear the new man entering her life talk so admiringly about the man he knew had already been so intimately connected to her. The respect she held for Breyton and her admiration toward was intensified by the strong friendship he obviously felt for Sam.

Gertrude could not help but wonder how Sam would react when he learned of her prospective marriage. She was scarcely able to eat, as her belly was becoming ever more full on the knots growing there.

As lunch rolled on and the conversation turned away from Sam to the glamorous life of a prince that Sawsha was so interested in hearing about, Galina noticed how attentively her daughter watched Breyton. Too, she saw the bashful way the pair crumpled when their eyes met. There was something secret, something of wanting between them. As a protective mother, she concluded that while Sam was out and about this morning, her daughter and her recovering guest had shared an unplanned rendezvous. She expected the gentleman to have reached a higher level of intimacy than she deemed appropriate for a pair who were only beginning to become well acquainted. To Galina, this man, however honorable on the outside, was taking advantage of her baby. She was suspicious of those Malleus men. After all the time she'd spent with her husband at court where she observed the conduct of the former king, Donovan, and Herod, she thought she knew what to expect from a man whose blood ran with the same drive for women as his kin. "Gertrude," Galina called during an interlude in the conversation. "Would you mind taking Sawsha over to the paddock to check up on his pony while I have a private word with our prince?"

The sudden change in topic surprised Gertrude, but she obeyed. "Come on, Sawsha, let's go see that pony of yours." She stood from the table and held her hand out to the lad. Sawsha stood from the table and put his hand in Gertrude's. As the two walked out of the room, Gertrude looked back over her shoulder. She wanted to see if she could receive any signal of what this was about, but her mother simply smiled. A sign that did not necessarily mean that everything was going to be alright.

Breyton looked mildly frightened at the unexpected removal of her company.

Out of the house and into the humidity's reach, Sawsha and Gertrude strolled. The white-fenced paddock held within its grasp the horses and one pony that had been removed from the barn during the morning's troubled scene.

By himself, in the neighboring training ring, Gertrude's horse ran about, doing his best to entice all the other horses from the shade to play. Currently, he was reaching over his fence into the paddock to groom a palomino, seemingly sweetly grooming the old girl's neck, but that did not last. The tender moment was shattered when he playfully nipped at the light-colored horse's back, whinnied triumphantly, then ran away. The palomino kicked at nothing, too tired from the sun to be swayed out from the shade of the tree.

Sawsha climbed up onto the rails of the paddock to get a better view of the horse causing the trouble. "Is that your horse?" Sawsha asked, pointing to the lone steed while clutching onto the wooden post with an elbow.

Gertrude protectively put her hand on Sawsha's back in case she needed to catch him if he slipped. "Yes, the one causing the ruckus is mine."

"What's a ruckus?" Sawsha asked.

"It means that he is causing trouble where there does not need to be." Gertrude looked at Sawsha, whose dark eyes watched her stallion. *He looks so much like his father,* she thought, *except for his nose. He has his mother's nose.*

"Is what happened this morning a ruckus?" Sawsha inquired.

"Yes," she answered. "That is a perfect example."

"Is Papa still sleeping?" Sawsha looked to Gertrude.

She nodded her head. The urge to cry overwhelmed her, but she opened her eyes wide and inhaled, staying the tears. "Yes, dear. He needed to rest after we were all up so early this morning."

"Are those bad men who set Babu's shed on fire going to come back?" His little eyes peered deeply into Gertrude's.

"No, precious." She kissed his brow and shut her eyes tight. She did not want to let him go, knowing this would be her last time alone with the boy she loved as her own. "The people love your babu. They swore to her this morning that they would defend her lands from anything and anyone."

"Look!" Sawsha shouted, pointing at the horses, dropping the matters at hand.

Gertrude's horse had stuck his nose into a feed bucket and was now flailing about, trying to fling it off. He whinnied loudly, flung his head every which way, and kicked at the bucket with his forelegs.

"I'll help him," she said after asking Sawsha to come down off the fence.

Having learned from previous dealings with her steed, Gertrude was able to calm him with tender cooing and removed the bucket from his face. With the lead rope attached to his halter, she walked her horse to the stall adjoining the paddock to clean him. The barn still smelled of smoke, so Gertrude decided it best for her and Sawsha to spoil her horse outside.

Under the supervision of Sawsha, Gertrude fastened the cross ties in the wash stall to his halter and began to groom her horse. She slowly walked him through the process, showing Sawsha how to care for horses. She had Sawsha help her use the hard brushes to leaves and twigs out from her horse's hair. Finally, Gertrude showed him how to finish with the soft brush to give the steed a beautiful shine.

"He looks brilliant," Galina said as she joined the pair. "He'll be the envy of the paddock, as he always is."

"You shoulda seen it, Babu!" Sawsha excitedly said as he ran over next to Galina. "He, he got his head stuck in the bucket, and he couldn't get it off, and he swooshed his head all-around all over, but it just wouldn't come off!"

"Really? Silly horse." Galina patted and scratched the furrow in the horse's brow. "Sawsha, would you mind going over to the buttery and getting him some carrots?"

Sawsha nodded enthusiastically, then darted back toward the house.

"So, Mata, what do you want to talk about?" Gertrude asked, knowing that this was the reason why her mother wanted Sawsha to leave.

Bending down stiffly, Galina picked up the brush that Sawsha dropped. She started to stroke the horse's back before saying in a guarded tone, "I talked to Breyton, as you know...He asked me for your hand and then told me that he'd already asked you and that you said yes."

For a moment, Gertrude tried to determine where this became a question or where it was going, because her mother's face gave her no hint. "I'm sorry, Mata, but was there an inquiry in that?"

"It's more of a discussion starter," Galina corrected while still combing the horse. "So, are you to rush into the marriage like you did the engagement? Or shall I arrange for you to have a chaperone?" she heatedly pushed.

Stunned by the thought, Gertrude rebutted, "Mata, don't you think I'm a bit old and it a bit too late for me to be followed around by a 'virtue-protecting' nanny?"

Galina scoffed, "Yes, but wouldn't you know? You've taken full advantage of the absence of such supervision while you lived under my roof, so with this new man in your life, I do believe that a formal chaperone will be necessary regardless of your age or the circumstance. Especially as you seem to be acting like a child by running into plans to marry that man!"

Gertrude could not compose a response. She was too stricken by the intensity of her mother's stinging words.

Galina inhaled deeply in an attempt to calm herself, for her intention was not to scold her daughter. "Gertrude, it's been a *long* day. Given that I believe that our home was nearly set on fire this morning in an attempt to murder Breyton, I'm frightened for you. Even without that threat, I fret because you barely know Breyton. You don't know how much of a Malleus-man he may be. How much do you know about him? Are you sure, *absolutely* sure, that you are ready to fly into this marriage at this time? He said that you've decided to wed before winter comes, for heaven's sake!"

The pair had made their decision in their excitement together on the porch. Nodding, Gertrude confirmed her mother's statement.

"Yes, it's going to probably be in the second half of October to avoid the intolerable cold."

"So soon? With everything happening," Galina questioned, "are you doing this merely to get out of the union with Herod?"

"Would you rather me marry Herod under these circumstances?" Gertrude returned. "I do not need a reminder of the current political situation. This isn't merely an act of desperation to get out of marrying Herod. I just, I *do* see myself being happy and supported by Breyton, and I know that my emotions toward him are going to grow." She sighed heavily, then decided to admit one of the many things that were weighing on her heart. "Mata, I only have so many years of childbearing capabilities left, and I cannot have those wasted on a fruitless affair. I *want* to be a mother. I want children of my own to love." This was a side of Gertrude that even her mother rarely saw. "Breyton is a *wonderful* man. He supports my ambitions and defends them. I'd be a damn fool to let him pass."

"Gertrude, I'm just worried about you," Galina admitted as tears began to form. "You're my baby. I know you're strong, but have you yet told Sam? What will this do to him?"

"No," Gertrude said, finding a wave of defensive frustration building within her. "No. Mata, please. I haven't had the chance to talk to Sam. I didn't want to tell him before he was able to rest."

"Oh, that's considerate of you," Galina snidely remarked. "How about Herod? When are you planning to tell the king that you're marrying his older brother?" she asked as she came around the back end of the horse to speak to her daughter. "They're not just loose ends, Gertrude! They're decent human beings, and you can't hide these things from either of them. Especially the king!"

"Mata, I wish you'd stop!" Gertrude took a few steps back. "I've only been engaged for two hours!" Gertrude calmed herself when she saw Sawsha coming back with a full bushel of carrots in his arms.

She stepped close to her mother and whispered, "Please don't worry, Mata." Her gentle voice assured her, "I'll tell them both. I'll tell Sam today, and I'll write Herod soon. Trust me, I mean it when I say that I cannot continue to carry on the guilt of being with Sam any longer, and I want to start a life with Breyton. It's time I stopped being the lover of a man who already has a family, so that I may at last start one of my own."

~*~*~

"Psst, Gertrude," Breyton hissed from around a hall's corner.

"What are you doing?" Gertrude asked the prince, who was plastered against the side of a wall and kept looking around as if to ensure that no one was coming.

"Your mother scared the hell out of me earlier today. I just wanted to make sure that the coast was clear," the gentleman said, standing proper and coming to Gertrude's side with the cane's assistance. "Did she talk to you too?"

Though this conversation was heavy, Gertrude was grateful for the distraction from her impending conversation with Sam. Nodding, she somberly answered, "Yes. Did she yell at you at all?"

Breyton shrugged. "Not really, but she was stern. I hold no grudge against that; she's a mother trying to protect her baby. Considering the hell her husband gave her, I can see where she's coming from."

Gertrude pulled Breyton over toward an open window. "A week ago, I told her that I was starting to fall for you and that you fancied me, and we've been spending all this time together..." Gertrude's voice waned when Breyton lifted her chin to bring her eyes from their shameful stare at the ground to look at him.

"There, now I can see those pretty eyes of yours." Breyton gave her his adorable smile, and in an instant, Gertrude's consternation with her mother was gone.

She exhaled deeply, then said, "There was a point my mother

236

brought up that was valid: we seem to know each other fairly well, but we don't actually know a lot about each other."

"How do you mean?" Breyton asked while pulling out a handkerchief to wipe some sweat from his face.

Clapping her hands twice quietly, Gertrude bit her lower lip, then answered, "Right, let's do it this way: we'll play a game...sort of. We both come up with facts about ourselves, but not too many, as that may remove the fun of mystery from our lives. I'll start." The woman paused for a moment and looked up to the ceiling as she tried to piece together what random facts she could offer, but it was difficult with her prince staring at her so expectantly. "Right, here goes: I am absolutely, positively scared to death of the ocean. I won't even go down near the sand. The waves terrify me and make me almost paralyzed if ever I get near. Try to imagine the joy I had crossing the ocean as many times as I have. My middle name is Faye, which was my mata's mother's name. Alright, and lastly, hmm..." Gertrude checked behind her, then looked down the hall in the other direction to ensure that she and Breyton were alone for the next fact. She took a step closer to the prince, then said only a little louder than a whisper, "You could probably make me do anything for you if you figured this one out, but I'll save you the trouble: I love to have the back of my knees touched."

Breyton smiled spryly. He turned a shade of pink as he imagined exactly what that suggested. Crossing the arm that held his cane across his chest, then leaning the other atop it so that he could contemplatively stroke his goatee, Breyton took a moment to appreciate the idea before starting his facts. "I am a swimmer. Back home at my estate in the east, every morning when the weather is good, I hike down to the river and swim for as long as I can. I've been doing it all my life, and it feels lovely even when it's cold. So, Gertrude, should ever that dreaded ocean take you as a hostage, I'll be the one to jump in and pull you out.

"Well, what else…hmm, you already know that I race horses." A proud noble smile beamed from this man. He did not have to say it, but it was well known that Breyton was one of the best riders in the entire country. "Here's something: I cannot shoot an arrow for the life of me, but I seem to be fairly good with a sword. I was five years old when I had my first kiss with a four- or five-year-old girl who 'loved' me. We were engaged to be married for about three days, I proposed, but I broke it off with her when I saw her talking to another five-year-old, which made me extremely jealous. Let's see…well, ironically, though I love to swim in water that is freezing, I truly hate being cold. Winter is not for me. I bundle up like mad during the winter; I look like a four-hundred-pound puff-ball with all the furs and sweaters and scarves I have tucked around me. Especially nights—I can't stand being cold at night. So it'll be nice to have someone in bed with me again to cuddle up with when the ice comes to claim our country." Breyton took a step forward, wrapped his arms around Gertrude's back, and held her close. "And lastly," the prince kissed Gertrude's forehead and cheek before whispering in her ear, "I would love to massage, kiss, or touch the back of your knees or any other part of your body whenever you please."

29

Loose Ends

Gertrude went to check on Sam. She felt sick with worry after she left Breyton. She imagined how she would tell Sam that the time had come for them to end their romance. She did not know how to tell him that she was already engaged to Breyton.

The tightness in her stomach somehow intensified when she knocked lightly on the door and entered without waiting for an answer.

The gentleman jumped when the door first opened, mildly startled that the knocker would enter without waiting, but his heart settled when he saw that it was Gertrude. "You scared me," he admitted with a smile, bending to pick up his vest from the edge of the bed.

She was not surprised to see Sam awake and in the process of getting dressed. "You know me," Gertrude said, closing the door, "I like to make an entrance."

As the lady drew nearer, Sam could see that there was something off about Gertrude's body language. "Sweetheart," Sam called. He took a step closer and picked up the faintest hint of tobacco coming from her body. He gave her the gravest look of concern. "Gertrude, please, can you find it within yourself to share what's driving you to smoke again?"

Gertrude crossed her arms. She suddenly became furious. Her pursed lips barely parted as she said, "Sam. A lot is happening..."

"Sucking on the butt of a pipe is not going to relieve you of anything, Gertrude," Sam scolded. He stared so critically at her that she could barely look at him. "You are too smart to be dealing with whatever issue you're facing that way! Please, Gertrude, don't burden yourself in this manner. Tell me what's wrong; we can talk it out. Is it the threat of Absalom? Is that what's bothering you?"

"No," she succinctly answered, taking a small step back and turning her face away.

Sam took a step forward and wiped the sweat from the day's heat from his forehead with his sleeve. "Is it about Herod, then? Don't worry about that; we'll sort something out."

"It's not that either," Gertrude grumbled, still falling backward with her steps.

Sam saw the sudden flux of tears rise in Gertrude's eyes. "Then, Gertrude, what is it? God, please tell me. Is it the threat of the revolution?"

"No, no, no," she muttered and scrunched up her face in her hands. Her back hit the wall.

In desperation, he closed the distance between himself and her. He grabbed her wrists and pushed her hands off her face. "Is it Sawsha? Damn it, Gertrude, tell me what's wrong!"

"I *can't!*" Gertrude shouted as she violently wriggled her way out from between Sam and the wall, shooting herself over next to the bed. "Sam, I...I am *so* sorry, Sam, I'm so sorry," she cried. Though they had already discussed that this was coming, the wave of emotion that struck her now felt like it was ripping her out to sea.

"Gertrude," Sam said, more calmly now. "Please, love, just tell me, or my imagination will drive me mad." His words were welcoming, but Gertrude doubted that she could speak.

She turned her back on Sam and dropped herself on the far side of the foot of the bed. She clung onto the dark wooden bedpost and prepared to grant his request. She stared blankly into the sun's rays that fell into the room as she dryly, quietly answered, "Breyton proposed to me..."

Sam's heart stopped.

"...And I said yes."

Like a lost and empty soul, Sam's body crossed the room in front of Gertrude, who watched carefully. She was deeply fearful of what he might do with his sword and the open second-story window at such temptingly close proximities.

His walk to the windowpane was short, but every step felt like bare feet on shattered glass and burning coals.

So this is hell, he finally thought as he leaned heavily on the open window's ledge, looking out at the cloud-filled sky above. The weight that consumed him was like nothing he had ever known.

"Sam?" Gertrude called, scared to death that he might fall out the window. From her alarm, she stood, but she slowly lowered herself back on the bed at the reassurance of Sam's subtle wave.

He felt sick.

"So soon?" was all he could say as he clung to his turning stomach.

Gertrude enclosed her hands over her mouth as she hiccupped a sob. She nodded and squeezed her eyes shut.

"Does he know about us?" Sam asked, still staring blankly out into the gardens, which seemed to be losing their blooms below. "Does he know about our affair?"

"Yes," she answered. "He said he's known for some time, but that he's alright with it..." she swallowed hard and finished with, "...so long as we're done by the time he and I marry."

Sam scoffed and turned around to look at the woman he loved. "I just can't...You've only seriously known this man for a few weeks. It's a bit of a shock...So this is it, then?" he asked, but a string, a cold cord of cruelty, was heavily braided in his words. "The end?" he added with a slightly crazed look in his eyes and a shrug.

"We knew this would happen, Sam," Gertrude said while wiping the tears from her eyes. "We've both always known."

Snorting, disgusted at his own naiveté, Sam bitterly responded, "You mean I should have known that Prince Breyton's charming smile would have captured you? No, really," Sam added with a flat hand in the air as Gertrude made to argue with him. He inhaled deeply and calmed his elevating temper because it was reaching a range that rarely showed its head. "I should have known," Sam quietly said. "We've talked about it recently enough and, huh, I was with him when he met his first wife, so why shouldn't I have some sort of hand with his second?" Sam rubbed his head in response to his eyes being temporarily blinded by the flashing memory of Breyton kissing Gertrude.

A second wave hit him—one of complete and utter grief. The force and brutality of this undulation humbled Sam to the ground. He slid down the wall and landed flat and hard on his rump, but he did not feel it. Sam cupped his hands over his crying eyes as his body shook from sorrow.

Gertrude had never seen Sam in such a state. It was startling, but she did not hesitate a second. She launched herself from the bed to sit beside her protector, who needed to be guarded against inward destruction. She wrapped her arms around him and cradled his head in the crook of her shoulder and neck. She rubbed her cheek against his brow.

He clutched onto her. He did not know how he could let her go. He loved her. Everything he did was for her. What would he do now that she belonged to another?

"What'll I do, Gertrude?" he asked through his sobbing. "What'll I do without you?" He held tighter to her and added, "You're my everything."

"Without me?" Gertrude asked incredulously with a hint of jest to her words. "You're hardly in the arms of an angel, Sam. You'll do what you did before me, and you'll do fine. You have your son, and you'll tend to him the same as you always have, better even. Do you hear me?" Sam nodded. "Sawsha needs you now, and he will always need you, and it's not as though we have to cut contact entirely with each other. You're still my bodyguard, after all." Gertrude snuffled deeply, then let out a shaky breath. "I need you more now than ever."

Sam buried his head deeper against Gertrude, but he turned his face out so that he could still be heard. "Gertrude, I think that when Breyton says he wants us 'over,' he means entirely. I can't be your bodyguard when you are his wife. We'll find too much distraction in each other's company. There are too many memories between us to allow space for you and Breyton to grow. It's not as though we've fallen out of love. You've just, I guess, grown to love another, or at least to accept another."

It was painful to imagine life without Sam, but she knew what he said was true.

"I'll head home today," Sam offered. "With the protection of the entire valley now watching out for Absalom, you'll be safe. Sawsha's school starts next week anyway."

A breeze brought by the impending threat of fall came in through the window and landed on the lovers. Gertrude looked out through the window. From what little sky she could see, and from the breath of the wind, she knew that on this September morning, the great warm and loving summer was over. Looking back into the room, Gertrude kissed Sam's brow and whispered, "You know that you will always be in my heart."

Sam sat up and looked at Gertrude's puffy, red eyes. He smiled, framed her face with his hands, and kissed her brow. "I know," he said while sweetly rubbing his forehead to hers. "As you will always be mine."

For hours they sat together on the floor, side by side, fingers interlocked. They did not speak, for what else could be said when both had made it clear that their sweetly held and sacredly secret love affair was dead?

30

Word from Maltoro

The first of fall's rains had come. The early October storm's angry wind that whipped against the windows harkened of the darkness overtaking the lands.

"You're certain this is true, Mikhail?" Gertrude's words begged of the man before her.

"Yes, my lady," Mikhail answered, pulling a handkerchief to wipe the water running down his neck.

"We saw it ourselves," Adrian gently reminded her. "One of them at least. What do you want us to do?"

Gertrude could scarcely wrap her mind around the consequences of what was happening, let alone to give these messengers from the capital orders. She tapped her fingers on the top of the desk she stood behind. "Fifty silos and granaries ransacked and burned?"

Nodding, Mikhail responded, "And counting."

"That's more than half of the capital's supply," she calculated.

"For now," Mikhail said as he clenched his fists. "If the king's men can't guard the rest from the rebels' thieving hands in time, the people will starve."

"They may try to give the grain to the people," Gertrude tried to hope.

After what they had seen, the men had their doubts.

"The king needs you, my lady," Adrian pleaded. "The city, *we* need you back."

Gertrude inhaled deeply. She nodded. "Take a moment to warm up, have a meal, and rest if you must. Then, gentlemen, I must ask you to return to Maltoro. Inform the king that I will follow as soon as this storm ends. In the meantime," she sat at the table, grabbed a square of parchment, and reached for her pen. She hastily dipped it in ink. In quick, messy strokes, she wrote, *"My king, to prevent further unrest, open the royal stores of grain to the people. Ration it, but offer it. I will follow soon. —Gertrude."*

Looking up, she saw Breyton preparing to enter. He took a step back, seeing that she had company with her in the tearoom.

Gertrude folded the note. Grabbing the lit candle on her desk, she melted a red stick of wax over the back of the envelope. Her stomach began to twist as she watched drops of wax drip onto the paper. "Take this with you." She pressed her seal into the wax. "See that this gets to the king."

The older of the messengers took the note, but the two men exchanged looks instead of following her directions.

"With all due respect, my lady," Mikhail began, "what if the rain doesn't stop? How long?" He took a step closer to the table where Gertrude sat. His tightened muscles did little toward that line of respect. "How long before you return?"

In a moderate tone, she answered, "The rains will stop. They always do. I will be back in Maltoro within a week."

"The city may not last that long!" Mikhail pounded his fist to the table's top.

"Gentlemen!"

The men turned around, and Gertrude jumped.

Breyton was in the room with a smile on his face and his hand on the tang of his sword. He said to the messengers, "Now our Gertrude here will continue to do everything in her power to try to stop further harm to the people. She has been and will continue to be *your* greatest ally."

The tension in Mikhail's shoulders eased slightly, but before the men could realize that they were talking to the brother of the king, Gertrude cleared her throat and said, "Let's stay focused on protecting our city and securing the ones we love. Thank you, Mikhail, Adrian."

They bowed their heads and headed off to find a fire and comfort in her mother's home.

Breyton watched the men go.

"Everything alright?" Breyton asked after he closed the door to the tearoom.

Gertrude rolled her eyes and slumped in her chair. She shook her head and reached for the bottle of wine on her desk. She offered Breyton a glass while she filled hers close to the top.

"It seems that I'll have to return to Maltoro a bit sooner than planned," she informed him. She pulled a deep sip of wine.

"What's happening?" Breyton asked. He took a seat in the chair nearest to the desk.

While slowly rotating the wine in her glass, Gertrude answered, "Those men were messengers from Herod. The rebels have been looting the grain from the silos and freestanding granaries all around Maltoro. It was a concerted effort, all done in one day, but the fear is that they will continue to strike."

Breyton leaned back in his chair. "How many?"

"More than half of the city's supplies," she answered. She took another mouthful of wine. "Enough to more than sufficiently devastate the city this winter. The people were starving as it was, and now this…"

247

"Why would they do this?" Breyton asked. "It's a very poor move to gain sympathizers."

Shaking her head, Gertrude elaborated, "Many of the people doing this were bearing the Malleus flag." She shrugged and emptied half of the wine glass down her throat.

"So that the people will think this was Herod's doing," Breyton realized.

"Or yours," she said, pointing at him and looking him squarely in the eye. "It's stupid, it was a desperately stupid move, but it'll spark rage no matter who did it, and that may be what the rebels are after. All of Herod's and my work these last three, four weeks," she looked to the rain beating on the side of the window, "for nothing."

Breyton stood, rounded the table to her, and took her hands in his. "I don't believe that. It tells me that you and Herod are making change; the rebels fear that. They know that they're losing ground with the people, and this is their desperate attempt to cling to power." He turned her face up to look at his. "Don't give up now, my love." He ran his knuckles down the side of her face. "What do we do next?"

She chuckled. "It would be nice if, for once, *I* could be the one to ask that." She kissed the back of Breyton's hand. "I'll have to return to Maltoro; I've given those messengers a note to give to Herod to open the royal stores. It may be too little at this point, but we must try."

"What about reaching out to the other major cities?" Breyton suggested. "Ask them to supplement the capital. Make Herod loosen the coin with the people; have his crown pay for the subsidies. If he is not willing, then I'll pay for it myself."

Gertrude grunted. "I may need your help convincing him of either of those measures."

Breyton copied her grunt.

"Ha, I know, *trust* me," she said with a smile, "I know. He's been away from the influence of Absalom for over a month now. He's had time to see what his blind trust in that man did to the people. We may be able to convince him." Gertrude yawned the last two words. "I'm so tired."

"If you're to return to Maltoro, then it's best you try to rest tonight." Breyton helped Gertrude up from her chair. He held on to both of her hands, pulling her away from her unfinished wine. "Though I'm not exactly sure I want you going back to the capital right away. The road may be dangerous."

"I don't disagree with that," Gertrude responded, following his lead out from the tearoom and to the hall. "I'll have to plan a route and determine who to take with me." She wished she hadn't said that last part. She missed Sam's company, his friendship, but he was gone and had been for weeks now.

Breyton squeezed her hand. "Maybe I should go first," he offered.

"You're not going alone," Gertrude corrected. They continued down the hall toward her room. "Breyton, I already almost lost you once on the road. I'm going with you."

"I respectfully disagree," he responded. "You'll be far safer without me. I'm the one whose flag is being waved about over carnage and destruction right now, remember? If anyone has a target on his back, it's me. You sure you want to marry into this?"

Gertrude did not have much choice in that matter, but her fondness for Breyton had grown over the last month. "I'm certain, you great oaf. Let's not think about it now. We'll figure this out in the morning, as if I'll be able to sleep at all tonight."

They stopped at her door. Gertrude leaned on the wood and brought her eyes up to Breyton. The soft smile on his lips and the light in his eyes told her what he was thinking. Her cheeks flushed. Looking away, Gertrude quietly said, "I'll likely be up fairly early tomorrow, so I'd better get to sleep now." She opened the door and said, "Good night, dear."

Breyton leaned forward and kissed her dearly on the brow. "Good night, my Gertrude."

The energy between his lips and her skin sent pulses throughout her. Her head suddenly felt so light.

He slid his hands from her sides and drew himself back. His intense eyes held her gaze as he walked past her through the open door.

Gertrude continued to stand in the hall, processing what just happened.

"Coming, Gertrude?" Breyton's voice called from inside her room.

Smiling, she entered the room and closed the door behind her.

As the prince wrapped his arms around her, she thought, *I imagine I will be.*

31

Departure

A pair of hands softly enclosed their fingers on her bare shoulders. Sitting at her desk, Gertrude's body quivered from the unexpected contact. His lips kissed their way across her shoulder and pushed off the blanket she had draped over herself so that it fell to frame her hips. The gentleman's hands softly followed suit, running down her arms.

Gertrude trembled again and put her quill, still dripping from the ink of her signature, atop the desk. She ran her ink-stained hand against his cheek, bristly from the negligence of not being shaved this morning. With her other hand, she encouraged the gentleman's touches to explore as freely as they wished. "Oh, sir," she whispered as the man's fingers indulged, and as his lips kissed her cheek. "Oh, my Breyton."

The good prince smiled beyond the point of satisfaction to hear again his lady call his name. "Yes?" he asked as he kissed her ear, knowing that she had nothing at all to say. Breyton withdrew his hands, putting them back on her shoulders and giving the back of her head one more kiss.

"I suppose my mother was right; she should have hired a chaperone."

Breyton came around from behind the chair to lean against the desk. Gertrude quietly asked as she restored the blanket to cover her shoulders, "Why do you tease me so?"

He shrugged incredulously and asked, "You think last night was a tease? Gracious, what sort of act am I following?"

"Huh," Gertrude scoffed at the thought that last night was anything to be regarded as a tease. "Breyton, I should hope you realize how much pleasure you afforded me last night," she bashfully admitted.

Breyton chuckled and gave that adorable smile that made his blue eyes twinkle.

"You're going to drive me mad, aren't you?" she asked.

"I hope not," Breyton answered. "Who else am I going to talk to once you're gone? Myself? I'm rather rotten company," he ended with a wink.

"I'm sure you would find yourself satisfying enough company, Breyton," she responded with a chuckle, picking up her quill again and stroking the face of her letter with its feathers.

Looking down at what Gertrude was earlier fiddling over, Breyton scratched his shoulder, straightened out his shirt, then asked, "What're you working on?"

Exhaling loudly, Gertrude answered, "I'm drafting letters to the various cities, as you mentioned, asking them to aid the capital. Hoping that if I can present these notes essentially already done, that they'll force Herod's hand a little."

"If I am to leave for the capital today, shall I hand deliver these to Herod for you?" he offered.

The idea wasn't so bad. They had talked in the night of how to transport the pair of them safely to Herod. "Perhaps." Gertrude considered. "It would save me the trouble of finding and paying a post rider if I decide not to leave the safety of Forsythia."

Breyton chuckled. He knew that there was nothing that could stop her from returning to the capital.

The small bowl of apples on Gertrude's desk called to Breyton as he read the letter. "Huh, interesting," he said, disregarding her answer entirely as he snatched a lovely red apple from the bowl.

"Excuse me," Gertrude sharply snapped with a smile. "*That*, sir, is not yours."

Breyton rubbed the apple against his shirt's arm as he said, "Yes, yet neither is your bed, but I certainly slept in it last night anyway, didn't I? And, technically speaking, missy, I put my labor into collecting this apple, so it is thus rightly *my* property."

"Uh, do not go political-philosopher on me, sir," Gertrude waved her finger at Breyton, "for it was *I* who brought the bowl and the apples into the room; it was already removed from the supposed 'common good' and already established as my property. So, *you, sir*, are a thief driven by your competitive desire to take what is mine, so that your property is more significant than mine, thus reasonably making you the greater as well."

Breyton stared at Gertrude for a moment, only to take a bite from the apple anyway. "Really? I thought I was just driven by hunger. Well, since you are the dominant judiciary figure here, what are you to do about my crime? Hmm? Anyway, I worked hard last night; I think I deserve the right to eat this apple to rebuild my strength." Breyton continued to eat his apple as he walked to the other side of the room to gather his pants from the ground where they were left by the bed.

"That you do," Gertrude assured him, turning back to the desk to return her quill to its post. She removed herself from the table and walked to the bed with the blanket still draped over her shoulders. She sat on the mattress and watched Breyton with entertained curiosity as he pulled on his pants, holding a half-eaten apple in his mouth. His light acrobatics were amusing for a brief time until he made a loud sucking noise on the apple so that he would not drool on himself. He took the fruit out from his mouth. "You try it sometime," he said to Gertrude in response to her questioning expression.

"No, I'm fine, thank you," she replied. Gertrude sighed and kept her watch on Breyton as he finished dressing. There was something on her mind that she could not contain. When he sat next to her so that he could tie his boots, Gertrude put her hand on his back and said, "Breyton…I know that we talked about this last night, but…do you, er…I wish you would not leave today. Not alone."

"Gertrude, I'm going to have Braum, three other of your mother's men, *and* my mate Rurik, who will meet us a half a day's ride away from here to keep me company," the prince assured her. He finished tying his shoes, sat up, and looked properly at her. "You just don't want me to go without you." He smiled. He thought it was lovely how Gertrude turned away and wrapped the blanket tight around herself. She did not want him to see how concerned she was, even though it was apparent. "Gertrude, I have to go," the prince added, stroking the loose hair from around his lady's face, pushing it back behind her ear. "On top of the influence of support you think I'll have over him, I have to be the one to tell Herod that you are not going to marry him and that you are instead to wed me because I'm simply a million times better." Breyton paused, kissing Gertrude's shoulder quickly enough to stop her from making a smart response. He pulled back and gave her a shy smile. He rubbed Gertrude's back and added, "It's hilarious to think that he thought he had a chance with you."

"Go easy on him, will you?" Gertrude asked Breyton, looking back over the blanket on her shoulder to implore the seriousness of her meaning. "I think he really might actually love me, as odd as that may sound."

Stroking the sides of his goatee, Breyton shrugged and responded, "Gertrude, if he really loved you, he would have listened to you from the start, and if he would have, our country would not currently be on the brink of disaster."

~*~*~

The front porch of Forsythia Valley had with it such somber associations of being the place for goodbyes. Hardly anyone was ever greeted here by the ladies of the house, and it seemed only too often that Lady Galiova lost her company here. This was where she said goodbye to her sons on two sad and separate occasions. This was the place where she and her daughter waved Sam and Sawsha goodbye nearly a month ago so that the lad could start his first year at school. What a sad occasion that goodbye had been! Sawsha was crying because he did not want to leave. The pain afflicting Gertrude's heart for her breakup with Sam was intensified more than she imagined possible upon seeing that boy's tears.

Today, Galina and her daughter said farewell to Breyton and his companions. While Galina busily stuffed sandwiches she'd personally made for these men into the hands of Braum for their voyage, Gertrude stood a step above Lord Malleus, holding onto his hands and giving him a Heltkor blessing. When she was finished, she raised his hands to her lips and kissed his fingers.

Breyton rubbed his thumb against Gertrude's chin, then pulled her face to his. They kissed. Galina observed how intimately the pair interacted, so much more than they had the day before.

"*Please* be careful, Breyton," Gertrude said between kisses, shivering a little from the early-fall-morning breeze. "I know that I'll be just a day behind you, but I hate that we're not going together. I'll be so worried about you."

"Don't be. This is best for *your* safety," Breyton assured, stroking the sides of Gertrude's face with his knuckles. "We'll be together again in just a couple of days. I wish we could go together so I could ensure your safety myself, but it's just too dangerous for you to be on the road with me. I'm delighted that your mother will be going with you.

The people love her. You'll have nothing to fear so long as she is with you. As we discussed last night, it will also be better for me to speak with Herod alone first about everything." He turned a bright, bashful smile toward her. "Just think, in a few more weeks, we'll be married, and we can officially start our lives and family together."

"Doesn't it feel just a bit awkward, though? You know, us getting married at Herod's castle when Herod's the one who wanted to marry me first?" Gertrude asked, worried for the sake of respect and decency toward the king.

Breyton shrugged and said, "It's a tradition for the Malleus men to marry at the castle no matter the circumstance. Don't you worry about my brother. I doubt that we will have any problems with him. After all, it's because of *me* that he wears his crown." Breyton gave a finalizing nod, then lightly tapped the tip of his finger to Gertrude's nose. "I have to go now," he said before giving her one more passionate kiss.

Galina not so subtly cleared her throat to suggest to Breyton that he had taken quite enough of her daughter's attention for the time being.

"Be safe," Gertrude whispered to Breyton as he pulled away and as she gave his hands a quick squeeze.

The gentleman gave Gertrude a quick wink and a smile before going down the stairs and mounting the chestnut thoroughbred that had been sent over from his home in the east a week ago. The former racehorse looked back over his shoulder and gave a loud and happy exhale, glad to see his favorite rider in his saddle again.

Galina joined her daughter and held up her hands at the men on their horses. She gave to them the same blessing Gertrude had given Breyton. When she finished, she smiled and concluded with, "God's speed, gentlemen."

The men bowed their heads to the ladies and turned their horses away from the manor, and to the path toward the coast. Breyton hesitated a moment to have one last good look at his lady to give him strength for the ride.

"I love you," Gertrude said to him as he looked longingly at her.

Breyton's face erupted in a beaming smile. It was the first time she had said it, and it filled him with the courage he needed. He winked and said, "Who wouldn't?" He then turned his horse away, cantering off to catch up with the others.

Gertrude rolled her eyes and smiled. She was full of worry but still able to appreciate her lover's humor. After a moment of watching the men ride off, she turned to go back into the house, but she was stopped by the way her mother leaned her back against the wall, her arms folded crossly over her chest. "Is everything alright?" Gertrude asked.

Galina licked her lips, then coldly asked her daughter, "So how are Breyton's scars healing?"

The young lady did not answer at first. She did not care for the tone of the question. "I don't know what you mean," she finally uttered.

"Come on, Gertrude, I know you've seen them recently," Galina said disapprovingly. "Please don't try to deny it."

"Mata, please," Gertrude begged. She was not in the mood for this sort of confrontation. "It's not that serious, and it certainly was not planned."

"Oh yes, it is serious," Galina corrected, shoving her arms down to her sides. "It sure as hell is a big deal if you conceived, because I'm fairly sure that Breyton has not been drinking Galicofort tea to keep you two from conceiving as Sam did throughout your affair!"

"Shh!" Gertrude hushed her mother, pleading with her eyes for this conversation to be kept private. "Breyton and I are getting married in three weeks. If I'm pregnant, then I'm pregnant! No one will take the time to etch out my conception date!" Gertrude passionately argued as quietly as she could. "And how do you know Sam was drinking

Galicofort?"

"How stupid or blind do you think I am, Gertrude? Unless you're
sterile, which I highly doubt, why else would you not be pregnant after
so many years of an affair?" Galina asked quite angrily. "Gertrude,
what if Breyton doesn't, God forbid, make it to the ceremony?"
Gertrude was too stunned to respond, so Galina continued, "Gertrude,
listen to me. Don't think that I do not care for or approve of Breyton;
it's just that under Sam, you were guaranteed protection, but as
Breyton's wife..."

"What are you saying?" Gertrude interrupted. "That you would
prefer me to have an affair than to be in a legitimate relationship?"

"No, Gertrude." Galina put her hands on her daughter's shoulders.
"As my daughter, you are relatively safe from the rebels' hands, but
your involvement in the castle tilts your luck toward doom regardless
of your political perspectives. Marrying a Malleus, Breyton or not,
they will only see that you are a sympathizer to the royal family."

Forgetting to care if anyone overheard, Gertrude shouted, "What
the hell does that have anything to do with me being pregnant? It is
already well known that I am a loyalist who speaks for the people."

Galina shushed her daughter, then answered, "Having Breyton's
baby puts you in the same predicament as marrying him, and who's
to say it wasn't the rebels who attacked him?"

"Couldn't I just claim the baby is Sam's?" Gertrude mockingly asked.
"Anyway, it can't have been the rebels; their acts have cried out for
attention. They want people to know who they are; the assassination
attempt on Breyton was quiet, anonymous. It was meant to go unseen
and unnoticed. Please, Mother, I beg of you, don't curse what I have
with Breyton. I already fear enough as it is that last night, our first
night, might be our last." With nothing left to say, Gertrude stormed
back into the house and retreated to her room.

As she lay in bed, clinging to the pillow that mildly smelled of

Breyton, she wondered, *Why doesn't Mother realize that Breyton and I have already thought of all of this? Why can't she understand that's one of the reasons why we're getting married so early? We don't want the violence of the rebels to swallow up our happiness before we even know its taste.*

32

Skeletons

The next day, Sam and his steed cantered down the road still fresh with the prints of Breyton's departure. In a light fog, a condition typical of the season, Sam brought his horse to the hitching post just outside the stables. He grabbed his small leather bag from his bay's saddle, patted the horse on the neck, then went to the kitchen door.

The rocks that had grown in the pit of his stomach since he received Galina's message somehow became larger as he approached the house. He wiped the mud off his boots and paused before reaching for the door. Through the window, he saw Gertrude sipping a cup of tea at the kitchen table.

It had been weeks since he saw her. A lifetime felt like an insufficient amount of time to him to patch over the hole she left in his heart. He shook his head. *I always knew that it couldn't last,* he thought. *And yet here I am, as raw as I was when I left. Galina, why did you have to send for me?*

He knew why. He was the only soul Galina could entrust the complete care of her daughter. With chaos taking over the lands, Sam was the one man she knew she could still depend on.

While holding his breath, Sam knocked so as not to startle the lady, who looked lost in reverie before he entered. "Good morning," Sam greeted as he came around the table. He stopped sharply at the chair closest to him and clutched onto its backrest. *This feels so strange,* he thought.

"Good morning," Gertrude returned, stroking the warm porcelain body of her teacup. "Mother told me this morning that she had sent for you to be my escort back to Maltoro." She wondered how Breyton would handle this news. She looked into the waters of the tea in her cup. "Thank you,…for coming."

The pair remained still, hardly able to look at each other.

Sam looked out the window. He took a deep breath, then said, "As if I could say no to your mother."

A heavy silence enveloped the kitchen. It weighed on them both like chains.

Clearing her throat, Gertrude asked, "It's early, Sam. How on earth did you get here so quickly?"

Sam pulled the wooden chair out and sat down before answering. "I left last night, and I stopped in Canaan just after dark." He ran his hand over his face to wipe the heavy moisture of the morning from his skin as he somberly added, "Unfortunately, I rode into nothing short of chaos. There was another attack."

Gertrude gasped, grasping her heart. "On whom?"

Exhaling slowly, Sam recalled the name of the noble house attacked. "The Bolgariers. The rebels stole their horses, slaughtered the livestock, and burned the apple orchard. Luckily, no one was killed this time."

"The Bolgariers were hardly loyalists!" Gertrude mumbled as she nervously bit the tip of her thumbnail. "I always thought them fair to the peasantry…The rebels don't seem to be just striking those who favor the king." She stared out into the mist and said, "This is becoming a class war: the rich, the nobles, and the people of the king."

"You'd better hope not." Sam leaned forward in his chair over the antiqued table. "The Bolgariers are just a half day's ride east of here. Your mother's home more than boasts success."

"The rebels won't come here," Gertrude distantly asserted. "My mother has done far too much good for the people, *especially* the poor. She provides them medicine and medical treatment without ever asking for anything in return—her entire life, she has ignored and fought social divisions. The people know that. They *swore* to protect this house. She will be safe." Gertrude's voice panned out toward the end of her sentence. She exhaled the fear of her mother's home being attacked again. The lady slapped her knees and stood. "Let's not think about that now, Sam. Can I get you anything? Are you hungry?"

Sam smiled and could not resist chuckling, "You cook?"

"Who said anything about cooking?" Gertrude asked with a smile. "I was just going to hand you a bit of cheese, some bread, and if you're really good, I'll also grab for you a small pot of honey." She walked about the kitchen counter to retrieve the items.

"Is Sam here already?" Galina asked as she bustled into the room. "Oh good, I thought I heard your voice," she added the moment she saw him at the table. "I was so worried; a post rider was just at the door telling me about the terrible occurrence at the Bolgariers. Did you hear anything about that, Sam?"

As Gertrude joined them at the table, Sam retold to Galina all he had heard in Canaan. The three exchanged their opinions, worries, and predictions about the growing rebellion while Sam ate.

"We all must be careful these days," Galina said, pouring herself a cup of tea. "Lord knows what could potentially happen to any of us."

"Especially since we have no idea who they're after. Not really, anyway," Sam said, accepting a cup of tea. "It's like there are multiple groups with various agendas. If only they'd go to war with each other."

"Hopefully, they won't band together," Gertrude offered.

Settling the teapot in its decorative cozy back on the table, Galina looked intensely at her daughter and added, "You, Gertrude, have to be especially careful. It's a fine line you're walking."

Gertrude opened her mouth to argue, but Sam stepped in instead. "Gertrude has always been on the side of the people. She has always stood up for their rights; why should she feel especially threatened? If anything, wouldn't she be considered a rebel sympathizer?"

"I'm hardly sympathetic to their means of violence," Gertrude inserted, still stroking her cup of tea. "If it is indeed the rebels who burned the grain silos. The chaos that will cause..." She shuddered. "That was so inhumanly cruel. I cannot imagine what we will find when we return to the capital."

Swallowing hard and rubbing her throat, Galina produced a response to Sam's question. "Gertrude has to be careful because once the rebels find out that she is marrying a Malleus, they're going to think her a traitor, and God only knows what then they would do to her." She snuffled hard, doing her best not to cry.

"Mata, please, I'll be alright," Gertrude insisted. "Please, stop jinxing my luck. It's bad enough as it is."

"Gertrude, with this new attack, everything is just getting too close to home, love. I am scared for you. I know that you're an adult, and you can think for yourself, but I am not comfortable with you marrying Breyton at that castle. I've just...I have a rattling feeling throughout the depths of my soul."

Gertrude had an ill feeling as well, but she was too stubborn to share that with her mother now. She looked to Sam for guidance but found only longing in those sweet eyes of his. Though her love for Breyton was budding, she could not help but reciprocate Sam's look. Gertrude knew that he only wanted her to be happy and, as such, would do whatever she asked in an instant—everything except stop loving her.

In their silence, Galina could hear the cry from her company's hearts for each other. How she wished that her daughter could be with Sam, even though she did like Breyton; she just wished that he was not a Malleus. There was something in the look between Sam and Gertrude, something secret and undefined, that dug out a long-forsaken memory. The deeply buried skeletons of her past dug their way out through the parting of her lips: "I envy you," Galina admitted woefully, "and pity the two of you more than you may ever know."

Sam and Gertrude exchanged equally confused looks with one another.

"What do you mean?" Sam asked.

Placing her hand on Sam's, Gertrude licked her lips and informed him, "She knows about us, Sam." Turning toward Galina, she said, "But I don't know what you mean either, Mata."

Leaning back in her chair with her arms crossed over her chest, Galina decided that it was time, at last, to set the skeletons free. Looking up to the wooden ceiling, she asked her daughter, "Do you even realize how lucky you are? I know what it is like to love one that you cannot have, but count your lucky stars that you've been able to share your love these past few years and that Sam is still with you today, and tomorrow's tomorrow if ever you need him."

Gertrude and Sam exchanged a second pair of confused looks. Neither knew where this was going, and neither could have guessed if they tried.

Galina gave a deep sigh, then told her tale: "I was very young when I was arranged to marry Absalom. Sixteen. I was the daughter of a lord of Ruishland who thought my best course in life would be as a peace offering to a lord of a different country's court.

"Sam here was just a young farm boy working my uncle's lands. I doubt you would even remember a man named Taivo?" she asked Sam, and he shook his head. "He was my twin sister's and my escort from Ruishlind when we were just girls. He was a couple of years older than I; he was eighteen when I married Absalom. He had the most intense pair of eyes I had ever seen. Simply marvelous. A vision that turned heads. He would visit periodically to ensure that I was doing alright because he knew how much I hated my husband and how much I loved him." Lady Galiova smiled as she remembered Taivo's smile, his eyes, his face, his kiss. "He and I were lovers for years, from 1308 to 1316, but he was taken from me, you see. He died in my arms from an illness that I could now cure, but then I had never heard of before. That's why I became involved in medicine, so that I could save others from having their hearts broken the way that I did.

"So Sam, Gertrude, thank God for every day you have together. Do not regret a day of the secret life you've shared, for you two are not being ripped apart by tragedy." Galina stood from the table and started to leave.

"Wait, Mata!" Gertrude turned sharply around in her chair to look at her mother after realizing the meaning of her choice to share the specific years of her secret romance. "Mata! My brothers and I were born within those years. Are any of us Absalom's?"

Galina smiled and left the kitchen without a word.

After a quick look back to Sam, Gertrude leaped from her chair and darted out of the kitchen after her mother. "Mata, wait!" Gertrude hollered, chasing her mother up the stairs.

"Don't run, dear— it's not ladylike," Galina said as she calmly proceeded upstairs.

"Please answer me," Gertrude pleaded two steps behind her mother's footfalls. "Am I Absalom's? Or am I Taivo's?"

On the top step, Galina turned around and took her daughter's face in her hands. Gertrude could see the love radiating from her mother, and she finally fully understood the real reason why she was her mata's favorite. Galina smiled again and stroked her daughter's forehead. "Oh, my little girl." She snuffled back her tears and said, "You have your father's eyes."

~*~*~

It would be an understatement to say that Gertrude was thrilled to know that she did not belong by blood to Absalom Kemen. This was something that Absalom must have known. It would explain why he hated her so fiercely. It struck Gertrude that it was that wicked man's pride that had saved her; he was too proud to admit that his wife was having productive relations with a foreigner, which probably saved her mother's life. If any of the high-borns had learned this, Absalom would have become the laughingstock of the Gatherers. A man who could not control his wife was nothing in their eyes.

Even though her mother said that Taivo was present during her early childhood, try as she could, Gertrude could not remember him. She was depressed by the fact that she did not know much about her true father, not the sound of his voice or any image of his being, aside from his eyes, which she inherited.

Throughout the rest of the day and the first hour into their voyage to the capital, Gertrude asked every question she could think of to learn more about her father. Galina shared with her daughter all she could remember. It was as therapeutic for her to speak of Taivo as it was for Gertrude to learn about him.

His hair was jet black. He was tall, lean, and tan. He did have a difficult time learning the Vitenkan language, unlike Galina, who'd grown up with it in her own house. He chose only to speak Heltkor when in the presence of Galina's children so that their heritage would not be forgotten. He loved to fish, and he was an only child, but most importantly, his name was Taivo Elu, and he was Gertrude's very own father.

The few but incredibly strong facts about him kept Gertrude distracted as she, her mother, and Sam rode in a covered carriage for the castle by the sea. Having these details to focus on, served as a fantastic distraction from the worry of not knowing if Breyton arrived safely, and the fact that she was trapped in a cart with Sam.

As every minute passed, Gertrude became more and more eager to see her future husband. Galina comforted her daughter with the little assuring comments that if Breyton or Herod had met a terrible end, the entire country would know by now.

With her face plastered against the window of the cart, Gertrude watched the countryside go by and did everything in her power not to look at Sam.

~*~*~

On the second day of their travel, a road washed out by a swollen river stood as an obstacle to their journey. The carriage had to double back before resuming in the right direction by a different, longer route.

"At this rate, you might as well reschedule your wedding for June," Galina joked as she stared out the window at the large drops of rain falling from the sky. "For that, we might just get you there on time."

Gertrude was not in a joking mood. This was yet another bump in the road between her and Breyton.

Through the rain, Galina looked out her window to see the hills separating them from where her twin sister lived as a nun in the nation's oldest convent. "You know," she quietly said while still staring out the window, "I really ought to go see Katerine. Gertrude, we're going to have to stop for the night anyway before making it to the coast. Would you mind if we stopped at the convent?"

"She hates me," Gertrude said childishly. "She called me a harlot last I saw her because I was involved in politics."

There was nothing to argue. Galina knew that Katerine disapproved of her daughter's lifestyle.

"Isn't there a town just another mile that way?" Sam asked, pointing in the opposite direction of the convent. When Galina nodded, he continued, "If you want to visit your sister, we could drop you off at the convent, then Gertrude and I could go to the town's pub and wait for you there. We can have dinner, and Gertrude can have an opportunity to talk with the people while you visit."

"I think it's for the best that you and Sam find an inn for the night and then come and collect me from the convent in the morning," Galina suggested, patting her daughter on the knee. "It will be a good opportunity for you to talk to the people in the town, Gertrude. Just don't leave me there long enough for Katerine to have much of a chance to condemn or convert me."

~*~*~

The convent on the hill was a dreary place. Gertrude was grateful that she did not have to stay there for the night. The daunting shadow of the convent's edifice loomed over her and Sam in a manner that she wished she could easily forget, but that feeling stayed with her throughout the night.

The small town of Torgard was where Sam and Gertrude found a room for the night. The inn, like the town, was quiet. Sam supposed that no one was doing any excess travel these days, with the rebels running amok, even though all of the attacks thus far were on homes in the central and northeastern areas of the country.

Gertrude stood in the pub, looking at the empty tables, as Sam negotiated with the keeper for a room. This was the first time she had ever seen a place like this empty. A chill ran down her spine. *What's happening to our country? God, I hope we're not too late.*

The pair followed the old keep to their room. The second door in the dark hall opened.

There was only one bed in the room they received, even though they'd requested one with two mattresses.

They voiced this mistake, but the older woman who escorted them was too haggard to hear them as she shuffled away, blissfully ignorant of her tenants' qualms.

Sam and Gertrude stood with their backs to the closed door, awkwardly staring at the one bed.

As if being in the carriage with Sam was not awkward enough, Gertrude thought.

Finding the moment to be a bit too uncomfortable for his taste, Sam cleared his throat and asked Gertrude if she was hungry.

"A little," she answered as she sat on the bed, sinking a reasonable distance into the mattress. "Hmm, a bit too firm, this," she said, patting the dusty mattress while Sam dug through his bag in search of the rye bread, cold sausage, and apples he'd packed.

"Here you are," he said, giving Gertrude a serving of each. She thanked him and took a small bite of the bread. Her stomach was far too full of butterflies to accept food. She waited for Sam to sit down, but he continued to hover by his bag, leaning against the wall.

"Aren't you going to sit?" she asked.

All there was to sit on in the cramped room was the old mattress. The gentleman did want to sit, but he knew that it was no longer appropriate for him to be on a bed with Gertrude in any way, shape, or position, even if they were simply sharing a meal. "I'd prefer to stand," Sam said, "Stretch m' legs a bit, you know? We've been sitting for so long. My back's just killing me."

Gertrude sat up straight and opened her mouth to offer to rub it for him, but denying her force of habit, she quickly shut it and shrank back on the bed. For a very long while, the pair remained in their positions of awkward and forced restraint.

Gertrude sighed and made popping sounds with her lips.

Sam touched his fingers to his arm or his face to scratch an imagined itch.

"How are we going to survive this, Sam?" Gertrude asked, shattering the uncomfortable reverie.

Shrugging, Sam answered, "We're just going to have to somehow." He clenched his jaw and shut his eyes. "I don't like it at all. I know you *have* to marry Breyton and that you can't be with me for so many reasons, but that doesn't make it any easier." He looked at her. The hurt in her eyes calmed his temper and returned warmth to his tone as he said, "Come on, Gertrude. You're strong. You'll be fine. You'll be so distracted with your marriage to Breyton, and the rearing of your family that I'm sure will come very soon, and I'll be the most attentive father and proprietor that this country has ever known." Sam offered a weak smile to assure Gertrude that his words were true, though he did not believe in them. "Life will go on."

Biting the tip of her thumbnail, Gertrude scoffed, then said, "So it'll only be in the quiet time, like late at night when sleep will not come, that it'll be alright for me to reflect and realize how much I miss you?"

"You can miss me anytime you want, Gertrude," Sam corrected, leaning as far back against the wall as physics would allow. "Just don't let the memories of me distract you from the time you have with Breyton and your future family." Sam looked straight up. It was the only thing he could think to do to keep tears from falling. *She's always been too good for you. Let her go.*

Gertrude ran her fingers up across her forehead and through her hair. She nodded. What else could she do? She inhaled deeply. Her heart was in her throat. Staring at the light from the hall creeping in under the closed door, Gertrude chuckled as she recalled the night of the ball. "Sam," she looked back up at him as she spoke, "the night of the ball, Breyton, the blighter, asked me if I ever 'danced' with you."

Sam rolled his eyes. He smiled, then said, "Of course he did. What did you say?"

Smiling, Gertrude took a deep breath, then answered, "I told him that we didn't because it was inappropriate or something." She exhaled, then added, "In reality, can you remember the last time we danced?"

No, he could not. Sam doubted that they ever had. The memory he procured seemed so gray, so outdated, that it felt more like a scene that came from a distant dream than from something that truly happened. Both slowly came to realize that they never had, but neither was willing to admit so sad a fact. Sam did not like the depressed look that crossed Gertrude. He could not stand to have a lady depressed in his company. Sam abandoned his post on the wall. He held out his hand. She stared at him, puzzled by his demeanor, but she was thoroughly content to see so charming a smile on his face.

"Will you dance with me?" he asked.

"Here? Now?"

Sam looked down. "We may never again have this chance."

She sighed and took his hand.

The gentleman led the lady to the largest spot of open floor in that cramped and dusty room. Wrapping his arm around her waist, he held her hand against his heart. As Gertrude put her other hand around Sam's back, she whispered, "But there's no music."

Sam took in a deep breath and slowly started to dance with Gertrude regardless of her statement. "If you listen closely," he whispered, "I think you'll hear the music playing."

Music or not, Gertrude failed to care. She was in Sam's arms. She rested her head against his chest as he started to hum a gentle tune.

While Sam and Gertrude indulged in their dance, back in Maltoro, Herod leaned on a windowsill staring out at the clouds hovering menacingly in the night, depressed and disappointed by the news that Breyton brought with him from Forsythia Valley. While Gertrude and Sam succumbed to their passions, and while Herod and Breyton shared their brotherly talk, the rebels waged war on the house of Philemon.

33

The Streets of Maltoro

ire will smite the high-borns from their might.

F"That's certainly welcoming," Galina commented after reading the sign written over the gate leading into the capital. She leaned back into the bench of the seat and said to Gertrude, "We can still turn back."

Gertrude stared out her window. There was now the immense amount of painted words on nearly every wall along the road to Maltoro calling for the king's head.

"No," Gertrude corrected. "There is no going back."

The cart rolled over the irregular cobblestone streets that beggars lined. The tattered rags that they wore were barely distinguishable from their flesh, both equally strewn in filth. The people looked more like spirits of the lost; their heads bowed down, their bodies barely able to sustain the weight of their skulls.

As their carriage rolled on, Gertrude spotted a woman, crouched on a corner, cradling her babe. The mother gently stroked her baby's face, love, and reverence upon her own, though death had already taken her babe away. The people passing by her did not give her a second glance, but Gertrude would never forget the look on that woman's face.

"How will these people survive the winter?" Galina asked, turning with tear-filled eyes to her daughter.

Gertrude's stomach clenched as she said, "Many won't. This is the worst I've ever seen them."

Hunger had taken over the streets of Maltoro, and hunger would soon drive the capital to its knees.

The carriage arrived through a series of security checks through the gates of the king's home.

"It's nice to see this much security," Sam said, hoping to make some light out of the darkness their carriage rolled through.

Gertrude did not answer. She was focused on so many things other than the people in the cart with her.

The cart rolled to a stop, and at that moment, the castle door opened. Everything around Gertrude disappeared.

There, waiting for her between the proud columns of Maltoro's entry, was Breyton.

Gertrude jumped out of the cart and threw herself into Breyton's arms. She held him as if it had been a year since they'd parted. The guilt she felt for her last night with Sam and her fear of never seeing Breyton again clashed and fell from her eyes in tears. "I was so worried," Gertrude explained into his chest.

Breyton held her tight. "It's alright," Breyton soothed. "It's all going to be alright." His words were strong, but he was not so sure himself. "I hate to ask this so soon, but did you hear about Yuri?"

Gertrude pushed herself away. "What about Yuri?"

Breyton looked up, his eyes lining with tears. He shut his eyes, then looked back at her. "He…his house was…"

Gertrude shook her head. "No, please, no."

Breyton cleared his throat and sighed heavily. "We heard just a few minutes ago: Yuri's home was burned to the ground. As far as we know…" He bit his lip. "As far as we know, Yuri was inside."

"Oh, Breyton." Gertrude pulled him back close to her. Yuri had never been her friend, but he had been a voice for the people and close to Breyton. "I'm so sorry. This doesn't make sense."

"Nothing makes sense." Breyton kissed her brow. When he looked up, he saw Sam helping Galina out of the cart. His stomach tightened. *Of course. Sam is back*, he thought. Breyton bowed his head to Galina as he held Gertrude.

Seeing the tension between the two men, Galina said, "With everything so uncertain, I called for Sam to escort us. We cannot be too careful now."

Breyton agreed with this. He nodded to Sam. "Thank you," said the prince. "Thank you for getting them here safely."

"Breyton," Gertrude said, still being held in his arms. "Yuri was just behind me in the favor of the people. It makes *no* sense that he was targeted. Have you had an opportunity to talk with Herod? Of the silos, of us? How important is it for us to be traditionalists and marry here? Forgive me, but I value our lives a bit more than archaic practices, no matter how sacred they may be."

"Gertrude." Breyton looked down solemnly. He ushered her away from her mother and Sam so that they could enter the castle and speak more privately. "Shall we?" he asked of their company. Sam and Galina saw the hint and respectfully remained a few strides behind.

As they ascended the stairs toward the entryway of the castle, Breyton quietly said, "I have spoken to Herod. He was not thrilled that you chose me over him, but he's a bit distracted with everything else happening. He has agreed to open up the royal stores, and he has sent out diplomats throughout the country to beg for aid."

"Who are the diplomats?" Gertrude quickly asked. "Who could he have possibly chosen?"

Breyton shook his head. "I don't know. That'll be a question for

Herod. As far as us leaving..." He looked over his shoulder, back at the city. He thought of the sunken eyes that he had seen as he rode in undercover, dressed like a merchant. He recalled the outstretched skeletal hands and the thought that had crossed his mind as he saw them: *Are they reaching out for coins or the mercy of death?* He sighed heavily, then said, "I don't think we'll be able to leave for some time."

Gertrude nodded. This had also crossed her mind. The pair wandered into the castle, leaving Sam and Galina to make their way.

Sam watched Gertrude for as long as he could until Galina placed a supportive hand on his shoulder and asked him to walk with her.

Down one of the halls, close to where they first met, Gertrude quietly asked Breyton, "Do we still want to marry amid all of this? It doesn't feel right to be celebrating our life moving forward while so many are suffering."

"We don't have much choice in that now," Breyton informed her. "Herod's picked a date for us."

Her shoulders dropped. "Please say that you're joking."

No charming smile rose between the prince's smooth, long cheeks. He put his hands on his hips and somberly answered, "He wants us to wait until the twenty-fourth. His diplomats are due back to report on the twenty-third. He thinks that things may be smoothed over by them."

"So long." Gertrude looked morosely out the window at the recently abandoned Council Hall. The Gatherers had stopped gathering indefinitely for fear of their lives. Too many concerns consumed Gertrude's thoughts for her to appreciate that her desire to see the Council dissolved had been fulfilled. "The rebels could raze this city to the ground and begin rebuilding in that time."

"I know, but..." Breyton looked up and down the hall to see if anyone was around. "Since I left your mother's house, I've sent letters to all the faithful men who served under me while I was in the military to come here to protect Maltoro. They have sworn their allegiance and their swords to safeguard the crown. They should all be here by then."

"How many men are we talking about?" Gertrude asked, knowing that "swords" meant the troops that officers called their own.

Quickly adding up the numbers in his head, Breyton answered after a moment, "I'll have a better understanding of how many soon, but as of right now, it's anywhere between twenty-five hundred to five thousand men."

"Breyton!" Gertrude exclaimed. "You have your own army."

"Just for you," Breyton said with a wink. "It wasn't for nothing I stayed in the military for so long."

"Thank God you did," Gertrude said, placing her hand lovingly on Breyton's heart. She swallowed hard, then looked out to the gray clouds lingering in the sky through a nearby window. She had always imagined that the weeks leading up to her wedding would be filled with excitement and planning. The nerves growing in her gut were not exactly the type she had anticipated, and they were not the distraction from pre-wedding jitters that she would have hoped for. "I want a small wedding, nothing loud or complicated. I want a private event, just our families and a few—a very few—guests, no bells and whistles or balls. We don't want to boast of our positions."

"You don't want something at least mildly fancy?" Breyton asked, somewhat surprised to hear a lady wanting a simple wedding even under the present circumstances.

Nodding, Gertrude answered, "Yes, of course. Breyton, it's not about the party or the church, the ring, or the dress. All that matters is the quality of the man." She kissed Breyton's chin and sighed.

"Speaking of rings…" Breyton reached into his pocket. "It's time I do this right." With the mild discomfort in his body that remained from the summer's scars, Breyton kneeled and held Gertrude's hand. "Though I already know your answer, I thought it'd be good to double-check." He revealed a ring that would shame the adornments of a god. The thick golden band with the shimmering marquise diamonds Breyton offered was the single genuine hint he had yet made of his wealth. "You still sure you want to marry me?"

She looked up to clear her eyes, and, for a moment, she thought she saw a face quickly dart behind a wall, but she ignored the brief sighting of a ghost to see the ring again. "I'd marry you, Breyton, even if you hadn't given me so fine a ring." She bent down and kissed the prince as he slid it onto her finger. He stood, and they continued to kiss. The ring was heavy, Gertrude noticed, and not for nothing: three small circular diamonds surrounded the large centerpiece, and the thick band was embellished with even smaller diamonds. She kept staring at it as Breyton held her. It felt curiously powerful, and that surprised her.

So this is what it is like to wear an engagement ring.

"Gertrude." Breyton slid his hands down to her elbows so that he could speak to her properly. "This is probably not the best time to say this, but Herod wants to see you…alone."

"To kill me, no doubt," Gertrude joked, but the weight of her words felt true. "Now?" Upon seeing Breyton's confirming nod, she sighed. "Well, alright. Will you come with me? I'll show you where I listen in on the king's meetings."

Hand in hand, Gertrude and Breyton turned and walked to the king's office together, but the phantom face that she had glimpsed headed in the opposite direction, snaking its way out from the castle's walls and into the city. Through the muddy streets mostly abandoned from the cold, heavy rains, the young, red-haired stranger trooped to a borough rarely seen by the likes of Gertrude and Breyton. The young man walked to the end of an alley to a shadow draped in a full-length cloak. The pale lad swallowed hard, then said, "I have the date for you, Duke Malleus."

"Be quiet, you fool!" the duke snapped, inflating his body to look as though he was about to strike the lad. "No one must know that I am here, do you understand? No one!"

"Y-yes, sir," the young man apologized, bowing. "Th-they're to marry on the twenty-fourth of this month, sir."

"You're sure?" Donovan asked, rubbing his neck. The twenty-fourth was so far away. He was worried that he would not be able to keep the rebels under his control for so long a time. Their resolve was in question, especially after they'd failed to dispose of his older brother. Donovan whispered to himself, "What in hellfire am I to do with them over the next few weeks?"

"I heard it from the horse's mouth, sir," the lad assured him, hearing the domineering man's conundrum. The lad was scared. He kept hoping that Donovan would live up to his promise to pay him for this intelligence and not strike him down instead.

Donovan slowly paced the width of the alley as the lad nervously watched. The duke wanted to strike on the seventeenth, but he agreed with his partner that it should be done on the day of the wedding since Gertrude had rubbed her way into his accursed family. Some sort of dramatic revenge on both their ends was now desperately needed.

"Sir, if you want, I could get more information for you—it was nothing at all," the cold and red-lipped lad said, unable to stand the insecurity of the silence.

"No, no, m' boy, you've done enough, and don't worry." Donovan reached into his pocket and pulled out two gold coins. "My word is as good as my honor." The duke tossed the two coins at the lad, who gladly caught them. The young man thanked the duke, turned his back, and started to head out from the alley.

But secrets may be kept by two people if only one is alive. A dagger pierced through the lad's back and out the front of his chest. The young man, paralyzed from the agony and the shock, fell to the ground, where the wound from the blade would eventually take his life.

The two coins slipped from the dying boy's hand and into the mud and muck of the alley.

Donovan stepped over the boy's body and knelt to teach the lad one final lesson: "It's a shame that my honor is not worth anything, isn't it?" The duke pulled his dagger out from the lad's back and took the coins from the ground. After cleaning his blade on the boy's shoulder, he left the alley with his hood pulled almost entirely over his head, while the boy's mother, contently awaiting the return of her boy, would not know for days that her only son was dead.

~*~*~

"Aleksie, will you excuse us, please?" Herod asked of his right-hand man when Gertrude arrived at his office alone. "Just stand outside the door and wait there."

Aleksie did as he was told. He left the room with a glare in his eyes and a scowl on his face directed solely at the woman who broke his king's best chance for securing his line.

I suppose I deserved that, Gertrude surmised.

"Now that we are alone..." Herod lounged back in his chair in a position so relaxed that he looked like he was preparing to settle in for a brief rest. The king had not easily caught sleep. Since Gertrude was last in his presence, he had matured. Dramatic aging was a consequence of being ripped from one's comfortable cave to stand naked in the light. Herod's entire world had turned. His empire of lavish indulgences was no longer at his fingertips. He had, at last, become fully aware of what he had personally engaged and inflamed.

The wall of rain cascading outside seemed to fit the sorrow reigning over his heart perfectly.

"Your Majesty," Gertrude started, but Herod shook his head and held his hand up. He wanted to speak first.

"Gertrude, I assure you that I am not angry," the king said, turning

279

his sad blue eyes to her. "I will not pretend that I am not upset about you denying me, but when we were children, Breyton always had the best of everything—the best education, the best military training, the best horses—so why should that change now? In your eyes, he is the better man. Breyton is the 'charming one,' after all." Herod gave a bland smile to Gertrude and he swayed a little in his seat. "Oh yes, he's also not the one who people are asking to be beheaded."

"Your Majesty, please." Gertrude walked to the opposite side of the desk from the king and implored that she be heard through. "It's not that Breyton is the 'better man,' it's just that I prefer his quiet lifestyle over yours. Please understand, Herod, I'm in my mid-twenties, and I'm already considering retirement. I've been in this castle for most of my life, and I am ready to start settling down in a tame environment away from court." Gertrude rubbed the tip of her finger on the top of the desk. "I cannot tell you how flattered I was and still am that you, Your Majesty, consider me honorable enough to be your wife and queen. You are a dear friend of mine, Herod, and my loyalty to you as my king is as resolute as ever it has been."

Herod smiled. He did understand. He did not blame Gertrude for not wanting to live in the castle, especially during these uncertain times. "Gertrude, can I say something to you that you won't run off to tell Sam or Breyton?"

Before nodding to the king, Gertrude stopped herself from looking at the double mirror behind which Breyton stood listening in on this interview.

Herod buried his head in his hands. The past few weeks without Gertrude had been a disaster with all the rebellions, abandonments, and betrayals raining down upon his fortress. He feared that soon the walls that he'd designed would be tumbling down on top of him. "Gertrude, I ruled this country without fear or any sort of reservation. I thought I was the ruler of its people, and I thought I had their respect and admiration. I used to gamble and host marvelous parties. I wore the finest outfits money could buy, but now I see that the throne I've perched on and preached from is made of nothing more than bundles of straw. My head may still bear the crown, but I do not rule anymore. I never did. *They* do. Absalom…the rebels…but never me.

"It won't be long before they come. I just hope that it'll be after Breyton's men arrive, as they will stand an honest chance against the revolutionaries.

"I can't sleep at night. I lie in bed and wonder how many more will have to die because of me. How many more innocents will be burned alive or butchered because of hatred against the king? A sovereign who could not provide for his people? I've let so many down, especially you and Breyton…He is so angry with me, and rightfully so.

"I can't even protect my people." Herod picked up from the table a half-empty bottle of vodka that Gertrude had only just noticed. He poured it straight down his throat, disregarding the sting. Though he had been with Aleksie, Herod had been drinking alone. "I pity whatever fool wants to be king," Herod mumbled under his breath. With another deep drink, he added, "I don't envy the next, but I wish him luck, whoever he may be. I can't help to wonder…would it have been this way…if Breyton had been king?"

"Your Majesty," Gertrude started, but yet again, Herod held up his hand to stop her.

"You may go," Herod firmly said.

Gertrude did not hesitate. She immediately turned to leave. As she hurried out the door, she heard Herod say, "Stay safe."

By the secret door at the tunnel to the king's office, Breyton and Gertrude met. "How was it?" the prince asked. "I couldn't hear what he was saying. It didn't look pleasant."

In a way, she was grateful that he hadn't heard it all. She knew the high regard that Herod carried for Breyton, so she prayed that he had not heard his brother's words.

Breyton would have been a stronger king, a better king. Things would be different now, but this was their reality. It did no one good to regret the past, but she knew that Breyton would if he did not do so already. Gertrude took a deep breath, then answered the only way she could. "Oh, well, it went brilliantly, but, um, Sam took my tobacco and pipe, so I'm going to meet my mother for a drink. Come along if you want."

The prince wanted to know what happened, so of course, he followed. Being careful to edit from the synopsis anything alluding to what their country would be like if Breyton were king, Gertrude divulged to her fiancé what had passed. Once he knew, he joined Gertrude and her mother to see if it was possible to drown their sorrows.

34

The Wedding

"Are you ready, my lady?" a servant girl asked the woman dressed in white.

The color did not feel appropriate, but the lady was not about to admit that in a church on her wedding day. Gertrude shrugged off the feeling and answered, "Almost. I'll be ready in just a few minutes. Please find my mother and bring her to me." Gertrude did not look away from the mirror she used to dab makeup on her face as she addressed the servant. She was too busy concentrating on getting her painted lines above her eyelashes right. She did not regret dismissing the servants who were sent to paint her face. She thought it shamefully lazy for ladies to have other people apply their highlighting.

The servant girl bowed and left the bride's waiting room to find Galina.

Gertrude was left alone to finish getting ready. She lightly stroked powdered blush on her cheeks with a soft, thick round brush. All that was left were her lips. She stared at the small, round vial of dark red paint in her hand, unable to do anything else. This entire wedding seemed much more like a scene from a dream than a thing of reality.

The past week had been riddled with silence, and that disturbed her beyond belief. The last attack from the revolutionaries happened nine days ago on a former general's home, a few leagues south of the city's gates. They could see the smoke rising from the castle's halls. She knew that this wedding was a horrible, wretched idea for these times and circumstances, but it was the king's wish. It felt much more like one of Herod's opulent parties than the humble wedding she had desired. However stupid, it had to be obeyed.

Gertrude and Breyton did what they could and spent as much time together as possible. They did not know how much time they had left. With her bodyguard Sam not far away, Breyton and Gertrude continued to send correspondence to their contacts throughout the people, trying to do what they could to prevent the creaking dam from breaking.

The castle was under quarantine from the outer world. The king did not want the rebels infiltrating the walls of this fortress he'd built. The castle was his lady, and he was doing everything he could to protect her. Soldiers had fortified the walls. From the guns at the docks, naval demonstrations of strength echoed loudly through the cobblestoned streets. The King's Guard and Breyton's men marched endlessly.

A knock came to the door, bringing Gertrude from her distant stare. "Come in," she said, thinking that it would be the reflection of her mother she would see in the mirror, but no. Her painted eyes looked into the glass and saw a man she loved come through the door.

Gertrude whipped around in the chair to look at Sam.

He was stunned. She had never looked more beautiful.

They stared at each other for a moment before he came slowly closer.

She stood.

The dress she wore was long and contoured to every curve of her body. The material was light, elegant, and looked ever so slightly like feathers. Sam smiled; he could not help but think that she looked like a swan. "You look beautiful," Sam was finally able to admit, though he felt like the sight of her tore away from him everything he knew, even speech.

"Thank you," she quietly said, looking down; she could not look him in the eye.

Sam saw how she bent her head as though in shame. He felt miserable, knowing that his presence did this to her. He looked down at her hand to see the impressive ring Breyton had picked out for her. Sam took her hand in his to have a better look at the diamonds he could never afford. "He did good," Sam said, complimenting the ring. He swallowed hard, then added, "But he got it all wrong."

Gertrude turned up her shimmering eyes.

Smiling ironically, Sam recalled what Gertrude had told him a long time ago. "You wanted a thin white-gold band, with five small round diamonds embedded."

Gertrude pulled him into a tight embrace. She sobbed into his chest.

He held her close and let his tears freely drop onto her shoulder. "Don't cry." He snuffled. "You'll have to do your makeup all over."

Gertrude took care to wipe her eyes without too seriously smudging her art, but her tears would not stop. Sam held her close. He could not let go. His eyes were so full of sadness, which made her worry deeply for him. Pulling away so that she could speak to him, Gertrude pointed her finger authoritatively at his heart. "Samuel Maison of Legrette, I want you to promise me something: promise me that no matter what happens, you'll always be true to yourself and your son. Please, Sam, I couldn't live a day if I knew you did yourself harm because of me."

He would never admit it, but the thought had crossed his mind. In the deepest recesses, it whispered sickly sweetly to him. However, the clarion that pulled him from the darkness was the thought of his son.

Sam pulled her closer. "I would never do that, Gertrude, but I don't know how I'll live knowing that you're willingly marrying into a family that the entire nation seems hell-bent on destroying. Even Donovan's house was attacked this morning."

"What?" Gertrude asked, pushing herself back to see if she'd heard correctly.

"It's true," Sam confirmed. "He wasn't injured apparently, but his stables and a part of his home were burned."

Gertrude fell into the chair behind her, clutching her face in her hands. She heard the wings of all her conspiracy theories about Donovan flutter out the window. She raised her gaze to the ceiling as if hoping the divine would present answers in pity of her situation, but all she saw was a crystal chandelier that needed a dusting. "What am I doing, Sam? You must think me such a fool."

"Not a fool," Sam assured her, kneeling in front of her and taking her hands in his. "You've such a brave and lovely soul. God, how I wish that it was me you were marrying so that you would at least be guaranteed safety. I will die if anything happens to you."

"You're here, Sam," she said, putting his hand on her heart. "You'll always be here with me. Always. Because I know this, I am not afraid. You will always be the strength in my heart."

The door opened.

Sam popped up from the ground, and Gertrude quickly wiped her face clean of the tears with her sleeve.

Galina entered the room with the maid a step behind her.

"Uh, will you go and see if the groom's ready?" She quickly pushed back the servant, being sure to block her from seeing Sam and Gertrude. The servant was not given a chance to answer. Galina closed the door in her face.

Galina walked to the two and put one hand on both of their faces. She smiled warmly, then said, "Bless you both for your strength."

She kissed Sam on the cheek. "To you for all your service to my daughter, your love, your devotion, and the protection you've given her unconditionally. Thank you, Sam." The mother started to cry. "And Gertrude, my baby girl." She framed Gertrude's face and rubbed away her daughter's tears with her thumbs. "Do not be afraid. You were made for this role, love. You are so strong, far stronger than I. You will see this through. You've more than proven your courage and resilience to any challenge this world presents you." She kissed her daughter and whispered to her, "I almost wish that Breyton was the king or that you were marrying Herod instead. With you at the side of the king, all of this would be fixed. You would have made a queen to be feared, loved, and remembered. Long would it be told, the legend of the queen who tamed the animal court."

~*~*~

The wedding ceremony went without a hitch. Breyton never looked more handsome to Gertrude in his military suit of black, red, and gold. When she saw him standing at the altar, all the stress and worry, all the fear and anxiety were gone. Breyton was there smiling brilliantly at her, for her, and that was all she needed.

They said their vows and sealed their marriage with the words of the priest. The small congregation clapped for the new couple. Galina was so proud of her daughter, yet she grieved for the man who sat beside her.

Sam watched quietly. He did not allow himself to cry. He loved her too much to ruin her garden that was just beginning to seed.

Following the ceremony, the dinner and the traditional dance were quiet like Gertrude wanted, but Herod still managed to add his decorative touch. The party consisted mainly of Breyton's friends and fellow officers, who arrived as predicted in time for their wedding. They ate in a room half the size of the dining hall where the court of animals dined and sinned. This was an event of innocence, so a clean environment was required. The room was beautifully decorated with banners of gold and white. Herod wanted this wedding, even though he was not a part of it, to be spectacular for his brother and sister-in-law. They deserved only the best. He watched Gertrude dancing in Breyton's arms, smiling and laughing to whatever it was his brother was whispering in her ear. She was so beautiful, so elegant on the small dance floor. Herod reflected on this as he sat with a woman he barely knew. This woman was pretty, though not at all like Gertrude. He'd brought her as his partner to this event with a brooding Aleksie looming not so far behind. The blonde beside the king would satisfy him for the night, but the thing between Gertrude and Breyton, the slightly drunk Herod had to think, *that* was forever. He wondered what forever felt like as he brought another shot of vodka to his lips.

Though the situation beyond the doors of Maltoro was spiraling beyond control, Gertrude and Breyton danced on the floor with hope in their eyes. They were happy. Genuinely happy. Nothing in the world could distract them from their night, their romance. Save one thing: toward the second hour of their celebration, Gertrude noticed that Sam was missing. She felt unnerved by this. She went to her mother while Breyton spoke to one of his friends. The new Lady Malleus let down her glass of wine on the table and whispered to her mother, "Have you seen Sam?"

"How many of those have you had?" Galina asked, pointing to Gertrude's drink, totally ignoring her daughter's question.

"This is only my second," Gertrude answered, even though it was her third. She asked again, "Have you seen Sam?"

"I have, but you do realize that it is *Breyton* to whom you are married?" Skipping the answer to her thickly sarcastic question, Galina motioned to the small balcony behind Gertrude. The young wife turned to see the man standing alone with his back to the party. Turning to her mother, Gertrude asked, "Do you think I should talk to him?"

Galina shook her head. "Looks like you don't have to." She motioned for Gertrude to look again. Breyton was approaching Sam from behind. Taking a sip from her fruited spirits, she added, "I'm sure it will be a civil meeting between them."

The glass in Sam's hand was nearly drained. The cold night air was refreshing to his hot cheeks and pinked face. He brought the glass to his lips again and finished off what was left. The night was dark. A dense cloud cover loomed overhead. Sam thought, *All of this will soon be covered with a thick and impenetrable layer of snow. How cold the winters here can be! So cruel. Hardly anyone travels for fear of the flurries and the dangers of the storms; well, anyone except Gertrude. She seems to find delight in the adventure of it all.*

Sam closed his eyes and squeezed the sides of his empty glass. He was trying so hard not to think about her, but he simply could not help it. Every thought always came back to her.

"Sam?" Breyton quietly called as he stepped out into the cold air of the balcony. "Do you mind if I join you?"

Looking at the prince over his shoulder, Sam permitted him.

A tad uneasily, Breyton stood beside Sam. The prince had come out intending to have a heart-to-heart with his old friend, but without the invitation to speak, he was not sure if he could. Clearing his throat, Breyton made several attempts to start the conversation until finally, after gulping a considerable helping of the oat stout from his glass, he plucked up the courage to say, "How're you doing?"

Sam shut his eyes and tightened his grip on the glass in his hand. "Oh, brilliantly," he responded. "Just brilliantly, Breyton. I get to sneak you and my former lover out of the city and back to your cozy country home in the north tomorrow, where you'll make babies while I get to go home to a marriage as cold as our winters…How do you think I'm doing?" Sam wished he had more liquor, but being a man of control, he knew he had already imbibed enough for the night.

However, Breyton was good for at least three more rounds, so he took a few more gulps from his thick, almost chocolate-tasting stout. "Sam, I think you have more than enough reason and right to hate me—"

"I don't hate you, Breyton," Sam interrupted peacefully, turning to face the prince. "I just can't stand the situation, you know? You don't love someone that hard, and that long for this…It's not supposed to be this way."

Breyton nodded, then added, "If it's of any consolation, I swear to you that I love her and that I will protect her with every breath I take."

Sam smiled softly. If there was any man in the world that he would want to take care of Gertrude if he could not, it was Breyton. "I know," Sam said. He extended his hand to Breyton. The prince and the protector shook hands, and while they did, Sam added, "Promise me that you'll always be there for her. She needs to have your constant love and devotion. Anytime she says she doesn't, that's when she needs your protection most."

"She'll always have it," Breyton swore, patting Sam on the shoulder. "I promise you that every waking moment she will have it."

"Breyton," Gertrude's soft voice beckoned as she stepped up to the balcony doors. She had been watching the whole time. "It's getting late." She nervously played with her wedding ring as she kept looking from Sam to Breyton. "If we want to leave early tomorrow, we'd better get some rest and, um, you know, sleep off the alcohol we've all consumed." Her light joke was not received as she'd anticipated, but at least the message was comprehended.

The prince nodded, then turned to Sam to wish him good night.

With a heavy heart, Sam watched Breyton loop his arm around Gertrude's as they left the balcony, the ballroom, and the hall. His throat was dry; he wanted to return to call for another scotch or two, but what would be the point? At any rate, he had a long ride ahead of him tomorrow. He did not want to take a headache along with him on the journey.

35

A Flash of Silver

1 A single scream shattered the night.
  Heart pounding, Gertrude was ripped from her comfortable sleep.

The sudden movement woke her sleeping husband. "What's wrong?" he drowsily asked.

With her eyes shut tight, she strained her ears to hear if anything else was stirring. After a while, she licked her lips, then quietly answered, "I thought I heard a scream."

"Is that what that was?" Breyton asked, quickly removing himself from the bed. "I thought I dreamt it." His hearing issue prevented him from being as disturbed by the sound as Gertrude had been.

Out in the courtyard below their room, a window shattered.

Breyton ran to the window, using the wall to shield him so his silhouette would not be seen by anyone below. He looked down at the courtyard, where he caught a disturbing scene.

"Gertrude, get dressed," Breyton ordered as he watched shadows creep across the baileys below with shining, silvery swords unsheathed.

"What's happening?" Gertrude inquired, her voice pleading with the hope that the revolutionaries did not choose her wedding night to unleash their cruel intentions.

"Nothing good. Come on, get dressed." Breyton rushed to his trunk on the side of the bed, threw it open, and pulled out appropriate clothes for the occasion. "Wear your travel clothes and your dark cloak, something inconspicuous."

Gertrude squirmed out from under the blanket and rushed to her bag, where her travel clothes lay atop already. She felt a little dizzy for a moment. Her head still felt light after drinking at the party only a few hours ago, but she was able to pull on her dress without too much difficulty. "What are you planning?" she asked as Breyton looped his sword sheath into his belt.

He turned to speak to his wife in the dark, but a hidden trap-door on the other side of the room swung open, landing with a thud.

Sam popped up from the secret passage with his sword drawn. "I'm sorry for the intrusion," he quickly apologized, "but there's no time for propriety. Breyton, *they're* here."

Turning away from her husband, into whose arms she had jumped, Gertrude looked at Sam as she fussed with tying her bodice to say, "How did you get here so quickly? We only just heard the scream."

"I was already aware of their presence before the scream, but Gertrude, this isn't the time; I have to get you two out of here." Sam, having never made it to his room for bed in the first place, said, "You're knee-deep in royal blood, and I'll not see either of yours spilled. Come on, you two, hurry up."

"Sam." Breyton finished strapping his boots, then walked over to his friend as his wife finished her dressing. "Your sister's place—it's not far from here?"

"No, not at all," Sam answered. "It's over on Falcon's Eye."

The prince nodded. The newly married man inhaled deeply, put his hands on his hips, then quietly said to the bodyguard, "I want you to take Gertrude to your sister's and wait there until I come to collect her."

"Excuse me?" Gertrude's piercing stare cut through the darkness to glare at her husband. "Breyton, you're coming with us."

The prince shook his head.

"But we've only just married." Gertrude's heart swelled with the fear that her first night with her husband would be her last. "N-no, Breyton, I won't let you. You're coming with us."

Breyton walked to Gertrude and pulled her against him. He hated that he would be parting from her in such a manner, but this was something that had to be done. "Gertrude, you're going to go with Sam. I have to stay and defend this castle. Even though I've turned my back on this city and the crown, Maltoro is and always will be my home. I have every intention of defending its keep from the pestilence that seeks to destroy these walls." Breyton kissed his wife dearly.

Sam looked away.

When the prince's lips left the lady's, he smiled brightly, gave her a wink, then sweetly said, "Now I am immortal." He kissed her again, then turned to Sam. "Don't let anything happen to her, Sam."

Gertrude squeezed her husband's hand, then went to her bodyguard. "Be careful, Breyton. *Please*, be safe."

The prince nodded and said, "God be with you both. Gertrude, I love you. I assure you, my love, you won't be able to get rid of me this easily." Breyton smiled and winked at his wife. He waited to ensure that she and her bodyguard were through the secret passage before exiting through the room's doors.

She hoped the heels of his boots disappearing beyond the secret door was not the last she would see of her husband.

A long set of dark, narrow stairs twisted their way through the castle and down to the sewer system below the city. Sam and Gertrude trod these stairs quietly with a small torch.

"What about my mother?" Gertrude asked, stopping in her tracks. "I won't leave without her, Sam."

Being a few steps ahead of his lady, Sam stopped and swiveled back on his heels. "We would have to leave this passage," he grimly pointed out. "We won't be safe."

"I don't care," Gertrude quickly rebutted. "I can't leave her here."

The thought of leaving the safe halls to enter those potentially crawling with bloodthirsty revolutionaries was not appealing to Sam. Still, he realized that he could not live with himself if anything happened to Galina.

The pair changed direction and went down another landing's worth of steps to leave this passage for another. The vast system of tunnels in the castle was a network of complex webs that luckily Gertrude knew by heart. The flat secret hall they followed would lead them to the proper floor on which her mother was settled, but the exit would drop them off nowhere near the room where she would be sleeping. They would have to be extremely cautious if they were to make it through this alive.

When they came upon the painting that would allow them entrance into the well-trod halls, Sam whispered to Gertrude that she was not to make a sound in reaction to whatever they saw or heard. They could not be caught.

Leaving the torch in a bracket in the hall, the two were ready.

Pushed slowly open by Sam's hand, the painting unveiled the hidden aperture. Sam hopped out with his sword at the ready.

He peered up and down the hall. All looked still.

He gave a hand to Gertrude to help her jump down from the painting, for the hole was several feet from the ground. She clung to his side as they scurried down the dark passage headed for her mother.

They heard men grumbling not too far from them in a nearby hall as they came upon the right door. Without hesitating, Sam opened it.

A flash of silver swung for Sam's neck.

36

A Red Night

Sam dropped to the ground, the blade just missing him.

Gertrude jumped into her mother's room, seeing two other men holding Galina hostage.

The man who swung at Sam did not hesitate, swinging again at him.

Sam lurched from the ground and hit the opponent's swings match for match. The clanging of their blades clashed loudly in the small space.

Gertrude watched helplessly as her bodyguard fought.

Sam's swings were matching the foe's until Sam tumbled over a trunk. With a thud, he fell onto his back.

His opponent raised his blade to strike.

Sam kicked the offender's knee, which made a sickening snap.

The opponent dropped his sword and screamed as he collapsed.

"Kill her!" he shrieked from the ground to his compatriot, who had been watching the fight before him.

Terrified of what he may have caused, Sam looked up to the man who held a knife to Galina's throat. The villain gave her cheek a quick kiss.

But before he could press the blade to her skin, a vase shattered over the back of his head.

The brute fell over unconscious with glass rammed in his skull, dragging down Galina with him. Gertrude stood behind, holding the remnants of the vase in her hands.

The conscious brute on the floor squealed in pain, grasping at his knee.

"What about him?" Gertrude asked Sam as she drew her mother from the ground.

Sam hovered over the man writhing in pain. He kicked the downed man's head, knocking him unconscious. "That should take care of him for now. We don't have much time," Sam said to the two women, who both looked shocked by his action. "Come. Let's hope they're not coming through the way we intend to leave."

Tucked in the shadows, the three crossed the halls.

Hearts pounding, they pressed themselves flat against the walls as rebels darted across the opening of passages a short distance away. The walk to the secret passageway may have been a short distance, but it felt like crossing eternity.

Sam held his arm back as they were about to make the final turn, stopping the women from proceeding.

Holding his breath, he watched two rebels enter the room two doors down from their escape. He waited until the men were entirely out of sight before whispering to his wards, "Go."

They raced across the hall. Sam ripped open the painting and shoved the women through the hole.

Screams were starting to fill the castle, reverberating throughout the halls.

Gertrude prayed as Sam closed the painting behind them, *Lord, let the innocent outlast the night.*

Back in the secret passageways, the three wound their way down the long flight of stairs headed to the sewers. They moved in silence, listening for anything that might be ahead and fearing that even the sounds of their hearts pounding might betray them.

As the smell intensified and the air thickened, they knew that they were getting close.

The stairs ended and emptied into a long, wide tunnel a story beneath the castle's basin. They had made it to the city's sewer system.

Sam stepped down into the thick water. It surrounded him up to his knees. "Come," he said, turning back to the ladies and offering them his hand. "We're halfway there."

Sam led them southward to the heart of the city. Gertrude and Galina stepped into the reeking waters, the skirts of their dresses weighing them down, absorbing the sewage into the fabric. The filth and the rats in the tunnels were ignored by the women, who clutched tightly to one another.

The three made a turn into a smaller tunnel, only to run into three vermin far larger than rats.

"Good evening," the short, heavily armed rebel greeted them. "What have we here? Look it, boys," he announced to the men beside him. "Look at the luck we have. The prime minister's daughter—oh, excuse me, the *princess* herself—running around the tunnels like a rat? Tut, tut, missy, this won't do for a lady like you."

"Let us pass," Sam growled as Galina used her own body as a wall to protect her daughter. "These women have only ever been servants of the people. Gertrude only married into the Malleus family so that they would listen to her. *Please*, let us pass so that she can continue to be a messenger for the people."

"Samuel Maison?" One of the other men recognized Sam. "Oh, aye, lads, this man's alright. Come on, Maison, you know these women are only as good as the men that control them. Think of it, Maison, you're one of us. Not them. What do you owe them, eh? They feed you rich but keep you away with a ten-foot stick, don't they? Come off it, lad, be true to the countrymen who accept you and not the wives of pigs."

The first man who spoke spat at the ground. "What do you say, Maison?" he asked, holding his sword out to the side to prove to Sam that he would not hurt him if he did not have to. "Look, mate, our orders are to find that little bitch there," he said, pointing to Gertrude. "Just give her up, and we'll take her to our man in charge. No one gets hurt down here, especially not you, mate—if you're one of us, that is."

He was not one of them. He was neither a noble nor a serf. He had made himself; he had toiled and sacrificed and created a life of comfort through the strength of his courage and the company of the ladies he now stood to protect. Sam hesitated a minute, trying hard to keep calm to figure a way out of this situation. Handing Gertrude over to these blackguards was out of the question. However, Sam lowered his sword.

Galina pushed her daughter farther back. Neither woman could believe what they were seeing.

"Alright, I told you he was on the right," the fair-skinned rail of a man who knew Sam said. All three were thrilled to see this change in attitude from their comrade. "Joe," the man turned to the youngest of the three, "go tell the head that we've got her. Go tell him so he can see for himself just who ought to get the most gold tonight."

"So that's it, then," Gertrude bitterly said. "You're being paid for this violence, aren't you?" For the first time this evening, rage filled her. All of the hours and hardships she had personally endured fighting for the rights of the poor, and this was how the revolution was being carried out—by those summoned by the call of a coin. "This isn't a revolution from the heart at all. You're just mercenaries. Pity; I thought your intentions noble, fighting for a legitimate cause."

"Shut up!" the man who was in charge shouted, his voice echoing throughout the sewers. "A job's a fucking job. You don't know nothing about what it's like to scrimp for food like rats. To beg. To watch children die because they ain't got nothing in their bellies. To decide if it's better to whore out your daughter or your wife so at least one of them may have a bed for the night." He shook his head, disgusted by this woman who not hours ago enjoyed what they had heard to be a lavish wedding while their bellies were empty. "How can you *possibly* call yourself our champion? You've dined and drank and been fucked by the king *and* his brother. Your cup has always been gold. You don't know us. You don't know our suffering, and I'll be damned before I'll take your pity. This is a revolution. A raise, as it were, for the hardworking men like us. If spilling a bit of rich blood is what it takes, if that is how we are to earn our bread, then there it is."

Inspired by his mate's speech, the third man ran off in the opposite direction, his leader's voice trailing after.

Never before had another person's words cut her so deeply.

Sam watched the other man until he was sure he was far enough away before turning around to face the women. "I am sorry, ladies," he said. "But, they're right." Sam winked at the women.

They were not sure what his plan was, but at least they knew that there was something hatching. Sam turned back to the other men and pointed his sword at the women. "Go on, then," he said, "Take them."

The thin man said, "You're alright, Mr. Maison, you're alright."

Both men walked past Sam to collect their bounty, both men falling straight into the trap.

Sam whipped out his knife.

Gertrude slapped her hands over her eyes to shield herself from actually seeing what Sam did.

The two men's bodies fell with a thud and a splash into the sewer's mire. One, squirming and clutching at his neck that poured out blood. The other, reaching for his back, Sam's sword still sticking out from it.

Sam returned his knife to his belt and pulled his blood-soaked sword out from the fallen man.

The men continued to twitch and struggle in the sewage as Sam said, "We have to go."

Gertrude stared at the fallen men. Her heart longed to bring them back to life, to plead with them to understand the truth about her years of trying to save them from this or other dooms, but there the horrible truth was, soaked in excrement and blood.

"Come along, Gertrude," Sam insisted, pulling her away from the scene. With both women beside him, Sam bolted from the sewers, knowing that the third man would return soon. The three ran and ran through the maze of underground tunnels that hardly any soul knew, hoping that their tracks would not be pursued.

Above their heads, a battle of no truly declared good or evil was waged in the alleys and the streets, but most heavily concentrated in the castle of the king.

~*~*~

With the sole prayer in his heart reserved for the safety of his wife, it was not long before the lone prince encountered the enemy.

Two men emerged from a room of their slaughter to find the prince with his sword in one hand and his dagger the other. One of these men was dressed like a king's guard.

Breyton shook his head. *All of this time, they were the spies in our halls.*

"Put down your weapons, and I'll do you no harm," Breyton advised.

The men laughed. They narrowed in on him.

A club from the left swung for Breyton's face.

Breyton blocked the club with his sword and plunged his dagger into the belly of his attacker. The club dropped with a clap to the ground.

The other man lunged, sending his blade straight for Breyton's neck.

Breyton let his dagger fall with the body of the first man and pulled back his sword to block the strike. His elbow bashed against the man's arm, pushing the knife away, sending his sword to slam against the man's face.

The man reeled, hollering fiercely as he desperately pressed the loose flap of his cheek to his face severed by the blade.

Breyton grabbed the man by the shoulder and drove his sword into his core.

The screams turned to moans and then to silence as Breyton collected his dagger and returned to his mission of defending his home.

Seeing no other immediate threat in this area, Breyton headed toward Herod's room to see if his brother was alright. A strange feeling crept through him. War was underfoot, but hardly anyone seemed awake and aware to challenge the changing status.

The king's guards must have faltered, Breyton reasoned. *These vermin are moving through far too quietly. Where are my men?*

Screams began to fill the halls. The silent murders taking place were dissolving into a night full of horror and blood.

From a dark T-section of the hallway, a man leaped out and rammed himself against the unsuspecting prince.

Breyton slammed against the other side of the wall with a loud thud. His sword dropped to the ground from the impact.

Igor Mislov growled a chuckle as he pushed the prince into the wall and took a step back. He kicked Breyton's sword down the hall.

"I've waited to fight another man of the military all night, but it looks like you brought a butter knife to a sword fight, Your Highness," the enormous, gruff man teased as he shifted his weight back and forth. "Never guessed that I'd be the one to kill the prince. They'll make a right nice statue in my honor."

Breyton held the tang of his dagger firmly. "To die for what is right, sir, will be the true honor," the prince said firmly, holding tight to the

strength given to him from the kiss of his wife.
With a tumultuous roar, the bear charged.

37

Dust of a Red Dawn

B y the end of the night, a red rain would fall into the mire of the sewers. The gutters would run with blood as the lone harvest moon shone down upon Vitenka's darkest hour.

On the far opposite side of the city, past the capital's surrounding walls, Gertrude, Sam, and Galina crawled out from a drainage pipe into a river fouled by the city's waste. The escapees could not see the castle or the streets that they had left behind. The night was still a window of darkness.

An hour of silence that lasted an eternity passed, with every minute screaming at Gertrude to turn back. She wanted nothing more than to see her husband alive and unscathed. She knew that it was mad, but she knew that he needed her desperately. The feeling would not cease. It kept clawing and ripping apart her panicked mind and heart.

A pale dawn was rising, but the great star would only bear witness to a castle turned slaughterhouse.

As the three exhausted beings approached the top of a hill, Gertrude sighed heavily. Words came from her lips, the first she had said all morning: "What's the point of anything if man can so easily kill for a belief that's as mighty as a grain of dust?"

Galina did not know how to answer. She was surprised to hear her daughter questioning the revolution, but realized that the encounter with the men in the sewers had tarnished her. The divisions between the classes, the ignorance on either side, was why blood was spilled in the night. The poor fought for they were cheated at birth. The rich refused to bend because they knew nothing other than their birthrights. Enclosing her arms around her daughter, she proceeded to guide her up the hill. Support was all she could presently offer.

It pained Sam to hear the silence from Gertrude all morning as they walked out from the city's territory and into the hill country, but he did not know what he could do for her other than keeping his eyes on the alert. They were almost to his sister's home, where they would be able to see the castle and the city through the clouds of dawn. What they would see, he could only imagine with a shudder.

Falcon's Eye was a small town, and its inhabitants were all still soundly asleep, entirely unaware of the turmoil in the capital. They were ignorant of the barricades that were raised to keep the inhabitants of the city from leaving and ignorant of the hell that was waged in the king's very keep.

When they reached the top of the hill, the cloud cover over the coast was still too thick to be penetrated by the naked eye.

Gertrude stared into the gray and whispered her husband's name.

Seeing no point in waiting in the cold for the clouds to part, Sam pulled Gertrude and her mother in the direction toward his sister Beth's home. The walk was not far from the crest of the hill.

The downward slope was a relief to the women's bodies, which throbbed and ached all over from the abuse of the night. Sam brought the ladies to the door of his sister's cottage. The goats in the pen beside the house looked up at the travelers, and even these bleating beasts did not appreciate the way these two-legged animals smelled. One bayed angrily at them, turned his back, then defecated in their general direction. Gertrude was the only one who saw any of this, but she was too exhausted from worry to have appreciated the humor in the scene.

A small knock at the door drew Beth's husband from bed to investigate the early and unexpected visitor. Efrem shuffled his feet through his modest home, still contently half asleep, to see who on earth would ask for entrance at such an early hour.

Efrem was brought to full attention to see his brother-in-law covered with blood and filth, accompanied by noble ladies covered in the same sort of grime.

The women were brought into the house, and the rest of the morning passed like a misty blur before Gertrude's eyes. The lady of the house helped to bathe her and put her in a fresh pair of clothes that fit loosely, but comfortably.

The house was quiet, and it drove Lady Malleus near to insanity. The others wished to stay hushed so that if a rider came, they would hear his approach. However, in her confinement in their daughter's unoccupied bedroom that Beth and Efrem gave her, Gertrude could not imagine anything more torturous than the silence.

It did not seem possible that anything but conversation could stifle the troubling clishmaclaver of her thoughts: *Where is Breyton? Is he alright? What about Herod? Does he still claim life? The castle, does it lie in ruin? What in God's name is happening?!*

Unable to stand the ripping and tearing noises of her thoughts, Gertrude snuck out the window in the bedroom of the one-level house to return to the crest of the hill. She decided that this was where she would wait for the clouds to part.

I have to see it, she thought. *I have to know what's happening.* Her exhausted body fell onto the bench erected for those who appreciated the view of the capital.

The town was slightly more awake than before. A few people

took notice of the woman, who looked like the countless others who enjoyed sitting on that bench to stare at the city and dream. While it was all too common to see the dreamers lost in reverie staring out at the brilliant sea, Gertrude could not dream. She was too busily engaged in a nightmare.

Though she was dressed in humble, clean clothes, she was not a stranger in this town. People began to recognize her.

"Is that Lady Gertrude?" she distantly heard one say.

"I think she's Lady Malleus now," one replied.

"Didn't she just get married last night? What is she doing here?"

The clouds parted.

Gertrude's gasp startled the gossiping passersby, who turned their heads.

The highest tower of King Herod's castle was ablaze. Tongues of flame licked at the sky as the peaks of Maltoro were devoured. Great plumes of smoke floated over the city, which too seemed deranged and mutated from the attack of the war waged in the night. The woman looked to the city streets, too far to be discerned individually. Too many rooftops to be counted or were also being consumed by the wicked cravings of the fires.

"NO!" she screamed toward the city. She dropped to her knees, dug her groomed nails into the earth. "Please, God, no." She sobbed.

People surrounded her, but she did not hear them.

Her porcelain-complexion touched the earth. Pebbles and dirt pressed against her cheeks as she wept uncontrollably.

A stranger knelt beside her, held her, and tried to console her.

In the crowd that now surrounded her, none could believe the sight. The startled mumblings around Gertrude were white noise.

Her husband was in that castle somewhere.

"Breyton!" she screamed as she was pulled up from the ground.

Sam plucked Gertrude from the ground. He began to carry her back to the house.

"No! Sam, no!" She fought and punched and kicked at him as he carried her. "We have to go back. We have to do something!"

Sam kept his mouth shut. He had seen the flames. He knew that there was nothing they could do.

Hearing her screams, Beth rushed to the door to open it for her brother. Sam carried the hysterical Gertrude to the back room. She clawed at the walls, digging her nails into anything she could, trying to escape his arms.

He dropped her onto the bed.

"Sam! *Please!*" she begged.

Galina rushed in and clutched Gertrude in her arms.

"We can't just leave them!" Gertrude tried to get up, but Galina dug her fingers into the arms of her baby.

Sam buried his face in his hands. He leaned his back against the wall.

"Mata," Gertrude pleaded, tears running down her face. "We can't just leave them."

Galina pulled her daughter into her chest and squeezed her tight. She looked at Sam.

He looked down and shook his head.

"Right." Galina bit her lip and shut her eyes. "Sam," Galina said, her own eyes starting to fill with tears. "You know what to do."

Sam nodded. He wanted to hold Gertrude, to console her, but he had to begin the effort to book them safe passage out from Vitenka, which included fetching his wife and his son.

Galina clung to her daughter for hours, comforting her as best she could.

As the hours rolled on and no news emerged from the city, Gertrude fell into a state of shock.

Her thoughts began to drift as her mother lay beside her on the bed, holding her hand. *I am not a swan,* she thought ruefully, reflecting on the words of her husband, who she believed would never come home. *Nor wolf, nor wife, am I. A rat, a filthy rat I am! I escaped, like a coward. I crawled below it all, and I will live to scurry away another day. A swan would have defended her nest. The home of her mate would not so easily have fallen. A swan would have stayed, come whatever foe. A swan would have died trying, but at least she would have tried.*

~*~*~

An evening star drew over the town, shining through the patched clouds.

They waited for any word, any at all from the city. Aside from what they already knew, there was no news.

Beth brought Gertrude a bowl of thick, steaming stew, bread, and goat milk to ease her mind. Gertrude gave her a polite smile for the gesture, but she could not procure speech. Sam and his sister exchanged worried looks for Gertrude's sake. Beth left them to eat in peace.

It did not take Sam long to realize that his lady was not eating. He had spent the day arranging for their travel, hoping that they could depart first thing in the morning, and all he wanted to do was sleep. However, he and Galina had just changed shifts watching over her.

He put his food aside on the nightstand to help Gertrude get something in her stomach. He took the spoon from the bowl, filled it with the thick stew, blew on it, then held it up to her mouth.

She looked up at him. "Am I so pathetic?"

"Yes," he answered, hoping to make her smile. When she didn't, he insisted, "You have to eat, Gertrude—you haven't eaten all day." He pushed the spoon closer to her.

Gertrude took the wooden spoon from Sam and shoved it into her mouth. Food and eating seemed like foolish tasks at this moment. There were so many images burning in her heart that it made her stomach turn. The image of the man holding a knife to her mother's throat, seeing Sam slaughter two men, and her overly active imagination guessing left and right how her husband must have died made little room in her appetite for food.

"I'm sorry I'm like an infant," she quietly apologized, placing the spoon back in the bowl. "It's just, I haven't even been a wife for twenty-four hours yet, but I may already be a widow." She scoffed, "What sort of deal is that?" She played with the spoon in the bowl, then added after a chill ran through her body, "There hasn't been any word of who lives. My husband could be at the bottom of a pile of rubble or on top, but we just don't know. If he is lost, what then? And, God above, what if I am pregnant? Carrying the child of a man now gone. We'll have to go on the run like thieves in the night, but instead of goods we'll have stolen, it'll be our lives." The desperate pleading in her demeanor hit Sam like a charging bull. Her being pregnant was something he had failed to think of himself. "If the rebels did take the castle, they're going to know I'm with you and that you probably brought me here. They'll find us. We should never have come here. I'm putting your whole family at risk. We cannot stay."

Sam rubbed Gertrude's shoulder. "Gertrude, I've already arranged for us to leave. First thing tomorrow, we—"

Sam's proposition was interrupted by Beth barging back into the room to suddenly announce, "Gertrude, there's a messenger here from the castle."

Gertrude leaped from the bed, the bowl of stew spilling everywhere. She rushed to the front door to see a man dressed in the red and black military uniform of their country, a colonel she recognized as one of Breyton's friends.

"Lady Malleus?" the soldier with his heavy southern accent asked to ensure his message found the right person. "You are she?" He looked uncomfortable with the small crowd watching him—the

Shaws' daughters, and five other adults.

"I am she. What news do you bring?" Gertrude inquired, briefly looking at all the faces in the house gathered in the same room. "Have you word of my husband?"

The colonel nodded. "Let me first assure you, my lady, that your husband is alive."

The whole room sighed from the lifting weight of their relief. Gertrude cupped her hands together and thanked God for this incredible news.

The soldier continued, "He has sent me to tell you that the rebel resistance has been thwarted. We have won the night. He has asked my men and me, a small lot that will secure the perimeter of the house, to stay with you and this household until morning to ensure everyone's safety. He will call for you after he's sorted everything out." The soldier then did something that no one expected: the colonel approached Gertrude, knelt, and bowed his head. "Hail, Queen Gertrude. Our king is dead. God save the king."

Every eye in the room turned to Gertrude.

She stared at the kneeling soldier at her feet. "What?" She felt like her head was spinning and that the floor was falling out from under her. "What do you mean? Herod? What happened to Herod?"

Remaining on his knee, the soldier looked up to his queen and answered, "I regret to inform you, my queen, that King Herod, God save him, was found...dead. Your husband's been unofficially declared king, Your Majesty." He bowed his head to her once more.

"That's not possible," Gertrude muttered. "The crown was to be passed to Donovan, *not* Breyton. How can this be?"

"I dunno, m'lady." The sympathy that he felt for her was lined on his brow. The soldier stood as he further answered, "But it is."

The others bombarded the soldier with questions about the state of the city, the number of casualties, and who was to blame. But the colonel only knew so much. Most of their inquiries, he could not gander to answer, considering that the battle ended only a few hours before. What he did know was that the rebels were a combination of untrained and highly trained factions that were hell-bent on seeing the royal family destroyed. Gertrude listened intently, but she did not ask any questions other than those concerning the state of her husband. The soldier kept assuring her that Breyton was alright and that he was handling the situation like he was born to lead. The colonel's words barely penetrated Gertrude's heart, for her thoughts were far too occupied with the irony that the pair who least wanted to be king and queen were now condemned to wear the crowns.

38

The King and Queen

Through the October morning chill and fog, men from the
city made their way to Falcon's Eye.

The leading soldier quietly knocked on the door, hoping
that the inhabitants would already be awake even though it was very
early. He felt terrible, disturbing a whole household at such an ungodly
hour.

For the second morning in a row, Efrem shuffled from bed to open
the door. He stared blankly at the small entourage of military men
on horseback looking expectantly at him. Mr. Shaw smacked his lips,
then casually said, "Good morning," naturally following the customs
of the country.

"Sir." The soldier bowed his head. "Is Her Majesty here?"

Efrem nodded. "Aye, shall I fetch her?"

"We've come to fetch her," the soldier informed him. "The king
believes that we've made safe the city and requests that his wife joins
him in Maltoro."

Gertrude was immediately behind Efrem. "What news do you have
from my husband?"

"My lady." The soldier and all the men behind him bowed or bent down their heads, even if on horseback.

This is going to take some getting used to. Gertrude turned a bright shade of pink.

The soldier righted his stance and said, "King Breyton is well, my lady. He wishes to see you."

"I'm ready," she said. However, she held up her hand and asked, "May I bring my mother?"

The soldier smiled and said, "My lady, forgive me, you don't have to ask permission to do much of anything any more; you are queen."

~*~*~

Their small carriage wound through a specific route that had been mostly cleared of rubble and debris. The capital city that days ago had been lined with the outstretched hands of the poor felt deserted.

It broke Gertrude's heart as they rode through, wondering who had survived, who was imprisoned, and who had died.

What happened to Luda? She wondered. *It's been ages since I've seen her. Is she wounded? Did she run? Was she among the ones who rebelled? God, I hope she's alright.*

Galina sat across from her in their close cart, looking at the soldiers who surrounded them. They rode in a box drawn by one horse, their knees pressed up against one another. She looked to the rooftops as their covered carriage rode past countless boarded and shattered windows, praying that arrows would not fall from the sky onto their convoy.

What did rain down from the sky was ash that fell like snow. The whole city was covered in soot. The women covered their noses with the backs of their hands as their carriage carried them onward through streets unrecognizable.

It took nearly twice as long as usual to reach the gates of Maltoro. When they entered, neither of the ladies in the cart could believe their eyes.

A silence overwhelmed Gertrude as she stepped out of the cart. Lazy tufts of smoke drifted out of gaping holes in the western buildings of the castle. Remnants of fires reached out from the shattered windows in long streaks of ash-blackened fingers up the concrete walls. Two of the stately columns that stood as part of the entryway into the main hall had fallen, their tremendous broken stones cast across and upon the stairs. Nothing remained of the park on the bailey where families used to gather, and the Council building had been reduced to timber and stone.

Seeing the bailey, Gertrude scoffed and rolled her eyes. Amid the rubble, that damn fountain somehow still stood. It was partially buried, but there it was. She looked hard at it and thought, *I'm coming for you.*

The soldier that had come to collect her handed her and her mother handkerchiefs to cover their noses as they walked to the hall least damaged.

Gertrude thought of that morning when her mother's home had been attacked with fire, how the community had jumped on the opportunity to help her clear the rubble. *Will we be so fortunate?* Tears began to form in her eyes. *Oh, Herod, this castle was supposed to be your legacy, but now . . .* She was about to hang down her head, but she stopped.

From behind her handkerchief, she looked at the group surrounding her. They were looking to her for strength now. She had to be strong for them. She snuffled, blinked her eyes quickly to clear the tears, and stood a little straighter. *I am their queen now. I have to be strong.*

"This way." The soldier pointed through the hall to an area that had been mostly missed by the violence.

They wound through a passageway whose shattered windows let in a cool breeze.

A chill ran down Gertrude's spine. *How is this real? How is any of this real?*

The four soldiers armed with spears who stood at attention before the dark wooden double doors were enough of a sign to Gertrude that her Breyton was just beyond those doors.

Her heart jumped into her throat.

The soldier signaled to the gatekeepers, who clanked the butts of their spears to the floor, signifying respect to their queen.

The soldier-guard pushed the doors open into the library.

The room was alive with movement. Men bustled here and there, fussing over maps and communicating their plans for what next.

Somewhere from the room, someone shouted, "All hail, Queen Gertrude! Long live the queen."

Her stomach tightened.

"Hail, Queen Gertrude. Long live the queen!" a hundred voices inside returned. All the men in the room stopped what they were doing to bow to their queen.

Gertrude nearly fell over from surprise. She had never received a third of this respect from men before in her life. She was overwhelmed with emotion, but her expression did not betray her.

The room fell to silence as they watched her approach the center table.

A group of men stood before it; some she knew, many she did not. They bowed as she approached and parted, so she could see who stood on the other side.

The room around her dissolved.

My Breyton.

There he stood, his blue eyes looking longingly at her.

Gertrude wanted to leap over the table to hold him but knew that she could not. Not yet, at least.

"Everyone," Breyton began. He wanted to leap over the table too. "If you'll excuse us. I'd like to speak with my queen."

The men in the room knew what that meant. The soldier who had guided them helped to shepherd everyone out of the room as quickly as possible, including Sam and Galina.

Gertrude stood still in the center of the room, waiting for the door to close. Breyton, from his post behind the table, did the same.

The second the door shut, Gertrude ran to her Breyton and jumped into his arms.

She clutched onto him, kissing him dearly.

King Breyton Malleus held her tightly. He kissed her and thanked God above that they'd both survived that wicked night.

"Sweetheart, you're hurt!" Gertrude motioned at Breyton's cane, his wrapped knee, the bruises on his face, and the bandage on his hand. "Breyton, what happened?"

"I'm alright; it's not as bad as it looks," Breyton assured her, smiling. He stroked the sides of her face. "It's nothing your mother can't fix." The husband pulled his wife close once more and kissed her again—his joy for seeing her beamed from his eyes. "You're so beautiful. God, I love you, Gertrude. I'm so glad you're alright."

"Where's Herod, Breyton?" Gertrude asked with her face pressed against her husband's chest. "What happened to him?"

This was not something Breyton wanted to tell Gertrude quite yet, but he knew that she would not rest until she found the answer. "Gertrude, do you mind if I sit?" Breyton's leg was throbbing from the abuse he'd sustained during the battle. "I've been standing to make a statement that I'm alright, but I think I'm pushing it a bit too much."

"Of course." Gertrude helped him to a bench where they both could sit. "What happened, Breyton? Where's our Herod? *How* are *we* king and queen?"

Breyton licked his lips and organized his thoughts around the red night. "We're still not sure how they got in, but I have every reason to believe that the King's Guard was infiltrated. Igor Mislov, the bloody head of the Guard, likely gave full access to the rebels that night. Many of the guards were likely among the rebels, leading the first wave of the slaughter. They murdered as many nobles as they could in their beds. We found so many bodies, so many men *and* women that were slaughtered in bed, undoubtedly sleeping when it happened."

Breyton looked away from his wife. The carnage he saw was not easy to forget.

"There was one man...one of the first that I encountered. He was dressed as one of the King's Guard. He was a member of the Guard, I'd bet...I stabbed him." He turned his gaze back to Gertrude. "I stabbed him in the back. Before I pulled my sword from him, I had this...this urge to say, 'Now you know what it feels like...to see a man who swore to protect your family turn his sword toward your blood.'" Breyton hung down his head. "I didn't, but I suspect that those words will stay with me for some time.

"We—my men and I—once we'd settled everything and regained control of the castle about three hours after the sun rose, I went to see if Herod escaped or if he was in his room. I hadn't seen him that whole night. It didn't take long after everything settled for me to find out why." Breyton turned his now tear-filled eyes back to his wife. "Herod is dead, Gertrude. They killed him, executed him. He and the lady he took with him for the night were...from what we could tell, the rebels tied Herod's and the young woman's hands, made them kneel, and..." Breyton took several deep breaths before he could say what he and his closest men conjectured from the evidence at the scene. "It looked as though the rebels beat them both mercilessly." Breyton's eyes drifted to the center of the room. "They killed the girl and...they beheaded my brother." The king swallowed hard as it flashed before his mind's eye. "They piked my brother's head and stuck it before the rotting fountain by the Council's hall."

Gertrude felt sick. She squeezed Breyton's hand and wiped away her tears. "Herod did not deserve that; no one deserves that."

Breyton nodded. He, too, felt ill, but he had not yet had the time or opportunity to properly digest that his little brother, the boy who had always looked up to him, adored him and loved him, was gone.

Breyton leaned back in the soft couch and felt his achy, tired muscles relax in the comfortable seat. He could not remember the last time he slept or even the last time he sat down properly. The gentleman rubbed his head, which was still sore from being banged into a wall from that bear. "Gertrude, there's something else: Absalom and Mislov were there. They were with the insurgents."

"Absalom *and* Igor Mislov?" she exclaimed. "That's not possible. They both hated the lower classes. Why would they help them?"

Breyton shook his head. "I don't know about Mislov, the bastard. I took him on myself." Breyton clenched his fist. "I'd like to owe my knee injury to him, but I got him. Stabbed him with my knife. There's no room in this world for monsters like him." The new king sighed and rubbed the side of his wife's face. "You know, I think your father—"

"He's *not* my father," Gertrude quickly corrected. She smiled and leaned close to her husband. "Just between us...Absalom is *not* my father. It turns out, I am the result of another."

Breyton smiled. "You know, the more I learn about your mother, the greater my admiration for her becomes." He kissed Gertrude's brow. "Well, I think that Absalom was not there so much as another arm in the battle. I think he may have been *guiding* them. I think that maybe all of this—the battle, the whole damn revolution—may have been masterminded by him. We have him contained. He may have survived the night, but..." Breyton held her hands tightly. "He *will* be executed."

The words settled over her like a tumultuous wave, but then, the waters receded, and she suddenly felt at ease.

"Would you want to see him before…" Breyton asked.

She shook her head. "No," she answered. "He means nothing to me." Gertrude squeezed her husband's fingers. "He is a traitor and deserves a traitor's fate."

Breyton scratched the sides of his unshaven face, then continued, hoping to distract her from retreating into the horrible memories of her childhood. "A takeover of the castle would have required extensive knowledge of the city, the castle, and the rooms where all of those loyal to Herod slept. I found that our room was raided. Lord knows what would have happened to us if we did not wake up or if Sam had not come to collect us."

It still did not make sense to Gertrude that Absalom would risk his life for a takeover with the peasants. He was too smart to make such a gamble on a class of men he was known for despising. And then it hit her. "The blood and the crown," she whispered, staring off into the distance. "That's what he meant." Gertrude turned to her husband, who did not understand where she was going with repeating the phrase Sam's late brother used to scream. Gertrude anxiously asked, "*Why* are we king and queen? What happened to change the will from Donovan to us?"

"Aren't you going to explain what you mean by 'the blood and the crown'?" Breyton asked, but when his wife ordered him to answer her question first, he shrugged and replied, "I should have told you this: a few weeks ago, before you came to the castle, Herod and I had a little discussion between Aleksie and us." This conversation was not one he had hoped to ever have with his wife, but present circumstances brought forth the necessity. The words came like boulders rolling from his tongue. "He determined from our constitution that in the absence of the Gatherers, the king was the ultimate executive. So in what very well may have been his first true and last executive act, Herod changed the order so that I would inherit full authority over our lands and the crown."

"Does he know about this?" Gertrude quickly asked. "Does Donovan know that he's been excluded from the devolution?"

"Not that I am yet aware," Breyton answered, feeling his eyelids growing heavy. "But he will soon enough."

There was nothing left at the moment to do but to elaborate on her revelation. "I think that the conspiracy against the crown has been alive for years, and I believe its birth is owed to Absalom *and* Donovan. Now let me explain." Gertrude held up her hand to stop her suddenly more awake husband from interrupting. "What if the people who tortured Sam's brother Brody into looking like a conspirator were the conspirators themselves? My connection with 'the blood and the crown'—my father always wore that disgusting blood-red cloak of his, that's why he was called the 'Bloody Prime,' and what if the crown that Brody was referring to was the crown prince? He knew who they both were due to Sam's and my involvement with politics, however small then. Sam also saw the two of them together in an alley exchanging what he thinks was the poison that was used in the attempt to kill Herod. If Donovan is still under the impression that he is to inherit the throne on Herod's death, wouldn't it make sense that he would do absolutely everything in his power to obtain the crown? I bet you anything that within the next few days, he comes to claim his bounty."

"Gertrude, there's no hard evidence that connects Donovan to any of this," Breyton dissented, praying that his awful brother would not be so deranged as actually to murder their baby sibling, "only assumptions. And his house was attacked—how do you explain that if he's supposedly in control?"

"If he is still alive, then he must have faked the fire," Gertrude rebutted, as all the pieces of her thoughts suddenly formed one coherent whole.

"We survived the fire that started at your mother's home," Breyton delicately reminded her. He did not want to believe Gertrude on this.

"I'm telling you, love, wait and see—Donovan will come for the crown." Gertrude stopped trying to convince her husband any further. She could see that this was hurting him on a deeper level than his injuries. She shut her eyes, and the shock of everything reverberated through her spine and sent shivers all over her skin. "I can't believe that any of this is real."

"I know," Breyton drowsily agreed. He was exhausted. "We have a huge mess to clean up, too, and I don't simply mean the rebuilding process of the castle and the city." Rubbing his wife's hand with his thumb, Breyton added, "I'm sure you of all people know what all of this means."

She most certainly did. Her years of studying history and politics told her precisely what they would have to do in the following months. She never expected those courses at the Northern to be preparation for a life she'd studied but never wanted. Gertrude exhaled deeply, then said, "We're going to have one hell of a first year wearing crowns. I'm sure that's at minimum how long it's going to take before we can effectively root out all of the bad seeds. We cannot leave any standing, none at all." She sighed. "It will be a very delicate line, balancing bringing justice and not becoming tyrants."

After a moment of her husband's silence, Gertrude leaned back and kissed her king on the cheek. "We'll get through this," she promised, while softly rubbing Breyton's injured knee. "With my brains and your good looks, we'll knock down any opposition that objects to your standing as king." She winked, hoping to ease the moment in any way she could.

Breyton smiled, then wrapped his arm around her. "What're you talking about? This is a partnership, Gertrude; we are in this together. In my eyes, we're both kings."

The wife tucked herself closer to her husband and rested her head against his shoulder. He held her close as they both sat still and wondered about the violence that lay ahead. The two exhaled in unison just before a knock came to the library's door.

"Help me to stand," Breyton asked of his wife.

As quickly as she could, Gertrude helped her husband up from the bench.

They beckoned the knocker, and in came the colonel who had visited Gertrude the night before.

"Pardon my intrusion," the colonel with his heavy southern accent hesitantly started. "Your Majesty, the men would like to talk to you about further safeguarding the city. They need your opinion, Sire."

Breyton did not want to depart from this intimate moment with his wife, but he was king now even though a proper ceremonial coronation had not yet taken place. For the rest of their lives, the country would have to come first. No matter what happened henceforth, the eyes of the country, and possibly the world, would be ever on him and his wife.

"Gertrude, do you mind, love?" Breyton softly asked. "I have to go."

"I do mind," Gertrude said very point-of-fact. "I'll not let you leave or make decisions without me." Breyton opened his mouth to argue, but Gertrude continued over his protesting, "If you say we're partners, Breyton, then it's all or nothing." She held her hand out to her husband. "If the city needs a king to help it rebuild, then most certainly, it will also need a queen."

39

Following the Fall

Gertrude had barely slept in the weeks following the fall of Herod. There had hardly been a night since their wedding that she spent with her husband. Their duties were divided as such so that the pair were parted continuously from each other's company. Queen Gertrude's duties compelled her to stay close to the castle so that she could administer the immediate reconstruction of Maltoro. She also mediated and moderated the immediate political implications of this failed attempt at civil war. At the same time, her husband and his men hunted down every lead and every name the imprisoned interrogated rebels had for them.

She hated that he was out there. It made no sense for him, the king, to be, but she knew he was trying to prove to the people that he was willing to risk his life for them.

Until this morning, there had barely been time for Gertrude to worry about her husband, but now in the silence, her head ran wild with fear.

From what she knew, Breyton's injuries had not improved much. His riding abilities were gravely impaired, but the pain he was experiencing at great extent did not halt his fury for the crimes committed against his family and his country. Galina confided in Gertrude that she doubted a full recovery to the injury his knee had sustained with his persistence of being on the front lines, noble as it was of him to try to be a pillar of strength for his fellow men. Galina could not find it within herself to tell Breyton that his racing days had probably reached the finish line.

At her vanity in the royal chambers, the place that Herod had called home, Gertrude stared at herself in the oval mirror. The reflection she saw told her that she had aged years since her wedding morning when last she stared at herself. On that morning, she held a whole different mess of fears swelling in her heart than those which plagued her head today. Now, she worried about a second attempt to overtake the castle while her husband and a majority of his men were gone, the chance of losing her husband forever to a faceless assassin, the daunting task of being queen with or without her husband, the horrible ways that she and her king would be marking their coronation ceremony with crimson ink, and the newest addition of concerns that her mother had doled onto her plate this morning.

Her eyes drifted to the small smoldering piece of charcoal her mother had lit not long ago. It slowly helped to release a frankincense essential oil from the burner, dispersing its warming scent throughout the room. Galina had said that it would help her and Breyton to find clarity and oneness with their inner divine in these unclear times, but as of right now, the scent was only irritating her upset stomach.

Gertrude dropped her head to the vanity's surface. She held her forehead and the tip of her nose to the cool, dark wood as a shiver passed through her body. Pulling the blanket she had earlier draped over herself closer, Gertrude whispered to the wood, "Where are you, Breyton?"

The king was supposed to have returned early this morning so that together, he and his wife could partake in the official ceremony that would forever embellish their names with the titles King and Queen. Gertrude thought the rite a bit too flashy, considering how everything had come to be. Still, the clergy and the political traditions insisted that the country keep true to such formalities for the sake of stability. With a sigh, Gertrude sat up properly. Back into the mirror, her mixed eyes stared. From her education, she knew how necessary it was for some political traditions to remain while she and Breyton made radical changes to modernize their nation. Gertrude chuckled. She found it ironic that to "modernize" the political systems of the country, she would have to take a step backward. She kept trying to construct a way to explain to the people that the changes they were bringing would plant seeds of stability and were not merely stages of progress for the sake of progress, and yet, a chill ran down her spine. She recalled the hatred that man in the sewers had thrown at her.

Throughout her career, she had thought of herself as the people's champion, the one who listened to them and the one they looked to, but was that true? *Do they all think me a liar?* She wondered. *Do they all think me no better than the rest of my class? Do they see me as no more than a snake in the grass?*

The doubt that one man cast upon her would haunt her for the rest of her days.

As she wondered if the people would ever believe a word she said, on the other side of the door, Breyton stood.

After dismissing the guards from their post at their bedroom door to give him a moment of privacy, he leaned against the wall beside the entrance to recuperate from his dash back to Maltoro from the northern coast. He did not want her to see him like this. He could not let his wife see him out of breath and nearly entirely diminished from these pressures. However, at the same time, he needed her. Her voice, her touch, would be the best tonic for his tortured soul and tarnished skin. The king rubbed the back of his head against the wall. He tried to remember the feel of her skin against his, but the memories of their last night together were fading from the weight of his fatigue.

Breyton reached his fingers, stiff from the freezing late November winds, into his vest pocket to retrieve his handkerchief. Knowing how haggard his appearance was, he wiped his face and neck of whatever dirt and grime he could before stuffing the thing back into his pocket. At least he had managed to remove any trace of the battles he had recently engaged. He reached for his cane, the item he could not hide from her. The king made a quick prayer that his wife might still be in bed asleep as he opened the door.

From the click of the knob, Gertrude spun around in her chair to see if the sound was imagined or true. There stood her Breyton. Although he was bruised and tarnished from wear, she had never been more grateful to see him.

The couple stared at one another, both thinking the other a ghost before Gertrude moved to stand.

"No, sweetheart, stay there," Breyton softly commanded. "I'll come to you." He closed the door and did his best to hide his limp and to lean less heavily on his wooden cane. He did not want his wife to think him an invalid.

Gertrude watched her husband closely. She felt wretched for obeying his command. It was clear that he was in considerable pain. She squeezed the frame of the chair's backrest as she denied herself the urge to dive into his arms to spare him so long a walk.

Breyton stood beside his wife. The king softly pressed his knuckles to his queen's face.

Gertrude leaned her head into his touch that, though cold on her skin, felt so right and wonderful.

Breyton chuckled lightly, then said, "Oh yes, I remember you."

"Thank God for that." She jumped up and threw herself into his arms.

Breyton inhaled her deeply. Her scent was intoxicating and divine. However, a deeper inhale brought another smell to his senses, making his nose snuffle. His eyes scanned the immediate surroundings to see light smoke rising from a decorative brass incense burner on the vanity. "Gertrude, what is that burning?" he asked into her shoulder. "It smells familiar."

Gertrude said into his chest, "It's frankincense. It's burned in church. It was one of the sacred gifts. Mata said it would be centering, or uplifting, something like that, for us."

Breyton wasn't sure how to interpret Gertrude's explanation, but regardless, it was uplifting to know that his guardian angel Galina was still around. Though he did not want to admit it, he knew he would require her medicinal services soon.

Mutually pulling apart, Gertrude swallowed, bracing herself to look over her husband. As if sensing his previous thought, she said, "Perhaps you might consider my mother dropping by to see you, Breyton." She paused to touch her hand to his face. "She can help."

The king shook his head. He knew she could help, and he would not deny medical attention, but right now, all he wanted was to be with his wife. "I'll be alright," he answered, sounding much like a child. "I just need a bath and a nap, and I'll be fine."

Realizing that Breyton would eventually need to see her mother, Gertrude exhaled slowly. She did not want to be pushy, but it was trying to be patient. Deciding to change direction, Gertrude asked, "Are you certain that those are the only comforts you'll need, my husband?" Her richly spoken words and the glow from her eyes communicated her hunger for his attention and love.

Breyton's face parted in that crooked smile of his. "Well, I suppose that I was not specific enough; what I meant to say was a bath *with* you, and a nap with you tucked closely to my side...to say the least."

Gertrude smiled as well. "That sounds much better." She sank back into her seat. As thrilled as she was to be back in his arms, her body needed to sit.

Breyton did not mind. He bent over and laid his lips to hers. The touch assured her that his presence was real and not imagined. She pulled his face down so that she could properly kiss her husband. Their passion swelled, but just as she began to stand, her hand ran over a sore spot on his back.

The king winced and drew away.

"Oh, Breyton, I'm so sorry—are you alright?" she asked.

Nodding his head while pressing his hand on the back of his rib cage, he insisted, "Yes, yes, I'm fine. Please, it's nothing to worry yourself over."

"Breyton, please, before anything else, what has been happening in the world outside of Maltoro? I've been so consumed with what's been happening in this city, and reports and rumors have been flooding into the castle from every which direction. It's all turned to babble. I hardly know what to believe anymore. Please, Breyton, what have you seen?"

Breyton did not want to talk about this now. He wanted to make love to her and then sleep for days, but he knew that Gertrude would not be able to rest, nor would she let him rest without this information. Shifting himself around so that he was practically sitting on the vanity, he crossed his arms over his chest. "I do not know exactly what you have heard, but what is going on in our country is nothing short of chaos. The revolution was not just at our castle. It spanned the entire country. This was more than a centralized revolution, my love; this was a massive coordinated attempt to divide our nation in a civil war.

"We managed to settle the discrepancies, to soften it a bit, here in the northwest. My men are presently addressing the heart of the country, and as far as we are aware, the south is practically untouched, so I'm focusing all charges on clearing out the garbage from one town at a time in the east and north. Thanks to the information we have, it has been slightly less than impossible to weed out the bad seeds." Breyton sighed heavily. "These rebels are not falling easily." He scratched the side of his head, brushing off some dried mud that he'd missed with his handkerchief earlier. "Katia has been the nastiest front thus far; that's where I sustained the bulk of my scrapes."

Gertrude bit her tongue from saying *they're hardly scrapes*. Instead, she said, "I hate that you are fighting, Breyton. You are the king."

"I assure you that I'd rather not be," he said, trying at a light joke, but Gertrude was not laughing. "They need a leader right now, Gertrude. A king that they believe in. That's why I've been out there, but..." Breyton cleared his throat and looked down at the bottom of his cane before quietly, almost shamefully, saying, "I don't know that I'll be able to do much more. My horse and I were taken down outside of Katia, Gertrude. A couple of men leaped out from very well-hidden posts buried underground on the sides of the road; they startled my horse, and he reared. We both went down..." Gertrude could see that her husband's voice was waning. She knew where this story would end. "I bruised my ribs and back, but, m-my horse, my best, most loyal steed...his ankle snapped in the fall." Breyton paused again and pressed his fist to his lips. There was hardly anything worse for a rider as skilled as Breyton than to lose his partner in the race.

"Oh, my dear one." Gertrude stood and gently pulled him into her arms. The once famed racer and his noble steed were out of the game. She held her husband close as the stress, strain, pain, and anxiety of everything that was happening removed themselves from him. He had lost so much in the past few weeks. It was almost more than a man could bear. Gertrude comforted her husband with her soft voice and gentle strokes from her fingers to the nape of his neck. He sobbed into her shoulder for a long while. It was the first time she had seen her Breyton cry. It was the first time he had been granted

331

the opportunity to express his grief from all that had passed.

He felt ashamed for collapsing before his wife, but there was nothing that he could do to stop it. He knew that Gertrude would understand.

"Come, love," Gertrude directed, "let us go to bed. We've still several hours ere we're needed again. Come, come rest, Breyton." She helped to guide her limping husband to the bedside, where she also helped him to undress. It was then that the extent of his injuries was revealed. Gertrude said nothing, but the bruise-dinged spots on her mate were too many to count.

After pouring water into a warmed bowl, Gertrude returned to her husband sitting on the side of the bed. He watched her as she cleaned his face, neck, and hands. The warm, wet cloth was so refreshing. She washed him of everything that had recently passed. As warm drops of water that had dripped from the cloth ran down Breyton's temple caught by Gertrude's attentive fingers, a new sensation began to emerge inside the king. For the first time in his life, Breyton truly felt at home within Maltoro Manor, the castle by the sea. He felt safe and secure, warm, and at ease. He smiled, for he knew that this feeling would never have surfaced if not for the graces of his darling, gentle Gertrude.

When she was nearly finished, Breyton wrapped his arm around her to show her his thanks and praise. He rolled her into his embrace within the bed of the king.

Gertrude was careful to touch her husband tenderly and softly so as not to hurt the poor man unintentionally.

The king ran his hands down his wife's arms and sides as he kissed her. He pulled her velvet dress from her body.

Gertrude wanted to be able to focus on her husband and the thrill of making love to him once more, but there were shadows in her mind that would not let her rest. These shadows ran like wild voices in her conscience, screaming, *Tell him, tell your husband! Tell your husband to keep him forever at your side! If he knows, he will never leave again.*

However, as their desire to be with one another grew, her thoughts began to fade.

All that was before her was Breyton.

Being with him was intoxicating.

Though every part of him hurt, being with her, unifying their passions, made him feel immortal. He kissed her forehead as he gently slid himself into her.

She clung to him, praying that she would never have to let him go.

They summited the mountains, new breath filling their souls with new life.

As he gently touched the soft skin where her neck met her shoulder, the thoughts from before resurfaced.

She thought as she peered into his eyes, *I have to tell him.*

Gertrude rolled on top of Breyton, and in her husband's good ear, she whispered, "I'm pregnant."

"What?" the king questioned, gently pushing her back to ensure that he was hearing her correctly.

Gertrude licked her lips before taking hold of her husband's face with a gentle frame of her hands. "Mata thinks I'm pregnant. Apparently, I have all of the signs."

Breyton's eyes locked onto those of his wife as his mind processed her words. "Pregnant?" he asked, unable to do much more. However, when Gertrude shyly nodded her head and shone a brilliant smile, what more could the king do but reflect the same expression? "Pregnant!" The excitement building within him was the strongest tonic against the pain he had yet known. "Are you sure? How long have you known?"

Gertrude shrugged bashfully before answering, "I only just found out this morning. I have had a hunch for some time, but Mother confirmed my suspicion earlier today." She sighed contentedly, then said, "We're going to have a baby, Breyton."

A look of euphoria consumed Breyton. All the pains of his body mended in that instant. "Oh, Gertrude!" Breyton kissed his wife a dozen times.

The queen chuckled as she rode the wave of her husband's excitement. She was pleased that he was too distracted by the notion of having created life to have realized that the conception likely happened before their wedding night. "Can you believe it? We're going to be parents. I'll bet you're going to be a damn good father."

To this question, Breyton paused from his mirth to look Gertrude in the eyes. The only child that he had genuinely interacted with was Sam's son, Sasha. Those interactions did come easily enough, but Breyton was not sure if that was merely a show to impress Gertrude or if he indeed was a natural with children. The paternal instinct historically had not been a part of his family, and his first wife had been too ill to have carried a child, so he never deeply considered how he would be in the role. A chill ran up his spine as a dreaded thought arose: *What if I turn out to be like my father? Negligent and coarse to my children and my wife.* Breyton looked deep into Gertrude's eyes. A wave of grace passed from her to him. It calmed him. With her by his side, he felt like anything was possible. This burst of confidence made Breyton sit straight and wonder if he would be the one to challenge and change all reputations chained to the Malleus name.

Nodding and determined to make significant change, he affirmed, "I know that neither of us had exactly ideal paternal figures in our lives, but I can promise you, Gertrude, that our children will."

"If you say this, then mean it, Breyton," Gertrude said, sitting up so that she could be taken more seriously than she could from a flattened position. "Please, Breyton, no more cold, sleepless nights. I beg of you, my husband, do not leave me alone again. I cannot bear to spend another night without you, worrying that you will never return.

Breyton, I implore you, my love. Let your men handle the monsters out there. *I* need you, Breyton, ever so much more now that I am carrying your child." She turned his face toward her. "I love you, Breyton, and I know that what I ask of you is not best for our country, but it is best for our family." She slid one of his hands onto her lower abdomen. "Do not risk our child not knowing his father because of the victory of some hell-worthy assassin."

Breyton sighed heavily. He wanted to be an involved father. He wanted to give his son or daughter the affection and attention his father never showed him. "You know," Breyton softly started as he pushed a lock of Gertrude's hair behind her ear, "as much as I would like to deny this, I am not a young man anymore." He took a moment to recall all the aches stirring in his muscles before these turbulent times. "My dear wife, I cannot promise that I will be able to stay by your side every night what with the mess our country currently is in, but I will say, Gertrude, that for now, I will try. I want to see your belly grow, and I want to be here for you every step of the way. I want to hear the sound of our infant's first cry."

"And to see him take his first few steps and marry and all that too, yes?" Gertrude added as she realized that her eyes were beginning to water.

Breyton chuckled, then with a nod, said, "Of course."

The king and queen pressed their foreheads together as the excitement of the new lives they were building together swept between their souls. Hope had been born from the ashes of their home.

"We'll attempt to make a life for our children as humanistic and normal as possible, Gertrude," Breyton whispered as again, he started to kiss his wife tenderly. "They will not be raised as pampered brats as my brothers, and I were, but as proud and respectable, loved children," he continued. "We'll take them to the country as often as we are able so that they can grow in the woods barefooted and with dirt on their hands, just as I always imagined I would've when I was a child."

Gertrude chuckled, "And they will grow in the loving and protecting embrace of my mother's garden."

The king's kisses of victory to his wife for what he believed to be his greatest triumph led to what eventually became a very fine doze.

However, the day for this reunited pair had only just begun.

Later, that same day, the first frigidly cold day of winter, with crowns of gold worn firmly on their brows, the king and queen oversaw the executions of the seventy-two remaining rebels who had invaded Maltoro. It was a melancholy event on that last day of November, the official coronation ceremony of the Malleuses paired with the deaths of so many men. With somber, hardened expressions, the new king and queen watched the snaps of seventy-two ropes. It would be remembered as one of the darkest days of their reigns. Grim and horrible as it was, the deed was necessary to sear into the eyes of those rebels who still roamed the country that King Breyton and Queen Gertrude found it far better in their favor to be feared than admired.

The effects of her pregnancy alone were enough to make Gertrude ill, but watching the life be ripped from so many who had wanted nothing more than to provide a better future for their children was gut-wrenching. With every drop and every snap, she thought of those men who had confronted her in the sewer. Yes, their means had been ghastly wrong, but their desire was to provide for their own. She swore as she watched so many souls leave this world that though burdened with the crown, she would use this scepter to bring her people out of the dins and dredges of society and into the light.

Contrary to what Gertrude had predicted, Donovan did not arrive at Maltoro Castle. He stopped his victory trail to the castle about midway when word reached his ear that the castle had not fallen and that Breyton was the declared king. The world and all of his plans tumbled around him as the messenger told him of Herod's changed will. Donovan knew that the unexpected alteration in Herod's testimony would bring Breyton and his fury against those who betrayed the crown. He further understood that if sufficient evidence was gained or if one of those damned rebels betrayed him, he would not be excluded from the list. The duke was infuriated to hear that Absalom failed what should have been a foolproof invasion and that his minions across the lands were falling just as quickly. Donovan was sorely disappointed to learn that Breyton's men found the former prime minister first because he would have gladly killed him for his insolence. Absalom was the last of the men to drop. Gertrude wanted to ensure that his death was the last that the crowd saw, the one that they would remember.

~*~*~

The hunt for the supporters of the revolution and the reconstruction phase of the city was hardly easy. The entire project took several years, but eventually, the country once more came to peace. The scars of the revolution would always stay with the king and queen even though things were easier to manage without the self-serving intentions of the Council.

As peaceful and as still as the country eventually became once reconstruction was ended, the king and queen could never truly be at rest. There would always be foreign and domestic affairs to delegate and moderate.

So long as they lived, the obligations toward the duty they'd never wanted would never be complete.

* * *

Keep reading for an excerpt for the continuation of Breyton and Gertrude's Story in the sequel, *Foreign & Domestic Affairs*

Foreign & Domestic Affairs

He was the first to wake on the pale March morning.

His back felt stiff. His leg was asleep from the weight of his wife's knee on his thigh. Even though he did not sleep, he was pleased to see that Gertrude had slept and remained curled up beside him. Rest did not come to Breyton. His thoughts had been consumed by grief, and every memory that brought them to this point. Neither wanted what they had received, but here they were, nearly nineteen years later, king and queen.

Breyton lay still in bed, thinking back on the dreams the pair of them had made so long ago to settle in the country at his estate. The only involvement they had hoped to have with the crown was to help Herod from afar when needed. It would have been paradise.

The king scoffed to himself, *What a waste of thought.*

The country was better off now, *far* better. Regardless of how challenging things had been for him and Gertrude, and how difficult they continued to be, their homeland was prospering. He and Gertrude had proven themselves to be worthy, albeit reluctant, bearers of the crowns.

Finding himself smiling at the irony, Breyton looked at his sleeping wife. Until recently, it had been a while since he genuinely looked at her. Even after everything that had passed between them, and there had been as many fires of passion as fires from hell, she remained to be his everything.

From the provocation of her husband's fingers stroking her face,

Gertrude stretched and came to life. Her eyes took longer to focus than they used to when they first opened in the morning, but after blinking hard a couple of times, Queen Gertrude saw her husband looking down at her. She tucked herself as close as she could to Breyton's side. It was a cold morning. The warmth of his body was a great comfort. "You look lost in reverie," she observed. "Anything in particular?"

Breyton nodded and pulled the blankets tighter around his wife. "I remembered some of the things that we've been through." Before his wife had the opportunity to respond, Breyton realized that their son's teddy bear remained tucked between them from last night. She did not seem to notice, so he quickly decided not to say anything for fear of stirring her grief once more.

The queen chuckled, "That's certainly not a shortlist. Have you been awake very long?"

"No, not really," Breyton lied. He did not want to add to her worries, with everything else on her mind.

Gertrude saw the heavy bags beneath her husband's eyes, but she said nothing.

Breyton sighed, then somberly said, "We'd better get up."

His wife did not particularly wish to leave the warmth and privacy of her bed to go to a grim and cold ceremony. She wanted to curl up, fall back to sleep, and wake up last summer, before the nightmares and the numbness began.

"Do you think it'll snow today?" she asked, hoping that the weather would be merciful for once.

Breyton looked over toward the window, but since the curtains were down, all he could see was a gray glow coming from behind. "It's snowed every day this month; I don't see why it won't snow today."

The cruel, bitter weather was the reason that the influenza epidemics struck so hard in this country and why Gertrude's mother could not be here to help. "I wonder how long it will be before we find out how hard the epidemic was this season. It seems to get worse and worse every time it comes around."

The king and queen rose from their bed and began to dress for the funeral.

They dressed in silence. The blanket of loss encompassed them completely, allowing them to contemplate little else.

Hating the void between them, Breyton decided to make conversation to distract them from their cold reality. "I can't wait until the waters are at a reasonable temperature again," he said under his breath as he reached high, then twisted his back right and left. "I can't stand not being able to be free in the water; I feel so much better when I can swim."

"You're a fish, Breyton," Gertrude said over her shoulder as she pulled on a warm, thick under-layer that would be hidden by her dress. "I'm surprised you survive so long without being submerged." She slipped into the black first layer of her dress and then tied her corset loosely. From the closet, her husband brought her the black garb that was the appropriate item for such an occasion. She quietly thanked him while she wished that she could wear any other color than black.

In the mirror, Gertrude stared at herself. Dabbing on cover-up or worrying about how she appeared seemed so superficial after losing her son.

Her hands grasped the sides of the vanity. She inhaled deeply, but it felt like she could no longer breathe.

"Breyton." She sobbed. Her eyes were unfocused, filling with tears.

Though he had not heard her whisper, his hands were on her shoulders, his lips to the side of her face.

"Our baby," she uttered.

Breyton wrapped his arms around her and dropped his face into the nape of her neck.

In the sacred privacy of their bedroom, the husband and wife clutched onto one another and displayed their mourning. The funeral for their youngest child was inevitable, but this grief that they shared was one they would not be able to show beyond their bedroom door. However, the impending hour of that black ceremony drained all monarchical duties and expectations from the royal couple. For now, they could be mortal.

Amid her sobs, Gertrude said, "No parents should have to suffer the death of their child. None. I don't care who they are. This suffering is too cruel to bear."

"We have to get going," Breyton reminded her, though all he wanted was to stay here with her. He drew away from his wife and finished buttoning his thick, fur-lined jacket up to his neck. He collected for his wife her long, fur cloak and his own.

Gertrude nodded. She wiped the tears from her face and did her best to repair the cover-up. Once she finished, Breyton draped the heavy, long, dark coat over her shoulders.

From their wardrobe, Gertrude pulled out what many viewed as the essential pieces of their outfits. The pair that she removed was not as weighty or as loud as the others. She offered Breyton his as she kept her own looped around her wrist.

The king capped on his head the thin silver crown.

For a brief moment, they stopped and stared at one another. The love they shared was their tridents, their crowns, their curse.

The king reached out his hand to his wife. Together they walked through the castle toward the snow-covered bailey, where they would join the procession to the royal burying grounds. It was time to put their youngest son to rest.

Near the exit to the courtyard, the king and queen were welcomed by a small crowd. The queen barely paid any attention to the people around. She was too busy looking for her surviving children.

"Where are our children?" she asked her husband and their longtime friend Ivan. "I thought we were supposed to walk out with them?"

Ivan shook his head, then answered, "Their nursery maid has them waiting on the other side in the hall so that when you two come out, they'll still be warm, or something like that."

The king looked at his queen and could see that she was yet again displeased with one of the nursery maid's decisions, but right now, that was not important.

"Majesties, they're ready to start whenever you are," Ivan informed them.

The pair nodded and prepared themselves for the sorrow that was soon to envelop them the moment their son's small coffin rolled past.

The doors to the frozen courtyard swung open. A rush of biting wind and a blinding light from the natural order of the world flashed, beckoning forth the king and queen.

About the Author

S. Faxon is a creative warrior. She has written fifteen novels and has many more to follow.

In an effort to help other authors and creatives on their journeys, Sarah interviews other authors on her YouTube channel to share their stories with the world. Sarah also co-stars in the writing-podcast, Semi-Sages of the Pages, available on all of your favorite podcast apps.

She loves the sound of rain and the scent of ink on legal pads. Sarah lives in San Diego with her life partner, her two cats, and too many statues of dragons.

You can connect with me on:

- https://sfaxon.com
- https://twitter.com/readingescape
- https://www.facebook.com/authorsfaxon
- https://www.goodreads.com/s_faxon

Subscribe to my newsletter:

- https://rb.gy/e22ccf

Also by S. Faxon

Foreign & Domestic Affairs

In the sequel to The Animal Court, whispers from abroad and shadows in their court threaten to dismantle all that the king and queen labored to rebuild. While mourning the unexpected death of their youngest son, the king and queen are faced with the impossible decision of prioritizing their family or their thrones. With the eyes of the nation upon them, will the new foreign and domestic affairs tear them and their beloved Vitenka apart?